No Place To Hide

Praise for Susan Lewis

'A gripping story of love, uncertainty and betrayal . . . a guaranteed tear-jerker that will keep you at the edge of your seat.' *OK!*

'A master storyteller.' Diane Chamberlain

'Spellbinding! You just keep turning the pages, with the atmosphere growing more and more intense as the story leads to its dramatic climax.' *Daily Mail*

'Utterly compelling.' *Sun*

'Expertly written to brew an atmosphere of foreboding, this story is an irresistible blend of intrigue and passion, and the consequences of secrets and betrayal.' *Woman*

'Sad, happy, sensual and intriguing.' *Woman's Own*

Also by Susan Lewis

Fiction

No Place To Hide

Susan Lewis

arrow books

3 5 7 9 10 8 6 4 2

Arrow Books
20 Vauxhall Bridge Road
London SW1V 2SA

Arrow Books is part of the Penguin Random House group of companies
whose addresses can be found at global.penguinrandomhouse.com.

Penguin
Random House
UK

Copyright © Susan Lewis Ltd 2015

Susan Lewis has asserted her right under the Copyright, Designs and
Patents Act 1988 to be identified as the author of this work

First published in Great Britain by Century in 2015
First published by Arrow Books in 2016

www.randomhouse.co.uk

A CIP catalogue record for this book is available from the British Library

ISBN 9780099586494
ISBN 9780099586524 (export)

Typeset in Palatino Ltd Std by Palimpsest Book Production Limited,
Falkirk, Stirlingshire
Printed and bound in Great Britain by Clays Ltd, St Ives Plc

To Dorry and Channing Mitzell with love

No Place
To Hide

Chapter One

'Hope' is the thing with feathers
That perches in the soul,
And sings the tune without the words,
And never stops – at all . . .

Emily Dickinson

Present Day – Culver, Indiana

So this was what it was like beyond the corn-silk veil.

Others called it a curtain, but she preferred veil. This allowed for a more dreamlike connection between the blue skies and still waters of this hauntingly beautiful town, and the world out there, filled with cornfields, highways, cities, oceans – the world, the family, she'd left behind.

To get here she'd flown through storms and time zones, driven for mile after mile across vast swathes of farmland, forests, and yet more farmland, taking perfectly straight roads through the heart of it all. She'd passed poor and jumbled communities, stopped in flashy highway oases, spotted birds of prey swooping and soaring Icarus-like to the sun, and all the time she'd wondered what kind of a place she was heading towards.

1

It wasn't anything like she'd expected. It was a town of many contrasts, hidden stories, troubled history, settled on a lake that glistened like a lost jewel in the middle of nowhere.

It was the second week of September now. Summer was officially over, though the sun continued to warm the immaculate streets, and flowers bloomed as eagerly as the birds sang. The tourists who'd swelled the population to many times its normal size throughout the season had vanished with Labor Day, leaving the place as tranquil, as perfect as a photograph, and for long moments at a time as still.

Justine Cantrell was standing at the edge of Lake Maxinkuckee, her bare feet sinking into gritty sand, her fine, honey-coloured curls bobbing on a wayward breeze. The sunlight was so bright on the water that she had to narrow her green eyes to peer across to the opposite shore, perhaps two miles distant. The magnificent multimillion-dollar mansions nestling amongst the greenery were barely visible from here.

'Are you crazy?' Matt, her husband, had protested when she'd told him where she was going. 'You can't.'

'Where else would you suggest?' she'd countered quietly.

'I don't know, but so far . . . Justine, you're not thinking straight.'

She could almost have smiled at that. 'Are you?' she'd asked.

He didn't answer, because they both knew he wasn't.

Neither of them could, and probably never would again.

'It's been so many years,' he'd stated, as if she didn't

know. 'You have no family there now. You don't know anyone to help you get started.'

'Isn't that the point? To go to a place where no one knows me?'

She could hear their conversation as though the rippling water spread out before her was carrying it to her across the miles, sighing its meaning, its pain and hopelessness into the very depths of her heart.

Eighteen Years Earlier – London, UK
'They're here!' Matt called out as the entryphone's buzzer rang down the hall.

In the bedroom Justine smiled, not only because of how pleased Matt always was to see his brother – he was already opening the front door and shouting down the four flights of stairs to ask if Simon needed any help – but because of the way thirteen-month-old Abby began bouncing gleefully on the bed. It was debatable what Abby loved most in the world, visitors, since she was nothing if not Miss Sociable, or music. And it was music of just about any kind, they were rapidly discovering, for they could play her virtually anything from Dire Straits to Billie Holiday to Blur and she'd either dance in her awkward toddler way, or try to sing along, or simply sit with Matt and listen, appearing rapt.

In spite of being almost nine months pregnant, Justine managed to scoop up their adorable daughter, who instantly shrieked 'Dada!' and shot out her chubby arms.

Matt was standing in the bedroom doorway, his

deep-set smoky grey eyes shining with love as he took Abby into one arm and put the other around Justine.

He was a little over six feet tall, had a loose, rangy physique, and thick, dark hair that curled wilfully around his high cheekbones and slender neck. Though he was undeniably good-looking, at least to her mind, it was his remarkable eyes with their flecks of violet and lazy glimmer of intrigue that had drawn her to him when they'd first met as students. There was also his smile, so captivatingly radiant it had actually made her blink.

She loved everything about him, and knew what he loved about her: the silky honey tones of her hair, the riot of freckles that darkened her creamy skin, the throaty laugh that encouraged his jokes, the way she embraced his impulsiveness, and often matched it with a spontaneity of her own.

Almost since they'd become a couple everyone had wanted to be around them. Their enthusiasm, recklessness, sheer *joie de vivre* was as infectious as their generosity. By the time they married, at the age of twenty-two, it already felt as though they'd known each other all their lives.

With his degrees in politics and Arabic Matt's internship with the BBC news channel had soon resulted in a permanent position, while Justine started her working life as a teaching assistant at a nearby primary school, mainly to fill time until their first child – conceived around the time of the wedding – came into the world. Her qualifications in drama and business studies would always come in handy further down the line; what mattered for now was giving their unexpected little treasure the very best start in life.

Abby was certainly thriving in the love that surrounded her. However, her speedy growth, and a new baby on its way in a couple of weeks, meant there was simply no way this cramped attic flat at the top of a four-storey town house in south London was going to be able to contain them all. It didn't even have a lift, nor could it boast a second bedroom, nor enough space for anything more than was already crowding the open-plan kitchen-cum-sitting room.

'Where is everyone?' Simon shouted, coming in through the front door.

Laughing, Matt planted a kiss on Justine's forehead, and carried Abby out to the sitting room where her aunt Gina was starting to unload their sixteen-month-old son, Wesley, from the carrier on his daddy's back.

With no preamble Simon declared, 'We've got just the place for you guys. OK, I know you don't want to look right now with the baby being so close, but it's not going to stay on the market for long.' He shrugged the carrier off and smiled at Justine as she came into the room. 'You know where I'm talking about. Have you got the details?' he asked Gina.

'Give me a chance,' she replied, setting Wesley on his feet and watching him make his way straight to Abby's playhouse. 'It's in the envelope at the top of my bag.' To Justine she said, 'How are you? The baby's going to pop out any minute by the look of you.'

'Please,' Justine implored, rubbing her massively swollen belly.

'And here's my little angel,' Gina smiled, taking Abby from Matt.

'Mum, mum,' Abby murmured in response, and gave a whoop of delight as her aunt swung her up in the air.

'You're such a pretty girl,' Gina said gently, smoothing her wispy blonde curls.

Abby drew back to look at her, showed every one of her new white teeth in a beguiling grin and promptly waved her fists in the air.

'So where is this place?' Matt was asking as he took the estate agent's details from Simon.

Simon grinned. Unlike his brother, he was almost as fair-haired and blue-eyed as his wife, though his and Matt's features and height were similar, as was their zest for life. 'You tell me,' he chuckled, clearly enjoying the moment.

As he looked at the property details Matt frowned in confusion, before raising his eyebrows in amazement. 'You're not serious,' he said to his brother.

'Absolutely,' Simon confirmed.

Gina gave a laugh of excitement.

Intrigued, Justine took the details from Matt and experienced a bolt of astonishment as she recognised the house for sale.

'You're kidding,' she said to Gina.

'Honest to God, hand on my heart, this isn't a joke,' Gina assured her. 'OK, I know you weren't thinking of moving out of London, but you'd get so much more for your money if you did, and it's not an impossible commute for Matt. Plus, you'd be *our neighbours*. That surely has to seal it.'

The Candlemass Road

George MacDonald Fraser

Now available in paperback

'Here is any one of you, in a lonely place, with no neighbours or friends by. There approach great thieves, crueller than any devils, who will surely torment and slay you. There is no help for you at all . . . But as ye lie in terror, a knock falls on the nether door. . .'

To the young Lady Margaret Dacre, raised in the rich security of Queen Elizabeth's court, the Scottish border was a land of blood and brutal violence, where raid and murder were commonplace, and her broad inheritence lay at the mercy of the outlaw riders and feuding tribes of England's last frontier. Beyond the law's protection, alone but for her house servants and an elderly priest, she could wait helpless in her lonely manor, or somehow find the means to fight the terror approaching from the northern night – and hope for that 'knock on the nether door'.

From two forgotten incidents in the State Papers, the author of the standard work on Anglo-Scottish border history, *The Steel Bonnets*, has woven a tale which presents the vivid reality of life and sudden death on the reiver's frontier of four hundred years ago, when lawlessness was 'the custom of the country', and the only safety lay in the lance and the sword and the will to use them.

It is a story told with the meticulous attention to historical detail, and grasp of character, dialogue, suspense and action which have made George MacDonald Fraser's Flashman series world-wide bestsellers.

ISBN 0 00 647720 8

The Pyrates
George MacDonald Fraser

'An unfathomable delight' *New Yorker*

The Pyrates is all the swashbucklers that ever were, rolled onto one great Technicolored pantomime – tall ships and desert islands, impossibly gallant adventurers and glamorous heroines, buried treasure and Black Spots, devilish Dons and ghastly dungeons, plots, duels, escapes, savage rituals, tender romance and steaming passion, all to the accompaniment of ringing steel, thunderous broadsides, sweeping film music, and the sound of cursing extras falling in the water and exchanging period dialogue. Even Hollywood buccaneers were never like this.

'Fabulous. . . You'll want to stay up all night reading this one'
Washington Post

'The most wonderfully idiotic lovesong to swashbucklers ever set to Korngold trumpets. Fraser again proves himself a master'
New York Times

'A sort of Christmas pantomime which incorporates every pirate story and nearly every period melodrama ever written in a huge burlesque. I recommend the book with all my heart'
AUBERON WAUGH

ISBN 0 00 647017 3

It was definitely a bonus.

Justine's eyes went to Matt, who was clearly finding it as hard as she was to take this in.

'You said yourself, when we sneaked a look round it last month,' Gina continued, 'that it was your dream place, or would be when the renovation was complete. Well, it's kind of done now, and I can tell you, you're going to more than love it. It's straight out of *Grand Designs*, but homelier, more liveable. The way you thought it should be.'

'But what happened?' Justine wanted to know, glancing at Matt again and wondering if he was starting to feel the same flutters of excitement that she was. But it was hopeless; this place was so way out of their league that she had to wonder what sort of income Simon and Gina thought they were on to imagine they could afford it. 'I thought the owners were fixing it up for themselves,' she said to Gina.

'That was the plan, but apparently the wife's mother is sick so they've decided to move close to her which is somewhere up north – Carlisle I think.'

Justine could hardly believe that a couple would put so much effort into creating a dream home, only to abandon it the minute it was ready.

'It's a fabulous place,' Matt declared, responding to Abby's outstretched arms and settling her on his hip, 'but we have to get real here, we'd never be able to afford it.'

Justine only wished she could disagree.

'I know, let's jump in the cars and go take another look,' Gina suggested rashly. 'We can stay at our place tonight instead of camping out here, and if you end

7

up deciding to go for it . . . Well, I'm sure something can be worked out.'

So that was what they did, and a little more than two hours later they were driving in separate cars through the quaintly crooked village of Chippingly Moor, passing its two old-fashioned pubs either side of the high street, the post office-cum-mini mart, Susie the hairdresser's, and three different types of gift shops. Further on were a couple of fashion boutiques, a florist, two charity shops, a butcher, a baker and even an actual candlestick maker, who supplied many of the nation's major department stores.

Turning off right between an insurance agency and Ruby's flower shop, they descended sharply around a bend. Passing a kitchen showroom and a dozen or more old stone cottages either side of the street, they wound on round another bend and arrived at the humpback bridge that unofficially marked the start of Chippingly Vale. To the left of the bridge, after Brook Cottage, was the entrance to the walled-in park, to the right was a narrow road that snaked randomly around more cottages before branching off up the hill to where Simon and Gina's small Victorian villa enjoyed views of the vale.

Straight ahead, at the top of a steep, grassy bank was the magnificent farmhouse – the dream home – that Justine would kill to own . . .

Present Day – Culver, Indiana
In spite of the sun, Justine shivered as her mind drew a veil over the past and gently reconnected her with her surroundings. The lake was quiet, so quiet she

might have been the only person around. The roaring speedboats and jet-skis that had chopped up the waters all summer were under awnings now; no fishermen were throwing lines, at least not today; there was barely even the sound of a passing car behind her making its way along Lakeshore Drive.

In the next bay of the lake, hidden from where she was standing, were the imposing Culver Academies that formed, arguably, one of the nation's most exclusive boarding schools for boys and girls. She'd learned the other day that the Equestrian Centre often provided the sleek black horses and straight-backed riders for presidential inaugurations. It was hard not to be impressed by that, and by the dazzling number of billionaire alumni the place could boast.

There was nothing like this in the world she'd left behind.

Though the Academy wouldn't, or shouldn't, affect her life in any way, she often saw the students, smart in their uniforms, easy in their freedoms, milling about downtown, lunching at Café Max, shopping in one of the Main Street boutiques, or heading over to the elementary school to help run the after-hours boys' and girls' club.

Thinking of children brought her heart to an abrupt halt.

Where was Tallulah?

She glanced around in panic until she remembered that her three-, almost four-year-old, daughter wasn't with her today. Leaving her at day care for the first time since arriving in Culver had been a terrible wrench, so bad that Justine had felt the trauma of separation like a physical tearing inside. Only she had felt it. Lula was sunny and brave, chatty, bursting with the excitement of meeting new friends.

'She's going to settle in very well,' Felicity Rodnam, Director of the Child Care Ministry, had assured her, taking Lula's hand and smiling playfully into her eager eyes. Justine had melted at the look Lula had given in response. How could anyone not adore her beautiful, impish, enthusiastic little angel of a child, with her fluffy tangle of strawberry-blonde curls and pixie face?

Every mother thought their child was irresistible, she understood that, but not every mother had so many complex and conflicting emotions threatening to undermine the love of that child.

Tallulah wasn't to blame.

Justine knew that in her heart and in her head, but still the thought, the horror, rose up like a demon in unguarded moments to wreck the inner peace she was trying so hard for – the peace that she must attain or she would surely lose her mind.

How could she wish the most precious little person in her life had never been born? Even if she hadn't, would it really have made a difference?

Inhaling the clear, fresh air, she allowed her gaze to drift to the buoys further out in the bay, there to warn swimmers to go no further. She and Lula had swum a lot this past month, not only here at the beach, but at the south shore of the lake, closer to their home.

Enjoying the spectacle of a heron coming to land on the jetty nearby she waited for it to fly on, deciding she would leave when it did. It seemed to be in no hurry, but nor was she. She was telling herself, gently, that she had no need to feel fear, or apprehension, longing or shame. She could lose herself in the tranquillity of this vast, shimmering lake, in the promise of escape, the chance of shedding her old self like a second skin and becoming somebody else.

It was starting to happen.

A new name. A new beginning.

All the same, memories of her previous life kept rolling across the miles, as though to gather her up and return her to that fateful day when she and Matt had made the impulsive drive to Chippingly Vale.

Eighteen Years Earlier – Chippingly Vale

'I'm almost afraid to go in,' Justine whispered as she and Matt approached the old farmhouse. 'If we do, we might never leave.'

'I know what you mean,' he murmured, his dark eyes tense with purpose as he took in the rambling old place with its freshly restored limestone window frames, rebuilt chimneys and gleaming red front door. It looked so stately, yet settled and inviting, on the brow of the vale, so full of promise and cheer, that Justine could almost believe it was calling to them.

Because they'd tramped around the grounds the last time they were there she knew there were potential grassy gardens either side of the house, a cobbled courtyard and three old barns ripe for conversion at the back, plus an overgrown vegetable patch, a fully stocked orchard in much need of attention, and acres of farmland beyond that dipped and flowed, thrust and tumbled into the hazy distance. Who wouldn't want to bring their children up in such an idyllic West

Country setting that wasn't much more than an hour by train to London, and tucked in behind the thriving village of Chippingly Moor?

By the time they returned to London on Sunday evening Matt was so convinced the place should be theirs that he'd already left a message on the agent's answerphone saying he wanted to make an offer.

'Keep visualising,' he told Justine. 'Keep seeing us in it and somehow it'll happen.'

So that was what she'd done throughout the following two weeks, even while giving birth to their son, Ben. It was where she wanted to bring him up, so somehow they had to make the place theirs. Even if it broke the bank now, which it would, it was definitely their forever home, so they simply didn't care how hard they might have to struggle for the first few years. Why should they when everything about the house felt right? In the spacious kitchen the original flagstone flooring had been restored and replaced, and a shiny black Aga had been tucked snugly into a niche next to the fireplace. There was a vast centre island with a salad sink, extra storage and built-in wine racks, and still plenty of room for a dining table and even a sofa. At the far end of the ground floor was the perfect study-cum-library for Matt, with walls already full of shelving, a small cast-iron hearth in a corner and a view from the double French doors down over the steep grassy bank in front of the house to the park at the heart of the vale. At the other end was an ideal space for a children's playroom that opened on to a side yard that they could easily lay to lawn and cover with trampolines, slides, swings and see-saws. A large sitting room with arched sash windows at the front and back and huge inglenook fireplace was between the kitchen and study, while a massive oak staircase rose from the entrance hall to a bedroom each for the children with two more for guests, and a master suite for Justine and Matt that was so spacious and luxurious she hardly knew how she was going to fill it.

They soon learned from the agent that their first offer had been refused. So was the second. Then someone put in a bid that Justine and Matt had no hope of matching.

Their dream was being crushed by a stranger.

Could they really let that happen?

There had to be a way. The house simply had to be theirs, no matter what . . .

Present Day – Culver, Indiana
Justine's heart fluttered as the sound of a speedboat starting up further along the shore brought her back to the lake. Nevertheless, it still took a moment for her to fully remember where she was – and why.

They used to come to Culver for summer vacations as children, she and her younger brother Rob. They'd lived close to New Hope, Pennsylvania then. Their busy parents, Camilla and Tom, used to hand them over to Camilla's mother, Grandma May, each June to make the long drive across country to the summer house on Lake Maxinkuckee – or Lake Max as it was more generally known. Neither Justine nor Rob had any clear memories now of the times they'd spent here; they'd stopped coming around the time Justine was six, Rob four. Their father's job had taken the family to London, and as far as either Justine or Rob could remember Grandma May had never come to visit them there, nor had they ever returned to Lake Max.

Justine wished she could remember her grandma. She felt sure there had been a special bond between them – why else would Lake Max have presented itself so clearly when she'd realised she had to leave England and start again somewhere else, to become somebody else? It had felt as though her grandma was calling to her, telling her she'd be safe here; that she wouldn't have to worry about anything ever again.

Grandma May had passed on some thirty years ago when Justine was around twelve, but that didn't mean Justine couldn't feel her spirit lingering today, watching from somewhere close by, understanding her and caring. Imagined or not, it helped her to feel less alone. She wished she could picture the old lady in her mind's eye, or hear distant echoes of her voice, but she couldn't. She was sure there used to be photographs of her around their London home, but she had no idea where they were now. Presumably with her mother, Camilla, at Camilla's elegant town house in Chelsea, or perhaps at her country pile in Hampshire, though they weren't on display in either of those places either. Camilla never talked about her mother. There again Camilla rarely talked about anything other than gardening, her passion and claim to fame.

'Oh, hell, Justine, I don't know where those pictures are now,' she'd sighed when Justine had asked for them a few months ago. 'Why are you even interested?'

'Because I've decided to go and live by the lake.'

Her mother's eyes had widened at that, not so much

with surprise as something that had seemed like alarm. 'You surely don't mean Lake Maxinkuckee?' she'd protested.

'Yes, that's where I mean.'

Camilla's stare hardened. 'I understand your reasons for leaving,' she'd finally managed, 'but why on earth would you go to a place you don't even know?'

'Isn't that the point? To go where no one knows me?' Justine said, repeating what she'd said to Matt when she'd told him of her decision.

'But why *there*?'

'Give me one good reason why not there.'

Camilla's fleshy cheeks flushed with confusion. 'Because there's nothing there for you,' she cried. 'It's all gone, years ago, and no good will ever come out of running back to a place you can't even remember.'

'I'm not expecting a home to be waiting for me. I realise I'll have to rent a place at first . . .'

'You've got the whole world to choose from . . .'

'And I've made my choice. Exactly why is it a problem, Mother?'

Camilla drew back, as though offended.

Justine waited, her eyes holding the challenge.

Camilla turned away. 'I've already agreed that you need a fresh start,' she said, 'and I'll support you in any way I can, but please, do yourself a favour and forget about Lake Max.'

Had her father still been alive Justine would have sought his advice – or his opinion, anyway – but he'd died suddenly when she was in her late teens. By then her parents had been divorced for at least seven years. Justine and Rob had always remained close to their father, even after he'd moved to Seville with his new Spanish wife.

Camilla had married again too. In fact she was now on her fourth husband, Bill.

The last time Justine and Camilla had spoken was when Justine had rung to say goodbye. 'I've sent you my new email address,' she'd told her mother. 'Please don't pass it to anyone else.'

'Of course not,' Camilla promised. 'Rob tells me you've already rented an apartment in Culver while you look for something more permanent.'

Her mother sounded so peeved and agitated that Justine said, 'Would you rather I stayed here, in England? Perhaps I should move in with you. That would be fun, wouldn't it, us all under the same roof, sharing your precious garden?'

'Don't do this, Justine,' Camilla implored. 'You know coming to me wouldn't be the answer . . .'

'It would damage your reputation.'

'It's damaged all our reputations.'

Justine had rung off at that point, not wanting her mother to know she was crying.

Only Matt had witnessed the tears.

'Please don't go,' he'd begged, the day she'd booked the flights to Chicago.

'We agreed, I have to, for Tallulah's sake.'

'But I can't bear to think of you so far away.'

'No more contact between us,' she'd reminded him, her heart breaking into a thousand pieces as she connected with the real meaning of the words. 'It's for the best.'

Though they'd gone round and round in circles that

day, as they had on so many other occasions, talking things through in every possible way, seeking advice from Rob and his wife, Maggie, from the police and an army of counsellors, that was where it always ended, because as far as they could see it was the only way.

Justine had to leave. She needed to make a new home for herself and Lula, and since she was American by birth it made sense, at least to her, to return to her roots.

She could have chosen New Hope, Pennsylvania, but she hadn't, because she'd felt sure that Culver, Indiana was where her grandma wanted her to be. Of course, as a ghost, Grandma May would never be able to fill Matt's place – no one, living or dead, could ever do that – but in a quietly instinctive way Justine knew she'd made the right decision.

How she ached for Matt now, for everything that had once been theirs, the home, the friends, the dreams, the safety, the countless things they'd taken for granted.

One day – a few single moments in the day – had brought it all to an end.

Except that wasn't how it had happened. It had been coming for a long time, but no one had wanted to see it and by the time they had it was too late.

Stop, stop! You need to let go, to forgive yourself and start afresh.

The flimsy fabric of her dress floated around her knees like ripples in the breeze; her normally pale skin had turned golden in the summer sun. There were lines around her once lively green eyes bearing the unreadable story of her grief; shadows darkened their rims like spectres, palpable evidence of long, difficult nights during which sleep was rarely a friend.

Yet there were still moments when she could smile and feel her heart lifting at the beauty of nature, at how blessed she was in Tallulah and being able to make her home in this unexpected delight of a small town.

Lake Maxinkuckee had got its name from its first inhabitants, the Potawatomi Indians. She and Matt had found that little nugget on Wikipedia several years ago when they'd toyed with the idea of visiting the place for a family holiday. Camilla had immediately discouraged it. In fact she hadn't seen any point in them returning to the States at all, when there were still so many places in Europe and the rest of the world to discover. Camilla, who'd never lost her American accent in spite of being a committed Anglophile now, was nothing if not expert at tearing up roots. She did it at least once a week, in a literal sense, usually for an audience of thousands who tuned in to her highly rated afternoon TV show. Glamorous, erudite, flirtatious and undeniably gifted in her field – actually her garden – Camilla Gayley was nothing short of a goddess when it came to horticultural planning and landscape management.

That was what the press called her, the Greenfingered Goddess.

She was also something of a socialite, had a column in a national newspaper, and an Internet site that received hundreds, possibly thousands of hits a day. She was as active as a teenager on Facebook and Twitter, was forever posting selfies with the many celebrities she entertained at her mini estate and had, only in the past year, been invited – somewhat hilariously – to pose nude for *Playboy*.

Thankfully she'd turned it down. At fifty-eight she'd decided it wouldn't be seemly. (Nor was it at sixty-four, her actual age, Justine had thought at the time, though she'd refrained from saying so.)

Being a guest on *Desert Island Discs* – which, luckily for Camilla, had aired the week before all hell had broken loose – had, for her, been some sort of high spot in her glittering career. Justine had dutifully listened, cringing at all the name-dropping and self-adulation, while raising an eyebrow at stories she strongly doubted were true. Most outrageous of all was Camilla's luxury item: a photo album of her grandchildren that her dear son Rob had put together for her fiftieth birthday.

'Lucky no one asked her their names,' Justine had remarked to Matt as the programme ended. She knew the barb was unjustified, for her mother was actually much better with the children than Justine was ready to give her credit for, although it had to be said that she didn't see them very often.

'And of course,' she'd run on irritably, 'she didn't stop to think that it was too long ago for Tallulah to be in the album.'

'Don't let it get to you,' Matt cautioned. 'Lula's too young to know the difference, and we've got plenty of other things to worry about.'

Why was she thinking about her mother now? Most likely because she was the link to her grandma, an integral part of the connection that couldn't be made

19

real, or completed, unless Camilla allowed it. Or maybe it was simply because she hadn't heard from her mother once since she'd arrived.

'But you told me not to be in touch,' Camilla would protest if Justine got around to calling her.

It was true, Justine had asked her not to be, but she could send emails to the new account Justine had set up, in her new name.

When making the change she'd considered going back to her maiden name, but Camilla had retained custody of that.

'Gayley isn't exactly common,' she'd pointed out, 'and I'm sorry, I don't mean this to be hurtful, but I'd really rather people forgot that you're related to me.'

'Mum, for God's sake,' Rob had cried in angry protest. 'You're not even married to Dad any more, so why don't you change your name to Bill's and let Justine do what she wants?'

'Don't be absurd. Everyone knows me as Camilla Gayley. I can't just change it when it's all over our products, programme graphics, website . . .'

'It's all right,' Justine had interrupted. 'I'll find something else.'

In the end it was as though Grandma May had come to the rescue again, offering up her own name for Justine to take. So now Justine and Lula were no longer McQuillans, they were Cantrells.

Giving up Matt's name had been devastating. The day her new documents had come through she'd felt so panicked, so truly afraid that had it not been for Lula she was sure she'd have backed out and stayed. She kept thinking of the day she'd become Justine

McQuillan. How happy she'd been; how young and in love. She loved Matt as much now as she had back then. More. Much, much more, although that wouldn't have seemed possible at the start when her feelings had been so strong, and her determination so fierce, that she'd taken matters into her own hands to get them the farmhouse they so desperately wanted.

Eighteen Years Earlier – London, UK
Justine was in her mother's elegant study overlooking the Victorian lamp posts and leafy gardens of Chelsea Embankment. Camilla's severe, though attractive, face was already made up prior to a lunch engagement, her short fair hair combed to within a millimetre of perfection.

She'd expressed no surprise when her husband, Bill, had showed Justine into the room, nor had she raised an eyebrow when Justine had told her why she was there. She'd simply taken the estate agent's details, given them a slow lookover and passed them back again.

'I can see its appeal,' she stated, crossing one silk-stockinged leg over the other, 'but you'll never be able to afford to heat it, never mind buy it.'

Biting back a cutting retort, Justine said, 'We've worked it all out, and OK, it'll be tight at first, we might only be able to live in one part of it, but they're talking about making Matt an editor at work and if I can get a business going . . .'

'What sort of business?'

'I want to open a deli.'

Camilla's eyebrows rose. 'Mm,' she commented shortly, either not taking it seriously, or saving her opinion for another time. 'Twelve thousand pounds is a lot of money. Are you intending to pay me back?'

'I asked for a loan, not a gift,' Justine reminded her. 'We'll set up a standing order. It won't be much at first, but . . .'

Camilla's hand went up. 'You can pay it back when you have it. I don't want it turning up in dribs and drabs. It would be too annoying.'

Justine regarded her steadily.

'I'll give you the money,' Camilla continued, 'because it's only fair that you should have the same as Rob, which means the cheque I write will be for twenty thousand pounds, not twelve.'

Justine was dumbfounded. 'You gave Rob twenty thousand pounds?' she finally gasped.

'To help him and Maggie buy the house in Brentford. So it wouldn't reflect well on me if I didn't do the same for you.'

Still stunned by the news that her brother had received such an enormous sum and never mentioned it, Justine wasn't quite sure what to say. 'Have they . . .? Are they paying you back?' she asked.

'I hope so, though I haven't seen a penny of it yet and it's been over two years.'

Wondering if she'd ever have found out about the loan if she hadn't asked for one herself, Justine, determined not to be petty about favouritism, managed to say, 'I can assure you Matt and I will repay every last cent of whatever you choose to give us, and with interest if you'd like to set a rate.'

Sighing impatiently, Camilla took out her cheque-book, saying, 'Shall I make it out to you or Matt?'

'Either or both. We have a joint account.'

Camilla's smile showed what she thought of such foolishness.

'Can I call Matt now to tell him?' Justine asked as her mother handed the cheque over.

Waving her to the phone, Camilla said, 'I'll expect to be invited once in a while.'

'Of course, as often as you like,' Justine assured her, starting to dial. 'And thank you. I really . . . I mean, it's hard to find the words . . .'

'Then don't try. I know you're grateful. In your shoes, I would be too.'

And so, with not a single thought for being careful of what they wished for, they were finally in a position to buy the house of their dreams.

Chapter Two

Present Day – Culver, Indiana
'You look positively nymphlike standing next to the water in the sunlight.'

Justine smiled as the familiar sound of her brother's voice caught at her heartstrings and turned her around.

'I thought I ought to capture you on film,' he confessed, slipping an arm around her.

'But you didn't,' she said, making it part question, part warning.

'I didn't,' he confirmed. 'No photos, no video, no anything to take back with me apart from knowing that you're all settled in and ready to face the New World.'

Her eyebrows arched. 'I don't think they've thought of it that way for at least a couple of hundred years,' she commented.

'Longer,' he assured her, 'and you should drop the "of". Americans say a couple hundred, not a couple of hundred. Anyway, it's new to you, and that's what counts.'

Resting her head on his shoulder, she returned her gaze to the glittering, silky expanse of the lake. 'I keep waiting for a smell or a sound or something to stir a memory,' she told him, gazing towards the homes on the far shore, 'but nothing's happened for me so far. How about you?'

He shook his head. 'If we were able to find Grandma's old house, maybe that would get something going.'

'We don't even know if it still exists. Do you think it was on the East Shore?'

He cast a curious look towards the horizon, where glimpses of the luxury mansions gleamed white amongst towering sycamores and maples. 'I guess we know it was on the lake, because we both remember that much, but as for where, exactly . . . Obviously Mum's the person to ask, but we know we'll draw a blank there.'

Justine turned to look at him, drinking in his narrow, handsome face with its summer tan and guileless blue eyes. 'Aren't you intrigued to know why?' she pressed.

He shrugged. 'I guess so, but right now I'm more interested to know how my niece is getting along at day care. Any news yet?'

Feeling her heart tighten at the mention of Lula, Justine said, 'Not yet. They said they'd call if there was a problem, otherwise I should pick her up at three.' Her eyes drifted slightly as she went on, 'She's so adaptable, so ready to take on a new challenge, but I know she misses everyone . . .' As her voice fell into the abyss Rob tightened his hold on her. 'It'll fade,' he assured her, 'in time.'

There were parts that she didn't want to fade, now or ever, but she knew they would and she had to keep reminding herself it was for the best.

'Tell me,' he said as they started along the beach towards the re-creation of Vandalia Park Lighthouse sitting small and proud at the edge of the lake, 'have you noticed anything . . . odd, about the people here?'

She frowned thoughtfully. 'Odd in what way?' she prompted. 'Personally, I'm finding them incredibly friendly. And think of all the baskets of cookies and home-baked pies we've found on the porch.'

'Which are playing merry hell with my waistline,' he grumbled.

'I noticed,' she teased, pinching his middle. 'So, why do you think they're odd?'

'I guess I'm not expressing it well, and I certainly don't mean everyone, but there have been a couple of instances that have been . . . Well, take when I was at Hammer's, the repair shop, just now, checking how they're getting on with fixing your flat. When I mentioned the Jeep Compass belonged to Mrs Cantrell this old bloke wheels himself out from under a truck and gives me a very peculiar stare.'

'Did he say anything?'

'Yes, he said, "Haven't heard that name round these parts in a while."'

Justine smiled at his attempt at the local accent. 'Did you tell him about Grandma?' she asked.

'Yeah. I explained how she used to have a summer place here, at the lake, so maybe she was the Cantrell he knew. And he said, "Are we talking about May Cantrell?" I said we were, and he said, "Yep, I knew her," and with that he promptly trolleyed himself back under the truck.'

Frowning, Justine said, 'Didn't you ask any more than that?'

'I couldn't. He turned up his radio, making it pretty clear he didn't want to engage. And he's not the only one. Do you remember the old lady who brought us some leaflets from one of the churches? Did you catch the way she looked at you when you said your name was Cantrell?'

Justine shook her head.

'I admit I could have been imagining things, but it seemed for a minute that she was going to take the leaflets back.'

Justine wasn't sure whether she wanted to laugh at that or not. 'Maybe we look like a pair of heathens,' she suggested. 'Remember we're in the middle of Bible Belt here, and we don't have many credentials to recommend us on the God front.'

'How could I forget, when there currently seem to be more churches in town than kids?'

Justine couldn't deny that. In fact she'd been worried, for Lula's sake, about the lack of children once the summer crowd had departed. However, her mind had been put at rest when she'd discovered that plenty of kids were bussed in from neighbouring communities to fill the local schools, and there were a dozen or more who lived locally. Lula had already been on play dates with most of them. Her very best friend so far was four-year-old Hazel, daughter of Sallie Jo Osborn, the local realtor and owner of Café Max. In much the same way as Sallie Jo had taken Justine under her wing, Hazel had taken Lula under hers. Sallie Jo and Hazel had made moving into their new home so easy, and even fun, that Justine had found herself going for whole stretches of time without thinking about the reason why she, Lula and Rob were there.

Sallie Jo was a special person; there was no doubt about that. She and Justine could easily become friends; in fact they already were, but they were never going to be close in the way Justine had once been with Cheryl Manning. She'd met Cheryl at uni, had graduated with her, travelled with her, shared secrets, heartaches and dreams with her, and they'd vowed they'd always follow each other to the ends of the earth . . .

Cheryl would never come to Culver . . .

It hurt too much to think about Cheryl, so it was best to make herself stop.

As she and Rob crossed the kiddies' play park to where he'd left his car, opposite the Culver Coffee Company and Lakeside Grill, she felt a terrible sinking sensation drawing her down and down as though trying to bring her to her knees. Her brother would be leaving in a couple of days, taking the long flight home to his wife and daughter who'd been without him all summer while he'd come to the States to settle her in. God bless her sister-in-law Maggie for not minding about him being away for so long, or understanding it, anyway. Maggie would have come too if she hadn't already arranged to take Francine to her parents in France. At least Lula wouldn't have to say goodbye to her cousin and aunt when the time came for Rob to go.

Their journey to the Child Care Ministry, tucked in behind the United Methodist church towards the top end of town, took no more than five minutes, but each one of those minutes for Justine was filled with the dread of her brother's departure.

It wasn't going to be as bad as saying goodbye to Matt, she reminded herself. *Nothing could ever be as bad as that.*

She knew it could, but she wasn't prepared to go there, not when she was about to collect her precious little live wire of a three-year-old.

A few other parents were arriving in 4x4s and pickups as Rob and Justine pulled alongside the steps leading to the nursery's front door. They smiled and waved to those they recognised, but didn't get out of the car until they spotted Tallulah skipping down the steps holding hands with the jolly-faced director, Felicity Rodnam.

'Mummy, we've done lots of things today,' Lula cried as Justine scooped her up in a giant hug. 'I drew pictures and we played games and we had stories that were really good. Uncle Rob can we go to Papa's for pizza, please?'

Taking her gangly little frame into an embrace of his own, Rob said, 'I'm sure that can be arranged.'

'Yes!' she shrieked, clutching her arms around him. 'Will the naughty birds be there?' she wanted to know, referring to the vultures that regularly perched on the water tower behind the restaurant.

'Oh, I expect so,' he replied, knowing how their gloomy presence and sudden swoops fascinated his niece, as most things did.

Felicity Rodnam's eyes were shining. 'She's a joy,' she told Justine quietly. 'And quite advanced for her age.'

'She'll be four soon,' Justine reminded her.

Smiling at Lula, Felicity said, 'She told us lots about your home in England, so we got out the map for everyone to see where it is in relation to Culver.'

Though Justine felt a moment of unease, she managed a smile. 'Did you find it?' she asked.

'Sadly our atlas isn't detailed enough to include your actual village, but we worked out that it's quite close to London?'

Justine shook her head. 'Not very,' she whispered, 'a hundred or so miles away, but thank you for making her feel special.'

'It wasn't a problem,' Felicity assured her, looking fondly at Lula. 'Will you come again tomorrow?' she invited.

Lula immediately nodded. 'Can I, Mummy?' she remembered to ask.

'Of course.'

'Lula, you forgot this,' a little voice announced behind them.

Lula immediately slipped through Rob's arms to take the drawing a tiny dark-haired girl was holding up.

'Thank you,' Lula said earnestly. 'Mummy, it's a picture of our new house for you to put on the wall.'

'How wonderful,' Justine exclaimed, kind of seeing the likeness.

'I put a dog in the garden, in case you change your mind about us having one.'

Justine's eyes went to Rob and Felicity.

'Good luck with saying no,' Felicity murmured.

'Do you think we should call her Rosie?' Lula

suggested, glancing at Felicity, possibly hoping for support.

Justine's throat dried as Rob went down to Lula's height and whispered, 'If you do get a new dog I think she should have a name all of her own, don't you?'

Lula frowned, then nodded. 'Because Rosie is Rosie,' she informed Felicity. 'It would just get all mixed up if they were both called the same.'

'That's my girl,' Rob said, hiking her up into his arms again.

'So everything went well?' Justine said quietly to Felicity as Rob went to settle Lula in the back of the car.

'Indeed,' Felicity confirmed. 'She's a very sociable little girl.'

It was what Justine needed to hear. 'Thank you,' she smiled.

Felicity was about to turn away when she stopped and said, 'Am I right, she's an only child?'

It was what Justine had written on the registration form, so yes, Lula was an only child, she confirmed.

Whatever Felicity was about to say next was interrupted by a parent needing her attention, and glad to leave them to it Justine hastened to the car.

'What was that about?' Rob asked as she got in.

Knowing that Lula never missed a word, Justine said, 'Mrs Rodnam was just saying what a very good girl you've been today.'

Lula nodded eagerly. 'Mummy?' she said, as they drove away. 'Are there any days when I'm allowed to be naughty?'

Laughing, Justine said, 'Not when you're at day care.'

'No, because then I won't get any gold stars. I just thought if I forgot sometimes, it might be all right.' After a moment, she said, 'Can we ring Daddy when we get home?'

This was the first time she'd asked that question in at least two weeks. Knowing what a fool she was to have thought it wouldn't be asked again, Justine started to speak but found she couldn't.

'I thought we were going for pizza,' Rob jumped in. 'I think I'll have a taco fiesta. What about you?'

Immediately there, Lula said, 'I'm going to have chicken freddo.'

'Good choice. I bet you don't manage to eat it all.'

'If I don't we can put it in a box to take home. Mummy? There's a girl at day care called Abby.'

Feeling her head starting to spin, Justine said, 'That's nice.'

'She's four.'

'You'll be four soon.'

Lula suddenly yawned and sat back in her seat. 'I love Abby,' she whispered. 'I'm going to be like her when I grow up.'

Justine felt Rob's eyes turn to her. Neither of them spoke; there was nothing they could say.

It was as easy to get caught up in the energy and magic that was Sallie Jo Osborn as it was to love the perfect ranch-style house she'd found for Justine to rent. It was called Waseya, a Potawatomi name meaning sunshine and happiness, which alone might have decided Justine on the place. However, with its pale grey wood exterior, white-framed windows and huge wraparound porch it was everything she had hoped for, and in a picture-book setting. It was at the end of a tree-lined track that came off West Shore Drive and circled on round to a scattering of other properties, none large, but all in their own private space. So while Waseya was secluded in the woodlands at the edge of town, it wasn't isolated, and with its glimpse of the water through an opening in its front hedge that acted as a gate, it seemed almost shyly proud to be where it was.

As Rob drove in through the opening Justine felt her heart lift to see Sallie Jo waving from the porch steps where she was speaking on the phone while Hazel, with her tumbling dark curls and bright blue eyes, came dashing towards the car to greet Tallulah.

'Hey! I was just leaving you a message,' Sallie Jo called out as Justine climbed from the car. She was tall, curvaceous and about Justine's age, though with fewer lines around her eyes and none of Justine's newly acquired hesitancy. 'How are things?' Sallie Jo wanted to know. 'We came over to find out how Lula had gotten along at day care. Shame Hazel couldn't be there for her first day, but I bet she coped just fine anyways.'

'It was really good,' Lula insisted, rushing up to her. 'I did lots of things like colouring and counting and answering questions and they said I can go again tomorrow.'

'That's terrific,' Sallie Jo declared, swooping her up and giving her a kiss. 'I knew you'd be a superstar.'

Lula beamed, but quickly wriggled to get down as

she and Hazel had frames to climb, slides to swish down and secrets to share.

'And how did Mommy cope?' Sallie Jo teased, treating Justine to an affectionate hug. With her glorious sweep of raven hair, merry brown eyes and ready smile, the warmth of her personality had made her widely popular in the town.

'Mommy did OK,' Justine answered wryly.

'Hey, Sallie Jo,' Rob smiled, coming from the car with the groceries they'd just picked up from the Park 'n' Shop. 'We're going to Papa's for pizza in a while, if you and Hazel feel like joining us.'

Sallie Jo threw out her hands in dismay. 'Any other time you could count me in,' she replied, 'but I'm short-staffed at the café tonight. I think I know someone who'd jump at it though.' She turned to where Hazel and Lula were quietly watching a mother deer with its fawn at the edge of the woods. Though this wasn't a rare sight it was always entrancing, especially for Lula who adored all animals.

'We'd love her to come,' Justine assured her. 'She can stay over if you like and I'll take her to nursery in the morning.'

'You, my friend, are a lifesaver,' Sallie Jo informed her. 'I'm due to show a house on Pearl at eight thirty, so that would work out perfectly.'

'Great, that's settled then. Are you coming in for a cuppa?'

Sallie Jo checked her watch. 'I guess I ought to go home and pick up some things for Hazel.' Her eyes went back to Justine's. 'Oh, to hell with it,' she laughed, 'sure I'll make time for a cuppa.'

'We've still got a mountain of cookies and coffee cake to get through,' Rob warned, 'and no one escapes here without doing their bit to help out.'

'Believe me, I'm always up for a slice of Dorry Mitzell's coffee cake,' Sallie Jo assured him, 'please tell me there's some left.'

'If there is it'll be a miracle,' Justine informed her, tossing a dry look her brother's way.

'Hey, can I help it if Dorry's cake is as irresistible as yours?' he protested, pushing open the door.

'You bake?' Sallie Jo said to Justine in surprise.

'No, no,' Justine replied, flipping it away. 'He makes this stuff up,' and following him across the porch where a swing seat, two rockers, a stainless steel grill and various tools and toys were providing a haphazard sort of welcome, she held the door for Sallie Jo to step inside first.

The entryway led straight into the open-plan kitchen and sitting room, which comprised the entire single-storey front of the house. Large French doors opened on to the porch, while a wood-burner and carved beech fireplace dominated the sitting room's end wall and a huge picture window with twin butler sinks and gadget-covered worktops did the same for the kitchen. The furniture had a rustic charm with three sumptuous, though not new, brown leather sofas grouped around a coffee table in front of the hearth, and a sturdy square table in the kitchen covered by a red and blue check cloth.

There was no doubt the landlords had thought of everything when equipping the house for rent, providing a plentiful supply of linens, every conceivable type of pot and pan, and enough silverware, crockery and glasses to throw a party for twenty. They'd even installed a tree house, basketball net, swings, slide and climbers in the front yard in the hope of appealing to a family, with further thought given to this in the decor of the basement, where a whole host of children's favourite bears such as Barney, Winnie-the-Pooh, Paddington and Baloo were painted on the walls. The bedrooms and bathrooms were all in the two-storey rear section of the house, with Justine's behind the sitting room, and Lula's smaller, very pink emporium behind the kitchen. Two more bedrooms were upstairs, both with their own bathrooms and views of the lake through the trees.

'You want good tenants, you provide a good property,' Sallie Jo had declared when she'd first shown Justine around the place. 'Everything should be here, and if it isn't just let me know because I'm sure we can work it out. They're a great couple, the Stahls. My parents have known them for years. They have a cottage on South Shore Drive that they also rent out, but it sleeps fourteen and you said you didn't want anything that big.'

No, Justine definitely didn't. In fact she'd wanted nothing ostentatious at all, though she could certainly afford it. Just a simple place not too far from town was all she required. Somewhere she and Lula could feel cosy and safe, and where the contract for keeping the lawns pristine and flowerbeds well tended was taken care of in the rent.

'Safe?' Matt had protested incredulously when Sallie

Jo had emailed Waseya's details ahead of Justine's arrival. 'In the heart of the Midwest, where just about every redneck halfwit will own a gun?'

Justine had shuddered, as much at the prejudice, which wasn't typical of Matt, as at the reality. It wasn't that she hadn't thought of the USA's attitude towards guns, it had concerned her a lot when she'd first decided to come to Culver, but she'd run a thorough check on the town ahead of time and had found there was virtually no crime, gun or otherwise.

Indeed, now she was here it was hard to imagine anything spoiling the easy tranquillity of the place, though bitter experience had taught her to be very careful when it came to taking anyone or anything at face value.

Looking up from her tea-making as a cellphone rang, she was about to reach for her own when Sallie Jo said, 'Oh great, my ex-mother-in-law, at last. I'd better take it. Be right back,' and clicking on she wandered out to the porch to answer the call.

As the spring-hinged fly-screen clanged shut behind her, Rob said quietly, 'Sorry, I didn't think before I mentioned the cake.'

'It's OK, it doesn't matter,' Justine assured him. 'I just feel bad that I'm not helping out at the café when I know she could do with some extra staff.'

'Would it be such a bad thing to offer? At least it would give you something to do.'

Justine turned away to take mugs from a cupboard. 'Not that,' she said, and knew he wouldn't press it any further.

As Rob continued unloading the groceries, she fixed drinks for the children and checked the answerphone for messages.

As usual there were none.

Though she could hear Sallie Jo's voice on the porch, she couldn't make out what she was saying and nothing would induce her to eavesdrop. If Sallie Jo wanted her to know what was going on with her ex-mother-in-law then Sallie Jo would tell her, and Justine guessed she probably would when the call was over, since she was as open about her personal life as Justine was necessarily closed about hers.

It was one of the things she'd warmed to most about her new friend, the way she never pried, or seemed to expect a trade of confidences when she surely must be wondering about Tallulah's father and why he was almost never mentioned. Then there was the reason for this new start in life, the sudden departure from England, which Justine rarely mentioned either. And why choose Culver when it had only been a summer home for her grandmother, and one she could barely remember?

Sallie Jo's own reason for returning to Culver after being away for almost two decades had been to recover from a bitterly broken marriage. Since she'd attended the Academy between the ages of eleven and eighteen and her parents still owned a large and rambling cottage on the south shore, she'd more or less grown up by the lake so for her it was definitely home. For her parents it was a place where they spent various months of the year, while the rest of the time they were either travelling, or at their apartment in Florida, or visiting Sallie Jo's sister Cora Jane and her family in Indianapolis.

Sallie Jo's ex-husband was still in Chicago, and never in touch. After ten years of marriage he'd waited until Sallie Jo was pregnant to announce that the last thing he needed was to be a father, so if she wanted their marriage to continue she had to get rid of the baby. It wasn't that Sallie Jo was strongly pro-life, though her parents certainly were, as were most of the people she'd grown up with; it was simply that she'd longed to be a mother, so there was no way in the world she was going to get rid of her unborn child.

'It was him or Hazel,' she'd told Justine during one of their many chats over wine and dinner, 'and I can promise you I've never regretted the decision.'

The ex had married again only months after the divorce, while Sallie Jo remained single. 'If you're coming to Culver looking for romance,' she and several of her friends had laughed with Justine one evening, 'then you've sure got the wrong place, because there's none of that stuff going down here.'

Though romance was the last thing Justine wanted, she knew it wasn't the same for Sallie Jo, since she'd definitely picked up the frissons of attraction between her and David Clifton, the extremely popular editor of the *Culver Citizen.* In another time, another world, Justine was sure she'd be drawn to him herself, but only because he reminded her of Matt.

'Oh, I love him to bits, obviously,' Sallie Jo had admitted when Justine had remarked that she was sure David had a thing for her, 'but it's all too complicated. Much better for things to stay as they are.'

Though Justine wasn't entirely sure how they were, she was all for no complications.

'Great, that's that sorted,' Sallie Jo announced, breezing back into the kitchen. 'They want to come for Thanksgiving again this year. Mom and Dad were hoping they would, they're such great people, nothing like their son, and Hazel's gonna love having both sets of grandparents around. Oh my, what is it, honey?' she cried as Lula ran in sobbing.

'Mummy! Mummy!' Lula choked, rushing straight to Justine's arms. 'Hazel said I don't have a real daddy and that's not true, is it? I do have a real daddy . . .'

'Hazel, for God's sake, what got into you?' Sallie Jo scolded as a teary Hazel followed Lula inside.

'I'm sorry,' Hazel said to Lula. 'I didn't mean to upset you.'

Lula turned her head away. 'I want to speak to Daddy,' she wept. 'Please Mummy can we call him?'

Justine's eyes went to Rob. She was aware Sallie Jo was deliberately not watching them, apparently trying not to make them any more uncomfortable than they already were.

'Please Mummy, please,' Lula begged.

'You remember what I told you about time zones,' Justine whispered.

'*I want to call him now,*' Lula raged, her peachy cheeks turning crimson with temper.

Justine looked at Rob again, but he only shrugged and shook his head.

'OK, sweetheart,' Justine relented. 'We'll do it when we get back from Papa's . . .'

'No! Now!' and slithering to the floor she ran to fetch the phone.

Taking it from her as Sallie Jo discreetly ushered Hazel outside, Justine started to dial.

What else could she do?

When the number was complete she stood gazing into the trees behind the house, waiting for the connection and feeling it drawing her all the way across the Atlantic and back through the years to the time . . .

Eighteen Years Earlier – Chippingly Vale, UK

. . . a week before Christmas when she and Matt were finally able to move into the farmhouse. The wait, once the deal had been struck, though not long, had seemed endless, the excitement explosive, but at last a removal truck was lumbering through the festively lit village and down into the vale, and what little they had by way of furniture was being unloaded into their dream home. Though none of the barns had yet been renovated and all three leaked, this hadn't stopped Simon and Gina hiring in the necessary equipment to turn one into a massive party room-cum-Santa's grotto. They'd invited everyone from the vale to join in the festive welcome, plus dozens more from the surrounding village, while just about every spare bed in the local B & Bs, pubs and even their neighbours' houses was taken up by Matt and Justine's rowdy crowd from London. Justine's best friend Cheryl was there, of course, with her husband Brad and four-month-old baby, Chantal. They were staying over Christmas and New Year to help Justine and Matt unpack and settle in.

For Justine, leaving Cheryl was the only downside of moving to Chippingly, and it was quite a serious downside. She was going to miss her so much it could make her emotional simply to think of it, and it was the same for Cheryl.

'If anything ever comes up for sale in this paradise,' Cheryl shouted over the party din on the Saturday night, 'you've got to let me know, because I want to live here too.'

'Oh God, I'd love that,' Justine cried excitedly. 'Do you think Brad would leave London?' It was hard to imagine when Brad was an Essex boy through and through, and didn't even much like going on holiday unless it was to one of the towns on the south-east coast. Nor had he ever particularly excelled himself when it came to indulging his wife. In fact, Justine had always considered him a bit of a bully, which was another reason she'd have liked to have Cheryl nearby, to make sure his intimidation and selfishness didn't get out of hand.

'I can work on him,' Cheryl declared decisively. 'After all, if Matt's up for commuting I don't see why Brad shouldn't be.'

Going with the moment, Justine cried, 'Absolutely. And if you do come you can partner me in the deli.'

'Exactly what I was thinking. Imagine all the fab buying trips in France and Italy, and the upmarket dos we could cater if we expanded. There're loads of toffs with dosh around here. The polo club's not far away, is it?'

Laughing, Justine said, 'Nor's Highgrove, but that

might be setting our sights a tad high. Who are you looking at?'

'I don't know who she is,' Cheryl answered, peering through the crowd. 'The little piece of totty over by the Christmas tree chatting up Gina's dad. See her, all boobs and Bambi lashes.'

'Oh, that's Maddy Hawkins, the butcher's wife. They live in the cottage down by the footbridge.'

'Well I reckon you should keep an eye on her,' Cheryl cautioned. 'I caught her flirting with Matt just now and if I hadn't turned up when I did I reckon she'd've had him under the mistletoe by now.'

Justine choked back a laugh. 'Actually, Gina warned me she can get a bit out of hand when she's had a drink, but apparently she's harmless really. At least most of the time.'

Cheryl shrugged, and suddenly gasped as Simon poked her sides and yanked her on to the makeshift dance floor.

Leaving them to it, Justine wandered off to join a group of her new Chippingly friends at the bar. Everyone was being so welcoming, and doing so much to help them get settled – a couple had even put their plumbing and electrical skills to use to get them connected, and Terry Moore, owner of the local hardware shop, had popped in only this morning to set up their TVs. They hadn't even had a problem sorting out a babysitter for the night – Maddy Hawkins's mother had declared that she wasn't much of a one for parties, so she'd be happy to oblige. Having spent the past thirty years teaching at the local infant school she was something of an expert when it came to handling large numbers of kids, and there were currently eight all tucked up in sleeping bags on various chairs and sofas in the sitting room.

'Aha, there you are,' Maddy hiccuped as she squeezed in next to Justine at the bar. 'I just wanted to tell you what a fab party this is. We are sooo going to love having you as neighbours. You're just what this place needs, fresh and young and ready to rock 'n' roll.'

Laughing, Justine said, 'You're making it sound as though everyone else is old and past it.'

'Oh no,' Maddy protested. 'There's loads of young couples around here, thank God. Be a bloody miserable place otherwise. No I was meaning it's great that you didn't back out of moving in the way the other couple did. I told them it was a load of old nonsense about the place being cursed.'

Justine's smile faded. 'Please tell me I didn't just hear you right,' she shouted over the music. 'We were told that they decided to sell because her mother was ill, so they wanted to go up north to be with her.'

Maddy nodded. 'Yeah, I heard that too.'

Justine's eyes narrowed. 'But you don't believe it?'

Seeming surprised, Maddy slurred, 'Sure I do. I mean, who in their right minds would give up a place like this because of some crap about a curse? It had to be because of the mother.'

Justine regarded her warily.

'Relax,' Maddy giggled. 'I should never have mentioned it, because it's not even a curse really, more that everyone who lives here ends up having some sort of bad luck.'

Justine still wasn't liking the sound of this. 'What sort of bad luck?' she wanted to know.

Maddy shrugged. 'Things just kind of go wrong, or that's what they say, but I've never heard of anything and I've lived around here, or not far from here, practically all of my life.'

'So did you know the people who owned it before it was renovated?'

Maddy shook her head. 'It was derelict for ages until they came along. Ronnie, my old man, he says that's why the house got its reputation, just for sitting empty, because he doesn't know anyone either who had any bad luck from living here and he was born in Chippingly.'

Feeling slightly reassured by that, Justine said, 'Matt and I have had a really good feeling about the house ever since we first set foot in it.'

Maddy lit up. 'That's brilliant. I'm really glad, because that happens, doesn't it, houses like speak to you, and it could be it's been waiting for you to come along, so now you're all going to live happily ever after,' and clinking her glass to Justine's as though to seal the deal, she melted off into the crowd.

Chapter Three

Present Day – Culver, Indiana

It was Rob's last night. Justine was sitting with him on the moonlit porch drinking whisky as they talked, with blankets covering their knees to keep out the cool, damp air. Though they'd always been close the bond between them had grown stronger, more precious than ever this past year, since Justine's world had imploded. She really had no idea how she'd have coped without him, or what on earth her life was going to be like once he'd gone home and left them here.

'So what will you do about Lula and Matt?' he asked softly.

Though she'd known the question was coming, had braced herself for it, she still had no idea how to answer, so she simply shook her head.

Lula had left a message on the answerphone the night Hazel had accused her of not having a daddy, but Matt wouldn't have got it, which was why he hadn't rung back. Luckily Lula hadn't taken long to calm down and seemed to bear him no ill will, apart from saying, 'Naughty Daddy, he should listen to his messages.'

'It'll happen again,' Rob warned.

'Maybe, maybe not.' She wished he'd let it go, and seeming to sense it, he did. However, he didn't take them on to much easier territory.

'You need to get a job,' he said, 'if only to fill the time.'

'I know,' she replied. 'I'll find something.'

'Like what?'

'I'll have a better idea once I start looking. Don't nag, Rob, please. I'm still getting used to things, and you leaving isn't making it any easier.'

His dear, kind face showed how torn and worried he was, so she reached for his hand and gave it a comforting squeeze

'I need to be able to tell Mum – and Matt – that you're getting it together,' he said.

She raised a sardonic eyebrow. 'If Mum wanted to know how I am she could always pick up the phone or send an email. She's done neither since I got here, so why would you feel the need to assure her I'm OK?'

'You told her not to be in touch,' he reminded her, 'but I hear you, and I agree, she should have made more of an effort.'

'Has she contacted you?'

'A few times. She always asks about you and Lula.'

'And you tell her we're doing fine?'

'Something like that.'

'Is she still raising objections to me being here?'

'No, she hasn't said anything about it.'

Justine's eyes drifted to the moonlit lawn, where a cat was stealing through the flowerbeds and Lula's three-wheeled bike lay abandoned near the gap in the hedge that formed their entryway. She didn't want to ask the next question, but nor could she hold it back.

'Will you go to see Matt?' Her eyes were still averted; her voice was a small sliver of sound in a misty breath.

Rob was watching her closely. 'I should think so,' he replied. 'I'm sure he'll want to see me.'

She nodded. 'Yes, he will.' What she wouldn't give to be able to see him herself, but that was a thought she must quickly discard. *No more contact between them. It was the only way.* 'You should take some pictures of Lula to show him,' she said, wondering, as she spoke, if that would be the right thing to do.

'Don't worry, I have lots,' he told her.

Her eyes went to his.

'He'll want to see them,' he said softly.

She knew that was true, and since there was no more to be said, or nothing that would make a difference now, she downed the rest of her nightcap and led the way back inside.

The next morning turned out to be even harder than she'd feared. Lula couldn't bear to be parted from her uncle. She loved him almost as much as she loved her daddy. It dug painfully into Justine's heart to admit that Lula probably knew her uncle better than Matt by now. After spending the best part of last year with Rob and Maggie in Brentford, followed by these past two months in Culver, she'd grown very close to him, as he had to her.

She clung to his legs so tightly and hysterically as he made to get into the car that he swept her up in his arms and whispered a secret in her ear.

Lula liked secrets, even though she wasn't all that good at keeping them.

She managed to hold on to this one for a week before finally confiding to Justine that Uncle Rob had promised to come back at Christmas with Auntie Maggie and her cousin Francine, whose birthday was on Christmas Eve. Francine was going to be twenty.

A year older than Abby . . .

Don't go there. Don't even think it.

She hoped to God Rob meant to keep to his word, because Lula was already marking off the days on a calendar. He'd said in a recent email that he would, so she mustn't doubt him.

Lula was unhappy this morning because she'd insisted on calling Uncle Rob and Daddy before leaving the house and had got bumped on to voicemail both times.

'What do you want to talk to them about?' Justine asked, as they were about to get into the car to drive to day care.

'I want to tell them that we had another mummy deer in the garden with two babies,' Lula answered miserably. 'And there were rabbits, and we heard an owl last night.'

Relief released a few tight bands in Justine's heart. At least she hadn't wanted to beg them to come and get her, or to make Mummy take her home.

Where was home for Lula now?

Surely it had to be here.

'Of course you do,' she smiled, helping her climb into the car, 'and they'll want to hear all about it when they ring back.'

Since Lula had nothing to say to that, Justine got into the driver's seat and started towards the lake. A fine mist was swirling gently over its sunlit surface, masking the distant opposite banks where the Academies would already be in full swing, and shrouding the small jetty where she, Rob and Lula had often picnicked on summer evenings while watching the sun go down.

Aware of a car closing in behind her she waved out to Tamsin, one of her neighbours, and turned left towards town. Tamsin hooted and waved again as she headed off right – she was making drapes for the owners of a new build further along South Shore Drive close to the Venetian Village.

There were so many treasures around these shores, architectural, historical, natural, even mystical . . .

'Mummy?'

'Yes?'

'Can we sing a song?'

As the words echoed from the past, causing a harsh burn in her heart, Justine smiled and said, 'Of course. Which one would you like?'

Lula pouted her lips and wrinkled her nose as she thought – an expression that was all her own. 'I know,' she declared, and she promptly began in a sweet, tuneful little voice that drew up so many memories that Justine found it hard to breathe.

Abby had loved to sing.

'*Jesus loves the little children, All the children of the world, Red and yellow* . . . Mummy you're not singing.'

Obediently Justine joined in and kept going even when Lula missed the words, not focusing on their familiarity or meaning, but making herself register everything they were passing instead: the town cemetery with its grey headstones and clusters of flowers honouring the dead; cornfields with towering stalks almost ready for harvest; the Garden Court and Culver Bible church; Wabash, Tampa and Davis Streets where some of Lula's friends lived, until eventually they reached the Evil Czech Brewery where they turned on to South Main and Lula suddenly shouted the last line, '*Jesus came to save the children of the world.*'

'Well done,' Justine praised, hardly knowing how she was getting the words past the dryness in her throat.

Jesus came to save the children of the world.

Bitterness would never help her to heal, she had to quash it, deny it, damn it and be rid of it.

What would Matt say if he knew Lula was going to Christian day care?

Considering where they were, he must have guessed it would happen.

They'd never been religious, had never gone to services apart from attending various weddings or christenings, bat/bar mitzvahs, or other such milestones in a friend's or child's journey through life.

Maybe not having a God was where they'd gone wrong.

'Mummy! Mummy! Look!' Lula suddenly cried, jumping up in her seat as they slowed to cross Madison Street, where the sunflowers soaring grandly outside the B & B were starting to fade. 'What's that in Café Max?'

Pulling up outside Civvies, the clothing store, so

they could get a good look across the street to the café, Justine started to smile. Two banjo-playing skeletons with flashing eyes, mechanical jaws and swivelling heads were, presumably, chanting hillbilly songs in the front window. Halloween might be six weeks away, but most of the businesses in town were decorating already.

'They're silly,' Lula laughed delightedly. 'I wonder if they have names.'

'You can ask Hazel when you get to nursery,' Justine told her. 'We should go now or we'll be late.'

'We mustn't be late,' Lula murmured as Justine waved out to Naomi, the owner of Diva, another clothing store, this one a couple of doors along from the café, and one of Justine's favourite places to buy unusual jewellery, housewares and gifts.

All told there couldn't have been more than a dozen shops in the heart of downtown; most were on Main Street between Madison and Jefferson with the Corn Dance Café, Café Max, Fisher & Company and Diva amongst those on the west side, and a closed-down hardware store, Civvies, Gail's, a kind of New Age emporium, and the Culver Museum and Gift Shop amongst those on the east side. Further along, running north of Jefferson, were the bank, library and gas station, while tucked in behind the main drag were the CVS Pharmacy, Hammer's auto-repair shop, a post office, a florist, the police station, VFW Club and a dry-cleaners.

Running in each direction for several blocks from this heart of Culver were row upon row of uniformly laid-out residential streets, with an almost Stepford-like quality to their perfection. Every house was detached, and while some had white picket fences marking their borders, others had glassed-in porches making them useable year round, and a few could boast grand-looking gazebos or integral garages. What every single one of them had, no matter the condition or size of the house, was an exquisitely kept lawn, that flowed seamlessly into their neighbour's lawn, creating the illusion of a vast and lovingly shared garden that went on for block after block with very little sign of neglect to break the lull of precision.

Suddenly finding herself outside St Mary of the Lake Catholic church, Justine realised she must have taken a wrong turn somewhere – not an easy thing to do in such a small town and on a journey she'd made several times by now. It didn't matter, with everything following a grid system she'd soon end up where she needed to be, so driving on along Lewis, where grinning pumpkins and corn husks were already in evidence on some porches and pathways, she finally reached the Methodist church, where small children were skipping or dawdling into the day care ministry.

After signing Lula in and storing her jacket and lunchbox in her cubbie, Justine went down to her daughter's height for a kiss. 'Are you going to be all right?' she whispered.

'Yes,' Lula whispered back. 'Are you?'

Smiling, Justine nodded. 'I love you.'

'I love *you*,' Lula cried. 'Can I go and see if Hazel and Rochelle are here?'

'Of course. Off you go.'

Apparently suddenly thinking of something, Lula stopped and turned back.

'What is it?' Justine prompted.

Keeping her voice low, Lula said, 'Rochelle's brother is called Ben.'

As the name seared the wounds inside her, Justine said, hoarsely, 'Is that so?'

Lula nodded. 'Like our Ben, but he's just a baby.'

Justine swallowed. She could find no words, but as Lula went to break away she quickly held on to her. 'Did you tell Rochelle you have a brother called Ben?'

Lula's eyes grew wide as she shook her head. 'No, I never said anything,' she promised, a hand on her heart.

Hugging her close so she wouldn't see the tears, Justine said, 'That's my girl. You run along now. I'll be back for you at three.'

Half an hour later, after detouring to the liquor store at the top end of town, Justine let herself into Café Max, feeling profoundly thankful that she had somewhere to go and someone to meet, even though Sallie Jo had texted a few minutes ago to say she was running late. *New listing on Academy Road, owner hard of hearing so taking longer than expected.*

The café, with its deliciously welcoming smells of breakfasts cooking and friendly hum of chatter, was divided into two halves, side by side, with the entry half consisting of the reception desk, Sallie Jo's real-estate racks, a large stone fireplace and, for the next few weeks at least, the Halloween banjoists; while the other half was home to cosy banquettes and tables, a magnificent quarter-sawn oak bar that Sallie Jo had

had shipped all the way from Florida, and, hidden from view, the kitchens.

Marly, one of the regular servers, greeted her warmly and showed her through to the bar's window table where another server was already waiting to pour her a coffee.

'Let me guess,' Marly twinkled, opening up her notepad, 'a lean machine breakfast with extra fruit on the side.'

Justine smiled. 'I'll pass on the extra fruit this morning,' she replied. 'Just the oatmeal pancake, blueberries and banana.'

'Coming up,' Marly assured her, and with a playful little twirl she started towards the kitchens before being waylaid by more new arrivals, a couple of long-bearded men in overalls and wide-brimmed straw hats. Mennonite builders, Justine had been told a while ago, who, apparently, enjoyed more freedoms, such as breakfasting in a café, than their Amish compatriots.

Left alone, Justine flicked idly through the menu, feeling tempted, as she often was, by the savoury omelettes and quesadillas. However, she was only too aware of how easy it would be to gain weight given the size of the portions. Not that Café Max overdid it especially, and she had to admit she'd seen very few obese people in Culver; she just didn't want to get into a habit she might not be able to break.

As she set aside the menu she took out her phone to see if there were any more messages from Sallie Jo.

Nothing so far.

Since Rob had gone she'd started to worry about how dependent she was becoming on Sallie Jo. She'd even mentioned it a few evenings ago while she and her friend were drinking wine around the fire pit in Sallie Jo's garden, over on Lakeview, while the girls played hospitals in Hazel's bedroom.

'It's only natural to lean on someone when you're new to a place,' Sallie Jo had reminded her, 'and I promise I'm not having a problem with it. I enjoy your company, all the girls do, and I guess I'm just someone who likes to be helpful.'

'You're definitely that,' Justine assured her wryly, while wondering how anyone could enjoy *her* company when she was such a withdrawn version of who she used to be. And it wasn't as if Sallie Jo didn't have plenty of friends, because she certainly did, most of them female – other business owners from around town, teachers at the high school and Academies, divorced or widowed women who lived beside or near the lake. She really didn't have any shortage of company, nor was she ever anything other than generous when it came to including Justine.

Refilling their glasses, Sallie Jo had gone on to say, 'I hope you don't mind me bringing this up, but I kinda feel the need to apologise for what Hazel said to Lula about her daddy, back when Rob was here.'

Justine's heart twisted.

'I know you probably think she was repeating something I said,' Sallie Jo pressed on, 'but you have my word that she didn't get it from me.'

'I didn't think so . . .'

'I spoke to her after and she tells me she heard a couple of women talking in the Culver Coffee Company when she was there with a friend and her mother.'

Knowing it wasn't only heat from the fire that was burning her face, Justine said, 'I understand that people are curious, but I can assure you Lula does have a father who loves her very much and who misses her even more than she misses him.'

Putting down her glass, Sallie Jo said, 'I can see this is painful for you, so why don't we change the subject? I just wanted you to know that I have not been speculating about you with others . . .'

'I don't blame them, they're human . . .'

'Of course, and like most of the rest of the world they want custody of the ins and outs of everyone's story. They're particularly intrigued to know why anyone would choose *Culver* to start a new life. It's like they're hoping you might know something they don't, or maybe they think your choice somehow validates their own reasons for being here – you tell me what goes on in their heads. I just want you to be sure that I don't believe everyone else's business has to be mine, or that mine should belong to anyone apart from those I choose to share it with. We all have things we'd rather keep private, and it's our right to do that. But just in case, you might like to know that I'm a very good listener, and anyone who knows me will tell you that I'm totally discreet.'

Though Justine didn't doubt it for a moment, and though she would have loved, in those moments, to try purging herself of at least some of the terrible guilt and grief in her heart, she knew she never would. It would change everything between them; Sallie Jo simply wouldn't be able to see her as the same person again, and she didn't have the courage to jeopardise their friendship. It meant too much to her. As it was to escape her past that she'd come to Culver, admitting to it would be almost the same as bringing it with her.

It would get easier, over time, she kept telling herself. As she made more inroads into building a new life for her and Lula the past would be left behind, while Culver, and everything they were already coming to love about it, would become the focus of the future. She mustn't forget that only eight weeks had passed since her arrival, which really wasn't any time at all. And actually, she already accepted, on an intellectual level at least, that this was home now. In fact, even on a deeper, more spiritual level, she had to admit that there were moments, usually when she was at the lake, that she came close to feeling at peace, an accomplishment she hadn't achieved anywhere in England since leaving Chippingly.

So perhaps she really did belong here with her fellow Americans and the ghost of a grandmother she barely remembered. A grandmother whose name had stirred up some sort of memory for the mechanic at Hammer's, and for the woman who'd come calling from the Catholic church. And now she'd had her own strange encounter, just last evening, with Billy Jakes, whose trailer and barns were at the far side of the woods behind their house. Sallie Jo and others had already warned her that Billy wasn't quite right in the head, not that she had anything to fear from him, they'd assured her, it was simply that his claim of ownership to a dozen or more of the corn and soybean fields surrounding the town had him at constant odds with many of his neighbours, particularly the farmers.

'Your name Cantrell?' he'd shouted from his truck last night, startling Justine as she'd come on to the porch to water the plants. He was at the gap in the hedge, staring fiercely in her direction. She wondered, with a stir of unease, how long he'd been there. Though he wasn't an old man, exactly, probably fifty or so, the greyness of his lank, greasy hair and ragged beard made him seem vaguely decrepit, and creepy.

'Yes, it is,' she'd called back, wondering if she should go over to him.

'Related to May Cantrell?'

'She was my grandmother. Did you know her?'

'No,' he replied shortly, and putting his foot on the gas he'd promptly disappeared.

Recalling the encounter now, she made a mental note to share it with Sallie Jo when she arrived. Not that she expected her to have any idea what Billy Jakes might be keeping to himself, it was simply that the eccentricity of his behaviour would probably amuse her the way it had Justine – after he'd gone.

Picking up her coffee she sighed quietly to herself, and gazed around the café's wood-panelled walls where every imaginable piece of Culver memorabilia was hanging. There was everything from class-year photos dating as far back as the fifties, to vintage football jerseys from the high school and Academies, trophies from Culver's many sporting victories dating back to the twenties; there was even a horseshoe from Barack Obama's presidential inauguration hanging over the fireplace. It almost did a better job than the local museum of evoking the town's past, a fact Sallie Jo was extremely proud of, since her time elsewhere in the country hadn't in any way altered the fact that she was a Culver girl at heart.

On way. Be there in 10, Sallie Jo texted.

Since there was no such thing as heavy traffic in Culver unless getting caught behind a harvester on the country roads counted, Justine decided to use the time going through some of Sallie Jo's property details. She'd have to buy somewhere sooner or later, so it wouldn't hurt to find out what sort of home she could afford.

As she brought the latest *Homes & Life Styles* magazine back to the table, she spotted David Clifton, the local newspaper editor, outside chatting with Toby Henshaw, the craggy-faced, football-crazy chief marshal of the Culver Police Department.

Sallie Jo's little fan club, she'd tease if Sallie Jo were there, since it was widely known that Toby with all his gruff manliness, and old-fashioned views on a woman's place, had a soft spot for the glamorous café owner.

Were she in Sallie Jo's shoes Justine knew that she too would be more attracted to David, not only because he was single – widowed, in fact – and without kids, but because with his messy dark hair, sleepy grey eyes and winning smile he was very like Matt. Which was the reason, she quickly reminded herself, that catching sight of him unexpectedly had caused her heart to flip.

On the other hand, being a Tommy Lee Jones lookalike with boyishly cute dimples, a police uniform and an air of authority didn't let Toby down in any way. However, he was married with five kids, which had to remove him from any sane woman's wish list.

Waving out as David glanced her way, Justine felt pleased to realise he was indicating his intention to join her. Though she'd only met him a handful of times, and always with Sallie Jo, she was already starting to think of him as a friend.

'Getting the scoop for next week's front page?' she ribbed as he came in and greeted her with one of his typically ironic smiles.

'Not next week's,' he replied, setting his laptop and cellphone down on the table. 'Toby was telling me about a training exercise he's going to be involved in with the sheriff's department at the end of next month. Thanks, Marly,' he added as she brought him a coffee. 'He's invited me to go along, which could be interesting.' He was checking an incoming text, while taking a sip of coffee. 'So what's with the property mag?' he asked, putting his phone down again. 'You starting to look?'

Glancing at it, Justine said, 'Kind of. I guess before I do I ought to find myself a job. I don't suppose you've any useful suggestions?'

He shrugged. 'Depends what sort of thing you're looking for.'

Skirting her real skills, she said, 'My degrees are in business studies and drama, but they're about twenty years out of date by now.'

His eyebrows rose. 'Did you know the old movie theatre uptown's for sale? You must have spotted it, a couple of doors along from the Lakeside Grill. It can't be more than a hundred-seater, so how about bringing it back to life?'

She laughed. 'I've no doubt the reason it went out of business is because everyone watches movies on their computers and smart TVs these days.'

He didn't deny it. 'You could turn it into a regular theatre.'

'You mean with plays and musicals? Would anyone go? Would anyone even want to act?'

'Believe me, Culver's full of frustrated talent.'

She had to laugh. 'Still no good if we can't sell tickets, and actually I have zero experience as a producer.' Though this wasn't strictly true, it kept her on safer ground than if she admitted to anything from her previous life.

'So have you had any ideas yourself?' he asked, checking his phone again.

'A few, but I've no idea how viable they are.'

'Anything I can help with?'

'I'm not sure. Maybe. I'll let you know when I've given them more thought. Meantime, I've been considering trying to find out if my grandmother's old cottage still exists.'

Clearly liking the sound of that, he said, 'It could turn out to be Meredith Nicholson's *House of a Thousand Candles*.'

She cocked an eyebrow. 'Except you know it's not, because you wrote a piece about that place and its impressively philanthropic owners only a couple of weeks ago.'

'I guess I did, but it would be kind of cool, wouldn't it, if it turned out your grandma's place had a similar sort of literary, or musical, or arty connection?'

'Sure it would, but if it did I think it would have

come to light by now. To be honest, I'll be surprised if it's still standing.'

He grimaced and raised a hand as Sallie Jo came in and was immediately waylaid by Marly. 'It would be a shame if it's not,' he commented.

With a playful twinkle, Justine said, 'Because it would deprive you of a great front-page story?'

'I can't deny it, especially if you found a few skeletons.'

Needing no more of those, Justine was about to flip it away with a light-hearted riposte when Maddy Hawkins's words suddenly came echoing down the years. *I told them it was a load of old nonsense about the place being cursed.*

She tried to take a breath.

'Are you OK?' David asked worriedly.

Somehow extracting herself from the memory trap, she quickly smiled and said, 'I don't know about skeletons, but here's something interesting for you,' and leaning in closer she told him about the odd encounter she'd had with Billy Jakes the night before.

As they laughed Sallie Jo looked up curiously, and it seemed to Justine, when her friend joined them a few moments later, that she could be coming to some wrong conclusions about what she'd witnessed.

'What's the joke?' she asked, her eyes moving cautiously between Justine and David.

She really does like him, Justine was thinking as she allowed David to retell the story, and to her relief Sallie Jo seemed to find it as amusing as she'd hoped.

'I think trying to find the old cottage is a great idea,'

Sallie Jo declared enthusiastically. 'I can help you with that, if you'd like me to.'

'I'd love you to,' Justine assured her.

'OK. I mean, I guess you're prepared for the fact that it was sold at some point and razed to make room for one of the luxury palaces?'

'Of course. In fact, it's what I'm expecting, but it would be nice to find out *where* it was, exactly.'

'Sure. And I'll speak to my folks about your grandma. It could be they remember her. Did she only ever come in summer?'

'At first, I think. I know Rob and I used to come then, but I have a feeling she might have moved here permanently after we left for London. Don't ask me why I think that, I guess it must be something I heard someone say.'

'Surely your mom knows.'

'I've no doubt of it, but whatever the story might be, she isn't sharing.'

Sallie Jo's eyebrows arched in surprise as she looked at David. 'Well, I don't know about you, but I sure do love a good mystery,' she grinned.

'My favourite kind of story,' he responded. 'The House of a Thousand Secrets. Great headline. More intriguing than candles.'

No one disagreed – and no one seemed to notice how panicked Justine was suddenly feeling.

'Can I follow the search for the *Citizen*?' David was asking as he opened his laptop.

Justine swallowed, not sure what to say, apart from no, *please* don't. It wasn't that she minded about it featuring as local news – the hard copy rarely went any further than Culver. However, the online edition was available to anyone, anywhere in the world, and the very last thing she wanted was someone in England making the connection between Justine Cantrell and Justine McQuillan.

Chapter Four

Fourteen Years Earlier – Chippingly Vale, UK

It was crazyville! So much to do, so little time to get it ready and not enough people helping out. Added to which there was no sign of the electrician, the delivery van had a flat tyre somewhere on the M4 and Matt wasn't due back for another hour with the family estate car.

'We've run out of juniper berries,' someone shouted from across the kitchen.

'Cheryl's at the supermarket, ring her,' Justine shouted back, carefully spooning melted chocolate into a bowl of hot butter and cream.

'These tomatoes aren't ripe enough,' Gina complained, pushing hair from her eyes with the back of her hand. 'I can't mash them.'

'Try these.' Justine grabbed a kilo bowl of near mush from a giant fridge and skidded it across the worktop. 'Do we have enough stale bread?' she wanted to know.

'Loads,' Thomas, one of the kitchen assistants, assured her. 'What's it for?'

'A panzanella. Start breaking it up. Is there an alternative to coffee cake if the electrician doesn't turn up?'

'There's a whole carrot cake,' Becky, another kitchen assistant, told her, 'a pecan pie, a triple-layer lemon cake . . .'

'The lemon cake's for the kids later,' Justine cut in. 'Which reminds me, has Ramona dropped off the brownies yet? Anyone heard from her?'

No one had.

'She won't let us down,' Gina insisted. 'She never has before.'

'Ahha!' Justine exclaimed as Cheryl wheeled an overflowing trolley bag through the open barn doors while speaking on her mobile phone.

'OK, you're in the village?' Cheryl was saying. 'Great. Go down the main street, turn left opposite the old clock tower and wind down the hill past a kitchen shop and terrace of stone cottages. Did you get that? OK, go over the humpback bridge into the vale and you'll see . . . Yes, that's us, the old farmhouse up at the top. You need to come round the back to the barns. We're in the middle one. You won't be able to miss us. The electrician,' she informed Justine as she rang off. 'Any news from Linda? Flat tyre fixed yet?'

'Not that I've heard,' Justine replied, spinning round at the potential horror of a deafening crash.

A trayful of twenty-four individual trifles was all over the floor.

Becky was gaping at Justine and Cheryl, hands clasped to her open mouth.

Justine and Cheryl looked at one another, and to the young girl's amazement they started to laugh.

'Someone help her clean it up,' Cheryl called out.

'Thomas, are you doing the game pie for the deli tomorrow?'

'I am,' he confirmed, 'but we're out of juniper berries. I tried calling you . . .'

'Ahead of you,' Cheryl told him, tossing a jar his way.

'What are we going to serve instead of the trifles?' Becky wailed.

'We're going to make some more,' Justine replied. 'Do we have enough ingredients?'

'If we don't I'll go back to the supermarket,' Cheryl offered. 'Who's running the deli today, Maddy or Shona?'

'Both,' Justine replied, 'and apparently they've run out of green olives, stuffed sweet peppers and there are only two chickens left on the spit.'

Going to get more supplies from one of the two vast cold rooms, Cheryl said, 'Aren't you supposed to be picking Ben and Abby up from school today?'

'Hell!' Justine cried, noticing the time. 'Oh God! Is there someone else who can go? I can't leave here while we're in this mess. Gina, who's picking up Wesley?'

'Simon. I'll call and get him to collect your two at the same time.'

After making sure the chaos was under reasonable control and the newly arrived electrician was repairing the right oven – the last guy had spent nearly an hour on one that was working – Justine disappeared into her office at the far end of the barn to check if there were any urgent emails or phone calls, and to ring Matt to make sure he hadn't forgotten the school's end-of-term show tonight.

'It's tonight!' he exclaimed. 'I thought it was tomorrow.'

'No, tonight, and it's not at the infants' school, where we thought, it's here in the vale. They're already down there setting up the park.'

'Aren't you doing a wedding tea today? How are you going to be in two places at once?'

'That's why we have an events manager. I'll just make sure the tea's properly under way and the client's happy, then I'll leave Vikki in charge and come straight back. I should make it in time. Thank God I did their costumes last week. Now tell me, how did it go with the agent? I've been dying to hear.'

'Well, it was interesting,' Matt responded. 'On the one hand he thinks the book's great, has real potential, but on the other he kept banging on about how hard it is to find a publisher for teenage fiction.'

'*Teenage fiction,*' Justine cried, aghast. 'Is that how he sees it? I think you were with the wrong bloke. It's sci-fi . . .'

'For teens.'

She frowned. 'You've never said that before.'

'Let's say my eyes have been opened and not only to genre, but to video games.'

She blinked. 'Are you kidding? You mean games based on the book?'

'That's right. He reckons we could make a fortune, so he's going to pair me up with someone who's into all that stuff. A Japanese guy, living in LA. Apparently he's got a massive company already, and he only started up three years ago.'

Seeing Disneyland, Universal and glorious Pacific

surf, she said, 'Does that mean we're going to California? The kids'll love it.'

'We all will, but there's a chance this bloke will be coming here in a couple of weeks for some launch or other. If he does, I could meet him then.'

Justine was still grinning. 'So how do you feel about the change of direction?'

'Well, I guess I could handle becoming a multi-millionaire.'

Yelping with laughter, she said, 'I might fancy you even more if you're rich.'

'Bring it on,' he retorted wryly. 'Now remind me what's happening this weekend.'

'The disco for your nephew's sixth birthday?'

'Wesley! He's six already?'

Laughing, she said, 'You know very well how old he is, and we'll have to hold the disco in the playroom if it rains, because the party barn is hired out.'

'No problem. If the weather's good, we'll set up down in the park. Is your mother still coming on Saturday?'

'No, of course not. I had an email earlier saying she hadn't realised she has a prior commitment. Rob and Maggie should be here by five, they reckon. Francine's bringing a friend. I said that was fine, there's plenty of room, and your mother should be here around the same time.'

'Great. By the way, is Ben still planning to do his piece with Chantal for the show tonight, or has she backed out?'

'Don't even suggest it. He'll never forgive her if she does, but to hear them laughing and giggling when they're rehearsing I'm pretty sure she'll go through with it.'

'Have Cheryl and Brad seen it yet?'

'A couple of times, I think. It's a bit heart-stopping, Cheryl said, but if Chantal's up for it, she sees no reason why she shouldn't do it.'

'Is Abby going to join in?'

'Not as far as I know. She thinks they're amazing, she says, but she's determined to do her solo act. Don't forget you're in charge of the music. Oh, and I think she's changed her mind about *The Snowman*. Wrong time of year. She wants to do the one you've been teaching her. She won't tell me what it is because she wants it to be a surprise. Just keep in mind that she's not quite six. And I know she's good at remembering lyrics, but please don't let there be too many. She'll feel mortified if she forgets them.'

'Would I allow that to happen? She's going to be great. Promise. They both are.'

'And we're not biased in any way. OK, I have to go. How far away are you, in case the van doesn't get back in time?'

'About half an hour, but there's a load of stuff in the back of the car. We'll have to clear it all out.'

'Whatever it takes. I'll see you when you get here. Love you, richer or poorer, but richer would be better.'

As she put the phone down Justine was already dialling the deli on her mobile, while heading back into the barn where Cheryl had taken charge of the wedding tea, and Gina, who helped out on a part-time basis, was getting to grips with what they were going to serve after the infant school recitals later.

Not every day was like this, thank goodness, or she'd probably end up in a funny farm, but they'd been happening far more frequently lately as more and more requests came in following recommendations from satisfied customers.

She and Cheryl, who'd miraculously persuaded her stubborn, stick-in-the-mud husband to relocate to Chippingly only months after Justine and Matt had moved in, might have dreamt about enjoying a runaway success with their new business, but neither of them had really expected it to happen in quite the way it had. Their deli, Portovino, at the top end of the village high street, had first opened a little over three years ago following a joint family road trip round France and Italy gathering up ideas, wines and so much produce they'd threatened to sell the kids to make more room in the cars. They'd returned just in time to sign a lease on the shop and by the following year they'd knocked through into next door to make room for a palm court café with white wicker furniture and pale green accessories. It wasn't long after, with the kitchens finally fully operational in the middle barn, that they'd taken the plunge into catered events.

Part of the real joy of their business, they often liked to remind one another, was that neither of them had ever formally learned to cook. It was simply something they loved to do, and thanks to wall-to-wall TV programmes on the subject, it had never been difficult to add to their skills. Indeed, they owed much to Nigella, Jamie, Delia, Gordon, and at least a dozen others for some of their best-selling dishes, though they were always quick to point out that they'd added

– or even substituted – a little *je ne sais quoi* to make it their own.

As for staff, they'd found themselves with a whole host of neighbours willing to help out, either from the village, or the sprawling housing estate between Chippingly and the main town. There were now five women working on a full-time basis, alternating between the kitchen and deli, with eight regular part-timers backing them up, and still more they could call on for special events. They'd lately begun taking on graduates from various catering colleges, firstly to learn from them, and secondly to give them experience in the real world before they went on their merry way.

Meantime, the children were developing their own plucky little personalities; with all sorts of passions and talents that enthralled and amazed their parents on a daily basis. By the time she'd started school Abby could already play just about every nursery rhyme she knew on the piano, paint a picture of their house that actually looked like their house, and sing like an angel in front of the entire village, or playgroup, or wherever she'd been invited to perform. Her favourite place in the world to be, aside from the stage which made her nervous until she was actually on it, was the music room Matt had created in one of the barns, where she'd listen, rapt, to all his old albums and lately had even, with Matt's help, started writing little songs of her own.

As for Ben, even the health visitor had been dazzled by his hand-to-eye coordination when he was a baby, so it was no surprise that he was turning into a natural when it came to sports. And he was fast. Since starting school he'd won practically every race he'd entered, egg and spoon, three-legged, sack, and straightforward relay. He was on the football, cricket and rugby teams, and only a couple of weeks ago he'd won himself a legion of fans at the village fete when he'd kept hitting ducks with his bow and arrow and had generously, though solemnly because that was his way, shared out the prizes.

Though he and Abby fought on occasion, much like any other brother and sister, they usually made up in next to no time, though it had to be said that Abby was definitely the more forgiving of the two. Ben had a tendency to sulk, or perhaps it was fairer to say that he'd withdraw into himself and go to his room, or kick a ball around the courtyard on his own, or immerse himself in a movie until he was ready to bounce back.

They were a popular pair amongst the neighbouring children, with their cousin Wes living virtually next door, Chantal, Cheryl's daughter, whom they both claimed as a best friend, halfway down the opposite hill, and Maddy's kids Neil and Nelly in Brook Crossing Cottage at the edge of the park. These six formed the core group of friends; however there were at least a dozen more who came and went regularly from the farmhouse, known more generally as sleepover central, since all their little chums seemed to agree that there was always more to do at the McQuillans' than there was anywhere else in the village.

Plus there was always something amazing to eat.

By six that evening Justine had returned from the

wedding tea to find the park at the heart of the vale all set up ready for the recitals. At least six dozen white foldable chairs were cluttering up the spaces between the leafy beech and horse chestnut trees, while the stage, complete with a roof to hold up the curtain and lights, and roughly cobbled-together wings, was in front of the playground. Jolly triangles of bunting were swinging between low-hanging branches, while fairy lights in all colours were snaking up most of the trunks. A handful of local kids who weren't taking part in the show had already climbed up amongst the foliage to sort out the best viewing positions, or those closest to the catering tables, which were already set up around the fence.

Once satisfied that there was nothing more she could do in the park for now, Justine took herself up to the farmhouse to check on progress there. 'Is everyone dressed, rehearsed and ready to go?' she called out as she climbed the stairs.

'Mum! I can't find my hat,' Ben cried, rushing on to the landing in a panic. 'Where did you put it? Dad can't find it either . . .'

'It's all right,' she soothed, 'it's at the top of my wardrobe to stop it getting crushed.' Her eyes were twinkling with merriment. 'You look just the part,' she informed him, feeling quite proud of her own inexpert handiwork since she'd put the costume together herself.

His handsome little face flushed with pleasure, though he expertly ducked the quick ruffle she attempted to give his rapidly darkening hair. It wouldn't be long, she was thinking as she followed him into her and Matt's room, before he was the same colouring as his father, and she hoped for his sake that his freckles might soon disappear, since he considered them babyish. Ben detested few things more these days than being thought babyish.

'Here you are,' Justine declared, bringing the hat down from a top shelf and sitting it on his head.

'Is the feather right?' he asked, dashing to the mirror.

She watched the careful scrutiny of his reflection, and had to fight not to scoop him up for a cuddle. Apparently they had recently become childish too, apart from when he fell and hurt himself, or he was feeling unwell, when he might suffer one to make her feel better.

'Wow! It's William Tell!' Matt exclaimed, coming into the room with a green bob-cut wig in one hand and another in pink on his head.

'Dad, you look really silly,' Ben informed him.

'No,' Matt protested, checking himself in the mirror. 'I thought I looked cool. Do you think the green one instead?'

'None of them,' Ben retorted seriously.

'You need to lighten up, son,' Matt told him with a wink.

'I take it Abby's opted for the multicoloured wig,' Justine said, as Matt gave her a kiss.

'She has, for now anyway, and she looks a treat.'

'I'll pop in and see her. Ben, don't forget to go to the toilet before you leave.'

'I've already been.'

'Try and go again.'

'I want some tights like that,' she heard Matt

informing Ben as she went off along the landing to find Abby. On the way her mobile rang, so it was several minutes before she knocked on Abby's door and went in to find her sitting on the bed in the middle of her showbiz chaos, very close to tears.

'Oh no, what's the matter?' she cried, quickly going to her.

'What if I forget the words?' Abby whispered. 'Everyone'll laugh at me.'

Used to these pre-show nerves that generally dissolved the instant she was on stage, Justine said, 'No they won't, and besides you're not going to forget them because they're all up here locked in nice and safely.'

As she tapped Abby's multicoloured tinsel wig Abby turned her face into her mother's chest.

Smoothing the wig, Justine said, 'Why don't we try another rehearsal? Just you and me?'

'No, because it's got to be a surprise.'

'OK. So, did you remember it all the last time you sang it for Dad?'

Abby nodded. 'Your phone's ringing,' she told her.

Checking who it was, and fearing there was a problem at the wedding tea, Justine said, 'I have to take this, but I'll get Dad to come back and do another practice with you, OK?'

Abby nodded sadly.

It turned out that someone had forgotten to load the wedding cake – *the wedding cake* – into the delivery van, so someone – Justine – had to rush it over to the venue before anyone noticed.

'Sorry,' she said to Matt, finding him tidying up in

Ben's room while Ben shouted instructions from the toilet on where things went, 'but we can hardly have a bride without a cake, and you've always been better at cheering Abby up than I am.'

'OK, just don't drive too fast,' he warned, 'and make sure you get back here in time for the show or we'll never hear the end of it.'

Luckily she did make it, but only just, since the laughter and applause for the act before Abby's – Nelly Hawkins with her singing Jack Russell, Pip – was starting to fade as she joined Gina at the table full of trifles, brownies, cupcakes and a specially hired popcorn machine.

'Where's Matt?' she whispered, searching the audience for a glimpse of him.

'Backstage with Abby,' Gina told her.

'Is she OK?'

'She seemed to be the last time I saw her. I think he's worked out a way to be onstage with her in case she dries.'

Justine was intrigued, and as the curtain went up to reveal Matt taking bows in a pair of her diamond-patterned black tights, a red football shirt and green wig, and their friends and neighbours began whistling and jeering, she quickly realised what was happening. He was there to make sure that if anything went wrong he'd be the joke, not Abby.

It was only when Abby, in her glittery wig, slinky blue dress and bright red lipstick, glided on to the stage to a lively round of applause that Justine realised they were both wearing roller skates.

Chancy, she was thinking, with a little trepidation.

However, apparently uplifted by her enthusiastic reception, Abby gave a graceful pirouette in front of the mic before lifting it free. Though her eyes were shining with excitement, Justine could practically feel the rapid beats of her precious little heart.

Matt cued the play-in, Simon hit the karaoke box, and as the music began Justine wanted to cry as well as laugh. They'd chosen a song she used to sing with her dad when she was small.

I've Got a Brand New Pair of Roller Skates.

And her husband, she decided, her heart bursting with pride, was a genius, because there probably wasn't an adult present who didn't know the words, at least most of them, so there had never been any danger of Abby forgetting and feeling foolish. Everyone was joining in, keeping her going, and Matt was ready with a pratfall just in case something went wrong. However, Justine could tell from the sheer gusto Abby was pouring into her performance that she was completely on top of it. So much so that she even skated a little dance with Matt during the instrumental, and went on to honour three encores at the end.

Eventually Mrs Hayward, one of the teachers, gently eased Abby off to the wings to make room for the next act.

It was Ben, looking superbly merry-mannish in his Lincoln green costume, with Chantal, all floaty and femme fatale in her Maid Marian gown and wimple. However, Mr Grayson, Ben's teacher, was very quick to let everyone know that this was a scene from William Tell, not Robin Hood.

Once again the audience was right behind the

performers, stamping their feet and clapping their hands to the lively overture, while Ben strutted around the stage being very macho and Chantal ran hither and thither on tiptoe, trailing a silk hanky and touching the back of one hand to her brow.

They were simply too cute for words, and Justine and Cheryl were having to hold one another up they were laughing so hard.

At last Chantal took her position in front of a cardboard tree and carefully placed an apple on the top of her head. At the other side of the stage Ben was taking an arrow from his quiver and loading his bow.

As he took aim several teachers pantomimed a gasp.

Simon played in a drum roll.

Ben pulled back his arm.

Justine and Cheryl found each other's hands, playing along with the suspense.

Ben let go abruptly, the arrow flew and to everyone's astonishment it hit Chantal smack in the middle of her forehead – and stuck.

There was a second of disbelief before Chantal sank to the ground.

A teacher ran in from the wings, followed by two more. The audience began rising from their seats; Justine and Cheryl were paralysed with shock.

Then quite suddenly Chantal jumped up, plucked the arrow off her forehead and laughing uncontrollably, she and Ben joined hands to take their bows.

Finding her breath, Justine started to laugh along with everyone else. The little rascals had planned the shock, and the success of it was clearly everything they'd hoped for. She and Cheryl exchanged grins as the impish pair revelled in the praise and awe of their friends.

Cheryl said, 'I just love how much she trusted him. I mean, he could have taken her eye out.'

'Please, don't go there,' Justine protested.

'I might try and pull that trick on my old man,' Maddy quipped, 'only there might not be any rubber involved.'

'Oh, go on, you love him really,' Cheryl teased.

'Yeah, like a hole in the head.'

Realising what she'd said Maddy gave a whoop of laughter, and raised a glass of lemonade to her husband who was downing a beer over by the brook with a couple of mates. Though rumours abounded about the Hawkins – that Ronnie was having an affair with a woman from the estate, and that Maddy knew how to have a good time when she was out with the girls on a Friday night – Justine had no idea if any of them were true, nor did she particularly care. What mattered far more was that they were great parents to seven-year old Nelly and five-year-old Neil, who was currently in remission from a rare form of leukaemia. Knowing what the family had gone through during the darkest days of Neil's illness, and the fear they lived with every day that it might come back, never failed to soften Justine's heart towards Maddy's rougher edges, even though Maddy did make it hard at times.

Half an hour later, with everyone swarming around the refreshment table, Justine shouted, 'Anyone seen Abby? Abby! Where are you?'

'I'm up here, Mum,' Abby yelled from a nearby tree. 'It's so cool. Can we sleep up here tonight? Ben! We're up here,' she shouted to her brother.

'Is Wesley with you?' Gina asked, trying to spot him through the leaves.

'Yeah, I'm here,' he called back. 'We're all up here.'

Cheryl was looking in the other direction. 'Who's that going into the farmhouse?' she asked curiously.

Everyone turned round, but there was no one in sight. 'It must have been Matt, popped back for something,' Justine decided.

'It can't be,' Maddy told her, 'Matt's over there, packing up chairs.'

Seeing that he was, Justine turned back to Cheryl. 'Are you sure you saw someone?' she asked.

'Positive. He went in the side door, by the playroom.'

Justine frowned. Surely to God they didn't have an intruder, a burglar even, in the vale.

'Simon!' Gina shouted to her husband. 'We need you over here.'

Since Simon was an armed response officer with the county police force he was regularly called upon locally for off-duty action.

'What's up?'

'Cheryl just saw someone go into the farmhouse,' Gina explained, 'and we thought you ought to go and check it out.'

With eyebrows raised he turned to look up the hill. 'What kind of someone?'

'I'm sure it was a man,' Cheryl replied. 'It was pretty quick and it's difficult to tell from here, but I definitely saw someone.'

'Are you sure it's not one of your guys gone to get more food?' he asked.

Cheryl shook her head. 'There's only women on tonight, and we're all here.'

'Mm.' He gazed thoughtfully at the farmhouse again, before signalling for everyone to stay put as he went to investigate.

'What's going on?' Matt asked, coming to join them. 'Where's Simon going?'

'To check on the house,' Justine replied. 'Cheryl just saw someone going in through the playroom.'

Clearly not liking the sound of that, Matt said, 'OK, wait here,' and he started after his brother.

Watching him go, Justine felt her anxiety starting to build. 'It has to be someone we know,' she decided. 'I mean, who's going to carry out a burglary when there are so many people around? It doesn't make any sense.'

'There's no way out,' Gina added, 'not without coming back down the hill. Unless he wants to walk for miles across country to get to the main road.'

They watched in silence as Matt caught up with Simon and together they entered the house.

'I reckon it was a ghost,' Maddy murmured.

Justine threw her a look.

Maddy shrugged. 'Just a thought.'

'What's Daddy doing?' Abby called out from the tree.

'He's gone to get something,' Justine called back.

Long minutes ticked by with plenty of children still running around the glade, helping themselves to more food and climbing trees, until finally, to everyone's astonishment, Simon frogmarched someone out of the house.

'Oh my God, they caught him,' Cheryl gasped.

Justine's eyes were narrowed. 'It's Matt,' she declared darkly. 'They're larking around.'

'So who's still inside?' Gina wanted to know.

'I told you it was a ghost,' Maddy insisted.

In the end it turned out that Brian Grayson, one of the teachers, had experienced a very pressing need for a bathroom and hadn't wanted to satisfy it in the conveniences that had been brought in specially.

'We've left him there with extra loo roll,' Matt informed them. 'Poor guy would probably rather we weren't all standing around waiting for him to come back when he finally makes it.'

As they all laughed and turned away, Justine linked Matt's arm saying, 'Have you told anyone about the video-game thing yet?'

'Only you, and we don't know if it's actually going to happen, so we don't want to jinx it by spreading it around.'

Understanding that, she said, 'So when are you speaking to the agent again?'

'He's going to call sometime in the next few days to let me know if the Japanese guy's coming over to London. If he isn't, will you be able to get away for a trip to California?'

'I'll make sure of it. Two weeks max, I'd say.'

'Plenty long enough. It'll be a great treat for the kids. For all of us.'

'And we can afford these things now the business is taking off.'

Pulling her to him, he touched his lips gently to hers. 'You're amazing,' he told her. 'You deserve every bit of the success you work so hard for.'

'And yours is right around the corner,' she assured him. Not that his job at the BBC wasn't going well, because it was, but it didn't pay anything like the kind of returns she'd started seeing lately. Besides, in his heart he was desperate to write full-time – or design video games now that had come up – anything that made use of his creative talents and would allow him to work from home.

It was already dark by the time the children finally began to droop with exhaustion, with only the fairy lights and street lamps casting a dreamy glow over the park, and the smell of fresh grass, earthy water and buttery popcorn lending their own magic to the night air. Kegs of beer and bottles of wine had been rolled out hours ago, blankets spread on the ground, and Matt had plugged his iPod into a set of speakers for those who enjoyed Dire Straits, or Frank Sinatra, or Beyoncé – he had just about everything.

It could hardly be more perfect, Justine was reflecting, as she and Matt joined Simon and Brad under the tree to start getting the children down. A successful and memorable evening to end the infants' school term, with a long and hopefully hot summer stretching out before them. Maybe even a trip to California, as well as the villa she and Cheryl had booked in Tuscany for both their families, and whoever else wanted to come along.

Wesley was the first to drop from the branches, settling straight on to Simon's shoulders, followed by Chantal who slipped gently into Brad's arms before Cheryl came to take her. Next was Abby, awkwardly and head first so that both Justine and Matt made a grab for her. Neither of them realised that Ben was coming down too until he hurtled into his sister, and quick as a flash Matt grabbed him.

From there it seemed to happen in a terrible slow motion: Ben swung upside down, his leg slipped from Matt's grasp and as Justine gasped in horror his head slammed with sickening force into the concrete below.

Chapter Five

Present Day – Culver, Indiana

'Mummy,' Lula said quietly.

'Yes,' Justine answered.

Lula didn't look up, simply carried on crayoning at the kitchen table, her little head propped on one hand while the other made careful circles on the page so she didn't go outside the lines.

'Do you have something to ask me?' Justine clicked on her laptop to buy a new winter coat and snow boots for Lula from the OshKosh B'gosh online store. If they didn't fit she could always send them back, or perhaps she'd venture over to Plymouth or South Bend on a shopping trip one day soon.

It was odd how she was finding it difficult to leave Culver.

Perhaps not odd, more understandable, considering how safe she felt here. What was odd, she'd decided, was knowing she was surrounded by people who had guns and yet she still felt safe.

Actually, she had no idea how many of her new friends and neighbours owned firearms, though Sallie

Jo had already told her that she didn't, nor did David, nor any of their immediate circle.

'There are a lot of us anti-guns around here,' Sallie Jo had said, 'but it's not a battle we're going to win in this county, or even this State, so for a peaceful life it's a subject best not raised too often.'

'Anyways, it's mostly farmers and hunters who use them around these parts,' David had added, 'and I guess none of us really has a problem with that.'

Justine supposed she didn't either, since the situation was much the same in rural England: farmers and hunters had guns, although only with permits, and no one was ever allowed to carry one about in public. She wasn't sure if it was allowed here; she'd never spotted anyone with one, apart from the police of course, and even that seemed excessive to her, considering how tranquil the place was.

Chippingly had been every bit as tranquil. She'd felt safe there, until suddenly she wasn't any more.

'Mummy?' Lula said again.

'Ye-es?'

'When are we going home?'

Justine's heart thudded. Where had that come from? She hadn't asked it before, not even when she wanted to speak to Matt, or Rob. 'We are home, sweetheart,' she said, almost dismissively so as not to make a big deal of it.

'No, I mean our proper home with Daddy and Abby and Ben.'

With a dry mouth and wretched heart Justine got up from the table and went to busy herself at the sink. How was she going to answer the question? Why hadn't she prepared herself for it when common sense alone should have told her it was coming? Except not now. Last year, maybe, even just after they'd arrived here, but coming out of the blue like this when Lula hadn't mentioned Abby or Ben in such an outright way in months . . .

A torch beam flitting about in the woods suddenly caught her eye. She guessed it was Billy Jakes looking for rabbits. He was always out around this time of night. Thankfully he never came close to the house, even if there were rabbits on the lawn, and she'd yet to hear him fire a gun, so she guessed he must use traps. She didn't approve of those much either, but the last thing she was about to do was launch herself off on some kind of moral crusade.

People in glass houses . . .

'Mummy, you didn't answer my question.'

Justine carried on tidying the sink. More than anything in the world she longed to give her precious girl exactly what she wanted, but she couldn't. There was no home there any more. Matt, Abby and Ben had gone, just as she and Lula had, although in a different direction.

'I want to go home,' Lula whispered.

So do I, Justine didn't dare to say. She didn't even want to think it. They were at home here, and this was where they were going to stay.

How was she going to communicate that to Lula in a way that made sense and wouldn't upset her? And again she had to wonder why Lula was asking now, when it had been more than a year since they'd been together as a family. She'd felt sure Lula would forget. Being only two when she'd gone to Rob and Maggie, it seemed incredible that she still remembered her first home.

Justine wondered what her memories were, but didn't dare to ask. If she did it would bring them to life, and that wasn't going to help either of them.

'Why won't you answer me, Mummy?' Lula asked worriedly.

Going to her, Justine lifted her up and held her tight. 'We can't go back there, sweetheart,' she murmured.

'But why?'

'Because this is our home now. We belong here with Sallie Jo and Hazel. You like being with them, don't you?'

Lula didn't answer.

'Don't you?' Justine pressed, sitting her back so she could look into her eyes.

Lula nodded. After a while she said, 'Hazel's my best friend.'

'I know she is. Is it nice having a best friend?'

Again Lula nodded. 'She's nearly five,' she said. 'Older than me, but not as old as Abby and Ben.'

'No, she's much closer to your age. And there are all the other children at day care too. You didn't know many children your age before, did you?'

Lula shook her head. Her sky-blue eyes were avidly searching her mother's. 'I like it here,' she suddenly said and circled her arms round Justine's neck.

Knowing she was saying it to make her mother feel better just about broke Justine's heart. 'That's good,' she said softly, 'because I like it here too. And the best thing is that we have each other, so we can go exploring together, and find a lovely house for us to buy.'

'Can't we stay in this one?'

She needed some sort of stability, to know that things weren't going to keep changing, people weren't going to keep leaving.

'For a little while, yes,' Justine said, 'but not for ever, because it belongs to Mr and Mrs Stahl, our landlords. Do you remember, I told you about them?'

Whether Lula did or didn't remember wasn't clear as she laid her head on Justine's shoulder and wound a finger in her hair.

This was too hard. It was at moments like this that she started to doubt her ability to cope. 'Once we've bought a house it'll be all ours,' she said cheeringly, 'and we won't ever have to move again.' Had she said the right thing? Was that really a promise she could keep?

Lula yawned and snuggled in more tightly.

'Time for a tired girl to go to bed,' Justine smiled, and carrying her through to her bedroom she began helping her to undress. The room was almost entirely pink, with stars and angels and butterflies dangling from the ceiling and sparkling net drapes over the bed. It was so similar to the room Abby had had until she was ten, when Matt had helped her to redecorate to her own design, that it was all too easy for Justine to forget where she really was.

Don't think about Abby.

After bathtime Justine read Lula a story. Her favourite at the moment, because it was Hazel's, was *The Runaway Pumpkin*, but Justine didn't get any further than the first page before Lula was fast asleep.

Kneeling next to her, Justine smoothed a hand gently

over her honey-coloured curls, smiling through tears at the way she was cupping her adorably innocent face in her hands. She was like a little cherub who knew no wrong, had no understanding of what wrong really meant beyond arguing back to Mummy, or putting her dress on inside out. She did both often enough, but there was a sweetness to her soul and a very real gentleness in her heart that made her want to be good. Whether she would always be that way Justine had no idea, she only knew that she'd be a fool to take anything for granted.

'You will forget,' she whispered, 'I promise.'

As a wave of unbearable emotion surged in her heart she got quietly to her feet, and leaving the door slightly ajar she returned to the kitchen.

It was gone midnight in London, too late to call Rob, but she dialled the number anyway and after a handful of rings her sister-in-law's voice came down the line.

'Maggie, I'm sorry, it's me,' Justine said. 'Did I wake you?'

'It doesn't matter,' Maggie assured her. 'Rob's away for a couple of days, but how are you? Is everything OK?'

'Yes, it's fine. I just . . . I just . . .' She was starting to lose it, couldn't form her words.

'Take a breath,' Maggie urged gently.

Doing as she was told, Justine got herself back in control and finally managed to say, 'Lula was asking about . . . She still remembers them . . . I mean, I knew that, but she wants to see them.'

Sounding worried, Maggie said, 'What did you tell her?'

'I managed to get round it, sort of. Maggie, it's like she knows it upsets me to mention them, so she doesn't really want to do it . . . It's awful. I feel so bad.'

'Where is she now?'

'Asleep. I'm sorry, I just needed to talk to you or Rob.'

'You know we're always here.'

'Thank you.' After taking another breath she said, 'I've decided to get her a dog. I know she misses Rosie, so I thought it might be a good idea.'

'I think it is too.'

'David told me about a Coton de Tulear not far from here that needs a home. She's only a few months old, apparently.'

'Are they little white fluffy things, like bichons?'

'That's right.'

'Then she'd be perfect. Can I ask who David is?'

'The local news editor,' and so Maggie wouldn't read any more into it she added, 'he's a good friend of Sallie Jo's.'

'I see. How is Sallie Jo?'

'She's fine. Quite busy at the moment, so I haven't seen much of her.'

Maggie said, 'You mentioned in your last email that you were going to look for your grandmother's house.'

'Yes, I thought I might, but I'm not sure if it's such a good idea. David wants to write about it in the paper.'

Immediately realising the problem, Maggie said, 'And there's an online edition? Of course, there always is these days. Can't you just say you'd rather keep it a private affair?'

'I guess so, although he'll probably find it odd. Anyway, there's another issue with it, which is the way some people have reacted to my grandmother's name, and when you add to it the fact that my mother won't talk about her . . . Frankly, I really don't have the heart to deal with any more scandal, or disgrace, or shunning, whatever might be lying in wait.'

'No, of course not,' Maggie sympathised, 'but these issues, if there are any, would be from a long time ago. It wouldn't be the same. I mean, they surely couldn't hurt you now, after all these years.'

Sometimes it was hard to think of *anything* that wouldn't hurt her. 'No, I suppose not,' Justine agreed.

'What about a job?' Maggie probed gently after a while. 'Any progress on that front?'

'Not exactly, but there are a few empty shops in town. I've been trying to imagine what I might do with one of them, apart from turning it into a deli.'

'You did very well with the last one.'

'I can't go there again.'

Maggie's silence conveyed her understanding. 'Tell me,' she said softly, 'have you been in touch with Matt?'

Justine swallowed hard, but the tightness in her throat, her heart, didn't move, only lodged more deeply. 'No,' she answered. 'Have you?'

'Rob went to see him a couple of days ago.'

By now Justine was finding it hard to breathe. 'How – how was he?' she managed to ask.

'Fine, I think. Or as well as could be expected. He's still in the same place.'

'Of course.'

'You should be in touch with him. Rob thinks so too.'

'What does Matt think?'

'I don't know, but the two of you having no contact . . .' She went no further, Justine knew she didn't like to criticise, but it was clear she didn't agree with the decision.

'I'm starting to question it myself,' Justine admitted. 'Sometimes I feel so desperate to speak to him that it's like I'm going out of my mind, but I'm afraid, if I do, it'll just make things worse.'

'It's very hard to know what to do for the best,' Maggie conceded. 'I wish I could advise you better.'

'You're there for me, and you have been throughout,' Justine reminded her, 'that's what really matters.'

After a pause, Maggie said, 'Do you still feel Culver's the right place?'

'In so far as anywhere is right, yes, I guess I do. I kind of have roots here, tenuous though they might be, but they seem to help. And it's very pretty; the lake has a special quality that I know Matt would find as fascinating as I do.' Her voice faltered as she added, 'It feels strange to say that, when he was so against me coming.'

Clearly connecting with the despair in Justine's heart, Maggie said, very gently, 'Be in touch with him. I think he needs it. I think you both do.'

Justine didn't argue, she was too close to tears. How wonderful it was to hear Maggie speak the words she so longed to act on, even if she wasn't going to.

They'd known this initial period was never going to be easy, but it had to be got through.

'I should let you get some sleep,' she told Maggie. 'Thanks for the chat. I needed to hear your voice.'

'It was good to hear yours too. I'll tell Rob you rang. I'm sure he'll call at the weekend.'

After ringing off Justine went to pour herself a glass of wine. It was her first tonight, which was good, since she was often on her third or fourth by now. It didn't help, not even with sleeping, so she had no idea why she did it. A kind of Pavlov's dog reaction, she supposed. *When something goes wrong, reach for the bottle.*

Maybe she was already an alcoholic, she just hadn't realised it yet.

By the following evening both she and Lula were in much better spirits. Hazel was with them, and was staying until Sallie Jo returned from a meeting in Plymouth around seven. And, biggest boost of all, David was due to turn up at any minute with the new puppy. Justine hadn't meant him to go and collect it for them. When she'd called to say they wanted the dog she'd fully intended to go and fetch it herself, but he had insisted.

'Delong isn't far,' he'd said, 'and I'm going to be over that way later anyways, so I'll call to let you know when I'm on my way back.'

To have refused the kindness would have seemed horribly ungrateful, perhaps even hurtful, so after quickly confirming that the only reason the current owners were letting the dog go was because their son had developed an allergy, she'd thanked him and gone to break the news to Lula.

The last time she'd seen so much excitement was the day Matt had brought Rosie home for Abby and Ben.

Rosie. Oh dear God, Rosie, the retriever who'd ended up attaching herself so loyally to Lula that Justine couldn't understand now why she'd waited so long to get another dog. At least that was something she could do for Lula to make her feel happy and more settled.

'We've got a name for her,' Lula cried, dashing across the porch into the kitchen. 'It's a really good name. Hazel helped me choose it.'

Crossing her fingers that it wasn't going to be Rosie, Justine said, 'OK, let's hear it.'

'Daisy!' Lula announced proudly.

Justine's eyes widened. Not bad. In fact, she could think of lots worse, and not many better. Actually, none better.

'It's a flower, like Rosie,' Lula explained, 'but a different one because it's a different dog.'

'He's here! David's here,' Hazel squealed from outside.

Following Lula's dash out to the porch, Justine watched the girls race to David's car as he drove into the front yard, beside themselves with eagerness to get their first glimpse of his precious cargo.

Bringing a small cardboard box out to the lawn, David set it down gently, and Justine clasped her hands to her face as the most adorable bundle of white fur with two huge black eyes and a little button of a black nose poked her head out to say hello.

'Oh Mummy! Mummy!' Lula gasped, not quite knowing what to do.

'Do you want to hold her?' David offered, lifting her up in one hand. 'She's yours now.'

Lula immediately put out her hands and to her astonishment and delight the little dog leapt on to her shoulder.

'Look Mummy, look!' Lula cried, turning round for Justine to see. 'She's licking me.'

'She certainly is,' Justine laughed. 'She's absolutely gorgeous,' she said to David.

'And more or less house-trained,' he gladly informed her. 'They gave me food, a leash, bowls, bed and some toys,' he added, going to fetch them from the trunk.

'We got all that today, didn't we Mum?' Lula said, doing her best to hold on to a wriggling Daisy.

'It won't hurt to have more,' Justine assured her. 'Why don't you let Hazel hold her now.'

Clearly anxious not to leave her friend out, Lula immediately handed the puppy over and both girls started to giggle as Daisy treated Hazel to a healthy licking too.

'She's had all her vaccines?' Justine checked with David.

'Certificates are here so you'll see you're free to take her anywhere and everywhere just as soon as you like.'

'I have a feeling that's exactly how it's going to be, anywhere and everywhere,' Justine smiled, watching Daisy bounding about the grass and wondering if she'd ever seen anything cuter. 'Would you like a drink?' she asked David as he set the dog's belongings down in the porch.

'If you have a cold beer,' he responded, tossing a tiny ball to the girls to throw for Daisy.

'I'm sure there are some left from when my brother was here,' Justine replied, and going into the kitchen she found a Muller Kors and an already opened bottle of wine.

'I don't know if there's anything more guaranteed to make a person smile,' he remarked as they sat down on the rocking chairs to watch proceedings, 'than a couple of kids with a puppy.'

'She's been longing for one, ever since we arrived,' Justine told him. *Even longer.* 'I should have done it sooner – but maybe we should look at it this way, if I had, we'd have missed out on Daisy. What was her name before, by the way?'

'I believe it was Kayley, so not too different.'

Justine raised her glass. 'Here's to Daisy, may she be as happy here as we are.'

As he tipped the beer, David eyed her quizzically.

'It's home,' she assured him. 'We love the house, the people, the lake . . . When did you first start coming here?'

Going with the abrupt change of focus, though she could tell he'd noted it, he said, 'It was with my folks, back in '87, '88, when they bought the place in town, where I live now. I guess it was '88, because it was the year I graduated high school.'

So 1988, the year she and Matt met. 'Where did you go to school?' she asked, feeling faintly light-headed at the bizarreness – wrongness – of the fate that had washed her up here with another man all these years later.

'Indianapolis,' he replied.

'And after graduating, you went where?'

'To college in North Carolina where I got my Masters in political science and modern philosophy. After that, I landed an internship with the *Seattle Times* – my grandfather knew someone – and from there I had a series of jobs before I landed a position at the Pentagon press office.'

Justine blinked. 'I had no idea,' she admitted. 'You actually worked at the Pentagon?'

'It wasn't such a big deal,' he said modestly, 'but it was kind of interesting for a while.'

'Were you there for 9/11?'

He shook his head. 'Before my time. I only held the job for a couple of years before my wife got sick and frankly, she needed me more than they did, so that was what I did when we knew it was terminal, I took care of her until – well, until she didn't need me any more.'

Justine said softly, 'I'm so sorry. It must have been a terrible time for you.'

'It wasn't the best,' he conceded, 'but I'm a firm believer that whatever life throws at us, we learn to handle it and find a way to move on. Culver's been great for helping me to do that. No real pressures, lots of friendly faces, no complications unless you go looking for them ... My folks have been pretty amazing too, letting me use the house, the car, never getting on my case about what I might do next.'

Surprised and worried for Sallie Jo, Justine said, 'Does that mean you're thinking of moving on at some point?'

He shrugged. 'It's hard to say. There's plenty to keep me here, but maybe just as much to tempt me away.'

'Such as a more demanding job?'

'Sure, though I kind of enjoy the *Citizen*. It's been a good friend to me these past couple of years.'

Searching out the sudden yelps of delight, Justine laughed to see the puppy rolling over and over, like a star performer. 'It's hard to imagine a happier little dog,' she remarked, thankful for the tremendous boost it was already clearly bringing to Lula.

'Some relationships are made in heaven,' he smiled, 'and Lula's with Daisy appears to be one of them.'

'Hazel's being so sweet with them,' Justine observed, as Hazel passed the ball for Lula to throw. 'She's a very special little girl.'

'She certainly is,' he agreed.

They watched the puppy bounce after the ball, looking for all the world like a baby rabbit. The thought instantly sparked an alarm in Justine. 'Lula,' she called out, 'bring Daisy over here a minute.'

Quickly gathering up her new pet, Lula came rushing over, followed by Hazel. 'Do you want to hold her?' she offered. 'She's really soft and she loves being stroked.'

Taking her, Justine snuggled the little bundle against her cheek and promptly received a vigorous licking. 'We have to make sure Daisy doesn't go into the woods after dark,' she told Lula.

Lula's and Hazel's eyes grew big with concern.

'Remember Billy Jakes is around catching rabbits at night,' Justine explained, 'and we don't want him mistaking Daisy for one, do we?'

Lula and Hazel shook their heads. 'She's not a rabbit,' Lula said gravely, 'but he might not be able to tell the difference in the dark.'

'Precisely,' Justine confirmed.

'What does he do with the rabbits?' Hazel asked.

'I'm not sure,' Justine replied.

'He keeps them in the barn next to his trailer,' David told her, 'and when the time is right he kills them and eats them, or sells them to other people for them to make pies or pot roasts.'

Lula looked horrified. 'People don't eat rabbits,' she objected.

'Some do,' Justine told her.

'But that's horrible.' She looked at Hazel, and making all sorts of yuk and gagging noises, they took Daisy to the other side of the garden, well away from the woods.

'Maybe I'll ask the landlords if I can put up a fence,' Justine said, reaching for her mobile as it binged with a text. 'Sallie Jo's on her way,' she told David. 'I'm hoping she might stay for dinner, you're welcome to join . . .'

'No no, I really should be going,' he interrupted. 'The *Citizen* goes to press tomorrow, so lots to do.'

Justine got up to walk him to his car. 'It was really good of you to bring the puppy,' she told him. 'You can see what an effect she's already having.'

His kind eyes crinkled at the corners as he watched the boisterous play. 'I wonder who'll wear who out first?'

Smiling, Justine put out a hand to shake, and felt herself colour as he leaned in to kiss her cheek.

'Say hi to Sallie Jo for me,' he said, getting into the car. 'And anything you need, you know where I am.'

*

It turned out Sallie Jo was too short of time to stay for dinner that night, though she made a huge fuss of the puppy and reminded Justine to keep the following Tuesday evening free for her birthday celebration.

'I'll reserve a table at the Corndance Café,' she promised, 'there'll be five or six of us, so it should be fun. Or as fun as being forty-one can be. Oh, and my neighbour, Mandy Whitts, is happy to sit the girls. I guess it's OK with you for Lula to have a sleepover with us?'

Though Justine really didn't want Lula to stay away for the night, she had no good reason to object, especially when Hazel had spent so many nights with them, so she simply thanked Sallie Jo for thinking of everything, and including her in the invite.

'I'm sorry we won't be able to get together before that,' Sallie Jo said distractedly, checking her watch as they waited for Hazel to tear herself from the puppy and get into the car. 'It's parents' weekend at the Academy, so it'll be crazy busy at the café. Let's hope the weather stays good and all my staff decide to turn up. Hazel, honey, we have to go.'

Over the following weekend Justine deliberately kept a low profile, not venturing into town at all, spending most of the time finding new walks for Daisy. Though there weren't many British students at the Academy, a handful at most, she didn't want to risk running into any of their parents in case she should be recognised.

Sallie Jo rang on Tuesday afternoon to confirm her birthday dinner was still on and so a little before six

Justine dropped Lula and Daisy with Hazel, and managed not to utter a word about how anxious and bereft she was going to feel without her daughter *and* the dog. It was only one night, she kept telling herself, they would be fine, and so would she.

Now, here she and Sallie Jo were at the Corndance Café, enjoying cocktails while they waited for the others to arrive.

'I'm sure glad that weekend's over,' Sallie Jo sighed, after a generous sip of her Cosmo. 'Everything was great up till Sunday, when the cooks suddenly changed how they run orders. One was putting out in twenty minutes and the other in forty. It was chaos and soooo embarrassing. Why they change things on the busiest of weekends I'll never understand. Anyhow, we got through it. So how about you guys, what have you been up to?'

Justine smiled. 'Everything's about the puppy at the moment,' she replied, filling with affection for the little bundle of fluff that never ceased to delight.

Playfully rolling her eyes, Sallie Jo said, 'I'm not surprised; it's got to be the cutest thing I ever saw. Hazel's crazy about it, and now she's at David to find one for her too.'

'Do you want to get a dog?' Justine asked, picking up her drink.

Sallie Jo rocked a hand from side to side. 'If we could find one like Daisy I guess I'd be fine with it. We'll see.' She sipped her cocktail again and glanced around the cosy room with its Halloween decorations, linen-covered tabletops, and oak-beamed ceiling. There were only a handful of people already in, most drinking cocktails, though one table had just been delivered an enormous helping of firecracker shrimp, and some sort of creamy dip with pizza bread.

With time ticking on Justine was starting to wonder if the others were actually coming, and as though reading her thoughts, Sallie Jo looked vaguely awkward as she said, 'I arranged for us to be here earlier so we could talk.'

Though she couldn't imagine what it would be about, Justine felt herself tense with unease.

'It's kind of . . .' Sallie Jo shrugged. 'Well, I guess I want you to know that if you and David . . . I mean, I think he's attracted to you, and if you feel the same way . . .'

Justine was dumbfounded.

'. . . I want you to know that I'm not someone . . .'

'Please, you've got it wrong,' Justine broke in quickly. 'There's nothing between me and David, and I promise you there never will be.'

Though it was clear that Sallie Jo wanted to believe her, it was equally clear that she wasn't sure if she should. 'You say that now . . .'

'I mean it,' Justine came in forcefully. 'I'm truly not looking for a relationship, but even if I were, it really wouldn't be with him.'

'Because of me?'

'No, because of me. But yes, you too. I know you have feelings for him, and I'm sure he has them for you.'

Sallie Jo's eyes went down. 'Even if you're right,' she said quietly, 'I don't want to fall for him, because I'm sure he's going to leave sooner or later . . . He'll take a position in New York, or back in Washington. I know he's had offers already.'

'And he's turned them down?'

'So far, I guess.'

Not sure if giving advice was the right way to go with this, Justine said cautiously, 'Maybe if you opened up a little more with him, let him know that you're interested and he stands a chance?'

Sallie Jo's smile was wry. 'That's what everyone thinks,' she confided, 'but he's not stupid, he's got to know I have feelings for him.'

'Why would he be sure of you if you're not sure of him?'

Sallie Jo had no answer for that.

'If you ask me,' Justine pressed on, 'you've both been through a lot with him losing his wife and your divorce, and now you're both afraid of being hurt again. That's what's holding you back.'

Sallie Jo's laugh was hollow, yet hopeful. 'Do you think so?' she said.

'I really do, and so would you if you were able to see things from the outside. The trouble is we never can when it comes to sorting out our own lives.'

Apparently liking the answer, Sallie Jo suddenly brightened. 'Hey, we don't want to be talking about this any more,' she declared, 'we want to be talking about you . . . I've had an idea about a job that might be of interest to you.'

Justine felt herself starting to tense.

'I could really do with some help . . .'

Justine tried desperately to think up a way to head her off, certain she was going to ask her to help out at the café. Yet what excuse could she give when she owed Sallie Jo so much?

'So what do you say?' Sallie Jo prompted eagerly.

Realising she'd missed the details, Justine said, 'I'm sorry, I don't think I'd be right for the café. I . . .'

'Hell no, you don't want to work there,' Sallie Jo laughed. 'I'm asking if you'd consider going to view properties for me, you know, take down the particulars, measure up, photograph, write the blurb? If it appeals, you might even want to think about getting your realtor's licence?'

Realising it was a question, Justine felt herself flounder. 'Uh, it's not something I've ever . . . I mean, it's . . .' At last she started to smile. 'It's a great idea,' she declared, understanding it was what Sallie Jo wanted to hear, and actually it wasn't such a bad one now she came to think of it. 'I'm not sure about the licence,' she ran on, 'but I'd love to help out with the listing side of things.'

'That's terrific.' Sallie Jo clinked her glass to Justine's. 'I've kind of got this fantasy that we might even go into partnership together, but hey, that's me, I always get carried away.'

Remembering how often she and Cheryl used to get carried away, and how many of their dreams had come true, Justine gamely said, 'Don't let's rule it out. I'm sure I'll love the idea once I've had time to get my head round it.' *And once I've dealt with how much like a betrayal it might feel.*

Looking up as Naomi came in with Christina, a teacher at the high school who lived over in Knox, Sallie Jo waved out and quickly said to Justine, 'There's something else I need to tell you, but I won't go into it in front of the others. It's just I thought you'd like to know that I asked my folks if they remembered your grandma. My mother said she did, but she didn't want to repeat the rumours she'd heard, because she had no idea what was true and what wasn't.'

Justine's eyes widened.

'I'll get more out of her when she's here,' Sallie Jo assured her, rising to her feet, 'unless we've managed to find out for ourselves by then.'

Chapter Six

Nine Years Earlier – Chippingly Vale, UK

The farmhouse was overflowing with everything that made up Christmas. Trees were glittering merrily in the kitchen, hall, sitting room and playroom, each laden with decorations the children (mostly ten-year-old Abby) had either made or helped choose during shopping expeditions locally and in town. Coloured lights chased and flashed and twinkled all day and night, with trains hooting around the base of the play-room tree, and carols warbling from music boxes and dancing reindeer beneath the others. Abby and her friends had collected all sorts of greenery and berries from the orchard and wilderness beyond to make wreaths for the doors, while Ben, Chantal, Nelly and Neil had kept warm in the kitchen roasting chestnuts and making lists to send up the chimney to Santa. Even Matt's study hadn't escaped the festive spirit with silver snowflakes sprayed on the windows, as they were throughout the rest of the house, two modest red felt stockings hanging from his corner mantelpiece with Mum and Dad embroidered on the fluffy tops, and his very own Advent calendar offering him a chocolate a day from each little window. Abby and Ben's large and very hopeful stockings (both made by Abby) were dangling each side of the fireplace in the sitting room, where baskets of kindling and pine cones, sprayed with fake snow, were cluttering up the hearth, and a garland of gold-painted leaves, bright red poinsettia and rich green pine fronds was draped across the shelf.

With the delicious smell of brandy-laced puddings filling the kitchen, and the radio jollying things along with 'Jingle Bell Rock', Justine left Win, her trusty housekeeper, to carry on in her invaluably capable way while she took off down to the deli to help with the end-of-day rush. As she ran through the drizzly rain into the heart of the vale she felt cheered by the lights burning in everyone's windows, the glowing reindeer grazing in gardens, and fake icicles dangling from rooftops. Of course the children couldn't wait for it to snow so they could build snowmen, toboggan at top speed down the hillside, and turn the park and brook into an ice rink, but none was forecast for the next few days, so there was unlikely to be any for Christmas itself.

What was due to happen on the big day was the usual midday champagne and canapés at the farmhouse for anyone who cared to drop in – at least sixty or more usually did – followed by the traditional feast of a meal for around twenty that Justine and Cheryl always prepared together, using the kitchen barn. Both their families would be there, including grandparents – even her mother was threatening to grace them with her presence this year – Rob and Maggie would come

110

with Francine, naturally, and as usual a number of old folk from around the village would join in rather than be left on their own.

When added to the dozen or so parties they'd already catered this month, it was a heck of a lot of work, and by the end of it she and Cheryl would be more than ready for their regular new year skiing trip to Meribel. Vikki and Daniela, their senior managers, were perfectly capable of taking care of the events at that time, while the deli would close its doors from Christmas Eve until January 10th.

Digging around for her phone as it rang, she waved out to Simon as he rode into the vale on his motorbike, and clicked on the line to speak to Matt.

'Where are you?' they both asked at the same time.

'On my way to the deli,' she told him. 'The kids should be there by now.'

'Did they go to Longleat?' he asked.

'Ben did, but Abby decided to go shopping with Gina instead. How are things your end?'

'OK, I'm at the airport now, no delays apparently, so I should get into Heathrow around eight in the morning.'

'Which means you'll be home by ten. I can't wait to see you.'

'Same here. I've really missed you, and I've been worried out of my mind . . .'

'Stop, I'm fine, I promise.'

'But you shouldn't be up and about already.'

'The doctor said there was no reason for me not to go back to work, as long as I don't overdo it.'

'Which would be fine if he was talking to someone else; as it's you . . .'

'Matt, I'm over it, honestly. Everything's back to normal, and that's how we need it to be, for the children's sake as much as for ours.' She wasn't going to tell him, or anyone else, that her heart was still breaking over the second miscarriage she'd suffered in the past eighteen months. It wouldn't help anyone, least of all her.

'I shouldn't have left you,' he said. 'I felt terrible, I still do . . .'

'You had to go,' she reminded him, 'and once we knew it had gone there was nothing you could do here.'

'Apart from take care of you.'

'Darling, don't let's keep having this conversation. Cheryl and Gina did a great job of running everything . . .'

'I'm talking about you, not the business . . .'

'And they took very good care of me. As did Abby. She's decided she might be a nurse now, instead of a singer.'

With a smile in his voice he said, 'Heaven help the sick and wounded. Surely that doesn't mean the end of her girl band?'

'Never let it be said, except the members keep changing by the week. Wes has joined them now, so technically speaking they're not a girl band any more. And only time will tell how well that's going to work out.'

Laughing, Matt said, 'Is he planning on singing with them at the village hall on Christmas Eve?'

'As far as I know, and he's a part of the surprise they have planned for when you get back in the morning. I think you're going to enjoy it.'

'Having you all there would be enough for me,' he said, 'but I'm intrigued to find out what it is.' With a sigh he added, 'LA's a great place to be when you're all with me, but this is the fourth time this year I've had to come on my own and I'm not liking it much.'

'But you're loving the reason you're there.'

He didn't deny it.

'Matt, flight's up,' she heard someone say.

'Who's with you?' she asked, turning into the village where rows of dazzling Christmas lights were strung across the high street, adding their own seasonal splendour to the German market stalls crowding the pavements. There were fewer people around than she'd expected, probably thanks to the rain.

'Hayley,' he reminded her.

Of course, his editor, who might be joining them for Christmas if she could get out of a prior commitment.

Justine couldn't say she was much looking forward to that, since Hayley wasn't her favourite person. 'She must be very pleased with the way things have gone,' she remarked, blowing a kiss to Ruby, the florist, who blew one back.

'Everyone is. We'll just have to wait and see if it all comes together now. Sorry, I should go. I'll call as soon as the plane gets in.'

After ringing off Justine popped into the butcher's, where Ronnie and his assistants were red-cheeked with the cold and a short queue of locals were waiting to be served. Catching his eye she helped herself to a

113

dozen eggs and carried them off, knowing he'd add them to her Christmas order. It was usually Matt who picked up the eggs from a nearby farm shop, but she didn't want to ask him to call in on the way through in the morning. He'd be eager to get home, and she didn't want him to end up feeling bad if he forgot.

It was incredible the way things had taken off for him over the past few years, in fact since their first trip to California when they'd met the video-game genius, Hachiro. Within a year Hachiro and his team of technical wizards had turned three of Matt's stories into action-packed, interactive challenges for all major consoles, and thanks to a highly organised and targeted marketing campaign they hadn't taken long to catch on. So there were now McQuillan's Masters, McQuillan's Majors and McQuillan's Monsters, which had recently launched in time for Christmas. This one was causing some controversy, since the previous two had been suitable for all ages, whereas the British censors had slapped Monsters with a 12 certificate.

Matt was leaving others to deal with that. His interests these days were more focused on the political thriller he'd taken three years to complete, which was now enjoying a huge success. The McQuillan name had some currency, it appeared, for he'd been reviewed and interviewed extensively leading up to publication, and the book was now sitting at number seven on the *Sunday Times* best-seller list where it had been, in various positions including number one, for five straight weeks. And the reason Matt and his editor had flown to the States ten days ago was to meet his new US publisher in New York, before going on to LA for discussions with a major studio who had offered a substantial sum for the movie rights.

'Seems like some people have all the good luck,' Maddy had commented grudgingly when Justine had broken the news of the possible movie deal on her first full day back at work. 'While the rest of us have to pick up the bad.'

Justine had breezed past it. She was used to Maddy's snipes by now, and she certainly wasn't going to remind her of the reason she'd recently been off work. Losing a baby could hardly be called good luck, any more than the previous miscarriage could, or the countless other stresses and challenges they dealt with as a family or in the business.

Finding Maddy behind the counter now as she let herself into the deli, Justine clocked the handful of customers, some at tables, others browsing the shelves – apparently the rush was over – and after making sure everything was running smoothly she went to join Ben and Chantal at a window table.

'Hey you two,' she said, sitting down with a steaming cup of camomile tea. 'How was Longleat?'

'Yeah, it was cool,' Ben answered, his eyes glued to the portable console he and Chantal were using to play Monsters. As Matt's son he'd had no trouble getting hold of a copy, and as far as Justine could make out, he'd been playing it morning noon and night ever since.

It surely wasn't good to be so obsessive; in fact, Ben was so single-minded and rigidly focused at times that it had ended him up in all sorts of scrapes simply for being unaware of what was going on around him. On the other hand, he'd always thrown himself, body and soul, into everything he did; he was determined to master whatever was put in front of him, and why would she want to change that when his grades were so good and it pleased him so much to do well?

'Did you see the lions?' she asked.

'Yeah, they were awesome,' Chantal responded, as distracted as Ben by the game. She was like a china doll, petite and pretty with feathery dark curls and huge sea-green eyes.

'And the meerkats?'

'Yeah, they were awesome too. Ben, no! No! He'll get you if you do that.'

'No he won't. I'm going through the tunnel.'

'He'll be at the other end and smash you up.'

'He can't be. Look, watch.'

Sipping her tea, Justine took a moment to watch her son, knowing she must soon go to help Maddy and the part-time servers who were on today. It had taken some time, but she'd just about stopped having a heart attack every time he climbed a tree now, which was something he seemed to do a little too often; she sometimes even wondered if he did it purposely to scare her. Or perhaps not to scare her, but to remind her of what had happened when he was five.

Amazingly, unbelievably, considering how hard his head had hit the ground that hot July night, he'd ended up suffering no more than a mild concussion, and a cut that required as few as four stitches. Nevertheless, the emergency doctor had decided to keep him in hospital overnight, just to be on the safe side, so Justine and Matt had stayed with him while Simon and Gina had taken care of Abby. Justine wasn't sure if Matt had ever truly forgiven himself for the accident, they didn't tend to talk about it any more, but she knew there were still times when he woke up in the dead of night panicking that he might have let his son fall to his death.

Thank God it hadn't happened, but it had felt so close – or that was how it had seemed that night – and she could never think of it now without turning cold to her core as she heard the sound of Ben's head smashing into the concrete.

The love she felt for him and Abby surpassed everything, and never had it seemed more profound, more overwhelming even, than during the times she'd failed to carry a baby to full term. It was as though she was being reminded of how blessed she was to have them, how meaningless, worthless her world would be without them. Nevertheless, it didn't change the loss that churned in her heart or turned her empty arms heavy with longing. It was a cruel trick of nature, the mind making itself ready for new life long before the body could deliver. It was as though she'd already held her baby, felt its breath on her skin, its hunger as it fed, its tiny fingers wrapping around hers, and unlike the fragile life in her womb, the feeling wasn't yet ready to go away.

Whilst lying in bed recovering, she'd wondered if the loss was some kind of punishment for the way she worked so hard. Her conscience was always telling her that she should spend more time with Abby and Ben, take more of an interest in their music and sports, treat them to a day out at Longleat herself instead of relying on someone else to take them, but it never quite worked out that way. She tried, she really did, and it wasn't often that she missed one of Abby's concerts, or an important match of Ben's, but the pressure of the business was such that she was always being distracted by something, or forced to be somewhere else, and it was much the same for Matt. He did his best as a coach and a roadie, a homework assistant and improviser of musical instruments, but his commitments these days were even more pressing than her own. However, at least she was always there to see them off to school – being the ages they were now, they didn't need her to take them when it was no more than a ten-minute walk with dozens of others along the back lane to the end of the village – and she was at home most nights to eat with them, and listen if either of them wanted to talk.

Though she felt sure that what she did with them wasn't enough, they were the first to tell her to stop worrying, they were fine and didn't need to be babied. Indeed, they were a pretty independent pair, with, she quickly reminded herself, reassuringly good school reports, and more friends than she could remember the names of. At least, Abby's social skills were good, and her friends were certainly plentiful – and noisy. By contrast, Ben's character was more introverted and sombre, while his circle of friends wasn't a large one, mainly due to his unusual sense of humour, Justine and Matt suspected. Even they had to admit it was strange at times, especially when things that simply weren't funny had him laughing uproariously, or when he'd blink in mute confusion, even disdain, at a joke that had sent everyone else into paroxysms. Still, that was Ben, and just because he was a little different in some ways, didn't mean they loved him any the less – perhaps it made them love him more. Even his violent temper didn't detract from the fact that he was probably one of the most generous children around when he wanted to be. He also continued to excel at sports, though his aggressive tactics often got him into trouble, had even earned him a few suspensions over the last couple of seasons. And his Uncle Simon, who'd started taking him clay-pigeon shooting with Wesley, had repeatedly threatened to leave him behind if he didn't learn to wait his turn.

Looking at him now and feeling her love for his complexities warming her heart, Justine resisted smoothing his hair because he didn't like it, and started to stand up. A sudden dizziness made her sit down again and a moment later, to her surprise, Ben said, 'Mum? Are you all right?'

'Yes, I'm fine,' she replied, knowing she would be in a second or two.

He and Chantal were both looking worried.

'I lost my balance,' she explained. 'I thought you two were too engrossed to notice.'

Letting go of the console, Ben suddenly stood up and put his arms stiffly around her.

Melting, she hugged him back, and found herself wishing he could be this affectionate more often.

'Shall I let you into a secret?' he whispered in her ear.

'Yes please,' she whispered back.

'We know Father Christmas isn't real.'

Her eyes widened in shock. 'He isn't?' she cried. 'So who brings all the presents?'

He glanced at Chantal.

'Mummies and daddies do,' Chantal told her.

'But where are we supposed to get them from if Father Christmas doesn't exist?'

'From the attic,' Ben informed her. 'Me and Abby saw Uncle Simon hiding them up there.'

'Oh you rascals, you were supposed to be asleep.'

'Abby came and woke me up. I think there's a new bike up there for me.'

'Oh do you now?'

'Chantal's having one too.'

Chantal nodded eagerly. 'We sneaked into our attic to see what was there, didn't we, Ben, and we found this pink bike with gears and a basket and a bell. You won't tell Mummy we went up there, will you, Auntie Justine?'

'OK, as long as you promise not to tell Uncle Matt that Father Christmas isn't real, because he still believes in him.'

'No he doesn't,' Ben scoffed. 'He's too old to believe.'

'Well you know Dad, he's not like other people. Now, I'd better go and help out. Do you want another hot chocolate?'

'Yes please,' they chorused.

'Are we having tea here or at home?' Ben wanted to know.

'You can have it here if you like. You should let Mum know if you're not going home, Chantal.'

'Her mum and dad have gone to pick up her granny,' Ben reminded her, 'so she's staying with us tonight.'

'Of course. Sorry, it slipped my mind. You can have tea wherever you prefer. I'll be here until eight, or Win's at home if you'd rather have it there.'

'We'll stay here,' Ben declared decisively, and sitting down again, he promptly returned to the video game.

Going over to the counter where Maddy was serving someone with a large carton of Cheryl's home-made fig béchamel cheese sauce, Justine handed one of the servers her teacup and took an apron from a hook on the kitchen door.

'Are you sure you're up to it?' Maddy tossed over her shoulder. 'I can manage on my own; we're not as busy now as we were earlier.'

Catching the subtext, that she was a bit late in the day to be of any real help now, Justine said, 'I'm fine. In fact, if you want to go early . . .'

'No, I'll stay. We don't want you overdoing it.'

After topping up the bowls of sun-dried tomatoes, pesto rice salad and paella, Justine took over the till while Maddy helped an old lady out to her car. This was the thing with Maddy, as cutting and belligerent as she could be at times, she had a genuine soft side that never failed to remind Justine of how brave, resilient and caring she was. Heaven only knew how she got through each day with the fear that her son's blood cells might turn on him again. Every time he appeared overtired, or didn't feel hungry when he should, or threw up, she and Ronnie surely had to be racked with terror.

Thankfully, for the past three years Neil had been exactly like any other normal, healthy child, though he was a year behind at school having lost so much time when he was ill, and he'd only just, in the last few months, managed to get on to the school football team. What a triumphant day that had been for the Hawkins family, and for the rest of the vale. Everyone had celebrated the occasion by throwing an impromptu party in the park. Justine had only found out later that Maddy, having downed almost an entire bottle of vodka, had tried to seduce Matt. And when that hadn't worked she'd turned her attentions to Brad, Cheryl's husband, who'd ended up helping Simon and Ronnie to carry her home before she got herself into any serious trouble.

As maddening and embarrassing as her drunken flirtations could be, no one ever held them against her, or reminded her of them later – how could they, when life had dealt her and her son such a rotten hand? She had to let go somehow and it seemed that for her flirting, or even full-blown sex – with someone other than her husband – and alcohol provided the necessary escape.

Looking up as the door opened, Justine broke into a smile as her leggy whirlwind of a daughter came rushing in waving a copy of the latest *NME* and wanting to know if her father was still coming back tomorrow.

'He's already on the plane,' Justine told her.

'Yes!' Abby shouted, punching the air. 'He is going to be totally blown away when I tell him that Eric Burdon's bringing out a new album in January. That's what it says here. Or no, we have to try to get it for him for Christmas. Do you think we can?'

'It's worth a try,' Justine assured her.

'And we have to get tickets for Madonna's tour starting in May. She's in LA first, so we either have to go there, or somewhere else she's playing, I haven't got all the details yet, but we definitely can't miss it.'

'I'm sure that won't happen,' Justine smiled, knowing that Matt, in spite of not being a big Madonna fan, would never let her down.

'Ben, Chantal,' Abby shouted, turning to them, 'come on, we're going to practise our carols. We need to have them right for when Dad gets home in the morning.'

'We're having our tea here,' Ben protested.

Abby spun round to her mother. 'Can I have tea here too?'

'Of course. Where's Wesley? Did he go shopping with you?'

'No, he's with his grandpa today. We need him for rehearsals though, so I should ring him, and I would *if I had a mobile phone.*'

'You'll have to see what Father Christmas brings,' Justine told her, adoring and fearing for how flighty and gorgeous Abby looked with her long wavy blonde hair, jaunty red beret and mascaraed lashes. She was growing up so fast. Already there was an air of sophistication about her that Justine was sure she hadn't had at that age, and she couldn't say she'd noticed it in many of Abby's friends either. Apart from those in her girl band, so maybe it was the music and pop-star ambition that was rocketing Abby so rapidly out of childhood.

She'd talk to Matt about it, see what might be done, as if anything could be. After all, they were hardly going to discourage Abby's love of music and performing, it meant everything to her, and as much as they might want their children to stay young for ever, it was never going to be in their power to make it possible. They probably just ought to come to terms with it, and feel proud of their many achievements.

Matt was as thrilled with the carols the children performed for him when he got back the next morning as they were with the gifts he'd brought from LA. There was something for everyone, including Chantal, Wesley, Nelly and Neil, although nothing too big with Christmas only two days away. For Justine, however, there was a two-carat diamond pendant from Tiffany that just about took her breath away. She realised, of course, that he didn't think it would make up for the baby, it was simply his way of saying how sorry he was for what she'd been through, and how much he loved her.

Quite how deeply he was grieving himself was hard to tell, as taking his cue from her he immediately threw himself into the children's excitement. What was the point of bringing him down by forcing him to talk? The baby was gone now, they couldn't bring it back, so it was important they focused on those they already had and loved so much.

Christmas Day turned out to be as hectic, emotional, hilarious and surprising as it was most years – surprising this time not only because of all the unexpected presents, but because true to her word Camilla came to stay. Though she wasn't known for letting her hair down and mucking in where needed, after a few glasses of champagne her high-heeled shoes came off, and she was spreadeagled against the sitting-room door where Wesley had hung his new magnetic dartboard. The game was to see how many darts he and Ben could throw around their human targets without hitting them. Since both boys were in the school archery team they were excellent shots, and luckily no one had been injured by the time the game ended in a draw. The next time Justine saw her mother she had a sparkly pink party hat perched rakishly on her perfect hairdo, and was singing 'Rocking Around The Christmas Tree' with Gina's dad into Abby's new karaoke machine.

Justine and Rob couldn't remember ever seeing her tipsy, never mind having such a good time.

'Who is this person?' Rob muttered as he passed Justine in the busy kitchen. 'And what has she done with our stuffy mother?'

Choking on a laugh, Justine said, 'We have to get her drunk more often, it brings out the human being in her – or the grandmother, anyway.'

'You're not kidding. Can you believe she's actually saying she wants to come and watch the rugby with us guys tomorrow?'

Justine nearly dropped a tray of roasters. 'Fifty quid says she won't,' she declared, allowing Cheryl to take the tray while Simon scooted in behind them to fetch more vino.

'We're not all as flush as you, so make it twenty and it's a deal.'

Justine won the bet. Her mother was way too hung-over the next day to venture far from the house. She even had to pull out of the shopping trip she'd promised Francine and Abby, apparently not having realised it would clash with the rugby.

Since it was raining again and the temperature had dropped to zero Justine didn't feel much like going out either, so leaving Maggie and Gina to take the girls to the Boxing Day sales, she bundled the boys off to the game with flasks of hot soup and plenty of home-made mince pies and felt a flood of relief as quiet descended.

Soon, however, she became aware of the awkwardness of being alone with her mother. This was a situation she couldn't remember being in since . . . Maybe it was since she'd asked to borrow the money to close the deal on the farmhouse. She'd taken great pleasure in paying it back, in full, some years ago, enclosing a stiff little note with the cheque that had gone along the lines of: *So kind of you to help out when needed. Hope repayment hasn't taken too long to come. Let me know if you'd like any interest. Jx*

She'd felt terrible afterwards, especially when her mother emailed her thanks with an assurance that no interest was required, and she would divide the sum between the children and put it into the accounts she'd opened for them after they were born.

'So, how are you?' they both said at once as they settled either side of the roaring fire with cups of hot coffee and a plate of Turkish delight between them. Though Justine couldn't stand the stuff herself, she was sure it had long been one of her mother's favourites, which was why she'd put it out.

'You first,' Justine insisted.

Camilla didn't look thrilled. 'I was sorry,' she began, 'to hear about the baby.'

As the words inflamed the loss, Justine's eyes drifted to the flickering Christmas tree.

'You don't want to talk about it,' Camilla stated.

Justine shrugged. 'I guess not. It won't change anything, so it's best to get over it.'

Camilla didn't argue, simply sipped her coffee and gazed up at the mantelpiece where the children's hand-made cards for their parents were proudly displayed. 'They made one for me too,' she said softly. 'I was very touched by that.'

'They do every year,' Justine told her, 'you're just not around for them to give it to you.'

Of course they could have sent it, but they'd always preferred giving their special cards in person, or Abby did. Justine didn't suppose Ben much minded either way, although he still made them, so she was sure he got just as much pleasure out of watching the recipients' eyes light up as Abby did.

'I enjoyed yesterday very much,' Camilla admitted. 'Rob's always told me I don't know what I'm missing out on, not coming here for Christmas, and he's right, you make it very special, for everyone.'

Unused to compliments from her mother, Justine shifted in her chair. 'You're always welcome,' she said, 'you know that.'

Camilla nodded and her eyes still didn't meet Justine's as she drank some coffee.

To fill the silence, Justine said, 'What kind of Christmases did you have when you were a child?'

As Camilla's eyebrows arched, a fleeting smile

seemed to warm her paleness. 'They were usually good,' she replied. 'Your grandmother was much like you in the way she liked to cook and entertain. I remember the house in New Hope was always full of people, heaven only knew who they all were. Arty types mostly, I think, and I guess some were family . . . My father liked to dress up as Santa Claus, and I seem to remember much alcohol being consumed.'

Liking the image, Justine asked, 'What happened to him? You never talk about him, actually about either of them.' Of course Camilla knew that, but for once Justine was sensing she might actually get somewhere.

Keeping her eyes down, Camilla said, 'He died when you were about three, Rob had just been born. We were still in the States then. It was a terrible shock. No one expected it.'

'What did he die of?'

'He – uh, he had a heart attack.'

Getting the impression that wasn't entirely true, Justine said, 'Were you close?'

Camilla swallowed as she nodded. 'Yes, we were.'

'What did he do?'

'He was in banking.' Camilla's laugh was empty. '"Neither a borrower nor a lender be," he used to say to me, which was odd coming from someone who made a fortune out of doing just that.' After a moment she said, 'He came to Europe during the war. That was before I was born, of course, before he even knew your grandmother. He was with the 82nd Airborne Division during the Normandy landings.'

128

Surprised, Justine said, 'You've never mentioned that before.'

Camilla shook her head. 'Haven't I? I guess he never talked about it much, so that's really all I know.'

'What about how he and Grandma met? Did they ever tell you that?'

Camilla's head dropped against the wing of the chair. 'If they ever did I've forgotten now. Actually, no, I think it was in Italy. Rome. That's right. She was on vacation with her mother and aunt, and he was some kind of diplomat at the US Embassy there. That would have been around '47, '48. Your grandma always used to tease him he was working for the CIA, but I don't think that's true.'

'How about her? Did she ever work?'

'Not really, or not that I ever knew of. Maybe after . . .' She stiffened slightly, and Justine could tell she was changing what she'd been about to say. 'After we came to England, you, me, Daddy and Rob . . . She might have done something then, but we weren't in touch so I never really knew what she was up to.'

'Why weren't you . . .?'

'Someone said she gave up the place in New Hope and moved to the lake house. If she did . . .' She took a breath. 'It doesn't matter now. It was all such a long time ago. I can't think how we even got on to this.'

'She was your mother, my grandmother, why wouldn't we talk about her?'

Instead of answering, Camilla got unsteadily to her feet. 'If you don't mind, I think I'll go and lie down for a while,' she said. With a fleeting smile she added,

'Please make sure I don't drink any alcohol today, I still haven't recovered from yesterday.'

As Justine watched her go to the door she wanted to say, 'Why do you always walk away? What are you hiding?' but before she could speak Camilla turned round.

'Bill has left me,' she said, referring to her fourth husband. 'He's found someone younger.'

'Oh Mum, I'm sorry . . .'

'Don't be. If he hadn't gone I probably wouldn't have come here this Christmas, and I'm glad I did. You have a lovely family, Justine, and I'm happy to say that Rob does too.'

Unsure whether her mother was surprised by that, or in some way envious, Justine said, 'You know you're always welcome.'

'Thank you,' and with a sad sort of smile Camilla left the room.

She'd already left for London by the time Matt went downstairs the following morning to make tea. He found a note in the kitchen thanking them for a wonderful time and saying she'd be in touch soon.

Three days later they were skiing in Meribel, whooshing down the snowy slopes by day like the true non-professionals they were, and living it up with too much food and wine in their chalet at night. Matt and Justine rented the place every year, and since it slept eighteen there was never any problem fitting everyone in. Even Maddy and her family had come this time, along with all the usual suspects, Simon, Gina, Cheryl, Brad, Rob, Maggie, and of course the kids. Abby had managed to pack her guitar and keyboard into the car so she was providing the live entertainment most evenings, while everyone but Cheryl and Justine cooked.

It was around ten at night on New Year's Eve, while Justine and Matt were in their room getting ready to celebrate the change of year, that he pulled her into his arms and kissed her deeply.

'So what was that for?' she teased, straightening his bow tie.

'I've been thinking,' he said, 'but before I make a decision I need to run it past you first, because it'll affect you too.'

'Go on?' she prompted, amused and intrigued.

He took a breath. 'I reckon I should get a vasectomy. No, hear me out,' he interrupted as she gasped. 'I know we'd both love another baby, but I don't want you to go through another miscarriage. We already have two fabulously healthy kids, and, if you think about it, maybe we're being selfish putting our needs before theirs. The age gap between them and a new brother or sister is going to be ten years or more . . .'

'Matt, no, I can't let you do it,' she cut in gently. 'I hear what you're saying, but if something were to happen to me, or to the kids . . .'

'It's not going to.'

'You don't know that for certain. There might come a time when you'll want to start a family with somebody else . . .'

'Don't talk that way.'

'I don't want to think it either, but we have to be realistic. We've got no idea what the future might hold and you're still young, Matt. A lot of men your age are only just getting started on having families . . .'

'This is the only family I want.'

'I know that, and hopefully it's the only one you'll have, but if you . . .' She broke off as his mobile started to ring. 'I'm going to guess Abby,' she said, rolling her eyes.

Taking out his phone he checked the ID. 'Hayley,' he told her.

Frowning, Justine said, 'Again? This has to be the fourth time she's rung since we've been here. Doesn't she know we're on holiday?'

'Of course she does. I guess she just wants to say happy New Year.'

Not liking that too much, Justine watched him look down at the phone as the call went through to voicemail.

'Should I be worried about this?' she demanded.

'About what?'

'The frequency of her calls. The fact you apparently don't want to speak to her in front of me . . .'

Matt laughed incredulously. 'Where the heck is this coming from?' he cried. 'Have I ever given you cause to doubt me?'

He hadn't, but she wouldn't be the first trusting wife to miss what was staring her in the face.

Was it?

Surely to God not.

'She's young, she's pretty,' she heard herself saying, 'and we know how attracted women are to you . . .'

'Justine, stop. For God's sake, there's nothing going on between me and Hayley and there never will be.'

'Have you told *her* that?'

'Why would I? I'm . . .'

'Has she ever come on to you?'

He flushed and she took a shocked step back.

'She has, hasn't she?' she persisted.

He threw out his hands helplessly. 'I – I guess so. I mean, I didn't encourage her, I swear it, but OK, I think she would like there to be something between us. If she'd come right out and say so I could tell her it's never going to happen. As it is, I don't really know what to say to her. She's my editor, she's put a lot behind me, and she's . . .'

'You need to change editors.'

'It's not as simple as that.'

'It can be, if you make it. You just tell your agent you want to move publishers for the next book, or go to a different division of where you are now.'

He regarded her steadily, a dark, almost angry look in his eyes. 'OK, I can do that,' he said carefully, 'if it's what you want, but you realise what you're saying, don't you?'

She eyed him warily.

'You're telling me you don't trust me, and I don't deserve that. Never, since the day we met, have I even looked at another woman that way, and I don't understand why you think I'm doing it now.'

Realising how much she was hurting him, she let her head fall forward as she exhaled her tension. 'I'm sorry,' she murmured. 'I didn't mean it that way. Of course I trust you.' Reaching for his hand, she brought it to her mouth and kissed it. 'I trust you,' she repeated, looking into his eyes, 'and I love you, and I don't want you to have a vasectomy.'

'Then I won't,' he said softly, pulling her to him. 'And you're to get it out of your head that I'm having an affair, unless you want to divorce me, of course, and then I'll have one with you.'

Chapter Seven

Present Day – Culver, Indiana
You think no one knows where you are, or what your name
is now, but you're wrong, we know exactly what you're
calling yourself, and where you're hiding. How does it make
you feel to know you've been found? You'll never feel as
bad as those you've left behind.

Justine's eyes were heavy with shock as she read the
email again. She was in the kitchen, the doors and
windows closed against the storm that had raged through
the night. Tallulah was at day care, she'd dropped her
half an hour ago; her instinct now was to go right back
and get her.

She didn't move, other than to lift her head.

As she watched the trees bowing and shuddering
in the wild gusts sweeping the woods, their golden
leaves flying and diving like feather-light missiles, she
had the sick feeling that someone was watching her.
Were they hiding behind the hedge, driving past in an
unfamiliar car, secreted amongst branches waiting for
her to come out?

No one is there. This is all about intimidation.

Ben used to hide in trees. He'd spend hours in them,

doing only he knew what. On occasions he'd refuse to come down even after he'd exhausted all patience. It was as though he enjoyed making people angry, or afraid, or just plain worried. She'd always wondered, especially as he got older, if he'd secreted himself in trees specifically to torment her and Matt, knowing how anxious it made them that he might fall and hit his head again, the way he had when Matt had tried to catch him and failed.

Ben's head hitting the ground.

The sound of sirens as the ambulance arrived.

Fear like she and Matt had never experienced before.

And all for a slight concussion.

It was how people – parents – overreacted.

She read the email again, her heart thudding with the kind of unease that could easily turn to panic if she allowed it. The message had been sent several weeks ago to her old account, the one she'd used for Portovino Catering. She wondered why the account was still active when she was sure she'd closed it down. She also wondered what had made her log into it this morning when she'd believed there was nothing to log in to. Was it some wayward habit that remained stubbornly connected to her reflex actions? Could it be possible for ghosts to give warnings, for hatred and vengeance to transmit itself along tele-pathic lines?

Crazy thinking.

That part of her life was over. The business had been sold, renamed and relocated, and nobody apart from her immediate family knew where she was. She was as certain of that as she could be.

Whoever had sent the email hadn't actually said what her name was now, or where she was living. So there was a very good chance she was right, it had been sent to intimidate her, for there were no other messages after that, nor, thank God, was there any mention of Lula, and that was really all that mattered.

She was going to close the Portovino account now, once and for all.

After carrying out the necessary steps she pushed aside the shocking start to the day and made herself carry on as though it hadn't happened. She had details to write up of properties she'd viewed for Sallie Jo; after that she'd upload them on to the website, and take down those that were out of date. She'd done enough by now for Sallie Jo to trust her without checking her entries first.

By lunchtime the storm had abated, so she took Daisy down to the lake. She was such a sweet-natured and obedient little dog that she didn't really need a leash, but Justine didn't want to take any risks. It would break Tallulah's heart if anything happened to her precious pet, and Justine had to admit it would have much the same effect on her.

What a fool she was to have logged into her old account; as a result memories were escaping all over the place, and she was finding it almost impossible to shut them down. She gazed out at the lake, and through the mist she spotted a small boat with a single fisherman on board. It made her think of Matt and Simon taking the boys fishing, in lakes, rivers, even deep sea. To stop her thoughts felling her with more images of faces, voices, hands, the turn of Matt's head, the curious look in Ben's eyes, the sound of Abby's voice, she turned the solitary figure before her into the troubled ghost of Paukooshuck, the son of an Indian chief, who was said to canoe across the lake on moonless nights in search of his father. It was daytime now, but she tried clinging to the story anyway, needing to conjure it to draw a mask over the troubled details of her own awful past.

'Hey! There you are!'

Justine turned around and felt herself relax with relief as reality returned in the shape of Sallie Jo striding towards her.

'I've been calling,' Sallie Jo told her, 'but I guess you don't have your cell.' She scooped up an excited Daisy to give her a hug. 'Boy, have I got some news for you,' she informed Justine with a playful grin. 'Are you ready?'

'If it's good,' Justine countered.

Sallie Jo shrugged. 'Hard to say for certain, but your grandma's house?'

Justine tensed.

'It still exists.'

Justine's eyes rounded, as her heartbeat seemed to flutter and slow. 'How do you know?'

'I did it the easy way – a friend who owes me a favour over at County Hall dug through the old records. The online stuff only goes back ten years or so, or I'd have been able to do it myself. Anyways, it turns out the place is on the East Shore and was built in 1951 when William Cantrell owned the land – your grandfather, I'm presuming?'

Justine nodded. That had certainly been his name.

'And following his death in 1973 ownership passed to May Cantrell.'

Justine couldn't think what to say.

Sallie Jo linked her arm as they continued back to the house. 'Now here's for the best bit,' she continued, 'in 1982 when May died her daughter Camilla inherited the place, and I'm going to guess that Camilla is your mother?'

Justine came to a stop. *Her mother inherited it?* 'Camilla Gayley?' she asked, to be sure.

'That's her. And now here's where it gets really interesting, because as far as the records show your mother still owns it.'

Justine couldn't believe it. *Her mother still owned it?* 'That can't be right,' she protested. 'I mean, it doesn't make any sense. Why wouldn't she tell us it was hers?'

Sallie Jo could only shrug.

'She never comes here,' Justine ran on. 'She didn't want me to come either.'

Sallie Jo had no explanation.

'This is bizarre,' Justine muttered.

Not disagreeing, Sallie Jo said, 'If you're interested, we could take a drive over to the East Shore. I've got the address right here.'

Justine wasn't entirely sure what she wanted to do, except of course she had to go, if only to be able to tell her mother that she'd actually seen *the house she owned* with her very eyes.

The journey around the lake through Venetian Village, up over Mystic Hills and along the county road past Culver Marina took no more than fifteen minutes. By then Justine was as intrigued as she was bewildered – and not a little worried, considering the peculiar responses she'd encountered to her grandmother's name.

What on earth were they going to find?

After passing more multimillion-dollar homes than she cared to count, all of differing styles and vintage, a couple of exclusive golf courses, a private road right opposite a tumbledown barn, Sallie Jo pulled up alongside an ugly chain-link fence that stretched for about a hundred yards between two solidly built stone walls that fronted the neighbouring properties. There was no name or number immediately visible on the fence, and until Justine peered through the trees towards the lake there didn't even seem to be a house.

'Are you sure this is it?' she asked, trying to pick up a sense of the place, an echo from across the years that might help her to connect with it.

Sallie Jo was studying the map she'd brought with her. 'This is it,' she confirmed.

Justine turned to look at her. 'Do you know if anyone's living there?' she asked.

'Not that I could find any details for.'

Justine's eyes travelled the fence again. 'There doesn't seem to be a way in, no gate or anything.'

'There's probably access from the lake if it has a mooring, and according to this it does.'

'So you can only get to it by boat?'

'Come on,' Sallie Jo responded, and pushing open the car door she walked towards the fence.

Justine and Daisy caught up with her as she reached the far end, where a small pedestrian gate was chained and padlocked with a sign reading *Private Property, Do*

Not Enter. Beyond it a narrow stone footpath wound through the trees and disappeared from view at the brink of a slope. The lawns, though strewn with stray twigs and leaves following the storm, were immaculately tended, as were the rockeries and flower beds.

'Someone's definitely taking care of it,' Sallie Jo commented.

Justine was trying to get a better look at the house. From where they stood all they could see was the upper floor with a modest form of Dutch gables equally spaced in the pitched roof, black beams running through the smeared whitewashed walls and two tall chimneys. The interior shutters appeared firmly closed.

'What do you say we climb the fence and go take a closer look?' Sallie Jo suggested mischievously.

Justine was all for it until she remembered where they were. 'We need to be sure no one's in there first,' she countered. 'We don't want to find out too late that it's a nutjob with a gun who's not keen on visitors.' *How would her mother know anyone like that? How come her mother owned the place at all?*

'Good point,' Sallie Jo agreed. 'I'll do some more investigations. If nothing else we ought to be able to track down the company or person who's taking care of the gardens. They've got to know who's paying them.'

After using her phone to take some shots of all they could see from the road, Justine was about to follow Sallie Jo to the car when Daisy started to tug towards the dense forestation on the other side of the road.

'What is it, sweetie? Did you see a squirrel?'

Daisy carried on tugging, clearly eager to chase down her prey.

Justine waited for a car to pass and allowed herself to be led over to a small opening in the trees. As she approached an odd sensation crept over her, a light-headedness, or a kind of déjà vu that had no actual form or vision, but it was simply an unsteady feeling.

She'd been here before.

'Did you find something?' Sallie Jo asked, coming up behind her.

'I'm not sure,' Justine replied, and passing Sallie Jo the leash she gingerly pushed aside some brambles and stepped into a tangled hollow in the trees. As she made to go forward her foot caught on something and she stumbled. Checking what it was she found a long, solid block of wood, like a railway sleeper, snarled up in the undergrowth. There turned out to be more than one – at least half a dozen were randomly spaced around the clearing – and the déjà vu was wafting back in peculiar waves. She glimpsed small feet climbing on to one of the blocks of wood, a boy bowing, a girl wrapped in a blanket for a cape. She and Rob used to play here, pretending to be grand people with servants who came to the lake long before Grandma's time, bringing their luggage in a private railway carriage that the train would unhitch outside their house before going on its way.

Sallie Jo broke into a smile as Justine shared the memory. 'That sure used to happen,' she confirmed. 'Wealthy people would arrive from Chicago or Indianapolis bringing half their households with them in rail carriages for the summer.'

'My grandma must have told us about them,' Justine murmured, still sensing the evanescent recollection. She looked around the scrambled web of bindweed, ivy, split tree branches and rotting leaves. It would have been less overgrown when she and Rob played here. They'd have been able to see the sky; sunlight had poured in on them, which would be right, considering the time of year they used to come here.

'So what are you going to do now?' Sallie Jo asked as they headed back to the car.

'Get in touch with my mother,' Justine replied. 'And my brother. He'll be as stunned as I was to find out Grandma's lake house not only still exists, but is still in the family.'

'Any ideas on why your mother would want to keep it a secret?'

'None, but if you knew my mother . . .' Astounded all over again, she cried, 'I can hardly believe that she's owned it for thirty years and never told us. I don't think she's even been here in all that time.'

'Would you know if she had?'

Only half listening, Justine said, 'Do you think it might be built on an Indian burial ground? I know there are supposed to be lots of them around here.'

Sallie Jo looked doubtful. 'Why? Are you thinking it might be haunted?'

Justine gave a laugh as she threw out her hands. 'I honestly don't know what I'm thinking, and I guess I won't until I speak to my mother, and even then . . . She's very good at avoiding the issue if she wants to, and the issue of my grandmother is one she's been avoiding for most of my life.'

As soon as Sallie Jo dropped her and Daisy off Justine went straight to her computer, uploaded the photographs she'd taken and sent them to her mother and brother with a message saying,

This is Grandma's house on Lake Maxinkuckee. It appears to be in very good nick judging by what's visible from the roadside, especially as it probably hasn't been lived in for thirty-odd years (still checking that out but if you know anything, either of you, perhaps you'd care to enlighten me). According to the records, Mum, you are the owner. I'm presuming you know that, so intrigued – do we have a mad relative you're hiding away? What's the big secret?

Having no time for anything else, she grabbed Daisy again, put her in the car and set off to collect Lula. She hadn't even reached town by the time Rob rang.

'What the hell?' he cried. 'I just saw your email. Are you sure about this?'

'As sure as I can be. Sallie Jo checked the records and there doesn't seem to be any doubt, our mother owns the lake house and has done since Grandma died.'

'That is so . . . Actually, I don't know what it is apart from beyond stupefying. And it's in good nick, you say?'

'The garden certainly is. We couldn't get close to the house, so I'm not sure about that.'

'Do you think someone's living there?'

'No idea. There's no front drive, as such, so no way to get a car in, and the only gate in the fence is pedestrian and heavily padlocked.'

Rob was clearly having as much trouble taking it in as she was. 'You know what I'm starting to think,' he said, 'that Grandma might have ceded the house to Mum, you know, to avoid taxes or something, and maybe she's still there.'

Justine almost swerved into the ditch. 'That's crazy,' she shrieked. 'Why would she say her own mother is dead if it isn't true?'

'I have absolutely no idea, but unless she comes up with a reasonable explanation as to why she's never told us she owns the house, I'd say your next task could be to find our grandmother's death certificate.'

Justine flinched at that. 'This is starting to get very weird,' she commented. 'Actually, I think the next step is to find out if the place is occupied. Mum should know, but as I don't have much faith in her telling us anything, I'll let Sallie Jo carry on with her investigations.'

After a pause, she said, 'I don't suppose you recognise the house from the shots I sent?'

'No,' he replied. 'What about you? Did it do anything for you while you were there?'

'Not the house, but I found some old railway sleepers in the woods opposite, and they gave me a kind of flashback. We used to play there, making out we were rich people with our own private carriage. Do you remember it?'

After trying to conjure up his own memory, Rob said, 'Not really, but I'm younger than you . . . Oh God, listen, I have to go, I just couldn't wait to ring when I got your email. We can catch up later if you like. If you hear from Mum get in touch straight away.'

'I will,' she promised. 'It'll be interesting to see if I do.'

It wasn't until she was pulling up at day care ten minutes later that she realised she hadn't told Rob about the email she'd found in her old account this morning.

It didn't matter. The account was deactivated now, the way it should have been when she and Matt had removed themselves, Abby and Ben from Facebook and Twitter. So if anyone had any further plans to intimidate her they'd find their messages either bouncing straight back or falling into a bottomless void.

A week later, still having received no reply from her mother, Justine agreed that Rob should go round to Camilla's Chelsea home and demand some answers. He went that very day and called Justine straight after. 'You're going to love this,' he told her, as soon as she came on the line. 'According to the housekeeper Mum's away filming on some remote Hebridean island, so it's possible she hasn't even got your email yet.'

'And you really believe that?' Justine scoffed as she climbed into Sallie Jo's golf cart to start a planned tour of the town.

'Let's say it's very convenient,' he agreed, 'but she's definitely not there; because the housekeeper invited me in to take a look if I didn't believe her. Any news on occupancy of the house yet? Ghost, mad relative, or Grandma?'

'No record of anyone being in residence, which the gardening company has confirmed to the best of their knowledge, although one of them said he was sure he'd seen a face at the window a couple of times.'

'Get out of here!' Rob laughed. 'Is her name Bertha, by any chance?'

'Bertha?'

'Rochester's wife. Who pays the gardening company?'

'OK, you're going to love this, because we just got an answer to that today. Apparently it comes from a firm of lawyers in New York who also pay the property taxes which, I hope you're sitting down for this, amount to twenty-eight thousand dollars a *year*. Every year.'

There was a beat of shocked silence before he said, 'You have to be kidding me!'

Justine ran on, 'It probably won't surprise you nearly as much to hear that the lawyers are not at liberty to divulge the name of their client.'

'But you asked if it was Camilla Gayley?'

'I did and was given the same reply. Not at liberty blah blah . . . How about here?' she cried to Sallie Jo as they approached the root-beer stand on North Lakeshore, closed for the winter.

'Where are you? What are you doing?' Rob wanted to know.

Justine knew this was going to baffle him. 'We're in Sallie Jo's golf cart organising a scarecrow placement for the Fall Fest,' she replied.

She almost felt his double take. 'A what? For what?'

'We're choosing where to position scarecrows for the autumn festival that Sallie Jo set up last year to promote local businesses and charities. However, if you're picturing things like Guy Fawkes, or Wurzel Gummidge, or sorry old broomsticks that hang around in fields, think again. These scarecrows are more like giant dolls or puppets even, and they're beautifully made by local kids at school or with their families. Lula and Hazel are making a mermaid.'

'Sounds impressive. So is Lula with you?'

'No, she's at home working on said scarecrow with Hazel and Petra Yates, one of the high school students who lives nearby. I think you met her while you were here.'

'I believe I did. Tall girl with mousy hair and a bit of a lisp?'

'That's her, but she recently changed her hair colour to a whiter shade of pale.' The erroneous words snatched at her harshly. It was a song Abby used to sing, taught to her by Matt, and she had no idea why she'd said that when what she'd meant was lightish shade of pink.

'I've no idea what colour that is,' Rob was saying, 'but I'm just a bloke. So what's the next move with the house?'

'You tell me. We can't do anything without keys unless we break in, and we're not keen to try that until we're totally sure no one's in there. Do you have any idea when Mum's supposed to be back from this Hebridean junket?'

'No, but she can't stay there for ever, so it must be any day now.'

'OK, let me know if you hear anything.'

'Same goes for you. Enjoy the scarecrows,' and he was gone.

'Mother done a disappearing act?' Sallie Jo asked sardonically as they turned into the Academy grounds, where she'd come to drop off a bag one of the students had left at the café.

'It would appear so,' Justine replied, 'but she can't run away from it for ever.'

'I hope not. It's got us all crazed with curiosity, that's for sure. I won't tell you some of the things folks are saying, you won't want to hear it, but David's theory is that she comes every summer to meet a secret lover whose wife has some kind of disability so he can't leave her.'

Justine shook her head and gazed around at the grand, red-brick buildings with their smartly turreted roofs, so pristine and elegant they might have been built a mere decade ago rather than a century or two. The late afternoon sunlight was burnishing everything as golden as the changing leaves, lending it an almost illusory feel. She was mesmerised by the air of learning, the sense of privilege and history, achievement and authority that emanated like rainbows from the Huffington Library, the Dicke Hall of Mathematics, the Eppley Auditorium, the Vaughan Equestrian Centre, the wavelike structure of the new rowing centre. So many buildings, more facilities than she'd ever seen at a high school, and then there were the sports fields: football, polo, lacrosse, baseball, hockey, the golf course, sailing school, tennis courts . . . There seemed no end to the sheer magnificence of the place sitting like a grand duke with his illustrious retinue of pupils and scholars on the banks of the legendary lake.

Would things have turned out differently if Ben and Abby had grown up here, gone to this Academy?

She wanted Lula to study here one day, and felt sure Matt would agree.

Waiting in the golf cart as Sallie Jo ran into a dorm building to deliver the lost bag, Justine tried to find the source of the music she could hear that seemed to be coming closer. At last the musician came into view and she felt immediately entranced by the unexpected vision of a young female student, no more than sixteen or seventeen, walking beside the water playing the bagpipes so expertly she must have been playing them for years.

Abby would have been entranced too . . .

'OK, that's done,' Sallie Jo declared, jumping back into the golf cart and starting the engine, 'and with locations sorted for all six of our scarecrows when they're ready, I reckon we can head back to find out how the mermaid's coming along.'

As they drove Justine could feel the almost palpable air of excitement that was building around town now the festival was so close. People were stopping their cars all over the place to admire the scarecrows already in position, while giant bales of hay had appeared in the town park to create a straw pyramid for the children to climb. There was to be a bounce house too, and later would come the thrill of a haunted castle. Apparently everyone was signing up for a moonlight canoe paddle on the lake, and the free wine and cheese social at the old hardware store was sure to pull in the crowds. The weekend was crammed with so many events that Justine could only wonder how many Lula was going to fit in. Knowing her she'd want to do everything from pumpkin painting, to pony rides, to dressing up Daisy for the pet-costume parade. She'd been talking about nothing else for days, and as Justine watched and listened and loved her with all her heart she was aware of the sadness inside her growing so heavy it was hard to bear. She longed to throw herself into the community, to be as much a part of it as she sensed Sallie Jo would like her to be, that Lula needed her to be, but if anyone knew the truth about her, if they had any idea, no one would want her there at all.

After arriving at Café Max and swapping the golf cart for Sallie Jo's car, they drove on out past the cemetery and down to the lake before turning along the track towards Waseya.

'Who's that by your mailbox?' Sallie Jo wondered as they drew closer.

Recognising the older woman with neat grey hair and slightly stooped shoulders, Justine said, 'It's Elise Gingell, one of my neighbours.'

'Oh sure it is,' Sallie Jo realised. 'Hey Elise,' she called out, coming to a stop beside her. 'Is everything OK?'

Turning round, the old lady broke into a friendly smile. 'Everything's fine, Sallie Jo. I was just leaving one of our newsletters for Justine.'

Sallie Jo muttered through her smile to Justine, 'Good luck with that.'

'So sweet,' Justine muttered back as she got out of the car. Though she had a fairly good idea what the newsletter was about, her heart still sank when Elise put the leaflet into her hand. *Marshall County Right to Life News.*

'You're very welcome to join us for our next monthly meeting,' Elise told her kindly. 'I know I won't be able to persuade Sallie Jo, but I'm hoping you're someone who sees things our way.'

Before Justine could summon the right response, the old lady continued. 'The meetings are the first Tuesday of each month at seven p.m. You'll find us in the Laramore Room at Plymouth Public Library . . .'

'I'm sorry,' Justine broke in more forcefully than she'd intended, 'but I'm afraid my views don't correspond with yours.'

Elise blinked, as though not sure if she'd heard correctly. 'Is it something you've really thought about, dear?' she asked in her sweet granny way.

'Enough to know that I can't agree that *every* child, no matter what, has a right to life.' Why was she getting into this? She should have said she'd think it over and get back to her.

Apparently unruffled, Elise replied, 'You're thinking of rape and incest, I know, and they're certainly powerful arguments against our cause, but let me say this to you, Justine, the Good Lord would not allow someone to fall pregnant if he did not want that child to be born.'

Before she could stop herself, Justine said, 'And you know this because the Good Lord told you himself?'

Elise was still smiling. 'What I know, because I've lived long enough to know, is that something good always comes from something bad, eventually.'

'Does it?' Justine snapped. 'Does it really?'

Elise nodded.

'Well I'm here to tell you that it doesn't,' and hating

herself for being mean to the old lady, while wanting to scream at the sheer, deluded naivety of it all, she stalked off towards the house.

'What is it? Are you OK?' Sallie Jo asked worriedly, coming into the kitchen behind her.

'Sorry, I'm fine,' Justine replied, scooping up Daisy. 'I just . . . I don't know . . .' She broke off as she realised Sallie Jo wasn't talking to her. She was looking at Petra, whose face was as white as the mermaid head she was holding. Justine's insides turned to liquid. 'What is it?' she demanded, starting through to Lula's bedroom. 'Where's my daughter? Lula?'

'Petra! What's going on?' Sallie Jo demanded.

'I don't know,' Petra sobbed. 'They were in there . . .'

'Lula!' Justine yelled, finding the bedroom empty. 'Lula! Where are you? This isn't a game.'

'I've looked everywhere,' Petra wailed.

'Are you saying they're not in the house?' Sallie Jo barked.

'I – I don't think so.'

Justine was opening every door and cupboard, searching under beds, even opening drawers. Her heart was thudding so violently she barely heard Sallie Jo ordering the girl to pull herself together and tell her what had happened.

'We were all here, in the kitchen,' Petra stammered, 'then they said they were going into the bedroom . . . I could hear them in there talking . . . I carried on with the mermaid, expecting them to come back any minute. When they didn't . . . I went to look for them, but they – they weren't there.'

'How could they not be there?' Sallie Jo exclaimed angrily.

'The back door is still bolted from the inside,' Justine told them.

'How long has it been since you saw them?' Sallie Jo demanded.

'I don't know. I mean, it must be ten minutes . . . I was about to call you when you – you came back.' She looked terrified and Justine was starting to feel the same way.

Sallie Jo marched into the bedroom. 'There's a window open in here,' she called out. 'Did you leave it that way?' she asked Justine, returning to the doorway.

Justine shook her head. 'Someone's taken them,' she choked.

Sallie Jo stared at her fiercely. 'I know what you're thinking,' she told her, 'but things like that don't happen in Culver.'

'They happen everywhere,' Justine almost screamed, starting for the front door.

'Please calm down,' Sallie Jo implored. 'They'll be out here somewhere . . .'

'It's dark,' Justine cried, almost falling down the steps. 'They know they're not allowed out alone after dark. Lula!' she shouted. 'Lula, where are you?'

They searched everywhere, the garden, the woods, the lake shore, they knocked on all the neighbours' doors, but no one had seen them.

Justine couldn't stop thinking about the email she'd tried to forget.

Someone knew where she was, and that someone now had Tallulah.

And Hazel.

Her voice was shredded with fear as she told Sallie Jo, 'We have to call the police.'

It had been long enough now for Sallie Jo to agree, and taking out her cell she dialled 911.

Chapter Eight

Five years earlier – Chippingly Vale, UK
Short of a police escort with blue flashing lights and outriders, or a private jet, or some sort of space shuttle, Justine and Matt were pulling out all the stops to make it home in time for Abby's 'massively important gig' as she'd described it in her text. *The Black Diamonds totally megaband and want me as support at Komedia in Bath.*

Apparently the megaband's producer had been shown several of her YouTube clips and hadn't wasted much time getting in touch.

Abby had been so thrilled to receive the call that as well as texting she'd rung her parents in the middle of the night in Sydney to shriek out the news.

'You've got to come. You so totally have to,' she'd informed them, clearly not prepared to take no for an answer.

So, no matter that Justine had been about to treat Matt to a much-needed holiday after a lengthy book tour of Australia and New Zealand, they'd cancelled the luxury hotel in Tahiti, rearranged their flights and would have made it back in time had the second leg of their journey not been subjected to a ten-hour delay.

'At least we tried,' Matt cried as Abby flounced off to her room the morning after the gig rather than welcome them home.

'You may as well go back now and have your *holiday*,' she shouted down the stairs. 'No one needs you here. We can manage perfectly well without you.'

Matt and Justine looked at one another. 'Great to be back,' he muttered sardonically.

Justine almost smiled. They were tired, fed up and not at all in the mood for a fight with their tempestuous fifteen-year-old daughter.

'She's making me feel guilty,' Matt complained.

Sighing, Justine walked around the suitcases and went to put on the kettle. 'She's good at that, especially where you're concerned.'

'She didn't even tell us how the gig went.'

'She didn't give us the chance to ask.'

Matt looked worried. 'She wouldn't be in this kind of mood if it had gone well.'

Justine didn't disagree, partly because she didn't have the energy. 'I wonder where your mother is?' she yawned, checking the time. Seeing it was just before midday she decided Catherine was either pottering about a Sunday market somewhere locally, or perhaps she was over at Simon and Gina's.

'Hey Ben,' Matt said into his mobile, 'just letting you know we're back. Did you get my message about the delay? It turned into a heck of a long flight so I expect we'll go to bed this afternoon. Give me a call when you get this.'

'Do you know where he is?' Justine asked.

Matt shrugged. 'Upstairs for all I know.'

Justine arched an eyebrow. 'Great homecoming, huh?'

Laughing, Matt pulled her into his arms. 'I know I've said it a hundred times, but thanks for coming with me. I'd have hated doing all that on my own.'

'I loved being there,' she assured him. 'And was I really going to let you go Down Under for three whole weeks without me?' In truth he hardly ever made a long trip without her these days, not only because Hayley, his editor, was always too keen to accompany him if there was a chance he might be alone, but because he insisted that the only person he ever wanted to share new places and experiences with was his wife.

'It's just a shame we didn't get to Tahiti,' he sighed. 'I was looking forward to having you all to myself on an exotic island for a week.'

'And we gave it up only to miss Abby's gig. Maybe she's right, we should get on a plane and go back.'

'If I could face an airport again, I would.'

After making a cup of tea, Justine said, 'I should go upstairs and talk to her. If things didn't go well last night, she might want a chat.'

'OK, I'll sort out the luggage and try to find Mum.'

Hearing a car pulling up outside, Justine said, 'That's probably her. I'll go and check.'

Finding her mother-in-law in the cobbled courtyard between the house and barns unloading at least half a dozen supermarket bags, Justine immediately pulled her into a hug. 'How are you?' she smiled. 'God, it's good to see you.'

Patting her back, Catherine said, 'I wanted to be here when you arrived, but it seems you've beaten me to it.'

'No matter. Tell me about the children, have they behaved themselves?'

Seeming to find the question amusing, Catherine replied, 'I never have any trouble with them, that's the best part of being a grandparent.'

'But three weeks is a long time.'

'I've done it before and I'd do it again.' She drew back to cup Justine's face in her hands, and Justine was reminded of how much she loved this dear lady with her twinkly blue eyes, and older, more feminine version of Matt's smile.

'You look tired,' Catherine told her, 'which is hardly surprising after that wretched delay, but don't worry, I've got everything under control and Cheryl's invited us all over to her place for a meal this evening.'

Relieved to hear that, and anxious to see her best friend and business partner since Cheryl's marriage, never good, had lately bordered on total collapse, Justine said, 'Did you get to Abby's gig last night?'

'I'm afraid not. I'd already arranged to play bridge at Saffy Morgan's and I didn't want to let anyone down.'

'Of course not. Do you know how it went?'

'She hasn't said. Well actually, I haven't seen her this morning. Is she up now?'

Justine's tone was wry. 'Sort of. How about Ben? Have you seen him?'

'No, he was off and out early, didn't say where he was going or what time he'd be back.'

'Did he take the dog?'

'Oh, no, Simon came for Rosie a couple of hours ago to take her for a run on the common. I expect they're in the pub by now.'

Suspecting the same, Justine hugged Catherine again and began helping her in with the shopping. Quite how they'd have managed without her these last few years Justine had no idea, for Matt's research and publicity trips had become more frequent as his books had grown more successful, and Justine would never have been able to accompany him had Catherine not retired from the hospice, leaving her free to take care of the children. Of course, if it was during school holidays they took Abby and Ben with them, Catherine too, if she wanted to come, but more often than not they found themselves travelling alone.

As for the running of Portovino Catering, it was so established and well-staffed now that Justine and Cheryl had worked out a system whereby they could easily stand in for one another with the help of the senior managers. This meant that Cheryl got just as many breaks as Justine, though she didn't usually go as far – either to her stepmum and dad's cottage in Burgundy with Chantal, or to Maddy and Ron's villa in Spain, also with Chantal, while Brad, grumpy as ever, generally did his own thing with his family in London.

'Hey you,' Matt virtually crooned as his beloved mother came in the door, and whisking the shopping from her hands he pulled her into a bruising bear hug. 'How are you? God, it's good to see you,' he enthused, echoing Justine.

'Mm, I imagine you missed me every minute of the day,' Catherine teased with a wink at Justine. 'Did the festivals go well?'

'He was a triumph,' Justine assured her. 'And we loved Australia. Actually, maybe we loved New Zealand more. Whatever, the whole family has to go next time. Everyone's so friendly over there, the scenery is like nothing you've ever seen before, the food is out of this world and don't get me started on the *wine* . . .'

'Started?' Matt scoffed. 'We could never get you off it. You should have seen her . . .'

'Don't listen to him,' Justine laughed, flipping his arm. 'Now what we really want to know is what's been happening here.'

Catherine threw out her hands. 'But I told you in my daily emails,' she protested.

'Yes, but have you been holding anything back? Something we need to deal with?'

Catherine rolled her eyes. 'We're all grown-ups now,' she reminded Justine. 'Or the children like to think they are, and they're really no trouble.'

Justine regarded her sceptically. Knowing her two as well as she did, 'no trouble' seemed a little unlikely. 'So everything's OK at school?' she prompted warily.

'Oh yes, at least as far as I know. There haven't been any complaints, let's put it that way. Oh, and I must tell you, I went to watch Abby performing in assembly a few mornings ago. What a treat that was. The other children adored it. They were all up and dancing. I must admit I nearly got with the beat myself.'

Laughing, Matt said, 'What did she sing?'

'Well, she didn't do anything of her own, which I thought was a shame, because she's very talented, as you know. She did two songs by Donna Summer, because apparently someone's told her she sounds just like a young Donna Summer, and I have to say I think they could be right.'

'Oh my God,' Justine gulped, 'which songs did she choose?'

'"Last Dance" and "I Feel Love".'

'She sang "I Feel Love" in school assembly?' Matt cried. 'Didn't the staff shut her down?'

'Not at all. They knew what she was going to do because she used the music room to rehearse, and I have to say half the teachers were dancing too. It was such fun. It put everyone in a marvellous mood for the day.'

Knowing that Abby often did that with her morning-assembly gigs, Justine said wryly, 'I bet Ben didn't dance.'

Catherine raised an eyebrow, but clearly didn't want to comment on how churlish her grandson could be at times. 'Chantal and Nelly were backing singers,' she said, 'and what a treat they were.'

Since Abby had abandoned her girl band long ago in order to advance her solo career, she'd invited many of her friends to accompany her on stage, with Chantal and Nelly always being her favourites. 'They're the best,' she would passionately inform her parents, as if they might not appreciate just how talented and supportive Chantal and Nelly were. 'And they're like family, which makes them extra special.' On the other hand she often said the same about the boys from the Sixth Form jazz band whom she'd known for most of her life, and who were always asking her to sing with them. The same went for the rock band who, in Matt's opinion, were almost as good as The Doors, as if anyone but him actually knew who they were; and for the gospel choir, which Abby had put together herself for an Easter concert she'd organised while in year nine.

Basically, as long as it was music Abby loved it, soul, punk, rap, new wave, folk, country, everything but heavy metal (which was more Ben's thing), and her ever-increasing song list already spanned many decades. She hadn't quite got to grips with opera yet, but hadn't ruled it out as something she might develop an interest in when she was older. From the way she presented herself it would have been easy to believe that day had already arrived, since she was extremely mature for her years, not only in her beach-model looks and sassy personality, but in the way she knew her own mind (which could be a bit scary, Justine sometimes found). Justine couldn't remember ever being so confident at fifteen, or as certain of the direction her life must take. There again, she'd never been as musically gifted, or as mad keen to make it to the top.

So apparently her darling girl was a young Donna Summer now, which, raunchy as Donna Summer might be, Justine decided she preferred to a young Kylie Minogue, or even Ruthie Henshall (this after playing Roxie Hart in a school production of *Chicago*) or Adele. In fact, Abby had been likened to so many artists in the last few years that Justine had forgotten who half of them were (if she'd even known them in the first place), and anyway, she and Matt preferred to think their daughter's talent was unique.

They were proud, but also exasperated parents a lot of the time, for as well as being highly entertaining, Abby could be extremely temperamental – and bossy, and opinionated and disdainful of those who just didn't get it (usually them). On the other hand she could also be as loving and playful as a kitten, as kind as her grandmother Catherine, and as generous as only someone who had no real understanding of limits could be.

Then there was fourteen-year-old Ben, who seemed hell-bent on doing everything in his power to make himself as unlovable and difficult as his sister was popular and admired. He was already as tall as his father, though had yet to fill out, his dark hair was as unkempt and unwashed as the rest of him, and he could be as gloomy as a bad-news bulletin, or as witty as any comedian, depending on his mood. More often than not he treated his family with contempt, as if their moronic presence had been assigned personally to him as some sort of cosmic punishment. His obsessive nature had expanded over the last couple of years to include yet more video games and violent movies, and he'd been thrown off just about every sports team due to his unpleasant attitude. Though he was fully capable of being a straight A student he showed little interest in trying these days, yet there was a time, not so long ago, when he'd had all sorts of career ambitions, from becoming a biochemist, to an astronaut, to a crimi- nologist, or maybe even a philosopher. Lately he'd declared an intent to become a drug addict (to annoy his parents), or a music producer (to needle his sister); or a transvestite (to shock his grandma); or a soldier, which he actually seemed more serious about, provided he got posted to a front line somewhere in order 'to get away from this fucking family', he'd rudely add.

Justine and Matt worried about him incessantly, as

did the school, whose counsellor had recently recommended a professional psychiatric assessment.

'I think for everyone's sake,' she'd told Justine and Matt, 'especially Ben's, we need to find out if there's a medical reason for his antisocial behaviour, because we can't keep putting it down to puberty.'

Justine and Matt hadn't resisted, in fact they'd been all for it; however Ben was no more interested in 'spilling his guts to some weirdo shrink', as he put it, than he was in thanking the head teacher for not giving up on him yet.

Whatever his feelings, everyone agreed that his behaviour, at least at school, had shown some improvement following the recommendation, and since he hadn't ever been in any real sort of trouble, nothing criminal anyway, there was hope that with a mind like his he'd soon be back on track and catch up on his lessons. Whether he'd manage to regain the power of speech when at home remained to be seen, since he still didn't seem capable of much more than monosyllabic grunts or surly shrugs and eye-rolls. And quite what he was doing on his computer all hours of the day and night only he knew.

'For all we know he could be enrolling for jihad in there,' Matt had commented more than once, 'or tormenting some poor kid on Facebook, or being threatened himself.'

'He's just weird,' Abby would wisely inform them, as if they should already know that and get over it.

'And you're a slapper with shit for brains,' Ben would inform her, should he happen to overhear her summary damnation of his complicated character.

Such was life with two teenagers in the house, rarely calm, frequently challenging, and almost never predictable. It was often a relief to get away, Justine felt, but only safe in the knowledge that neither Ben nor Abby would ever dream of playing up their adored granny the way they did their parents.

'So, how did the gig go last night?' Justine asked Abby, when she finally persuaded her to open her bedroom door.

'Like you really care,' Abby said tersely. She was sitting cross-legged on her silver satin counterpane, idly strumming her acoustic guitar.

Going to sit on the edge of the elaborate French-style bed with its silver-leaf headboard and zebra-skin throws (copied from an interior magazine they'd found while on a girls' weekend in Paris with Cheryl and Chantal last year), Justine looked around the room, taking it all in. It was a shrine to Abby's short life and many passions, with hundreds of photographs from across the last decade and a half arranged in splendid montages: Abby as a toddler in bikini and wellies splashing about in the brook; Abby with Ben on a donkey ride laughing fit to fall off; Abby playing at being a waitress in the deli; singing at a wedding, aged ten; with friends, parents, and a few celebrities they'd met over the years; outside the Café Wha in New York to honour Bob Dylan (Matt's idea); in front of Radio City Music Hall with her name Photoshopped on to the billboard; at the Cavern Club in Liverpool 'with' the Beatles; onstage (pretending to perform) at the Hollywood Bowl; at a Beyoncé concert in Las Vegas; at Madonna's Sticky and Sweet Tour in Toronto;

walking into Asia World Arena in Hong Kong with the real Rod Stewart . . . Then there was the wall of shots, most blown up into posters, of Abby actually performing or recording: moody, glittering, breath-taking images of a young girl who might already have been a megastar, the compositions and poses were so worldly and impressive.

Everything in the room had been styled, collected or chosen by Abby: the fancy modesty screen they'd found at an antiques fair in Toulon, now swathed in her performance gear – boas, bustiers, undies, belts and jeans – the black silk draperies covering the windows, the over-poweringly ornate crystal chandelier that hung from the ceiling like a preposterous birthday cake, the cluster of postcards, fridge magnets and museum brochures she'd gathered on her travels, awards she'd won for music, sports and art, her precious trio of acoustic guitars, a Korg PA arranger keyboard, a set of African bongo drums, a second-hand violin, two computers (one for school, the other for music) and a nifty, expensive Bose sound-mixing system.

Abby certainly didn't want for much, which made Justine worry at times that everything was happening too fast, too soon for her little girl. It was difficult to know how to slow things down, when so far the only brake she and Matt had been able to make work was to forbid her to audition for any of the TV talent shows until she'd finished her GCSEs. Though they'd been treated to some powerful sulks as a result of the decision, backed up with some red-hot tirades of lively abuse, they hadn't yet turned on the TV on a Saturday night to discover they'd been defied.

'So you think I don't care,' Justine commented, as though mulling this extraordinary misconception.

'You'd have been here if you did,' Abby retorted, striking an angry chord.

Justine regarded what she could see of her daughter's beautiful, miserable face, patched with colour, creamy smooth with youth. Her luxuriant hair with its natural waves and honey-gold sheen was scrunched into a knot at the nape of her neck, while her jean shorts and crop top exposed far more flesh and piercings than they could begin to conceal. 'We tried to make it,' she said, 'you know that, so what's this really about?'

Abby huffed, hit a loud G6 and shoved the guitar to the end of the bed.

'Did something go wrong last night?' Justine ventured.

'Noooo!' A tone that was meant to make Justine feel like an idiot.

Feeling no more than tired and slightly irritated, Justine said, 'OK, we can do this the long way and I'll keep asking questions, or you can just tell me why you're in a bad mood.'

'I'm not in a bad mood.'

Justine counted to ten. 'Would you rather I left?'

Abby didn't answer, which meant her mother was to stay.

Trying to move things along, Justine said, 'Grandma Catherine was very impressed by your assembly gig the other morning.'

Abby shrugged.

Being too tired to handle this well, Justine made the mistake of glancing at her watch. 'Abby, I'm jet-lagged, I need to . . .'

'See, that's it,' Abby cried angrily. 'You've never got time for me. You always put yourself first . . .'

'Stop this nonsense now . . .'

'If you'd been there last night that stupid bitch in the Black Diamonds would never have spoken to me the way she did, not in front of you, but I couldn't care less, because she's just a stupid, talentless, ugly waste of space who should find something else to do because she sure as hell can't sing.'

Justine gave it a moment. 'So what did she say?' she asked quietly.

Abby's expression turned mutinous.

'OK, if you don't want to repeat it . . .'

'She said I was too up myself for a kid my age and that I should get a reality check because I was already making a lot of enemies – and that just isn't true. I'm not making enemies, and anyway, how would she know anything about me when I only met her for the first time last night?'

Feeling for how hard it could be to rub up against the competition, Justine took Abby's hand and linked their fingers. 'Would I be right in thinking that you went on first?' she asked.

'Duh, I was the support act, so yes I went on first.'

'So she saw how good you are and felt the need to put you down.'

Slapping the bed, Abby cried, 'That's what Chantal said, but it was really horrible, Mum. She was such a cow, honestly, and I know it wouldn't have mattered half as much if you and Dad had been there. And it definitely wouldn't have if Harry had come, but he didn't, and he said he would . . .'

As tears filled her eyes, Justine realised they'd finally got to the heart of the issue. Harry Sands, the eighteen-year-old son of Melanie and Kelvin Sands who'd moved into the vale nine months ago, had clearly been too wrapped up in freshers week at his new uni to keep his promise. It wouldn't have surprised Justine to learn that he had no idea he'd actually made a promise, since Abby was quite good at convincing herself that something was true if she wanted it to be.

'Delusional, that's what she is,' Ben had snorted when the subject of Abby's crush on Harry had come up one evening. 'Why would someone like him be interested in her?'

'He *is* interested in me,' Abby had shot back furiously. 'Why else would he come and watch me sing at the summer fete, and why else would he invite me to go on a picnic with him and his mates?'

'He invited everyone,' Ben reminded her, 'not just you.'

'But he asked me himself, whereas he got Connor to ask everyone else.'

At the mention of Connor Sands, Harry's fifteen-year-old brother, Ben's expression darkened. There was no love lost between those two, and if pressed Justine would have admitted that she didn't care much for Connor either. He might be as good-looking as his older brother, an accomplished hockey player and a gifted student, but he had always struck her as sneaky and arrogant, someone who enjoyed causing trouble, or making others feel small.

Though his brother never came across that way, Justine had to admit (but never to her children) that his mother, Melanie Sands, did. It had to be where Connor had got the unpleasant side of his nature from, since his father was unfailingly friendly and ready to help out with all their community events, even providing many of the props, free of charge, from his film and TV hire company.

'Don't you think that's mean,' Abby wailed, 'saying he'll come then not bothering to turn up?'

'Did he actually say he'd be there?' Justine asked carefully. 'Were those the words he used, or did he say something more general such as he'd make it if he could?'

Abby scowled. 'He knows how much I wanted him to come. It was like a really big deal for me, playing with the Black Diamonds.'

'It's freshers week,' Justine reminded her.

'So what? You shouldn't make promises and not keep them.'

'Abby,' Justine said softly, 'I understand why you like him so much, he's a lovely boy . . .'

'He's not a *boy*!'

'OK, young man, which actually makes my point. He's too old for you . . .'

'Three years!'

'Which isn't much when you're older, but it is right now. He'll be mixing with girls his own age, going places, doing things you can't possibly get involved in . . .'

'Why not?'

'You know why not. Eighteen is very different to fifteen. For one thing it's legal for him to go to pubs . . .'

'I *sing* in pubs.'

'Only locally, and you're not allowed to drink. He is, and he'll want to do that with friends of his own age.'

'I don't mind if he drinks. In fact you might as well know that I'd have sex with him if he wanted, and I reckon he does.'

Taking a breath, Justine said, 'It's when you talk like that that you remind me of how very young you are.'

Abby's eyes flashed. 'I hate it when you say things like that. Fifteen's not too young to have sex. Everyone's doing it in my year.'

'Even if that's true, it's no reason for you to do it too.'

'I'm telling you I would if Harry wanted to.'

'Then we have to feel thankful that he didn't show up last night, and that he's going to be in Leeds from now on – or at least until Christmas.'

Abby's head went down, and Justine could feel her awful despair. 'I know he doesn't fancy me really,' she whispered shakily. 'Who would when I'm ugly and fat and totally up myself . . .'

Pulling her into a hug, Justine said, 'You're beautiful and slim and totally going to be famous one day, and if you still want him then I bet all you'll have to do is click your fingers and he'll come running.'

Seeming to like this idea, Abby nodded slowly.

'And remember what we read the other day,' Justine pressed on. '"Every bad situation is a blues song waiting to happen."'

Abby's head came up. 'That was Amy Winehouse,' she stated.

Justine nodded. Right now Abby had no greater idol. 'So maybe you should get writing,' she suggested.

Abby was clearly already there.

Deciding to leave her to her composing, Justine got up from the bed.

'Mum?' Abby said as Justine reached the door.

Turning round Justine watched her put down the guitar, unfold herself from the counterpane and come towards her, all long slender legs and smooth flat tummy with a crystal stud in her navel.

'I'm really glad you're back,' she said, sliding her arms round Justine's neck, 'and I'm sorry I was so horrid when you came in.'

'You're already forgiven,' Justine assured her, and tilting Abby's face up to her own, she whispered, 'Love you.'

'Love you too,' Abby whispered back. After a beat she added, 'Do you think I should text Harry to find out why he didn't come? I mean, he might be ill or something, because he didn't even get in touch.'

Justine was about to respond when Ben said, scathingly, 'You are such a stalker. Leave him alone, why don't you? He's . . .'

'*I'm* the stalker?' Abby hissed furiously. 'Look who's talking. You're even standing there now, eavesdropping on what other people are saying . . . He does it all the time,' she told her mother. 'You need to talk to him, because he is seriously psycho . . .'

Ben growled menacingly into her face.

Drawing back sharply, she said, 'See what I mean. Everyone's scared of him. No one'll have anything to do with him except Chantal, and she wouldn't bother if she weren't so sweet.'

'Why don't you fuck off and die,' he snarled.

'Ben, for God's sake!' Justine snapped. She'd thought, believed, he was improving . . .

He was walking away.

'You are so never going to make anything of yourself,' Abby shouted after him.

He simply raised a middle finger and disappeared into his room.

Before Abby could rant any more, Justine said, 'Please tell me you haven't been arguing like this the whole time Dad and I were away.'

Abby flushed. 'He just makes me so mad at times.'

'Abby, Granny really doesn't need it . . .'

'It didn't happen often,' Abby broke in heatedly. 'As a matter of fact we hardly ever saw him, thank God, because who wants to hang out with *him*?'

'Plenty of people,' Ben shouted, tearing open his door, 'they're just not dumbfucks like you and your . . .'

'See?' Abby broke in. 'He's eavesdropping again.'

'Drop dead,' he spat, and slammed the door.

Abby glared at her mother, clearly expecting some sort of reaction, but Justine was so agitated she couldn't think what to say.

'Aren't you at least going to tell him off for swearing?' Abby pressed forcefully.

Deciding to give her a hug, Justine said, 'I should go and help Dad with the luggage,' and before any more arguments could break out she ran down the stairs and closed the kitchen door behind her.

'I don't know what gets into them,' she said to Catherine and Matt. 'The way they wind one another up . . . Sometimes I don't know who's worse.' To Catherine she said, 'Please tell me what they were really like while we were away.'

'Oh for sure there was the occasional skirmish,' Catherine admitted, 'but you expect it at their age.

174

Teenagers are driven by hormones that haven't yet attached themselves to normal restraint or common sense.'

'Were Simon and Matt like it when they were that age?'

Catherine gave it some thought. 'Probably,' she replied, 'but to be honest, I'd say puberty is a bit like another form of childbirth, it can hurt a lot while it's happening, but when it's over you forget all the bad bits and only remember the good.'

Justine looked at Matt who simply shrugged as if to say, I'll buy into that one, and as if to back him up their sixteen-year-old nephew Wesley chose that moment to burst in through the back door with Rosie the retriever.

'Hey Auntie Just, Uncle Matt,' he laughed as Rosie barrelled between them, so excited by the surprise that she hardly knew who to greet first.

Leaving Matt to deal with Rosie, Justine went to hug Wes, who surely had to be six foot by now. With his young James Dean looks ('*Who?*' he'd protested when his grandmother had first commented on the likeness) and easy-going nature he was probably one of the most popular lads around. Although it had to be said it was only recently that he'd stopped being a nightmare for his parents, for he'd spent a good part of the past couple of years being sulky, uncommunicative, aggressive, sneery, with, thank goodness, the occasional burst of humour that filled everyone with heady relief as they were reminded that behind all the frontal-lobe chaos the real Wesley was managing to survive.

'The trip was wonderful,' Justine told him when he asked, 'the journey back was hell. How's everything with you?'

'Yeah, cool.' He was hugging his grandmother now, then shaking hands with Matt. 'Is Abby here?' he wanted to know.

'Upstairs in her room,' Justine told him.

'OK, I'll go see her. Oh, Gran, Mum wants to know if you told Uncle Matt and Auntie Just that Cheryl's . . .'

'. . . cooking dinner,' Catherine finished. 'Yes, I remembered, so you don't have to put me in a home yet.'

Laughing, Justine said, 'That is never going to happen,' and grabbing Wes's arm before he could leave she said, quietly, 'Ben's upstairs too. If you've got a moment would you pop in and have a chat with him? I think he could do with some . . .' How should she put this? 'Cousinly support?'

Though Wes didn't appear thrilled with the task, he managed a cheerful 'Sure thing' and, laughing at the way Rosie had pinned Matt to the wall, he took himself off to see his cousins.

Two days later Justine and Cheryl were in the kitchen barn, with no other staff around for the moment, preparing pies, salads, and sauces to stock up the deli. It was Justine's first day back after the trip Down Under, and though she was still jet-lagged it felt good to be behind the stove and worktops again while catching up with Cheryl.

'So he's still in the hospital,' Cheryl was saying, as Justine added more garam masala to a chicken curry and soberly absorbed the news that Neil, Maddy's son, was in hospital being tested for another type of cancer, this time in his spine.

'Poor Maddy,' Justine murmured. 'Poor Neil. It seems so unfair when he's been doing so well for so long.' She was picturing his cheeky grin, freckly nose and gangly limbs, and remembering how elated he'd been the day they'd thrown a party to celebrate his selection for the football team. When he appeared so healthy and full of life it was hard to accept there could be anything wrong with him.

'It might turn out to be a false alarm,' Cheryl reminded her. 'Let's keep our fingers crossed for that, anyway. The kids have all been going in to visit him, which is keeping his spirits up, Maddy says.'

'How is she coping?'

'She's there every day, as you'd expect, and she looks about as bad as she's obviously feeling.'

'Has she hit the vodka yet?'

'Not so far, but who could blame her if she caved in? The stress, the fear, must be unbearable.'

'Are things still good between her and Ronnie?'

'As far as I know.'

There had been much bawdy speculation on what might have happened between the butcher and his wife while on a second honeymoon in Greece a couple of years ago, for neither, to the best of anyone's knowledge, had shown any signs of playing around since. In fact they appeared to be closer than anyone could ever remember, and the effect their new harmony was having on their children was a joy to see. Neither Nelly nor Neil frowned quite so much now, nor did they seem as nervy or apprehensive, and there was, apparently, much improvement in their grades at school. This was one of the reasons why this latest scare with Neil felt so wrong and unjust.

'To be honest I don't know how either Maddy or Ronnie would cope if he turns out to be sick again,' Cheryl commented, as she removed a mixing bowl from the blender. 'Actually, how would any of us if it happened to one of ours? It's unthinkable. We forget sometimes how lucky we are to have normal, healthy kids.'

With some irony, Justine replied, 'I'm not sure I'd call mine normal, but I know what you mean.'

Smiling, Cheryl said, 'Chantal tells me Abby was sensational at the Komedia last Saturday night. Has anyone been in touch with her since, like the producer who hired her?'

Justine shook her head. 'She's managed to convince herself that the female singer in the Black Diamonds has it in for her, so now she'll never hear from the producer again.'

Cheryl grimaced. 'From everything you hear about the music industry I guess there's a chance she could be right.'

'As Matt says, she's going to encounter a lot of competition along the way, and a lot of sharks who'll be out to take advantage of her one way or another, so she'd better start toughening up now.'

Wiping her hands, Cheryl said, 'She can handle herself well enough. She's got the confidence and she's talented. No one can take that away from her, no matter what their intentions might be.'

Praying that would turn out to be true, Justine said, 'Speaking of intentions, she informed me the other night that she'd sleep with Harry Sands if he asked her.'

Cheryl's eyebrows shot up. 'Wouldn't we all?' she

retorted, making Justine laugh. 'He so drop-dead he actually makes me blush when he speaks to me in case he can read my mind.'

Spluttering on another laugh, Justine said, 'How's his delightful mother these days?'

Cheryl's expression collapsed. 'Please don't get me started on that piece of work,' she muttered. 'She's only got herself co-opted on to the parish council, so there's something for us all to look forward to. She's also appointed herself head of flowers at the church, she's starting up a new walking group, she informs me, and apparently she's arranging for various luminaries to come and give talks at the village hall.'

Justine's interest was piqued. 'What sort of luminaries?'

'Heaven only knows. I guess we'll find out when she's managed to book them. She sent Connor over the other day to invite me and Brad for drinks. I had to wonder why she didn't just ring up until Brad pointed out that it was probably the boy's way of getting to see Chantal.'

Curious, Justine said, 'Does Chantal like him?'

'Not as far as I'm aware, but you know Chantal, she's lovely to everyone so it's not always easy to tell who she does or doesn't like. I think she's still got a bit of a thing for Ben, but we hardly ever see him these days.'

Justine rolled her eyes. 'With the way he is you might think yourself lucky,' she commented. 'I thought things were getting better, but now I'm not so sure. He and Abby . . . The things they say to one another in the heat of the moment . . . I'm sure Rob and I never used to be anywhere near as horrible when we had fights.'

Shrugging, Cheryl said, 'Maybe that's the blessing of only having one, no scrapping, no sibling rivalry, just a peaceful life in that area . . . As usual, it's the parents making all the noise in our house.'

Justine regarded her worriedly. 'So things aren't any better with Brad?'

'They're never going to be, you know that. The only reason we've lasted this long is because of Chantal. Once she goes to uni . . . Well, hopefully he'll pack up and go and I'll be free to start a new life with someone who's not jealous of my success, such that it is, and who doesn't keep putting me down at every opportunity. Honestly, you don't know how lucky you are with Matt. OK, you do, but you're so close you two, and when the kids go you'll still have each other. When Chantal goes . . .'

Realising she was becoming emotional, Justine went to put an arm around her. 'When Chantal goes you'll still have me and Portovino, because we're not going anywhere.'

Cheryl smiled through watery eyes. 'Thank God,' she whispered, painting Justine's nose with a floury finger, 'because there are times when I really don't know what I'd do without you.'

'She wouldn't have to be without us,' Matt insisted when Justine related the conversation to him later. 'We've known her for so long. She feels as much a part of the family as Simon and Gina, even my mother says that.'

Rolling over on the bed where they'd just snatched a late-afternoon nap, Justine said, 'The question is, will

Brad actually leave when Chantal goes to uni? I hope so, because Cheryl's life has been on hold for too long already. She should be with someone who really appreciates her . . . Actually, wouldn't it be great if we could pair her off with Kelvin Sands, who's such a sweetheart – he really deserves someone as warm and wonderful as Cheryl.'

Laughing, Matt said, 'I'm guessing Melanie Sands would have something to say about that, but I know what you mean, he and Cheryl do seem well suited.' Reaching for the slender wand on his nightstand, he slipped an arm around her and changed the subject to something he considered far more important than the affairs of their neighbours. 'Are you sure,' he said softly, 'that you want to go through with this? I mean, if you don't . . .'

Justine turned to him in amazement. 'You surely can't be suggesting a termination,' she protested. 'Matt, this is *our* child . . .'

'I realise that, and I swear I want it as much as you do, but after the last two miscarriages . . .'

'They were a long time ago, and there's nothing to say it'll happen again. In fact, I have a good feeling about it this time. I really do.' It was true, she did, though she couldn't remember now if she'd felt the same way about the others.

Pulling her into his arms he held her close as he said, 'Then that's good enough for me, because I'd love to have another child, girl or boy, fat or thin, tall or short, clever or dumb, just please don't let it be as difficult as Ben.'

'Please don't ever let him hear you say that.'

181

'Of course not,' he promised. 'Actually, I wonder what he and Abby will say when we tell them?'

Turning on to her back with a sigh, Justine said, 'I'm guessing Abby will consider it gross, or something along those lines, but she'll be fine with it when it comes. Actually, she'll probably be too busy auditioning for *The X Factor* to notice there's a new member of the family taking up all the attention.'

'Oh, she'll notice that all right,' Matt responded drily. 'But as for this *X Factor* thing, I know I've said it before but I'll say it again, I really don't want her to do it. If they turn her down . . .'

'They won't.'

'But we both know it's possible. She's good, fantastic even, especially as a performer, but there's so much competition out there these days and I dread to think how she'll take it if she has to give up her dream.'

'She's far too determined to let anything stand in her way, you know that, and if something does . . . Well, let's worry about it when, *if*, it happens. Right now I'm more concerned about Ben and what he's going to do with his life . . . Or what he'll make of having a little brother or sister?'

Matt could only shake his head in bewilderment. 'I wouldn't mind knowing what he makes of anything,' he commented resignedly.

Feeling the same way, Justine said, 'Actually, trying to look on the bright side, do you remember how Wes once punched Simon when Simon broke down his door to find out what was going on in his room?'

Matt's smile was wry. 'It's a good reminder, because yes, I do remember, and it ended up becoming a kind of turning point between them. All that surging testosterone . . . I reckon it scared them both and look at them now, the best of friends.'

'He's a lovely boy,' Justine murmured, 'and Ben is too, underneath it all. And who knows, finding out about the baby might be a turning point for *him*.'

Matt's eyebrows rose, showing how doubtful he was of that. 'He won't say anything about it at first,' he decided, 'largely because he doesn't say much about anything, or not to us.'

Squeezing his hand, she said, 'Wes tells me they've got an archery tournament the week after next, and he thinks he's talked Ben into taking part. If he does, we must make sure we're there to support him.'

'If he wants us to be there, and I wouldn't put any money on that, or on him actually turning up now Connor's joined the same club.'

'Mm, yes, Melanie told me about that when she came into the deli earlier. I'm sorry, but that woman . . . She really gets under my skin. I try not to let it show, but she was going on today about it being all right for some swanning off to Australia and New Zealand, and she supposes the deli will be all beer and barbies from now on. I almost told her she was living in a cultural warp if she thought that was all Australia and New Zealand were about, but it's not worth getting into anything with her. She's so supercilious it makes me want to slap her.' Justine groaned as a depressing thought occurred to her. 'I'm sure she'll have plenty to say about late pregnancies when she finds out about me. In fact, she'll probably organise a midwife or obstetrician to come and give a talk at the village hall.'

Laughing, Matt started to pull himself up from the bed and promptly fell back again as Abby came charging up the stairs shouting, 'Mum! Dad! Where are you?'

'In here,' Justine called out.

A moment later the door banged open and Abby burst into the room, with Chantal close behind.

'It's Ben,' Abby panted. 'He's up a tree again, in the orchard, and he's throwing apples at the cows in the next field. It's really scaring them and he won't stop.'

Heaving a weary sigh, Matt got up and pulled Justine to her feet.

'You have to make him stop,' Abby insisted. 'It's cruel what he's doing.'

'He's not usually cruel,' Chantal piped up in his defence, 'but he got mad with Connor on the way home from school and now he's taking it out on the cows.'

After pulling on some clothes and hiding the pregnancy test, Justine followed Matt and the girls out to the orchard, where the smell of cow dung and wet grass was pungent enough to make her stomach churn. Sliding her hands into the rear pockets of her jeans, she peered up through the tangle of branches to where Ben was perched, ignoring his father as Matt tried to persuade him to come down.

'Please Ben,' Chantal called out, her pretty, heart-shaped face pale with concern. 'You promised to help me with my homework, remember?'

When there was no response, Justine said, 'Ben, you can stay up there as long as you like, but if you carry on throwing apples at the cows I'll call the farmer.'

'Who'll come with his gun,' Abby shouted, 'and shoot

you out. They can do that, can't they, Dad? Farmers can shoot people who mess with their livestock?'

'Why don't you go and get a life bypass somewhere?' Ben growled at her. 'And take Chantal with you.'

As Chantal's eyes widened with hurt, Justine put a comforting hand on her shoulder. 'He doesn't want you to see him giving in,' she whispered, hoping she was right, and leaving Matt to deal with it, she gently ushered the girls back through the orchard.

It was only a few minutes after she'd managed to dispatch Abby and Chantal down to the deli for any treat of their choice that Matt and Ben came into the kitchen. Seeing how tense they both looked, Justine quickly searched for something friendly to say.

'Don't just walk away,' Matt snapped angrily as Ben made for the stairs. 'You need to tell us what the hell's wrong, and something obviously is.'

To Justine's surprise, and relief, Ben stopped at the foot of the stairs, but didn't turn round.

'What happened with Connor?' she asked gently. 'Why did you fall out?'

'Because he's an asshole,' Ben grunted scathingly. His tone implied that she, a supposedly intelligent human being, should have understood that.

'What did he do?' Matt wanted to know.

Ben shook his head; his long, matted hair was masking his face, but Justine could see how tightly he was gripping the stair rail. A moment later, to her astonishment she realised he was crying, great hiccuping sobs, and by the time she reached him he'd dropped to his knees. 'It's all right,' she murmured, trying to help him up, or at least find a place for her arms that he would be able to accept. 'Everything's going to be fine,' she insisted, looking helplessly at Matt. This was the last thing either of them had expected.

'What is it, son?' Matt urged, as Ben turned his back on them. 'Why are you so upset?'

'What did Connor do?' Justine pressed, finding herself wondering if the crying was as real as it seemed, and hating herself for doubting it.

'It's not him,' Ben choked. 'It's you two,' and suddenly rushing up the stairs he charged along the landing to his room.

Matt was after him like a shot, getting there before Ben could lock the door. 'What about us?' Matt demanded, as Ben roared like an animal and flung himself down on the bed. He glared at Justine who'd come in behind him.

She was looking around. The room was a black hole of teenage-boy flotsam, with rugby and football boots, crossbows, cricket bats, old food and drink cartons, hockey sticks, video games and magazines cluttering the floor. The duvet was bunched into a heap against the headboard, towels blocked the way into the bathroom, clothes were spilling out of the wardrobe, and his computer and TV were haphazardly filling up the space between tangles of wires, consoles, keyboards and remote controls. The only order in the room was inside the cabinet containing his many sporting trophies, although Justine noticed that one of the glass panels was cracked. All four of the curtains at his double windows were hanging off the poles.

Going to sit on the bed, Matt put a hand on his shoulder.

Ben quickly shrugged it away.

'What have we done?' Matt said gently. 'Please tell us why you're so angry with us.'

'Just go away. Fuck off,' Ben snarled into the pillow.

'Sweetheart,' Justine said, kneeling beside him, and still not sure how trusting she was of this outburst, 'we can't make anything better, or even apologise, if you won't tell us what the problem is.'

As he continued to growl and rage into his pillow Matt and Justine looked at one another, not sure what to do.

'You don't care about me,' Ben seethed furiously. 'I don't mean anything to you. All you care about is Abby.'

'That isn't true,' Justine cried. 'We care just as much . . .'

'Liar! You wish I was dead.'

'That's just nonsense,' Justine protested.

'Why are you telling yourself these things?' Matt interrupted. 'You've got to know that . . .'

'You're always doing stuff with her. You never do anything with me.'

'Because you don't want to do anything,' Matt reminded him. 'But if you've changed your mind and you want to start going to games again . . .'

'You mean with Uncle Simon, because you never come anywhere with me.'

'Ben, how can you say that?' Justine exclaimed. 'We've taken you to World Cup matches, European championships, the Olympics, for God's sake . . . You've been to Twickenham, Wembley, Yankee Stadium with Dad . . .'

'You don't come though, do you?' he shouted. 'You're always too busy doing stuff with *Abby* . . .'

'Stop this right now,' Matt barked. 'Do you have any idea how lucky you are to have been to all the places you have? The experiences you've had, the things you've seen . . .'

'You even came back from Australia so you could be at the gig for *Abby* . . .'

'We'd have done the same for you if something special had happened,' Matt assured him.

'But you didn't, did you? I was supposed to be going to camp in the summer but you couldn't be bothered to come with me. All the other dads went, but I didn't have anyone to come with me so I had to stay at home.'

Matt frowned in confusion. 'When was this? You never told me . . .'

'Because you don't listen. Nothing I say is of interest to you. I'm just a waste of space. You're ashamed of me . . .'

'Stop talking nonsense,' Matt broke in forcefully. He was looking at Justine, clearly wondering if she knew anything about this summer camp.

Briefly shaking her head, she watched Ben sit up, plant his elbows on his knees, and hang his head down between them.

Carefully, Matt said, 'Did Wesley and Uncle Simon go on the camping trip?'

Ben muttered, 'It was just our year.'

'And you're sure you told me about it?'

'I brought a note home from school.'

Afraid that he might have and they'd somehow missed it, Justine asked, 'Why didn't you say something? We could have postponed the trip, or got Uncle Simon to go with you.'

'I didn't want Uncle Simon to come, I wanted Dad.'

Looking as wretched as he was clearly meant to feel, Matt said, 'I'm sorry I let you down, son. I promise it won't happen again.'

'Yeah it will, because it always does. Now why don't you fuck off out of my room, both of you, I don't want you in here any more.'

It wasn't until they were downstairs and safely out of earshot that Matt said quietly, 'Well, at least he's talking.'

Choking on a laugh, Justine put a finger to her lips and walked into his arms. Today, she decided, was definitely not the right day to tell Ben about the baby.

Chapter Nine

Darkness had fallen more than an hour ago; Lula and Hazel still hadn't been found.

There were people everywhere, crowding the lane, combing the lake shore, spreading into the woods . . . The state police had arrived, boosting the numbers of local officers. Everyone seemed to be shouting into radios and cellphones; blue lights flashed through the trees, over the moonlit water, across the house.

Justine was on the porch, desperate to act, not knowing what to do. Panic was trying to overwhelm her; fear was striking her heart with thick, violent stabs. The police had ordered her to wait here; they were handling things now. She was unable to make herself believe it was happening – it had to be a nightmare. No one had taken Lula and Hazel, they couldn't have, yet where were they?

She and Sallie Jo had already answered dozens of questions. Did they have any idea where the girls might have gone? Had they checked their phones for messages? Was there a friend they might have visited? Had anyone been to Sallie Jo's to find out if they were there? Had they ever been out alone at night before? What were they wearing? Could Justine check to see if anything was missing from Lula's room such as warm coats, boots, anything that might suggest they'd planned to go out?

As the news spread about town the festival arrangements were abandoned, cafés and restaurants emptied, as did the VFW Club on East Washington. They were all here, swelling the numbers of searchers, waiting to be told what to do.

Justine heard someone mention an AMBER Alert, and the world seemed to spin off its axis.

Too many nightmares were coming back to her; she couldn't cope with this. She had to make it stop.

'That doesn't mean anyone thinks they've been abducted,' Sallie Jo assured her, clearly trying to bolster herself as well. 'It's standard procedure in these situations. Isn't that right, Toby?'

'Correct,' the town's chief marshal confirmed, his face glowing blue, falling into darkness and glowing blue again. 'The alert isn't only about abduction. If they've wandered off . . .'

Justine wasn't listening. She knew in her heart that they hadn't wandered off, that someone had taken them. Surely the police had worked that out for themselves. The window in Lula's room was open; crime scene investigators were already there, carrying out their work. For Tallulah's sake she had to show Toby the email she'd received, even if it meant telling them who she really was, why she was here . . .

There was a sudden commotion in the lane. Something had happened.

Please God they've been found.

It turned out that two small bicycles had been discovered on an overgrown track in the woods. There were tyre marks from a truck nearby.

David took hold of Sallie Jo as she started to break down.

Justine's eyes were wide and raw as she watched a police officer duck the tape and come towards them. He spoke briefly with Toby and listened as Toby turned to Justine and Sallie Jo, saying, as gently as he could, 'We're going to need up-to-date photos and a full description of what the girls were wearing.'

With trembling hands Sallie Jo clicked open her phone. Seconds later a recent shot of Hazel was being sent on for processing.

'Justine?' he prompted.

Justine looked down at her phone, hardly knowing what to do.

'Let me,' David said, and taking the phone he transmitted a shot of Lula sitting on the porch with Daisy. *The one she'd wanted to send to Matt.*

'K9 unit's about ten minutes away,' someone announced over Toby's radio. 'Helicopters are up.'

Justine thought she was going mad.

'. . . you to identify the bicycles,' she heard Toby saying.

She tried to grasp the lifeline – the bicycles might not belong to Hazel and Lula – but it slipped away and she was drowning again.

She and Sallie Jo followed Toby through the crowd. Other officers escorted them, instructing everyone to be patient or to stand back.

Minutes later they were in a glaring pool of light deep in the woods staring past ribbons of police tape to where Hazel's and Lula's bikes were lying abandoned on the brambly trail.

Justine sank to her knees.

Toby came down with her. 'It's OK,' he murmured. 'You're going to be fine. We'll find them.'

'Yes, it's their bicycles,' she heard Sallie Jo whispering raggedly to another officer.

Justine's head was spinning. How was she going to break this to Matt? How would she even begin to explain that Lula had gone?

There was the sound of someone shouting further down the trail. A flurry of torchlight lit up the woods fifty yards ahead as Toby and others started running in the direction of the disturbance.

Without thinking Justine went after them. 'Lula,' she sobbed wretchedly, 'Lula, I'm here.'

With no warning a gunshot boomed through the night.

Justine reeled as if she'd been hit. Her ears were ringing; there was no breath to take.

Suddenly she started to run, panicked, desperate to find her baby, but she was grabbed by an officer and pressed against a tree.

Someone was shouting. 'Billy, put down the gun.'

'You're on my land,' Billy Jakes shouted back.

'Just put the gun down before someone gets hurt.'

'Get off my land.'

'No one's going anywhere till you put down the gun.'

'Come any closer and you'll be sorry.'

'Billy, two girls have gone missing. Do you know anything about that?'

'I said *get off my land*.'

'We need to search the area, Billy. If you don't let us we'll have to arrest you.'

A sudden silence fell. All that could be heard was the rustle of night creatures, birds, people moving stealthily, officers with firearms aloft sliding between trees.

Justine was still being held back. Sweat, tears, mucus poured down her face. She was shaking so hard she could hardly see or hear.

An officer up ahead shouted, 'OK, step away from the gun, Billy. That's right. Keep moving. I'm coming in now.'

'You're on my land,' Billy growled.

'We need to find the girls. Can you tell us where they are?'

'I don't know nothing about no girls.'

'Their bicycles are back there in the woods. Are you sure you haven't seen them?'

'Course I'm sure. Do you think I'm blind? Ain't no girls here.'

'Have you seen anyone else hanging around? Anyone come calling you weren't expecting?'

'Ain't seen no one all the day long, but I can tell you this, someone's been around here and when I find 'em I'm going to shoot their butts right out.'

'When you say someone's been here . . .'

'That's what I said.'

'How do you know if you didn't see them?'

'I always know.'

The woods fell silent again and Justine became aware of Sallie Jo standing beside her. She could feel her penetrating stare.

'You know something, don't you?' Sallie Jo muttered.

Justine flinched.

'You've got to tell us,' Sallie Jo hissed. 'Whatever it is . . .'

'I don't. I . . .'

'Is it true you're in witness protection? That's what people are saying.'

'No, no, I . . .'

'Has someone found you? Is that what's going on?'

As Justine tried to answer, a message squawked over a nearby radio.

'K9's arrived.'

'We'll find them,' she mumbled to Sallie Jo.

'We'd better,' Sallie Jo retorted, leaving Justine in no doubt that she'd hold her responsible if they didn't.

Moments later a burly officer with a close-cropped beard and wide, jutting face took a spaniel past the police tape to the bicycles, where it began sniffing around. Within seconds it was heading down the trail towards Billy Jakes's trailer.

'If Billy has them,' Sallie Jo whispered, 'he won't hurt them. He's never hurt anyone.'

Billy's voice boomed through the night. 'See, that's how I know someone's been here,' he yelled furiously.

What did he mean?

Suddenly David was with them. 'The AMBER Alert's gone out,' he said quietly. 'I've already had calls from Chicago and Indianapolis.'

Realising the calls would be from news organisations, Justine's heart wrenched with hope and dismay. If it helped find Tallulah she'd welcome every camera, reporter and satellite dish in the nation. If it didn't . . .

Another voice on the radio. 'Are Sallie Jo and Justine with you?'

'Affirmative,' the officer answered.

'OK. Someone's coming to get them.'

Why? What had happened?

Justine was already running forward, as was Sallie Jo.

The sheriff and two men came through the trees to meet them, and escorted them past Billy's dilapidated trailer and a tangle of uniformed officers towards a decaying old barn.

The doors were open, and from the cavernous interior Toby and another officer emerged into the light. In their arms were two small girls, looking terrified and bewildered and in very bad need of their mothers.

'Lula!' Justine sobbed, stumbling towards her.

'Mummy!' Lula cried, reaching for her.

Taking her, Justine held her so tight that neither of them could breathe. *Thank you, thank you, thank you,* she whispered feverishly. *Oh dear God, thank you.*

'Mummy, I was scared,' Lula whimpered, still clinging on hard.

'I know,' Justine murmured, 'but it's all right now. You're safe and I'm going to take you home.'

'I want paying for them rabbits,' Billy Jakes growled from the darkness.

Toby whispered to Sallie Jo, 'They set them all free. Every last one of the cages is empty.'

Justine's heart buckled. They'd come here to rescue the rabbits. No one had taken them after all.

As she turned away she could feel Sallie Jo watching her, and knew that in spite of the happy outcome this wasn't over yet.

While Lula slept that night, safe in Justine's bed with Daisy snuggled in beside her, Justine lay staring helplessly into the darkness, not knowing what she should do, or where she could go next.

She'd truly believed when she'd come to Culver that her grandma was trying to reach her, to bring her to a safe place where she could set down roots and begin again, but that belief felt empty, even delusional now. The events of tonight, the simple mission to free a few dozen rabbits, had turned itself into a brutal reminder that she was never going to escape the horror she'd left behind, because it lived inside her, would always be wherever she went.

The rabbit story was already making the news: two missing children, with the cutest twist of heroism at the end. The girls' photographs had been flashed up on screens for everyone to see; the sheriff had commented for the cameras, as had Toby Henshaw; someone had even interviewed Billy Jakes, who'd demanded compensation for his livestock loss and the damage done to his land.

Sallie Jo, holding Hazel in her arms, had expressed her relief at finding the children safe, though they were a little shaken up, she'd informed the reporters, by the man with the gun whom they'd hidden from behind the banks of hutches.

Justine had kept her head down as she'd mumbled an apology to the police for all the bother the children had caused.

The following day, because she had to, she took her little heroine to the Fall Fest in town, watching and somehow smiling as everyone made a fuss of her and admired the mermaid scarecrow she presented with Hazel. More photographs were taken of the girls to end up heaven only knew where, but it was certain they wouldn't stop at the Culver Facebook page and local paper.

She saw Sallie Jo and David several times throughout the day, on the café's street terrace, heading towards the history hayride, judging the scarecrows, helping to relocate the puppet show to inside the library. She felt sure they were keeping their distance, or perhaps she was avoiding them. She barely engaged with anyone, apart from on the most superficial of levels.

'Mommy! Mommy!' Lula cried, rushing up to her with Daisy. 'We won second prize!'

Mommy. Was this the first time Lula had called her that? She couldn't be sure. Did she mind? She had no idea.

What prize?

'For the pet costume,' Lula reminded her.

Of course, Daisy was dressed as Tinker Bell.

Even before they got home Lula was asleep in the back of the car. She'd had a wonderful day riding ponies, leaping about the bounce house, taking part in all sorts of contests and having her face painted like a cat's. She was as excitable and sociable as any child could be; the trauma of hiding in a barn from an angry man with a gun was clearly forgotten.

Days passed. Lula went to day care, Justine continued to assist Sallie Jo with the realty business, but didn't meet up with her. The requests to detail properties or update the website came by email, and Justine responded the same way. Their continued working arrangement suggested that Sallie Jo wasn't cutting her off altogether, but there were no phone calls or texts to invite her to the café, or to a girls' night, or to say she was coming over, unless it was to drop off Hazel for the children to share some playtime.

Since Justine didn't have a realtor's licence she couldn't take prospective buyers to view properties, so until Lula came home at three she spent each day with only Daisy and her computer for company.

More than anything else in the world she wanted to be in touch with Matt, to tell him what had happened, how she was feeling, to ask him what she should do. Though she'd missed him before, every single minute of every day, the need for him now was growing to a pitch where she could barely stand it. She wrote him dozens of emails and letters that she never sent. She spoke to him constantly in her mind, listened for his answers and sometimes felt sure she heard them.

Halloween came round, and she and David took the girls trick or treating while Sallie Jo worked at the café. Justine wondered if her friend was deliberately avoiding her, but didn't ask. She didn't want to seem paranoid – or to learn that Sallie Jo was. Hazel came out as a truly scary witch, while Lula was a dashing Jack Sparrow in an almost identical costume to the one Ben had refused to take off for days just after the first *Pirates of the Caribbean* movie had come out.

That very film was currently Lula's favourite.

Though David was friendly throughout the evening, humorous even, Justine was sure she sensed a distance that hadn't been there before. They were all, she, David and Sallie Jo, tiptoeing around the night of the rabbits and Sallie's Jo's accusations as though they were something too explosive to touch. They were, for her, but why was it so difficult for them? Why weren't they asking the questions Sallie Jo had thrown at her that night? What was holding them back?

As yet no one from the past had contacted her to say they knew where she was, but she was expecting it every day. Sooner or later it was bound to get back to those who were interested that she was living happily – they would probably say happily – in Culver, Indiana with her daughter Tallulah. Though Rob and Maggie regularly assured her that they'd neither seen nor heard any reports of the rabbit story on the news in Britain, they couldn't possibly know what might be happening online, and nor could she.

Two days after Halloween she returned from day care with Lula to find a small package in the mailbox from her mother. It wasn't a surprise since Rob had told her it was coming, though she had no idea what was inside. A letter, she presumed, but it clearly contained something more – perhaps the photos of her grandma that she used to ask about.

She wouldn't open it now; she wasn't entirely sure when she would. The house on the lake seemed to have lost its importance, even its intrigue. Whatever its story might be she knew it couldn't be good or it wouldn't be a secret, and having so many of her own she didn't feel able to cope with any more.

After fixing Lula a drink and admiring the paintings she'd brought home with her, she decided to check her emails. Only one had arrived since she'd left to collect Lula. When she saw it she sat down hard and covered her face with her hands.

'What is it Mommy?' Lula asked worriedly. 'Did something go wrong?'

'No, no, nothing's wrong,' Justine quickly assured her, trying to smile. 'I just got a bit of a . . . a surprise, that's all.'

'What kind of a surprise?'

Justine couldn't connect with the question.

'Is it a nice surprise?'

Justine looked from her daughter's face to the message on the screen. 'I – I'm not sure,' she answered.

We need to talk. Call me.

There was nothing to say it was from Matt, but she knew it was, and because it was what she'd been waiting for ever since she'd arrived she didn't hesitate a moment longer, and reached for the phone.

There was no answer the first time she tried, but after she'd put Lula to bed she rang again and he picked up straight away.

'I knew it would be you,' he said softly.

The sound of his voice after so long a silence, the familiar timbre that conjured the beloved image of his face, the depth that seemed to resonate all the way into her, made it impossible for her to speak.

'Are you OK? Are you still there?'

'This is crazy,' she told him brokenly.

'I know.'

'We need to be in touch.'

'We are now.'

'I need you to come, Matt.'

'You know I want to, but we made the decision we felt was right at the time.'

'I keep asking myself what were we hoping to gain?'

'A good, uncomplicated life for Lula.'

Of course, and it was still their most important concern, but to do it this way, never to meet, to carry on as though they didn't exist for one another any more . . . ? 'I can't keep to it,' she confessed. 'I have to speak to you, even if it's only once in a while.'

'I need to speak to you too.'

Dizzied by relief, she could only wonder why she'd left it this long to call. Why had he? Why hadn't they realised months ago that trying to shut one another out, to live as though they could embrace new lives while separated, was never going to work?

'How are you?' she asked, steeling herself for an answer she was afraid to hear.

'OK, I guess,' was all he said. 'I'm more concerned about you. Rob told me that Lula and her friend went missing, how worried you are that someone will hear about it and realise who you are. Has it happened yet?'

'No, I don't think so. I'm not sure.'

'Is Lula all right?'

'She's fine. She's started calling me Mommy.'

There was a moment before he said, 'I can't decide how I feel about that.'

'No, nor can I, but it was bound to happen.'

'Actually, it's a good thing,' he decided. 'She'll talk with an American accent soon, and as she grows up no one will ever know she was born British.'

Though the thought of that made Justine feel vaguely disoriented, she managed to say, 'Just like no one in Britain used to realise I was born American.'

There was a smile in his voice as he said, 'Even I used to forget until your mother served as a reminder.'

'I had a letter from her today.'

'Saying?'

'I don't know, I haven't opened it yet. Did Rob tell you I've found my grandmother's house and that my mother owns it?'

'Yes, he did. So what's that about?

'I've no idea.' Realising she didn't want to talk about any of that now, or even think of it, she started to ask about him, but he was already speaking.

'Tell me more about Lula. What happened with the rabbits?'

For the next few minutes she made him chuckle and sensed his pain as she told him about the rescue mission, the compensation she'd offered Billy Jakes that he'd actually turned down, the excitement of the Fall Fest, and thrill of Halloween. As much as it was hurting him, she realised he needed to know that Lula was settling in and appeared, for now at least, unaffected by the past. They'd done their best to shield her from it; maybe it had worked.

'She's called you a few times,' she confessed. 'She left messages on the answerphone at the farmhouse. You haven't disconnected the line.'

'I'm sorry, I thought I had. I'll make sure it's done. The place hasn't sold yet.'

'No, I know. Will anyone want to buy it?'

'There's always someone.'

Picturing their beautiful home sitting at the top of the vale, abandoned and boarded up with no one coming or going any more, was almost as harsh as trying to picture where he was now.

'Does Lula ever talk about . . . the others?' he asked quietly.

He couldn't say their children's names, and she wasn't sure she could either. 'Now and again, less than she did.'

'Rob was here last week,' he told her. 'Hayley's supposed to be coming tomorrow.'

So Hayley was still in touch with him.

They'd always been close, so she should have expected it.

'Does she come often?' she asked, feeling the despair of not being able to be there for him the way Hayley could.

'Not really,' he replied. 'Once a month, maybe.'

That seemed often to her, or certainly more often than he used to see his editor. She couldn't allow herself to feel jealous; she had no right, nor the heart, to deny him the contact. 'Are you writing anything?'

'Not really.'

She wasn't surprised, but it saddened her deeply to think of how frustrated and powerless the disconnect from his sure means of distraction must be making him feel, on top of everything else.

Needing to change the subject, she said, 'Tell me about . . . Tell me how the . . .'

'It's OK,' he said, apparently understanding what she was asking. 'Actually, it'll never be that, but I'm doing my best.'

Not doubting that for a moment, she started to ask more, but he interrupted, saying, 'I want to hear about Culver. Rob says it's a good place, that you were right to go there.'

'It feels right,' she answered, 'or as right as anywhere can without you.'

'Do you feel safe there?'

'I did, until the rabbit rescue, now I'm not sure. The trouble is, if I leave where would I go? Maybe I should have taken your advice and moved to a city. It's easier to be anonymous in a city.'

'But you felt your grandmother was calling.' There was no mockery in his tone, he'd never dismissed her conviction in any way; he'd simply been concerned about all the guns and Bibles, habits, ways of life they were so unused to. 'Have you felt any sort of connection since you arrived?' he asked.

'I think so, sometimes . . . Not lately though, probably because there's been too much else on my mind. It usually happens when I'm at the lake.'

'Rob tells me it's close by.'

'It's just a short walk from the house. We can see it from the front porch.'

He waited for her to go on.

'There's something magical about it,' she told him. 'When the light falls a certain way it makes you want to paint it, or write poems about it . . .' She smiled. 'Not that I can do either. Other times you feel an uncanny sense of everything it's seen, especially the Potawatomi Indians who used to live on its shores. They were rounded up by the US army in the nineteenth century and forced to leave. Yet another instance of the white man covering himself in glory.'

'Where did they go?'

'All over, apparently, but mainly Kansas. The route they were forced to march is known as the Trail of Death.'

As the words hung between them, invisible and powerful as the ghosts they'd never escape, she suddenly realised Lula was standing in the doorway holding Daisy. Knowing how hard this was going to be for Matt, but unable to ignore her daughter, she said, 'Hello sweetheart. What are you doing awake?'

'Who are you talking to?' Lula asked.

Justine tensed, not sure what to say.

'Tell her it's a friend,' Matt said gently in her ear, 'and give her an extra kiss goodnight from me.'

Over the next few days as Justine relived the call, everything that was said and not said, all that was meant and felt, she found herself more desperate than ever to see Matt, and yet, perversely, slightly easier about staying in Culver. Describing it to him, putting some of its detail and her feelings into his imagination, had made it seem as though they were sharing it, and though he clearly wasn't here, he no longer seemed as far away.

There had still been no contact from the past as a result of the rabbit rescue, so she was daring to hope that the connection between Justine McQuillan and Tallulah Cantrell had not been made.

All she needed to do now was find the courage, the will, to start going out again. The trouble was, in spite of feeling better for speaking to Matt, her confidence remained in shreds. Sallie Jo still wasn't making any signs of wanting to continue their friendship, and the rejection, the loneliness she felt each time she avoided Café Max was a cruel reminder of how much she missed Cheryl.

Cheryl, whom she hadn't spoken to in over a year, and would probably never see or speak to again.

It would get easier, she tried telling herself. She had no idea how, or when, but it would, because surely it had to.

It was the middle of the day on a Thursday, just after she'd returned from walking Daisy, that she heard a car pull in from the lane. Her heart thudded when she saw it was Sallie Jo. Part of her wanted to rush out and greet her warmly in relief; the other part hung back cautiously, suspiciously, especially when she realised David had come too. A crazy fear suddenly sprang into life. They were here to ask her to leave. They believed she was in witness protection and could bring them into danger, so for everyone's sake it would be best if she left.

Or worse, they'd found out the truth about her and

were giving her the chance to go without making a fuss.

She felt suddenly desperate for somewhere to run, or someone to turn to. She needed to speak to Matt, or Rob, but Sallie Jo and David were already coming up the steps to the porch. Randomly, foolishly, she grabbed the unopened package from her mother, as though it were some sort of protection. Later she would wonder if a hand had been held out to her, but in the moment she had no clear idea what she was thinking at all.

'Hi,' she said, trying to sound bright as she opened the door. 'This is . . .' She was going to say a nice surprise, but what she finally managed was, 'Unexpected.'

'Can we come in?' Sallie Jo asked, not smiling, but not seeming hostile either.

'Of course,' and standing aside she waved them to the table. 'Shall I make some coffee?' she offered.

Sallie Jo turned to face her as David said, 'We've just had some, thanks.' He didn't seem hostile either, but they obviously wouldn't want to cause a scene.

His eyes moved to Sallie Jo.

Justine's followed.

Sallie Jo's expression was stern, but the natural kindness in her heart was glowing through the darkness.

'Was everything all right with the uploads this morning?' Justine asked, clutching at the banality as a way of staving off the inevitable. 'I had some . . .'

'Everything was fine,' Sallie Jo assured her. She took a breath. 'Justine, we're here because we're worried about you.'

Justine feigned amazement. 'Why – why on earth would you be worried about me?' she stammered.

'Because you're a nervous wreck. Everyone's noticed it. You hardly engage with anyone these days, you stay shut up in here, you don't come into the café any more, you never call . . .'

'I'm sorry. I – I thought you weren't calling . . .'

'Hazel says when she's here that you act strange, like you don't seem to see her.'

'I'm sorry. I don't mean to.'

Sallie Jo's eyes didn't leave hers for a moment. 'I don't know what you're hiding, or running from,' she said bluntly, 'and it's probably not my business to know, but watching what it's doing to you . . .'

'I'm fine, really,' Justine insisted.

'No, you're not fine and we want to help, if we can.'

Justine clutched the package more tightly to her chest. She couldn't handle kindness; it was going to undo her.

David said, 'Fall collection starts tomorrow. Maybe your landlord forgot to inform the gardener that he needs to have everything ready for the pickup. If you've got a rake I'll go make a start.'

Realising Sallie Jo must have given him a cue to leave, Justine replied, 'There's one in the garage.'

As the door closed behind him, Sallie Jo sat down and folded her hands on the table. 'You don't have to tell me anything,' she said gently, 'but if you do I want you to know that it will never go any further than this room.'

There was no reason not to believe her, because Justine knew she was discreet – however, she also had no idea what kind of secret she was committing herself to keep.

Justine pulled out a chair and sat down too. For a while she stared at the package in her hands. Properly registering it, she said, 'It's from my mother. I think it contains some of the answers we're looking for surrounding my grandmother's house.'

'You haven't opened it?'

Justine shook her head.

Sallie Jo said nothing.

Soon they could hear the scrape of the rake outside. *Do not mix branches in the leaves; do not include pumpkins or rocks.* She remembered reading the instructions in last week's *Citizen*.

'Justine, I really think you should talk to someone,' Sallie Jo urged. 'It doesn't have to be me, but whatever you're bottling up inside, whatever's scaring you, you need to let it out. If you don't it's going to drive you crazy.'

Justine couldn't deny it. She felt it every day.

She was still staring at the package, thinking of the secret her mother and grandmother shared and wondering if it should stay that way, a secret. She of all people knew that some things should never be told.

At last she looked up and tried to imagine how appalled Sallie Jo was going to be by the truth. She noticed the fragile lines around her eyes that made her seem vulnerable, in spite of the quiet strength she exhibited every day. Justine didn't want to hurt her, or burden her with a secret too heavy, too awful to hold, and yet maybe it would be better if Sallie Jo heard the truth from her rather than from anyone else.

The question was how, where to begin? With Matt, with Abby, with Ben?

In the end she took a low, delicate breath, and heard herself saying, 'I used to live in a place called Chippingly. My best friend Cheryl and I had a deli there . . .'

Chapter Ten

Chippingly Vale, UK

It was a Wednesday afternoon at the beginning of November when Justine's waters broke, announcing the imminent arrival of Tallulah Catherine May.

'Ugh! Gross!' Abby squeaked, quickly stepping away from the gush.

They were in the deli, with Cheryl and a handful of regulars.

'I'm not due for another week,' Justine complained as Cheryl rushed to her side, abandoning a woman with a slice of cherry tart and no cup of tea. 'Matt's in London.'

'He'll be here in time,' Cheryl assured her. 'Abby, do something useful like call an ambulance.'

'Already done,' Janet Beasley informed them, bustling over in her matronly way. She used to run a care home near Colchester before retiring to the West Country, which didn't exactly qualify her to deliver a baby if the need arose, but she was always a comforting presence.

'I'm fine, honestly,' Justine assured her. 'I don't think . . .' She gasped as a sharp pain shot through her.

'Just take a seat,' Mrs Beasley instructed. 'No need to get into a fuss about anything.'

'Should I shut the shop?' Cheryl wondered aloud.

'Who are you calling?' Justine asked Abby.

Eyes bright with excitement, Abby cried, 'Dad. Who else? Oh God, it's his voicemail, what shall I say? I know – Dad, it's me, not sure I can cope without you, but going to try. She's all right for the moment, but think you should get here. Oh my God, it's totally amazing! I can't believe it's happening at last. I'm totally buzzing. Love you . . . Oh yes, baby's on its way.'

Laughing as Abby treated her to a goggle-eyed look, Justine loved her for the support she'd given over the last few months, and held her bump as she said, 'Does this mean you'll come to the hospital with me?'

'Are you kidding?' Abby retorted, apparently shocked her mother might think she wouldn't. 'I'm not letting you go on your own, but no way am I watching, right? I mean, there are some parts of my education that can definitely wait.' She looked at Cheryl. 'Chantal ought to be here,' she decided, opening up her phone again. 'She's the one who wants to be a doctor.'

'I don't think there's much she can do for the moment,' Janet Beasley pointed out kindly. 'Are you OK, dear?' she asked as Justine winced. 'Bit further along than we thought, mm?'

'Oh no, please no, not in the middle of the deli,' Abby protested. 'Anyone could walk in . . .'

'Shut up,' Justine laughed, knowing she was teasing.

'Someone should put up the closed sign,' Abby declared.

'I think I should drive you,' Cheryl insisted, going to lock the till.

'I can run things here,' Abby offered.

'I thought you were coming with me,' Justine reminded her.

'Oh yes. Definitely coming with you,' and throwing her arms around her mother, she said, 'This is like totally the most amazing thing ever. I might actually be the first one to see her.'

'I thought you weren't going to watch.'

'No, deffo not doing that. Why hasn't Dad rung back yet?'

'He's in a meeting.' Justine's eyes closed as a vicious spasm clenched her in its claws.

'I'm taking you,' Cheryl decided, and while Abby and Janet Beasley helped Justine out to the car she quickly ushered the onlookers out of the deli, set the alarm and locked up.

By seven that evening Abby was holding Tallulah in her arms, totally entranced with the magical little alien that almost looked human, while Justine rested her head on Matt's shoulder and wondered when she'd last felt this tired and happy.

Probably the day Ben had been born, which happened to be this very day fifteen years ago.

She wished he was with them now to complete the family – or did she? It seemed such a very long time since he'd been the son she'd found it so easy to love, the fresh-faced boy who'd tumble in from football covered in mud, eyes glittering with triumph as he powed and whoofed and kicked the air, reliving the game. The son who'd sneak into her bed on Sunday

214

mornings for a cuddle and tickle before going downstairs to wreak havoc in the playroom. The son who charged about the vale with friends he'd known since before he could walk, who played on all the sports teams, who came top of the class in science, maths and geography, who had friends she knew and was always kind.

He had yet to respond to any of the messages Matt and Abby had left on his voicemail about the baby, which wasn't particularly surprising when he'd shown no interest in it at all.

'I keep telling you,' Abby declared when Justine voiced her dismay, 'he's sulking because this is supposed to be his birthday, not anyone else's. He is soooo self-involved . . .'

'His phone's probably out of battery,' Matt interrupted, taking the baby from her.

'No way!' Abby protested. 'He's doing this to make you feel bad and it's working. You shouldn't give him the satisfaction.'

Justine said to Matt, 'You ought to go and find him, take him for a pizza, or wherever he wants to go.'

'Like he'd go anywhere with one of us,' Abby snorted.

'Don't be like that,' Justine chided, in spite of knowing Abby was right.

'Well! Tell me, when was the last time . . .'

'Enough,' Justine whispered, raising a hand.

Matt was gazing adoringly at the baby's sleeping face. Justine pulled back the blanket so she could see her too.

'Hello, Tallulah Catherine May,' she murmured,

touching a finger to the minuscule white spots on the baby's silky-soft cheek.

Lula's delicate eyelids flickered as her rosebud lips blew a little bubble.

'Why did you go for that name?' Abby wanted to know. 'I thought you weren't going to.'

'Ben chose Tallulah, you know that . . .'

'Only because you kept on at him for a suggestion, so he went for one he was sure you'd hate.'

'He chose it because he thought it was pretty,' Justine argued, 'and it is.'

'I like Lula,' Matt informed them, easing a little finger into his newest daughter's tiny fist.

They all laughed as Lula burped, opened her mouth wide and closed it again.

Looking up at Matt, Justine said, 'They'll probably let me go home after the next feed . . .' She broke off as Matt's phone rang.

Please let it be Ben, although not if he's going to say something cruel.

'Hi Simon,' Matt said, allowing Justine to take the baby. 'Thanks, mate. Yes, she's a beauty. Two point eight kilos, ten fingers, ten toes and everything seems to be working.' As he listened to his brother he whispered to Justine, 'Apparently Mum's on her way.'

Justine smiled. It would be good to have Catherine around for a while. She was always so unflappable and cheery and, perhaps best of all, she had a way with Ben that no one else seemed to have.

'Si, could you do me a favour,' Matt was saying to his brother, 'we're not sure where Ben is . . . You know it's his birthday today . . . Really? You saw him, when, where?' His eyes went to Justine. 'He's at home,' he repeated with a sigh of relief. 'He's not answering his phone,' he told Simon, 'which could be because he's stuck into some video game . . . That's great, Si. Thanks. Yeah, he'll love it if Wes goes too.' After ringing off he said to Justine, 'Simon's offered to take him into town for an Italian. If it happens I think I should join them so he doesn't feel we forgot him entirely today.'

'He wouldn't care,' Abby informed them.

'Says you,' Justine retorted.

'I'm telling you, he even boasts about it, that he couldn't care less about anyone . . .'

Cutting across her, Justine said to Matt, 'Don't worry about me if you go. I'll have my girls to keep me company.' She held out a hand for Abby's and taking it, Abby said, 'It's going to be so weird having a baby around. I mean, cool, but weird, especially when everyone's probably going to think she's mine. Oh God, I hope I don't get mistaken for one of those loser single mums who get pregnant just to live off benefits.'

'I don't think that's likely,' Justine responded drily.

Abby's face softened as the baby started to wake up. 'Hello, little Lula,' she whispered sweetly. 'I'm your big sister, Abby. I reckon you're going to look just like me. Let's hope so, anyway, because you definitely wouldn't want to look like Ben with his hairy face and spots . . .'

'Stop being unpleasant about him,' Matt chided. 'He's not in a good place, we know that . . .'

'That's the understatement of all time,' Abby snapped, 'because when's he ever been in a good place?

He should get over himself and give the rest of us a break.'

'Taking that sort of attitude doesn't help,' Matt reminded her. 'It just drives a wedge between the two of you, and that's not what we want. And I hope you don't speak about him that way to anyone outside the family.'

'Oh, that's right, let's all have a go at Abby now, why don't we? I'm only the one who helped get Mum here, who held her hand until you turned up, had to listen to her screaming and swearing . . .'

'I did not swear,' Justine protested.

'You so did. Even I've never heard those words before.'

Laughing, Matt said, 'What were you supposed to be doing this evening?'

Abby shrugged. 'I was just going to hang out with Chantal and Nelly. We thought we might rehearse some new stuff I've been working on.'

'What news on Neil?' Justine asked.

'He's cool, as far as I know. Chantal went to see him earlier and texted that he'll probably have to have chemo after the op, but he should be all right after that.'

Justine's heart ached for the boy. First leukaemia, then a suspected cancer of the spine, now a tumour in his neck . . . What hell it must be for Maddy and Ronnie. It seemed that every time they felt able to breathe again something else tried to strike him down.

And throughout it all Neil never failed to be anything but optimistic and cheerful.

How she wished she could say the same for Ben, whose

smile she hadn't seen since she couldn't remember when, unless she counted the ugly grimace when he'd shown her the tattoo on his knuckles – HATE.

It was largely because of Neil and their many visits to hospital wards that Chantal and Nelly had both decided on careers in medicine. Justine, agreeing with their parents, felt pretty confident that they were bright enough and determined enough to succeed – unless their ambitions changed along the way. This was always possible, of course, and no one was holding them to anything. In fact all anyone knew for certain these days was that Abby was no longer interested in auditioning for *The X Factor*, thank goodness, though not because she'd lost her ambition, far from it, but because Harry Sands had declared it to be for saddos minus a shame gene.

'Which means she should win hands down,' Ben had sneered when Abby had repeated this to her parents.

'Unless you went in for it too,' she'd shot back, 'then no one would stand a chance of getting anywhere near the number one spot.'

To Justine's surprise Ben had seemed to find this funny.

'Why don't you try saying something nice to one another for a change?' Justine implored.

'I say nice stuff all the time,' Abby insisted.

'Not to me you don't,' he grunted.

'Who would?'

'No one in this family, that's for sure.'

'Because you're a moron who hardly ever washes or cleans his teeth or changes his clothes.'

'And you are a seriously bad fucking singer who should do us all the favour of shutting the fuck up, for good.'

'Ben!' Justine snapped.

'Bad, bad, bad, that's what you are,' he continued taunting, 'and I'm the only one who's got the guts to tell you.'

Stricken, Abby turned to her father.

'Dad! Did you hear that? He is so . . .'

'Ben, go upstairs,' Matt told him. 'You're creating tension the way you always do, so don't come back until you're ready to apologise and . . .'

'Apologise for what? Telling the truth? You know she's crap, so why . . . Hey! Get your hands off me! What the f . . .?'

Hauling him out of his chair, Matt said, 'Go to your room, now, and when you come back the apology should be for all of us.'

'You'll wait a long time for that,' Ben snorted as he headed along the hall. 'You are such a bunch of no-hopers. I don't know what I did to be a part of this family . . .'

Matt slammed the door so they couldn't hear any more.

That unpleasant little scene, typical of so many, though not nearly as bad as some, had erupted only yesterday, the day before his birthday, and now Lula's birthday too.

Ben didn't go out with his uncle and cousin that night, nor would he open his bedroom door when Matt brought everyone home and tried to persuade him to come and meet his new baby sister. He simply cranked up the volume of his heavy metal music so that it boomed throughout the entire vale, like thunder. In the end Matt broke the door down, only to find the room empty. He'd escaped down a rope blanket, leaving his music blaring, and window wide open.

He didn't come home for the rest of the night, nor did he answer any texts or return their calls.

When he eventually showed up around eleven the next morning, reeking of beer and body odour, he helped himself to all he could carry from the fridge, and flatly refused to say where he'd been.

Over the months that followed there was no improvement in Ben's manner at all; if anything he seemed to get worse, especially at home. Fortunately, at school he didn't seem to be in as much trouble as before. However, after keeping a close eye on him for some time, the resident counsellor arranged for him to see a psychologist who specialised in the problems of adolescence to try and establish why he was finding it so hard to make or keep friends. He rarely turned up for the sessions, and even when he did he apparently had nothing to say, apart from denouncing his fellow students as a bunch of fuckwit tossers that no sane person would want to be associated with. Still, at least he wasn't causing any trouble as such, and since his grades, for the most part, remained above average, there was no reason for the school to insist on any further assessments.

Feeling the lack of outside support, Justine's and Matt's stress levels soared, and weren't in any way helped by their secret inspections of his home computer.

The so-called friends he was making online rejoiced in the kind of names and profiles to send chills down any parent's spine. Whether he actually met up with any of them wasn't easy to say, since he rarely told them where he was going or what time he'd be back, but at least he did come back, eventually.

It was around the beginning of year twelve that Ben took up smoking dope in the house, a gesture clearly meant to provoke, which invariably succeeded and ended in terrible showdowns between him and Matt. Heaven only knew who was giving him the money to buy drugs, or where he was sleeping the nights he didn't come home; he'd never say, no matter how many times they tried to force it out of him.

As time passed and the atmosphere in the house became blacker than ever, Matt began finding it impossible to write, while Justine knew if it weren't for Cheryl and the others her business would be on the verge of collapse.

Perhaps the most heartbreaking of all the torment he continued to inflict on them was watching how dismissively, even cruelly he treated Lula. It was as though he couldn't stand to be near her, which might not have been so hard to deal with if she didn't always want to be with him. She invariably broke into a smile when he came into the room; she took her first steps trying to get to him, only to be pushed over when she got there; she learnt to say his name before Abby's, an honour he greeted with an irritated roll of the eyes, and whenever she offered to share her toys it was always with him first, even though he often deliberately broke them.

'He is totally out of control,' Abby shouted at her mother after finding Lula in tears one morning. 'I saw him, with my own eyes, tearing the wheel off her toddlebike. He even seemed to think it was funny.'

'Where is he now?' Justine asked, trying to console Lula.

'I don't know. He stormed out when he saw me *and* he threatened me. He said if I told you and Dad I'd be effing sorry. Like I'm scared of him.'

Wondering if perhaps she ought to be, Justine said, 'I'll get Dad to talk to him.'

Abby wasn't impressed. 'Great, and they'll start fighting all over again, or Ben will make out he's crying, like he does, poor little him who gets ignored because he's not a girl, who doesn't matter to Mummy and Daddy because you never wanted him in the first place . . . He'll start listing all the terrible things you're supposed to have done to him, stuff that *never even happened*, and you'll feel bad and think you've got to make it up to him . . . Can't you see what he's doing? He even laughs about you behind your backs, telling everyone what dumbfuck parents he has, all he's got to do is turn on the waterworks and you'll do anything he wants.'

It wasn't the first time Abby had thrown this at her, and though Justine knew it was probably true, she and Matt had no idea what to do with Ben. Grounding him didn't work because he always found a way out of the house and sometimes he didn't come back for days on end, as though to punish them. Cutting off his allowance made no difference either, because he still seemed to have money. Imagining the various ways in which he might have been earning it made Justine feel physically sick, and often sent Matt searching the streets in the dead of night, not even sure of what he'd do if he found him.

'You have to confiscate his phone and computer,' Simon told them after yet another bitter episode that they'd all have preferred to forget, but couldn't. 'If you don't, he's going to end up in the kind of trouble you really won't want to be dealing with.'

'You think we haven't tried?' Matt cried desperately. 'He told us if we didn't give them back that something seriously bad would happen, and he's so . . .'

'Schizo,' Abby provided.

Matt threw her a look. 'I'm getting so I wouldn't put anything past him,' he confessed wearily. 'And you know what Lula's like with him. She adores him, though God knows why. She'll do anything he tells her to. You can just hear it, can't you – throw yourself down the stairs, Lula; run in front of a car, Lula; why don't you climb this tree with me and see what it's like to fly?'

Realising how close he was to the edge, Simon came to put a comforting hand on his shoulder. 'Shall I get Wes to have another chat with him?' he offered. 'It's seemed to do some good in the past.'

'He's always looked up to Wes,' Justine put in, unconvinced, but trying to stay hopeful. 'He's about the only one he does look up to now.'

'And Harry,' Abby reminded them. 'He thinks Harry's really cool . . .'

'Harry's at uni,' Matt interrupted, 'and even . . .'

'He's due back in a couple of . . .'

'I don't care, he's not family, and just because he's your hero doesn't make him mine. Or Ben's.'

Shuddering at the thought of Melanie Sands's reaction to the possibility of her precious boy being asked to help the delinquent, as she'd actually called Ben to Justine's face, Justine said, 'Dad's right, sweetheart, we have to keep this in the family.'

'So does that mean we should count Chantal out too?' Abby demanded hotly.

Justine looked at Simon and Matt. It was a heavy burden to put on a young girl's shoulders, especially one who'd only recently accused Ben of stalking her, but they were desperate. 'If Cheryl agrees,' Justine said, 'maybe we could ask Chantal to try being friends with him again. I'm sure it's what he wants – they were always so close when they were young, and if that awful Connor hadn't forced his way between them they still might be.'

To Abby Matt said, 'Is Chantal dating Connor these days?'

Abby shrugged. 'Not officially, but like they hang out quite a lot and I know that gets under Ben's skin. But honestly, the way he treats people, you can hardly blame her for backing off.'

'Where is he now?' Simon asked.

Matt and Justine looked at one another and shook their heads.

'Then this could be a good time to take a look at his computer and see if we can find out where he's going, who he's in touch with, what's making him tick these days.'

'Good luck getting into his room,' Abby retorted. 'He always keeps it locked.'

'Unless he *wants* us to go in,' Matt added, 'because he does that too so his mother or Lula can find his porno magazines, or used condoms – I'm guessing masturbation, because he's never brought a girl home that we know of. And as for his computer, I've checked it through a dozen times and the same goes, you only find what he wants you to find. Not that it's good, because it's a very long way from that – more porn, the kind of interactive games he's not even legally supposed to be playing, terrorist forums, animal cruelty . . . You name it, he's been there and if I try talking to him about it he just tells me to eff off, or he laughs. It's the way he laughs that makes it clear he knew damned well I'd go checking the minute I found his door open and computer on, so he set me up.'

Clearly feeling as helpless and frustrated as they did, Simon said, 'What about Mum? Have you told her how bad things are now?'

Matt shook his head. 'I don't want to worry her, or make her feel she has to try and sort it out.'

'He won't speak to her anyway,' Abby informed them, 'he already told me that. He said, if anyone calls Grandma Catherine about me I'll disappear and I might not even bother to come back. I told him he ought to do that anyway, because we'd all be a lot happier without him.'

Justine's eyes closed. 'That sort of comment really doesn't help,' she sighed.

'But it's true,' Abby cried, 'we would, because all he does is cause trouble and make everyone miserable and upset all the time. This is like a crazy house because of him. Just thank God I'm going to be out of it soon, that's all I can say.'

'Please don't,' Matt murmured.

Abby's eyes widened in shock. 'You mean, don't go on my gap year?' she exclaimed. 'You have . . .'

'I mean don't say that. We love you, we're going to miss you and the last thing we want is you feeling glad to be out of here.'

Obviously sorry she'd hurt his feelings, she went to give him a hug.

Reminding herself that they focused far too much on Ben, Justine said, 'How are your plans going for the world tour?'

Abby instantly brightened. 'Yeah, cool,' she replied, clearly excited. 'Wes – you know he's going to be my minder and manager, right?'

Justine glanced at Simon, who had evidently done a better job of taking this on board whenever it had been decided than she and Matt had.

'Right, well he is,' Abby ran on, 'and we've already been in touch with loads of venues around Europe, you know, sending them links to YouTube and my website and stuff to try and get some gigs booked in advance.'

'That's wonderful,' Justine smiled, so relieved to be hearing good news that she almost wanted to cry.

'Does Harry fit into this anywhere?' Matt asked.

Abby shrugged. 'Not really, he has to go back to uni when summer's over, but it's not like we're an item, or anything. We're just mates, you know.'

Since Abby had had a couple of boyfriends following

her crush on Harry, Justine was ready to believe she was as relaxed about that as she sounded. No doubt she'd find out more when he came home.

Glancing at the time, she said, 'I should go up and check on Lula. She ought to be awake by now.'

Abby didn't hide her disappointment. 'It's always Ben or Lula with you,' she protested sulkily, 'it's never about me.'

'I'm sorry,' Justine apologised, 'you know I'm interested in your plans, and I promise we'll talk about them later, but I can't just leave Lula . . .'

'What's wrong with talking to me?' Matt wanted to know.

'Or me,' Simon added. 'Come on, I'm dying to hear some of this new material. Wes tells me it's some of the best you've done yet.'

Clearly cheered by this, Abby said, 'My guitar and everything's set up over in the studio, so if you're really interested . . .'

Leaving them to it, Justine ran upstairs to check on Lula, and felt her heart flood with love to find her sitting on the floor of her room with a jewel-bedecked Rosie at her feet, listening to a story Lula was reading from an upside-down book. She was never any trouble, and hadn't been from the day she was conceived.

'How long have you been awake?' she asked, going to kneel down with them.

'This is Rosie's favourite story,' Lula told her, 'and it's mine too.'

Seeing it was *Miffy the Fairy*, Justine said, 'I expect you know this one almost by heart.'

Lula nodded her head up and down. 'Rosie can't read, because she's a dog.'

Hearing her name, Rosie thumped her tail on the floor and Justine ruffled her adorable head. She followed Lula everywhere, and had done since Lula had started walking. It was as though she was protecting her, ready to alert someone if Lula fell, or lend a handful of fur if Lula needed to pull herself up again. She slept beside Lula's bed, was always waiting when Lula came in from nursery, and seemed to prefer Lula to throw her ball when they took her for walks, in spite of it never going very far.

'Mummy, am I three?' Lula asked curiously.

Justine smiled. 'Not yet, sweetheart. In a few months you will be.'

Lula was frowning. 'Ben said I can't have a birthday this year.'

Trying not to show her annoyance, Justine said, 'You mustn't listen to Ben, he makes jokes that aren't very funny. Of course you'll have a birthday, and you'll be three.'

'And Ben will be *eight*.'

'Eighteen.'

'And before that Abby will be nine – tee.'

Laughing, Justine said, 'Nineteen. But there are still a few months to go before . . .'

'What I said,' Ben declared, making her jump, 'was that she won't be three.'

Justine turned to look at him, her heart racing, her mind spinning into chaos. 'I – I thought you were out,' she stammered.

With a shrug, he said, 'Maybe I was, and maybe I came back.'

Her eyes stayed fixed on his, and for once Lula didn't struggle to go to him.

He was thin, gaunt even, with hunted, haunted dark eyes that seemed too large for his face, and thick black whiskers that raged unchecked around his jaw and cheeks, mixing with acne, even specks of food or towel fibres, anything that seemed to pass them by. In spite of that he was still a good-looking boy, though she guessed that only she, as his mother, could see it, just as she was probably the only one who could sense the real him beneath all the darkness and contempt. He was her son: the bond that held them together was tightening even now, pulling them closer, not physically, but on a level neither would be able to put into words even if they tried. He was hanging on desperately to that bond because he needed her, and because for some reason he was afraid she might be letting him go. She had to let him know that would never happen.

Before she could speak, he said, 'I heard you talking about me downstairs.' His tone was so cold and aggressive that it snapped the bond like a useless stick. 'Save yourself the bother of calling Wesley or Chantal to the rescue. He's just a moron and she's a slag.'

'Don't say that, Ben, you and Chantal were always so close, and if . . .'

'She's with Connor now,' he cut in viciously, 'just like Dad's with Hayley. You have to get used to these things, move with the times.'

Justine hardly knew what to say. She was reminding

herself that this was what he did, played games with the mind, tied people up in knots, got them believing things that weren't true, and this wasn't the first time he'd taunted her with her old insecurity about Hayley.

'Come on, Mum, you know really, so stop pretending.'

'Why are you doing this?' she whispered. 'What's happened to you . . .?' She broke off as he pointed at Lula.

'*That*'s what happened to me,' he told her.

Justine's arms tightened around her daughter. 'Don't talk about her that way,' she protested. 'She understands . . .'

'She's a freak. No kids her age speak the way she does, or . . .'

'Ben, stop this now. I'm doing my best with you, I swear. You mean more to me than I can ever put into words, but . . .'

'*But*, there's always a but, isn't there, *Mum*? B is for Ben and B is for but. It would all be OK, but for Ben.'

She regarded him helplessly, this stranger, this precious, beloved son whom she adored, misunderstood and feared.

'It's all Dad's fault, you know that, don't you?' he stated.

She frowned. 'What do you mean?'

'I wouldn't be like this if he hadn't dropped me on my head when I was a kid.'

Realising he must have overheard her and Matt talking, so he knew this was Matt's worst fear, she said, 'Do you have some sort of listening device set up around the house?'

He simply shrugged, which might have been a

confirmation, she couldn't be sure. 'I want a car,' he announced, as if that were the most natural way for the conversation to proceed.

'You can't even drive,' she reminded him.

'That's what you think.'

'Who – who taught you to drive?'

'Wouldn't you like to know?'

The truth was she probably wouldn't.

'Abby got a car when she was eighteen, so I should have one too.'

'She'd passed her test by then, and you know very well that Grandma Camilla bought it for her.'

'So, let Grandma Camilla buy one for me.'

'Why would she when you never go to see her . . .'

'Nor does Abby.'

'Abby spent the whole of Easter in London doing work experience on Grandma Camilla's TV programme.'

'So she gets a car for sucking up.'

'She gets a car because she can drive and she deserves one.'

'So you're saying I don't.'

'What do you think?'

'What I think is if you want that thing there to become three, you'll get me a car,' and with a jaunty raise of his eyebrows he turned and walked away.

Matt's face turned white when Justine repeated the conversation. 'We have to get him out of the house,' he stated furiously. 'I'm not putting up with that sort of blackmail, much less the threats he keeps throwing at his sisters. Enough's enough.'

Though Justine didn't disagree, she knew it wasn't going to be easy, for either of them, telling him he had to go. And could she really do it? Could she actually watch her son walk away, not knowing where he was going, when or if she'd ever see him again? He'd end up getting even more involved with drugs and alcohol, possibly even crime. What earthly good could ever come of it?

'Justine, I don't know the answers,' Matt cried in despair. 'God knows we've tried to find them, we're driving ourselves out of our minds trying to help him, but we have to face it, he doesn't want our help. He doesn't even want to be part of our family.'

'I know he says that, but he doesn't mean it.'

'Are you sure?'

No, she wasn't, but nor could she convince herself that leaving their son to the mercy of the streets and whatever lowlife he was already involved with was the right thing to do.

They were walking across the field beyond the orchard, keeping to open land so they'd know if he was following. Not that he'd ever shadowed them on a walk before, or if he had they were unaware of it, much like they were unaware of any devices he might have planted around the house. They still hadn't found any, so perhaps they didn't exist, but he knew so much, always seemed to be a step ahead of them, had everything he needed to ridicule or torment them.

'I know this is going to sound crazy,' Justine began cautiously, 'but do you think we should talk to the vicar about him? Or the priest at the Catholic church?'

She half expected Matt to laugh, but for a long time

he didn't say anything, making her wonder if he'd even heard her. In the end, he said, 'We can't even get him to respond to a psychologist, so I don't think there's much chance of him sitting down with a cleric, especially when we've never been a religious family.' He glanced at her. 'Was that your mother's suggestion, by any chance?'

She nodded.

'So you've been talking to her about him?'

'Abby told her what was going on, so she rings now and again to find out if things are any better. For all her . . . idiosyncratic ways, I think she cares.'

Not taking issue with that in a way he might have done a while ago, he asked, 'What else does she suggest, apart from an exorcism?'

Justine didn't smile. 'She didn't actually say that . . .'

'But it was what she meant.'

'You're putting words in her mouth. What she actually said was that we might all benefit from some spiritual guidance . . .'

'Because she, God-fearing Christian that she is . . .'

'Matt, she's trying to help.'

After a few moments, he said, 'Did she have any other suggestions?'

'Not really, but she says we shouldn't blame ourselves.'

'Oh, that's helpful.'

'Please don't be sarcastic.'

'So who does she think we should blame? He's our son, just like Abby's our daughter, and let's be frank, I'm not sure we've done a brilliant job with her either.'

'Matt, stop . . .'

'It's true, Justine. She might not have *all* the same character defects as Ben, thank God, but she's not always a nice person. She's bossy, far too pleased with herself, vain, pompous, jealous of Lula . . .'

'Stop! I'm not listening to any more of this. Tearing our children to shreds isn't going to help them, or us.'

'Maybe not, but for your mother to say that we shouldn't blame ourselves is like offering us a way to absolve ourselves of a responsibility that couldn't possibly belong to anyone else. Which actually about fits the ticket with her, given that she never assumed much responsibility for you and Rob.'

'That's not fair. She might not have been as hands-on as your mother, but she was always there for us when we needed her. OK, not in the same way as yours was for you, but everyone's different, and let's not forget if it weren't for her we'd never have been able to buy the farmhouse. She made that dream come true for us . . .'

'All right, I hear what you're saying, but let's forget the church thing, OK? It's not only barmy, it'd be sure to alienate him even further, though perhaps God is the only one who knows how that might be possible.'

As it was starting to get dark by now they turned back towards home, each with their own thoughts and fears, most already shared, but some yet to be spoken. It was as if voicing them might in some way give life to them, and they already had more than enough to cope with. Besides, it wasn't as if Justine believed their house was in some bizarre, paranormal way connected to their misfortune. It couldn't possibly be true. They'd had far too many happy times there to start thinking now that it was capable of pouring some erstwhile dormant malevolence into one sole member of their family.

It was little more than a week later that Simon rang to let them know that Ben was in custody for stealing a car.

The point was immediately taken: if they weren't going to buy him a car, he'd help himself to one.

He was released the following morning on police bail, and a few days later they were told that no charge was going to be brought. Whether or not Simon had a hand in that they had no idea, nor did they ask.

Ben wasn't so lucky a couple of weeks later when he was caught breaking into a warehouse on the edge of town.

'He wasn't alone,' Simon solemnly informed them, 'he was arrested with three others, scumbags every one of them.'

Justine blanched. 'You know the others?'

'Not personally, but they've all done time, and chances are they're about to do more.'

'What about Ben? Will he?' Maybe life would be easier with him in prison, at least they'd know where he was and he wouldn't be causing all this upset at home.

What a dreadful thing for a mother to think, Justine told herself.

'I don't know,' Simon replied. 'It's a first offence, and given his age . . .'

'Where is he now?'

'In a police cell. He's due before the magistrate tomorrow. The others are sure to be remanded in custody. As for Ben . . .'

'Is there a chance they'll send him somewhere for psychological tests?' Justine broke in desperately. They needed help from someone, and were willing to accept anything from anyone.

Simon shook his head gravely. 'I'm afraid there are a lot worse kids out there than him,' he replied, 'most with a string of convictions under their belts, and even they aren't getting the backup they need. And with this being Ben's first offence, there's no way I can see him being singled out for special attention.'

Though she'd expected no less, Justine still felt crushed. There was something desperately wrong with their son, everyone knew it, and it seemed they were powerless to help him – unless he was willing to help himself, and he'd never shown any signs of wanting to engage with that.

Simon said to Matt, 'Will you go to the hearing?'

Matt's reply was a long time in coming. 'I'll go,' he said, 'but only to tell him he no longer has a home with us.'

'Matt!' Justine cried.

'I'm sorry, my mind's made up,' he declared, and before she could argue any further he walked away.

True to his word Matt went to the court in the morning, and when Ben was released on bail he handed him a bag of clothes and an envelope containing money. 'You're on your own now,' he informed him. 'We've tried with you, but there's no more we can do.'

Ben looked startled, almost worried. 'You mean you're chucking me out?' he cried, covering his surprise, maybe it was hurt, with a scornful laugh.

Matt didn't answer, he simply turned on his heel and walked away.

By the time he got home Justine had received a call. 'Dad refused to give me a lift,' Ben told her, 'so I'm getting the bus, and if I were you I'd let me in when I get there, because I can promise you this, it won't go well for anyone if you don't.'

Chapter Eleven

The day everything changed for ever in Chippingly Vale began with no indication of what was to come, no signs that this day was going to be set apart from all others. It was simply a typical early August morning with a warm, coppery sunlight burnishing the vale, dew sparkling on the grass and the sky overhead a tranquil cloudless blue.

It was just before nine when Justine set out to take Lula to playgroup, leaving Rosie to settle down with Matt in the study as she usually did while Lula was out, and Abby in the kitchen making lists of everything that needed organising for the summer disco, a task she'd taken over from Matt a couple of years ago. Being Abby she'd turned the event into a mini-concert, though she wasn't the only performer this year; in fact she seemed almost as excited by the other acts she'd invited from around the region as she was about taking the stage herself. As usual her able-bodied committee, Chantal, Nelly, Wesley and Connor, were on board for the event, and Neil joined in where he was able between his chemo appointments and the downtime that followed.

Today was a good day, so he'd be with them.

Ben never joined in, other than to ridicule their efforts, or to blast out his heavy metal sounds while they were trying to rehearse.

Justine knew he was in his room this morning, since he'd told her to eff the hell off when she'd knocked. As this had become his stock response when someone in the family tried to make contact with him, it hadn't surprised her, or even offended her particularly, it had simply made her feel more depressed than ever.

In fact, lately she'd begun to feel the same way as Abby and Matt, who wished he'd leave home and never even bother to visit. However, in spite of clearly detesting them all, he never showed any signs of wanting to move out. Instead, he came and went as he pleased, using the house like a hotel, his mother as some sort of skivvy and his father as a bank. It was as though he was holding them all to ransom, threatening all kinds of terrible revenge if they didn't give him what he wanted. Although Matt fought with him constantly, sometimes violently, Justine knew he'd never run the risk of Ben doing something to hurt Abby or Lula, or her, so it was always Ben who won in the end.

The worst part of it was that they could see no end to it, unless, please God, when the time came for his trial he was sent to prison.

After dropping Lula at the village hall Justine made her way along the high street, calling into the hairdressers to make an appointment for Abby, and on to the deli where Maddy and Cheryl, with the backup of two part-timers, were serving breakfasts. The smell of grilling bacon and freshly ground coffee made her tummy rumble with hunger, while the sound of 'Hippy Hippy Shake' in the background might, at another time, have had her shimmying playfully over to the counter. As it was she walked to where Wesley was whispering something in his mother's ear, and the way Gina laughed wrenched painfully at Justine's heart.

If only she could have the same easy-going relationship with Ben.

It would happen, one day. It had to.

'Hi, how are you?' Gina smiled as she spotted Justine. 'Looks like it's going to be a scorcher again today.'

After kissing her and Wes on both cheeks, Justine said, 'You're in early. I thought you weren't starting until twelve.'

'My son has offered to buy me a coffee,' Gina informed her, her eyes shining with irony, 'and who am I to refuse?'

'Except I forgot to bring my wallet,' Wes confessed, 'so now Mum has to pay.'

'Isn't that always the way,' Gina sighed. 'Have you got a moment to join us?' she asked Justine.

Though Justine would have liked to, she and Cheryl had arranged to spend the morning going through a list of potential new suppliers, so after assuring them someone would deliver their order to the table, she went through to the back room.

Though she wasn't feeling faint, exactly, she was aware of needing to sit down for a moment, and since no one was around she tucked herself in behind a desk and rested her head in her hands. She must be reacting to the heat, she decided, or more likely to the fact that she couldn't actually remember when she'd last eaten.

It must have been yesterday morning, before she'd become aware of raised voices in the vale and gone outside to investigate.

Since she'd come in at the tail end of the scene she had no idea what it was actually about, or even how it had started, she only knew that Ben was in front of the farmhouse, fists clenched, teeth bared like an animal's as Connor yelled up the hill, 'You're a fucking loser, McQuillan, a sad little tosser who's on his way to jail.'

'Come here and say that, you cowardly piece of shit,' Ben yelled back.

'No way am I going to contaminate myself coming near you,' Connor shouted. 'We've heard about all the diseases you carry.' Grinning, he looked to the group around him for approval.

Realising, with a sickening lurch, that he was surrounded by Abby, Wes and Chantal, Justine moved towards Ben. 'Come in,' she said softly. 'Don't get involved.'

He wasn't listening. He was boiling with fury and so tensed up she was afraid to touch him.

Down the hill Connor said something to the others, and everyone laughed.

Afraid of what Ben might do if Connor goaded him any further, Justine said, 'They're not worth it. Come inside.'

'Psycho boy,' Connor sang out.

Ben's eyes glinted with an almost sadistic pleasure. 'That's right,' he growled, 'and don't you forget it, *faggot* boy.'

'Psycho boy, psycho boy,' Connor chanted as Ben retreated into the house.

Justine glared down the hill at him. 'Don't you *children* have anything better to do?' she shouted.

'Come on, Mum, he started it,' Abby shouted back.

Not prepared to get into a showdown with her daughter for everyone to witness, Justine followed Ben inside. Unsurprisingly there was no sign of him downstairs, so she ran up to his room and knocked on the door. 'Ben, it's me.'

He roared so loudly at her to go away that she actually took a step back.

Accepting that he needed time to calm down, she took herself over to the kitchen barn to carry on with the recipes she was preparing for the deli, and to call Matt on his mobile. Since he was at the arboretum with Lula and Rosie where there was never a good signal, she left him a message to call back when he could.

'So where is he now?' Matt asked when they finally connected.

'Still in his room. The door's locked, as usual.'

With a sigh of dismay, Matt said, 'Abby must have told the others about his court case. How else would Connor know?'

'It could have been Wes, if Simon mentioned it to him.'

'I don't think he would have, but there again . . . I wish I knew what to say to you, Justine, how to make some sort of difference, but you're as aware as I am that we have no power over the boy. He's proving it to us all the time, so what's the point in trying to help him when he clearly doesn't want it?'

243

'But he must *want* to be here, at least on some level, otherwise he'd surely just go.'

'Would he? Maybe it's just too much fun tormenting your parents and terrorising your sisters.'

Hating how bitter he sounded, she said, 'I'm sorry I rang you now.'

'Yes, I'm sorry too, because I really don't know what you want me to do about this spat with Connor.'

Since there wasn't anything he could do without running the risk of some unholy eruption from Ben, Justine let it go. What was the point of getting involved? It was over now; the kids themselves had probably already moved on from it, so she should too. On the other hand, why let that ghastly Connor get away with his taunting and stirring? He was always trying to cause trouble, and the way he seemed to have enjoyed the upset made him every bit as despicable as his mother evidently found Ben. In fact, the only reason she didn't give in to the urge to go over there and treat Melanie Sands to a piece of her mind was because Melanie was still recovering from a 'delicate' operation that apparently hadn't gone terribly well.

And because Ben informed her, when she told him through the door that she'd take the matter further if he wanted her to, that if she did he'd set fire to the house.

'You know you don't mean that,' she protested, 'so why do you . . .'

'Fuck off!' he growled. 'I'm busy and you're getting on my nerves.'

'Busy doing what?' Matt demanded when she reported back.

'How on earth would I know?'

'And why on earth would we care?'

Still half afraid there might be listening devices planted around the house, Justine said, 'I admit he makes it difficult, but . . .'

'Difficult? I'd call it downright impossible, and frankly I'm sick to death of the way he's coming between *us*. We never have a conversation about anything else these days. I can't remember the last time we went out, or felt able to have anyone round, or even managed to make love, we're always so damned worked up or exhausted from dealing with him. He's destroying our lives and I'm telling you this now, if they don't end up sending him to prison so we can start living normal lives again then I won't want to be held responsible for my actions.'

Now, as Justine sat in the back room of the deli, feeling shaken all over again by Matt's words, she tried using the tenderness he'd shown her later when they *had* made love, to force them from her mind. She knew how torn, desperate and frustrated he was; she also knew what a gentle and kind man he was at heart. He'd never do anything to hurt Ben, or anyone else come to that; he just needed to let off steam now and again, and there was no one apart from her to let it off to.

Picturing him at the desk in his study, she picked up the phone and dialled his number. 'Are you OK?' she whispered when he answered.

'Sure. Are you?' he replied.

'Of course. I just dropped Lula off.' She almost asked if there was any sign of Ben, but decided not to. 'Is Abby still there?'

'I believe she's on her way to the deli with Chantal and Nelly.'

'I thought Nelly was working at the kennels today.' Nelly's vocation had changed this past year – she now wanted to be a vet rather than a doctor. 'Don't tell me Abby got her to change shifts.'

'Probably, knowing Abby. Apparently they're about to prevail upon you for a picnic to have by the brook while they continue their meeting.'

'Just as long as that dreadful Connor's not with them.'

'All I can tell you is that he wasn't when they left here.'

Ben's name continued to hang unspoken between them. In the end Matt mentioned him first.

'We need to decide what we're going to do about him while we're in Italy.'

Justine, Matt and Lula were due to leave in a couple of weeks with Simon and Gina, Rob and Maggie and Cheryl – Brad had better things to do, apparently. They'd expected the other children to do their own things now they were older, but it turned out that Abby, Wes, Chantal and Francine had decided they wanted to come too. It was only Ben who hadn't given them an answer, and like Matt, Justine desperately hoped he wouldn't want to come when he'd be sure to spoil the holiday. However, the thought of leaving him behind, and what he might do to the house while they were gone, made her blood run cold.

Maybe they should cancel the trip.

'He's a problem without a solution,' Matt murmured. Though she didn't like hearing it, Justine could hardly argue. 'I should go,' she said. 'I'll see you in a couple of hours,' and putting the phone down she turned on the computer ready to start work.

It was just after midday when they heard the first police siren wailing past. Since it wasn't unusual for an emergency vehicle to tear along the high street, Justine and Cheryl barely looked up from what they were doing. It was only when a second siren was followed by a third and a fourth that curiosity got the better of them – and the first stirrings of unease crept into Justine's heart.

Trying to convince herself this had nothing to do with Ben, she followed Cheryl into the deli to find it half empty as customers and staff piled into the street to watch even more police cars flying past.

'What's going on?' Cheryl asked one of the part-timers.

'No idea,' came the reply.

Justine felt distinctly strange as she began pushing through the crowd.

Everyone was asking the same questions: 'What's happening? Where are they going?'

Someone said, 'It must be the housing estate.'

Someone else said, 'No, they're turning into the vale.'

Justine started to run. Her heart was pounding, her breath hardly coming as she forced her way past more crowds knotted outside the florist, the bakers, the gift shop.

'. . . madman suddenly . . .'

'. . . gone berserk.'

'. . . accident . . .'

'. . . still on the loose . . .'

'. . . heard screaming . . .'

She kept going, arms pumping, legs burning as she charged into the vale. The shock of so many police cars below, so much chaos filling the valley halted her like a punch. This wasn't real. If she closed her eyes it would all go away.

It didn't.

She pressed on, past the workers' cottages, the kitchen showroom . . . Other people were running; she had no idea who they were, could barely even see them.

'You can't go down there,' someone cried, trying to grab her.

She shoved them away and tore on. It was as though an angry river was gushing between her and reality. She couldn't think, couldn't feel, couldn't hear, could only run.

She saw men, police officers, lying on the ground in the park, guns aimed towards a tree.

Someone grabbed at her again and forced her to stop. Two women in uniform.

'I have to get through,' she gasped.

'I'm sorry, no one's going in there.'

'What's happened? Please . . .'

'We haven't been told anything yet.'

More officers were clearing the way for other vehicles to get through. Police tape was strung across the entrance to the park, and a loudhailer was telling everyone to stay back.

'Abby!' Justine shouted in panic. 'Oh my God, my God . . . Please . . .'

As the officers tried to turn her around she spotted Matt through the chaos, slumped on the ground at the bottom of their hill, his head in his hands.

'Matt!' she yelled. 'Matt!'

When he didn't look up a terrible, stultifying fear engulfed her.

Tearing herself free she ran towards him, but she was caught again, this time by a man who clutched her to him, pinning her arms to her sides and turning her away from the park.

'Please, that's my husband over there,' she begged.

'Get those tents up,' someone shouted.

'Suspect's apprehended.'

'Five down.'

'For God's sake, clear the area.'

'That's my husband,' she repeated. 'I need to get to him.'

'Sorry,' the officer responded, pushing her back the way she'd come, 'no one's allowed beyond this point.'

'Let me go!' she screamed, and thrusting him aside she charged with a superhuman effort towards Matt.

Once again she was stopped, and as someone spun her round she stumbled to the ground. She tried to get up, but her legs were too weak. Then she saw Ben, his head down, his hands trapped behind him as he was pushed into the back of a police car.

'No,' she sobbed, 'no, no, no!' She couldn't allow the horror of these new suspicions to take root – *they must not become real*.

'Madam, you need to get up.'

'What's happened?' she begged as she was helped to her feet. 'Please tell me . . .'

The policeman wasn't listening as he tried to push her back to the gathering crowd. She strained to look over her shoulder, calling for Matt. A gap opened in the glade and she caught sight of Simon, on his knees, holding someone in his arms. His shoulders were shaking, and she realised he was crying, sobbing, howling in pain.

She tried to call out, but her voice had gone. The madness, the disbelief were so great that the world seemed to be dissolving into a dense, suffocating fog. She tried to breathe, but there was no air. She pushed herself forward again.

'I have to get through,' someone was sobbing beside her. 'You don't understand, my daughter is in there.' It was Cheryl, desperate to get to Chantal.

'Connor,' Melanie Sands was screaming. 'Connor, are you there? Please answer me.'

Then Maddy arrived, so stricken with fear that she could only sink to her knees, her hands clasped together as if in prayer. *Please let my children be safe. Please God, I'll do anything, just let my children be safe.* Her husband Ronnie put a hand on her head; his eyes were glassy, fixed on the inexplicable chaos still unfolding in front of him.

Time passed, Justine had no idea how much time, only that she was on the ground now with a blanket around her. It was too hot for a blanket, and yet she was icy cold. She still couldn't speak, could hardly think. She could only watch as tents were erected in the park, and people in white coveralls moved around them like aliens in a slow-motion movie. She heard a plane passing overhead, a car alarm in the distance, a dog barking. And all the time the terrible, incessant burbling of the surreal scene around her went on.

She saw Maddy and Ronnie being escorted into their cottage next to the footbridge. Melanie was with them, and Cheryl.

She became aware of someone next to her, sitting very close.

She turned and saw it was Matt.

How long had he been there?

'Mr McQuillan?'

They both looked up, squinting against the sun.

A slight woman with blonde hair and dark-rimmed glasses provided a shadow so they could see her. 'You're Ben McQuillan's parents,' she said. It wasn't a question.

Matt barely nodded.

'I'm Detective Sergeant Liz Purl,' she informed them. She gestured to a stocky man beside her. 'This is DC Hamish Cole. You need to come with us.'

It took a moment for the words to register.

Justine tried to get up, stumbled, and Hamish Cole caught her. 'My daughter,' she murmured, the words dribbling through terror, disbelief, denial. 'She's in there . . .'

'Where's Lula?' Matt asked.

She turned to him. How could she have forgotten Lula? 'She's at playgroup,' she answered. 'I need to . . . Do you have your phone?'

He didn't, so Liz Purl offered hers.

'Yes, Lula's here,' Justine was told, 'but I'm sorry, you'll have to come and get her. I know it's not her fault, but . . . Please, just come and get her.'

Justine handed the phone back to Liz Purl. 'I have to go,' she said absently. *What wasn't Lula's fault? Why would anyone say that?*

'We'll send someone for her,' Liz Purl insisted.

'She's been taught not to go with strangers,' Justine told her.

Firmly, but not unkindly, Liz Purl said, 'It's not a good idea for you to go.'

'But I . . .' Realising she was being advised to stay away for her own sake, Justine put her hands to her head. This nightmare had to end, *please*, it just had to, because she didn't know how to get through it.

'Take the dog,' Matt said hoarsely. 'She'll come if you have Rosie.'

They all climbed the hill to the farmhouse together, and a young female officer was dispatched with Rosie.

Hearing movements upstairs Justine was about to run up there, certain it would be Abby or Ben, but she knew on a level that didn't seem a part of her that it was the police going about their duty.

Abby! Oh dear God, Abby.

With a wrenching sob she turned to Matt, and clutching her hand between both of his, he pressed it to his mouth.

Her precious girl was down in the park . . . No, please God, don't let this be true.

Turning to the detective she started to speak, but Matt was already saying, in a voice roughened by shock, 'Where've they taken Ben?'

'I'll find out for you,' Liz Purl replied. Her eyes were hard, yet not unsympathetic.

Justine felt nauseous. She took a breath to steady

herself. She knew what she must ask now, but didn't know if she could bear to. Panic overwhelmed her and she started to shake.

'Sit down,' Liz Purl advised gently.

Justine sank on to a chair. 'What – what happened?' she finally blurted.

Before Liz Purl could answer Matt said dully, 'He used his crossbow – actually, it was the compound bow . . .' *Faster, lighter, more accurate* . . . 'I should have spotted him going down there, but I didn't. No one did. He must have been in the tree before any of the kids got there . . .' His voice cracked and Hamish Cole put a hand on his arm.

Liz Purl took a call on her mobile. When she'd finished, with very real anguish in her eyes she said to Matt, 'They're removing your daughter's body . . .'

'*No!*' Justine sobbed, jumping to her feet. 'Please . . . She has to come home. She's got a concert tonight.'

Drawing her to him, Matt said, 'Ssh, ssh. We have to pull ourselves together for Lula. She'll be here any minute.'

Liz Purl took Matt to one side and spoke quietly in his ear.

Turning back to Justine, he said, 'They want me to identify the body . . .'

Justine choked as she cried, 'No! No! She's not a body, she's our girl. Please Matt, bring her home.'

He looked so beaten, so wretched that she banged her fists into his chest.

'I'm coming with you,' she begged.

'No,' he said firmly. 'You need to be here for Lula.'

Liz Purl sat with Justine while Hamish Cole escorted

Matt down to the park. The crime scene officers were still moving about upstairs, or tramping in and out of the front door, speaking quietly to one another, occasionally glancing into the kitchen. The phone started ringing, and Justine suddenly realised that it had hardly stopped since they'd come in.

'It'll be the press,' Liz Purl said gently. 'I'm sure you don't want to speak to them.'

Justine shook her head. It would be all over the news by now, and she just couldn't stand the ruthless compounding of the horror with cameras, lights, speculation, blame and shame. She had to push it away, somehow keep herself aloof from it, as though it was happening to somebody else. 'I should call my brother,' she said. 'He could be trying to get through.'

As she went to pick up the phone Lula and Rosie burst in through the door. Lula was the palest Justine had ever seen her. *Dear God, how much did she know?*

'Mummy,' she whimpered, as Justine scooped her up, and wrapping her arms round her mother's neck she clung on tight and wouldn't let go.

It was early evening by the time the detectives and crime scene officers left, taking only they knew what of Ben's with them, leaving tape across his bedroom door preventing unauthorised persons from going in.

His parents fell into that category. As did his Uncle Rob and Aunt Maggie, who'd arrived about an hour ago. They were going to take Lula back to London in the morning. Chippingly was no place for her to be over the coming days, weeks . . . After that . . .

Justine stood with Matt looking at the sealed door to Ben's room, trying to imagine where he was now, what might be happening to him. Did he realise his life was over, that there would never be any going back from this? Did he care what he had done to his family, and the families of the children he'd grown up with? How long had he been planning this insane attack? What terrible, evil force inside had made him carry it through?

She knew now that Matt had heard the screams and run outside to investigate. When he'd spotted Kelvin Sands racing down the hill he'd followed, but by the time they'd got to the park it was already too late.

No one had escaped Ben. With lightning speed and terrible precision he had ended five teenage lives; one of them his own sister, another his cousin, another his lifelong best friend. For some reason the use of a compound bow felt worse than if it had been a gun. Justine wasn't sure why, except it seemed a more visceral act because of the way he would have had to hold the weapon, embrace it even, put a cheek against it and then let the arrow fly like a satisfied breath.

One, two, three, four, five.

Abby, Wesley, Chantal, Connor and Neil. Nelly had gone to the kennels after all or she would have been there too, and Maddy and Ronnie would have lost both their children.

Neil. Justine clutched her hands to her face. *He'd fought so bravely and cheerfully to hold on to his life, his parents had prayed for him every day, and now for him to go like this . . .*

Wesley, her wonderful nephew, Simon and Gina's only son and greatest joy . . .

Connor, Melanie and Kelvin's adored youngest . . .

Chantal, Cheryl and Brad's only child, beautiful and gentle, always kind and so full of life . . .

She turned to bury her face in Matt's shoulder. She couldn't bear to think of them any more. It would have to wait. She simply couldn't cope with the enormity of it.

And yet there would never be a day when she could cope, because she realised already that this was just the beginning.

Chapter Twelve

Present Day – Culver, Indiana

Justine was standing at the window of Waseya gazing through the steamy panes across the porch, down through the golden avenue of trees to where raindrops were spattering the lake. There had been a heavy downpour a while ago, shining, silvery blades streaming from the sky as though to cleanse this innocent place of the tragic ugliness her confession had brought to it.

She was still seeing it, feeling it; it would never let her go.

Her eyes refocused on the orderly piles of leaves David had left behind. He'd come into the house when he'd finished, but Sallie Jo had shaken her head, letting him know that it would be best for him to go.

Justine had expected Sallie Jo to leave soon after that, but she was still here, sitting at the table, her hands covering her face as though the pictures Justine had conjured were refusing to fade. Justine could see her ghostlike reflection in the window, a manifestation of the world's speechless horror.

She wouldn't tell Sallie Jo about the time that had

followed, when she'd had to be sedated to help get her through the shock and the grief. If it hadn't been for Lula she was sure she'd have ended it all, and was certain Matt had felt the same. They simply hadn't known how to cope, what they were supposed to do or say, how they could ever even begin to recover from what had happened. For a long time neither of them had been able to go out; they were too dazed, too ashamed and afraid of facing the world. They'd stayed at Rob's or with Camilla, alternating between them in the hope of avoiding the press. The stress caused a problem for Matt's heart and she'd had so many panic attacks, deep shuddering spasms racking her body and making it almost impossible to breathe, that her loved ones became afraid to leave her alone. No one went to see Ben although Matt and Rob tried, several times, only for him to refuse the visit. The two occasions they managed to see him happened across a courtroom when he was charged, and again when he pleaded guilty. Apparently he'd looked their way and winked, as though it was all a game and one he seemed to think he was winning.

Unsurprisingly, the media couldn't let go of the story. It was on every bulletin, every front page for weeks, maybe months. Nothing of this magnitude had happened in Britain before, a student from an apparently decent home and background setting out to kill his sister, cousin and friends, and succeeding in the most brutal and callous way. It was as though no one could quite believe it, and the fact that he was said not to be showing any remorse sent the pundits into a frenzy of opinion and hyperbole. It seemed everyone was analysing him now, declaring him psychotic, schizophrenic, sociopathic . . .

Justine and Matt were advised not to watch TV or engage with the press at all. They had no problem doing this; all they wanted was to hide from the world and work out how on earth they were going even to begin to move forward once all the fuss had died down. They were in regular touch with the psychiatrists assigned to Ben's case, spent many hours talking with them, so they were aware that their son was not, at this time, interested in any kind of mitigation that might help him.

Psychopathic tendencies was the phrase they heard most often. Apparently, it wasn't done to label someone Ben's age an outright psychopath. Tendencies allowed for change and rehabilitation.

Nothing was allowed for Abby, or the others. It was too late for them, and Justine's grief and anger were only surpassed by the helplessness and despair that made it all but impossible to face each day. God only knew how it was for the other parents. She and Matt sat for hours trying to compose emails of regret and apology, but no matter how carefully chosen and sincere their words, nothing was ever going to bring the children back. And that was all the parents wanted.

It was all they wanted, too.

When it came time to clear Abby's room Justine had to leave it to her mother and Catherine. One foot inside the door and she'd sunk to her knees, howling and sobbing and begging Abby to come back. Matt took her downstairs while the two grandmothers began packing, and Justine hadn't found the will to try again. It was as though each part of her shattered heart had a different way of coping and the strongest of them all, at that time, was denial. It helped her to carry on, mainly because it managed to convince her, once in a while, that Abby was simply away on her world tour with Wes. She, Matt and Lula would probably fly out to join them soon. They'd let Abby decide whether it should be Dubai or Bangkok or Singapore. She even surfed the Net for flights and hotels, made lists of what they should pack, and sent emails to Abby's account asking if there was anything she needed her parents to bring.

The first time she saw Ben after that terrible day in the vale was when he was returned to court for sentencing. The instant she saw him looking, oddly, exactly like himself – what had she expected, that he'd become physically transformed into some kind of monster? – she felt herself starting to burn with anger and loathing and so many other emotions that made her want to scream and rant and tear the smug expression right off his wicked face. Matt slipped an arm around her and she closed her eyes so she didn't have to look at her son any more.

The judge's voice was grave and steady. 'Ben McQuillan, you have been convicted of five extremely serious offences. You have shown no remorse, nor have you cooperated with the medical and custodial authorities. It is clear to me that you are an extremely dangerous young man, so I am going to order that you be detained at Her Majesty's pleasure. The authorities will determine when, if ever, you will be released.'

Now, here in Culver, Justine took a breath as though to step back from the words, but she would never forget them, never stop hearing their stern, dark reprimand, their damning summing-up of her evil son's character. If he'd been eighteen at the time of the crime there was no doubt the judge would have given a full life sentence. It was highly likely he'd serve that anyway.

Becoming aware of Sallie Jo getting to her feet she turned around, expecting her friend to go for her coat. Instead she filled the kettle and put it on to boil.

Finally breaking the awful silence, Sallie Jo said, 'It's like that book. The one about Kevin.'

Justine nodded. It wasn't the first time she'd heard it mentioned, and she was sure it wouldn't be the last.

Glancing at the clock, Sallie Jo said, 'The girls will need picking up soon.'

There was still an hour to go before they needed to get in the car, but if Sallie Jo wanted to use this as an excuse to leave, Justine would understand. Once alone she'd have to make a decision on what to do next, where to go, how she would explain to Lula that they needed to find another new home in a place far away from Culver and the new friends they'd made. The new friends who wouldn't want them in their lives now the truth had been told.

Should that place be in the States? Maybe Canada.

Perhaps they should return to Europe, but not England.

'I'm sorry,' Sallie Jo said softly. 'I'd never have forced you to relive that time if I'd . . .'

Justine shook her head. 'Please don't apologise. How could you have known? How could anyone even begin to imagine something like that?'

Sallie Jo's eyes went down. 'I guess we don't think so much about the people in your position, the parents who have to try to carry on. We don't imagine it happening in Britain either, although I remember the case now.'

Justine's breath caught on a sob she hadn't known was close. She pressed her fingers to her lips, then took a sip of tea from the mug Sallie Jo had passed her. It warmed her – she hadn't even realised she was cold.

'What followed was even worse,' she heard herself saying. She quickly corrected herself. 'No, nothing can be worse than what happened to the children, but trying to come to terms with it . . . There were two families who'd lost their only child, two more whose precious sons . . .' She gasped for air. 'We had to leave the vale, of course, there was no question of us staying, but within days everyone else had left. It was too hard . . . It was never going to be the place we all loved again. It was over. The sense of family, of belonging, of feeling safe and even privileged in our cosy community had been destroyed, smashed to pieces along with those five innocent lives. I'm not sure where everyone went, probably to relatives . . . Matt and I didn't ask, because we soon realised they didn't want us to know. They needed to cut them-selves off from us as rapidly and permanently as possible. I don't think Simon and Gina, or Cheryl, have ever actually blamed us for what happened, they just couldn't be with us any more. We understood that, of course. How could they possibly look at us and not be reminded of Ben? The others, Maddy, Ronnie and Melanie . . . They said some terrible things to us, and about us that got repeated in the papers, and online . . . Some of it wasn't even true, but who could blame them for wanting to hurt the parents of the monster when they couldn't reach the monster himself? That's what the press called him, McQuillan's Monster, after a video game Matt had devised a decade or more before.'

Suddenly afraid she was saying too much, forcing Sallie Jo through more than she wanted to hear, she said, 'I'm sorry, I shouldn't be running on like this . . .'

Sallie Jo's eyes held steadily to hers. 'I'm here for as long as you need me to be,' she replied gently. 'If you want to stop that's OK, if you don't that's OK too.'

Did she want to stop? Could she, now she'd started?

In the end she took a breath and found herself continuing. 'We didn't go to any of the other children's funerals,' she said, her mind travelling back to the pain of that cruelly perfect sunny day in August, 'and no one apart from my brother and my and Matt's mothers came to Abby's. They played some of Abby's music on the news that night. It received so many hits that someone got in touch to ask if they could sign her songs to their label.' Her lips twisted into a sad, ironic smile. 'Fame at last, but she wasn't around to enjoy it.'

Sallie Jo's eyes showed how sorely she felt fate had treated Abby.

'Matt said yes,' Justine continued, 'they could record an album of her songs if all the proceeds went to a children's charity, and we didn't hear any more after that.'

Sallie Jo arched an eyebrow. After a moment she ventured, 'Am I allowed to ask where Matt is now?'

Picturing Matt in his awful self-imposed loneliness, Justine looked down at her tea. 'He's with Ben,' she finally answered.

Sallie Jo frowned.

'We decided,' Justine explained, 'that in spite of what Ben had done we were still his parents and we couldn't just desert him. He'd told us many times that he felt abandoned, unloved . . . I don't know why he felt like that, because we were never aware of treating him differently, but he said it was our neglect, our favouritism that had driven him to do what he did.' She took a breath. 'As far as I know he's still never shown any remorse, which could be why Matt and I feel so much guilt ourselves, as though to make up for Ben's lack.'

Sallie Jo said, 'What does it mean exactly, to be detained at Her Majesty's pleasure?'

'Officially, that he'll be reviewed at various intervals to see if his behaviour or attitude have changed enough to make a difference to his sentence. In reality, he's very probably there for the rest of his life.'

Sallie Jo's hands clenched and unclenched, as though she was still finding it hard to get a hold of this. 'So Matt is . . . ?' she prompted. 'You said he's with Ben?'

Justine's eyes remained down as she answered. 'He's in a flat about a mile from the prison. In some ways it's as though he's serving his own kind of sentence, because he hardly sees anyone, apart from Rosie, our dog, who stayed with him, and the odd visitor now and again, my brother, his mother, his editor . . . And he goes to see Ben, of course.' She knew nothing about those visits, what he and Ben discussed, how Ben behaved, if they ever talked about her, or what he'd done, or how he felt about it now. 'We agreed,' she told Sallie Jo, 'Matt and I, that I needed to make a fresh start for Lula. It was clear that we couldn't stay in England, the case was too well known, and our faces were all over the news for weeks, months even, so wherever we went we'd always be recognised. Someone would know or find out and Lula would never be able to get away from being the sister of a mass killer. We couldn't allow her to grow up with that sort of stigma, or shame. It would be better if she never knows, though only time will tell if it's possible to keep it from her.'

Apparently understanding the need to protect their youngest child, Sallie Jo said, 'Does Lula remember Ben, or Abby?'

Justine swallowed as she nodded. 'I think the memories are fading, but yes, she does. It's mostly Matt and Rosie, the dog, that she remembers now.'

'And what about you and Matt? Do you Skype or FaceTime? Does Lula see him at all?'

Feeling her heart swell with yet more guilt and help-lessness, Justine said, 'No, she doesn't. We knew it would be hard, but we decided it would be for the best if we weren't in touch at all. We thought . . . We told ourselves it was the only way for us to have any kind of future, because Matt would always be where he is now, putting Ben first, and Lula and I would be here. We even talked about divorce, although we've never done anything about it . . . Lately we've come to realise that we were still so traumatised when we made the decision that we probably shouldn't have made one at all. We're in touch now, but I know he'll never be able to bring himself to leave Ben, and would I really want him to? He's our son, after all, and he doesn't have anyone else. Neither of his grandmothers, none of his relatives would go to see him . . . It's too distressing, and he'd probably treat them badly if he even allowed the visits. I guess he's the same with Matt, but he must want to see Matt or he wouldn't send the visiting orders. Perhaps he sees him because he gets some sort of sick pleasure out of making his father suffer, although Matt isn't a masochist, so I can't imagine he'd put up with it for long if that were the case. On the other hand he feels responsible, blames himself for the way Ben turned out. We both do. How can we not? We're his parents; we brought him up, so we must have done something wrong. There was never any doubt that some people blamed us, even in the media, who made our lives a double hell. There were so many articles, debate programmes, even documentaries trying to analyse Ben and what had driven him to do what he did, and the consequences of bad parenting. In our case we weren't accused of the conventional neglect or abuse, we were held up as examples of how damaging overindulgence can be, how it can breed a sense of entitlement and superiority, an inability to handle criticism or to accept any kind of failure. They said Ben obviously had an extreme nature, was possibly bipolar, or schizophrenic, and that we'd been too busy with our careers to recognise his cries for help.

'Actually, there wasn't much they could throw at us that we hadn't already thrown at ourselves, apart from the one thing we knew and the media have never found out. When Ben was small he fell out of a tree and landed on his head. Matt tried to catch him, but we were catching Abby at the time and we didn't see him coming until it was too late. Of course we have no way of knowing if the damage he suffered then somehow triggered all that came later. The experts we've spoken to have never been able to agree on whether it played a part. Some say it's possible while others simply rule it out. There are so many contradictions, and until Ben agrees to cooperate there'll never be a proper psychiatric assessment. The only person he'll see, or speak to, is Matt.'

'How about you? Will he see you?'

Justine's eyes drifted, as the memory of the only visit she'd made, a couple of months after he'd been transferred to Bristol to prison for life, emerged from the shadows to haunt her all over again.

Her Majesty's Prison, Bristol, UK
The first thing Justine noticed about Ben as he came into the visitors' hall was the dramatic change in the size of him. His arms, shoulders and chest were solid

muscle, his enormous thighs seemed too large for his trackies. In fact, she almost didn't recognise him with his shiny bald head and dark smudge of a beard. It was only when she saw his eyes, cold, darting and assessing, and all too familiar, that she realised this sly-looking, pumped-up thug was her son.

'So you came,' he said, sniffing as he yanked out a chair to sit the other side of a small, scratched table. 'I didn't think you would.'

'It's the first time you've added my name to a visitor's order,' she reminded him, trying to still her hands before she smashed them into his face, and let rip with the hatred she felt. This yob, this stranger who was her son had killed his own sister, her beautiful daughter whom she missed every minute of every day, and who hadn't deserved to die; none of them had.

He regarded her with what appeared to be lazy amusement. It was an act, she felt sure of it, but what it was covering she had no idea. 'I didn't want to see you,' he told her. 'Dad talked me into it.'

Aware of that, she said, 'I didn't want to see you either.'

His eyebrows rose. Though he seemed to find her response comical, she could tell he hadn't expected it. 'So shall we call it quits and bring this to an end?' he suggested.

Her eyes bored into his, showing him she wasn't afraid, that he couldn't intimidate her now, though her heart was hammering in her chest. 'If you like,' she retorted.

Neither of them moved.

In the end she was first to break the silence. 'Why

didn't you want to see me?' she asked, trying to change the tone by sounding reasonable, calm, maybe even caring.

He shrugged. 'What's the point? You never gave a shit about me while I was living under the same roof as you, so I can't see you losing much sleep over me while I'm under this one.'

He surely had to know how wrong he was about that, for she hadn't slept a single night through since he'd devastated her world. 'It's been a long time since you gave me a good reason to care about you,' she reminded him bluntly.

His smirk was vaguely sour as he said, 'So nothing's changed.'

'You've ruined more lives than you probably even realise . . .'

'Yeah, yeah, blah, blah . . .'

'Ben, for God's sake . . .'

'Enough,' he cut in, holding up a hand. 'I don't need to listen to any of it, OK? You want to blame me for what I did, go right ahead, I mean, I did it, so why not? But don't forget to take a look at the part you played in making me who I am.'

Turning cold to her core, she said, 'What the hell are you talking about? You come from a good family. No one played any part in what you've done to yourself . . .'

'You mean like making me feel inferior right from when I was a kid, second to everyone and everything . . . Nothing was ever about me . . .'

'For God's sake, get over the self-pity.'

'I did, a long time ago. I'm just saying, that's all.'

'But it's nonsense and you know it. Dad and I have always been there for you . . .'

'OK, let's stop with the bullshit. Neither of you thought I was worth anything before all this, so I don't get why you're trying to pretend now.'

'It's not a pretence! If we didn't care do you think we'd come?'

His eyes narrowed curiously.

'We're trying to understand where things went wrong, why you . . .' She broke off, startled, as he yawned and gazed around the room as though bored. 'Listen,' she snapped, sitting forward, 'I can walk out of here right now and never see you again. If that's what you want, just say the word.'

'The word,' he drawled.

Once again neither of them moved.

Aware of being watched by other inmates and their visitors, she kept her voice down as she said, 'Tell me what I did to make you like this . . .'

His head came forward so fast it almost hit her.

Jumping back, she took a moment to collect herself. 'Explain to me,' she said, 'if you're so full of hate and resentment towards me, why you didn't take it out on me? Why did you have to do what you did to Abby, to Wes, and Chantal . . .'

'What makes you think I'm not taking it out on you? It's my guess you're feeling pretty shit about it all, and nothing's going to make it better, so suck it up, Mum. Your turn to suffer. You've got a psycho for a son and *you're* the one who made me that way.'

'You've turned yourself into a victim of something that never even happened.'

'OK, have it your way. But then ask yourself, why are we sitting here? If nothing went wrong, what drove me to do what I did?'

'That's what everyone's trying to find out, but you won't talk to anyone.'

'I'm talking to you, trouble is you're not listening, because you don't like what you're hearing.'

'It's not making any sense.'

'What the fuck don't you understand about always putting Abby first? She was your special child, the one who could do no wrong. You went to watch everything she did right from when she was old enough to perform. You were always there for her, but you never had time for me.'

'Ben, I don't know why you're telling yourself these things when you *know* they aren't true. Dad and I were always there for you . . .'

'Yeah, right.' His sarcasm was so thick it seemed to curdle the already sour air. 'I've got to hand it to Dad,' he went on, 'at least he made an effort now and again, but you . . . You weren't interested in anything I did. You didn't even bother turning up if I won a trophy. You were always too busy with Abby, or your business, or you were away somewhere with Dad. Then your little brat came along, another girl for Mummy, wasn't the world just perfect? Let's all play with dollies and prams and go to watch Abby sing and dress ourselves up in whatever stupid crap you could get your hands on. It was like I stopped existing at all when *she* came along. Oh, don't get me wrong, I couldn't give a fuck about it now, but that kind of stuff messes with a kid's head.'

She could only look at him, wondering how on earth he'd managed to convince himself of so much injustice and neglect when she knew very well that she *had* been there when he'd played games and won trophies. She was the one who'd nursed him when he was sick, made all his favourite meals, driven him all over the countryside to take part in competitions and tournaments . . . She'd loved him with all her heart, had been so proud of him and had never once been aware of putting either Abby or Lula before him. Even if she had, it could never even begin to explain, much less excuse, what he'd done. Surely he realised that.

She looked down as he put his hands on the table between them, showing her his HATE tattoo, or maybe he wanted her to see the rawness of his knuckles. She felt a deeply visceral pang. What was happening to him in here? What sort of punishment was he really facing? What were they going to turn him into?

Nothing worse than he already was.

'What happened to you that day?' she asked steadily. 'What made you go down to the . . .'

'They mocked me,' he cut in mildly. 'You were there; you heard them. They thought they were better than me, they called me psycho boy, so I thought, yeah, that's who I am, and now they're going to find out what psycho boys do. Connor was the first to go. I wish I could get him all over again, fucking toerag that he is.'

No pity, not even the merest trace of regret or guilt.

She looked down at his hands again, tight fists on the table. 'Aren't you afraid in here?' she asked, wondering how much she cared and suspecting it was more than he deserved.

Something flashed through his eyes, so fast it wasn't possible to read it, but she felt sure it was unease or something akin to it.

Cockily, he said, 'I like it just fine, it's cool, they're my kind of people.'

'They're who you're going to spend the rest of your life with if you keep refusing to talk to the psychiatrists.'

His eyes stayed on hers as he nodded. 'Let's not kid ourselves,' he said, 'it doesn't matter who I talk to, the only way I'm ever getting out of here is if they move me to a place for the criminally insane, which might be cool, come to think of it, bit of a crack, a few drugs, knocking about with some wacky people . . .'

'Ben, you don't mean what you're saying. I know you regret what you did . . .'

'If you know that, then you know more than I do.'

'Can't you see that I'm trying to reach you, to show you that in spite of everything Dad and I are still here for you?'

'Then you're crazy. There's nothing either of you can do to help me, and nothing any psychiatrist can do either, because I'm not some schizo with voices going on in my head, telling me what to do . . . I'm in control of me, I'm the one who decided what I was going to do, and I'm the one who did it.'

'In a psychotic episode that you *couldn't* control.'

His eyes widened. 'Nice try,' he responded, apparently impressed.

'Am I wrong?'

He shrugged. 'Who knows?'

Without thinking she tried to grab his hands, but he pulled them away. 'Hey, hey, no touching,' he warned.

She stared at him helplessly, wondering what the point was of even being there.

'I don't know what you expect from me,' he said roughly, 'but face it, Mum, whatever happens, you'll never be able to forgive me for Abby.'

It was true, she wouldn't; she couldn't even bear to hear him speak Abby's name. 'If I knew you weren't able to help yourself . . .'

'If you knew that you'd be able to tell the world I was a nutjob, a full-on undiagnosed psycho, and that way you couldn't be to blame.'

She regarded him closely, trying to see her son past the stranger, a real human being who actually gave a damn. 'Before you did it,' she said, 'did you realise it would end this way, with you being locked up probably for the rest of your life?'

To her surprise he seemed to give it some thought. 'No, I guess I didn't think about that,' he replied, 'but it's OK. I can handle it.'

She gestured to his knuckles.

'Yeah, that's how it works in here. It's a different world. You don't want to know about it.'

She couldn't deny that, because she really didn't. All the same, it was hard to think of what he might be going through, even if some, most, would say he deserved it.

She shouldn't care either. After what he'd done, the way he'd destroyed so many lives, she should simply turn her back on him now, walk away and let him rot in this dreadful place.

Had anyone ever felt such a cruel conflict of loyalties

and emotions? If so, could they please tell her how to handle them?

'Tell me what to do,' she begged. 'What do you need . . .?'

'You can't fix this,' he growled. 'No one can.'

'But if you'd accept some help . . .'

'You're not listening. No amount of help is going to change what I did.'

'Would *you* change it, if you could?'

After a while he started to shake his head. It gleamed with the reflection of a light bulb overhead. 'Not Connor,' he said. 'Never him.'

'But the others. Chantal, Neil . . .'

'I know who they are, you don't have to spell out their names.'

'If it's too hard to hear them then you do have a conscience.'

'Whatever.' He suddenly pushed away from the table. 'Time to go,' he declared.

'Ben, wait,' she implored as he stood up.

'For what?'

'I haven't finished.'

'Yes you have. We've said everything we need to, and what we've decided is that you don't need me in your life, and I sure as hell don't need you.'

'I don't believe that.'

He shrugged. 'Your choice.'

'I want to come again,' she called after him.

Keeping his back to her, he raised a hand to wave goodbye.

'Then write to me, or ring.'

He didn't answer, just carried on through the door that led him to a place she could never go.

A week later she received a brief note at Rob's address that she'd kept with her ever since.

> *Dear Mum,*
>
> *I probably ought to say thanks for coming and even pretending you care, but it would have been better if you hadn't. It was kind of easier before, telling myself I hated you and that you hated me . . . It made sense of stuff, or I think it did. It's easier to be angry, it feels like who I really am, a shit psycho who's got to keep it together to survive in here. I can do that, but not if you come to see me. You make me weak and that's not good.*
>
> *So forget about me, Mum. Go on with your life and if it helps for me to say I'm sorry about Abby, then I'm sorry about Abby. She always hated me, but that's OK, I hated her too.*
>
> *Don't bother to answer this. I won't read it anyway.*
> *The person who used to be your son,*
> *Ben*

Culver, Indiana

Justine watched Sallie Jo fold the letter and take a deep, troubled breath as she struggled to absorb the enormity of it all.

How could anyone? It was outside most people's sphere of understanding, never mind experience.

In the end, looking up, Sallie Jo said, 'I can't begin to imagine how you felt when you received this, or how you feel now.'

Since she hardly knew herself, Justine simply shook her head. 'He's my son,' she said. 'That will never change, much as I wish to God it could at times. We'll never get past what he did; it'll be with us, all of us, for the rest of our lives. I had someone talk to me in the early days about forgiveness being the way to move on, but he's right, I'll never be able to forgive him for Abby. I don't think I've ever even properly grieved for her, because it's always been all about him, and in a way it still is. Matt's there, I'm here . . . He's made that happen. We tell ourselves it's for the best this way, but how can anything be for the best when so many families are ruined?'

Not even trying to answer the question, Sallie Jo said, 'Since he wrote this letter, has he shown any other signs of remorse?'

Justine glanced at her bleakly. 'Not that I'm aware of,' she said, 'but I've had no real news of him since I left. Matt and I decided it would be best that way.'

'Is it hard?'

'In some ways, yes. In others it's a relief.' She sighed and reached for the letter. 'To be honest I try not to think of him at all, but of course I hardly ever stop. He's always there, either as he was the last time I saw him, or as a boy . . . I hear him laughing, shouting, crying, roaring, swearing . . . I keep asking myself if I did put Abby first, and sometimes I think I did. Not deliberately, but I was so busy with the deli, or an event, the house was always full of people dropping in, or staying for a weekend, even a week, and I was often away travelling with Matt . . . I can see now that I didn't pay enough attention to my children and whereas Abby managed to cope with it, it obviously wasn't the same for Ben.' Her eyes went to Sallie Jo.

'It's why I want to make sure I'm always around for Lula. If I work it'll only be during school hours.'

'You have that now,' Sallie Jo reminded her.

'Thanks to you, and I'll always be grateful.'

Sallie Jo frowned. 'I'm sensing a but.'

Justine paused for a moment. 'I know you meant it when you said you'd never repeat what I've told you today, and I believe you, I trust you, but it will colour the way you feel from now on . . . No, it will,' she pressed when Sallie Jo tried to object. 'I've seen it so many times, and I don't blame you, how can you not be affected by knowing what you do?'

'But that's not *you* and who you really are. It's only a part of it, and we all have things in our past that we'd rather no one knew anything about.'

'Not like this.'

'OK, yours is bigger, which makes it harder, but you're here to try and overcome it, to prove to yourself that it is possible to carry on, and to give Lula a good life.'

'I want to believe it, I really do, but I can see now that I've been deluding myself thinking no one will ever find out. They will, sooner or later – not that I think you'll tell them, they just will, and once everyone knows my son, Lula's brother, is the McQuillan Monster they'll never be able to accept us the same way again. It's the first thing that'll come to mind every time they see us, and kids can be very cruel. So can adults. I don't want to live with the stigma, and I really don't want Lula to, so I need to start making plans to move on.'

Sallie Jo shook her head in quiet despair. 'But where

would you go that isn't going to throw up the same problems you're facing now? You can't live in total isolation, so there's always going to be a risk of new friends and neighbours finding out about Ben, and like you say, they probably will. So before you do anything hasty, why not give it some more time here?'

Justine forced a smile. 'It's really kind of you to say all that, and I appreciate it, I really do, but you haven't given yourself any time to think, and once everything I've told you starts to sink in you might find you're not keen for Hazel to carry on being friends with Lula. Ben's . . . problems might run in the family.'

Sallie Jo's eyebrows rose. 'I really don't think that's likely,' she protested, 'and I already know I don't want you to go. I've come to think of you as a friend, a real close friend, and I can promise you what you've told me today isn't going to change that.'

Justine wasn't sure what to say, she only knew that it didn't feel right to continue arguing.

'Listen,' Sallie Jo said, more forcefully, 'I understand that if it gets out you're going to face some prejudice for a while, ignorant, narrow-minded people who can't see any further than the backs of their Bibles, but you'll have me to help take care of that, and believe me, folks around here, they know better than to get on the wrong side of Sallie Jo.'

This time Justine's smile was real. It was true, Sallie Jo was a force to be reckoned with at times, and no one was ever going to take that away from her. 'I still say you should give yourself some time to think it over,' Justine responded.

'OK, if that's what you want, but I'm telling you my

mind's made up, and there won't be any changing it. What's more,' she ran on, a sudden light sparking in her eyes, 'no way am I letting you go anywhere till we've been into that house on the lake and found out all there is to find out about your grandma.'

Justine felt herself blanch.

'But I get that it isn't going to happen today,' Sallie Jo smiled.

Chapter Thirteen

Present Day – Culver, Indiana

It wasn't until a week later that Justine spoke to Matt again. By then a blaze of fall colours was gleaming like fresh candy up and down the streets of Culver, all around Lake Max and throughout the Academies. The whole town was glowing with the season's radiance, the people seeming uplifted by its brazen flamboyance. She couldn't remember the change happening so fast or so dramatically in Britain, which had something to do, she remembered once hearing or learning at school, with this being a continental climate, while the UK's was maritime.

Whatever the geographical or environmental reason, it was more beautiful than any fall she'd ever seen and made her feel ludicrously, though pleasingly, proud to be an American. As if nationality could lay any claim to nature!

When Matt called she'd just returned from viewing an apartment uptown in a block next to the Culver fire station, where Lula and Hazel had joined a group of other children at the weekend to climb all over the engines. Afterwards parents and kids together had traipsed across the road to the town park, where they'd picnicked, played on the swings and had some fun wondering about two empty Adirondack chairs that had appeared on the beach. Who had put them there? Would they ever come back? Maybe the chairs were just out to enjoy the weather. Were they contemplating a swim?

It had all been silly, innocent fun that Justine and Lula had enjoyed. Then Justine had spotted a group of girls from the Academy on their way into town, and it had seemed to drain the light from the day. They had looked so engaging in their navy blue uniforms, so full of easy laughter and untroubled confidence. Just as Abby had when she was their age, not so very long ago.

For no reason she could think of her eyes drifted to the top of the water tower behind Papa's, where two dozen or more vultures sat watching the world, ready to strike. It made her feel deadened and queasy, as she was reminded of Ben in the tree with his crossbow. Telling Sallie Jo about him had been like smashing open a piñata to find all her happy memories infested with bugs and poisonous things. She had to try to put it behind her, close a door on the past, but even if she could she knew it would always find a way in.

That night they'd gone to Sallie Jo's for supper, and to her relief no mention had been made of Ben. Sallie Jo had only brought the subject up once since learning the truth, when she'd said that she didn't intend to keep asking about it, but if Justine wanted to talk again, at any time, she would always be there.

'She seems to have taken it much better than I'd expected,' Justine told Matt after updating him on the conversation she'd had with Sallie Jo.

'Then she's gone up even further in my estimation,' he responded. 'Luckily not everyone's as uncharitable or unforgiving as some of the people we've encountered this past year.'

Shuddering even to think of those occasions and how shockingly ready people could be to throw out judgement and blame – as if she and Matt didn't blame themselves enough already – Justine said, 'I tried calling you at the weekend, but there was no reply.' His failure to ring back right away had left her imagining him in that brutal visitors' hall with Ben, or perhaps he'd been somewhere with Hayley.

'I was at the prison for some of the time,' he told her. 'The rest I was at my mother's and I forgot to take my mobile. I guess I get so few calls these days that it's no longer the first thing I reach for when I leave the apartment.'

Knowing it would be the same for her if it weren't for Lula, she said, 'I don't suppose Simon and Gina were there?' Even saying their names was hard; picturing them, imagining what they were still going through, how wretchedly empty their lives must feel without Wes, was enough to make her want to cower away in a dark, punishing place that might in some bizarre, merciful way alleviate the other families' pain.

'No, they weren't, but apparently they're settling into their new place, which is only a couple of miles from Mum's. I think they feel the need to be close to her, and she wants it too.'

Justine could understand that. After such a life-changing tragedy they'd obviously turned to one another for comfort and support, which meant that for a while Matt had lost his mother and brother on top of everything else. He and Catherine saw each other regularly now, but Simon never joined them, and she knew how much Matt missed his brother. She didn't doubt that Simon missed Matt too, but how were they ever going to spend time together without thinking of why their lives had been so brutally torn apart? 'Rob mentioned in one of his emails,' she said, 'that Simon had applied for a job with the Hampshire force.'

'Yes, and he got it. He's due to start at the beginning of next month. Gina's getting involved in all sorts of volunteer work apparently, a lot of it with Mum.'

Gina had always put herself out to help others, so it was no surprise that she was trying to provide support for strangers in spite of being so much in need of it herself. Justine remembered how desperate she herself had felt over this past year to reach out to those in need, to share compassion and understanding, empathy and warmth, but no one would have wanted it from her. It was strange how giving comfort to others could provide a kind of comfort itself. 'I don't suppose,' she said, 'there's any news of Cheryl and Brad?' Thinking of Cheryl was sometimes almost as hard as thinking of Abby, mainly because Cheryl was still out there, but had never tried to be in touch. They'd been so close, and Cheryl had relied so heavily on their friendship for moral as well as emotional support. At the very worst time in her life, she'd been unable to turn to Justine, and that alone nearly broke Justine's heart. How fortunate, yet undeserving she was to have found a new friend in Sallie Jo. Had Cheryl been able to find someone else to help her to face the future? Were she and Brad still together? How supportive had he been during those darkest, most horrific of days?

'Not that Mum mentioned,' Matt was saying. 'I think they stayed in touch with Simon and Gina for a while, but I'm not sure if they've kept it up.'

'What about the others? Melanie, Maddy . . .?'

'All I can tell you is what you already know, that they left the vale soon after we did and no one's been back. The whole area is deserted, apparently. No one goes down there from the village; it's only the ghoulish type of tourists who make the trek and post selfies on line: *Guess where I am?* I saw on the news that someone actually tweeted a picture of himself with a crossbow.'

Justine's eyes closed as though to shut out the sick image. 'Why was it on the news?' she asked.

'Because of its bad taste. There's a lot going on about that sort of thing lately.'

This was why neither of them belonged to any of the social media sites. They really didn't need to know what the world at large, mostly people who'd never even met them, thought of them or would like to do to their son. 'Has anyone managed to sell their house?' she said.

'Not that I know of. No one wants to live there.'

Who would, now? Yet it was still difficult to think

of that beautiful, special place with its quaint cottages and leafy park, the humpback bridge and trickling brook, the thriving village nearby, the countryside all around, in an abandoned, overgrown state, and no longer able to provide happy memories for families who deserved them. Yet another consequence of Ben's actions: people couldn't get their money out of their properties. She and Matt were in the same boat, obviously, but Matt had earned very well over the years, and a large catering company from Bath hadn't wasted any time in snapping up Portovino, absorbing it seamlessly into their own booming business, keeping their clients and a lot of their stock, but losing the name.

'So when did you get back from your mother's?' she asked, needing to move her thoughts away from the vale.

'This morning, and when I saw you'd rung I immediately cleared my diary and rang you back.'

She smiled. 'So you had a lot on today?'

'Masses, but it can wait.'

Knowing he was teasing, that like her he was struggling to fill his days, she said, 'Are we going to talk more often now?'

'I think we should, at least once a month.'

Thrown, she said, 'I was hoping it might be more often than that.'

'It would be hard to build a new life if it were.'

He could be right, but surely he wanted to be in touch as much as she did? 'Are we talking about you or me building a new life?' she heard herself asking, more tersely than she'd intended.

'Both of us. It's not ideal like this, we recognise that . . . Apart from anything else I need to know about Lula, what she's doing, how she's growing . . . Will you send some pictures?'

'Of course.' She couldn't, wouldn't ask him to send pictures of Ben even if he could take them, which he probably couldn't. She didn't want them, not of how he was looking now with his crudely shaven head and brutal stubble, presuming he was still like that. Perhaps he was even more thuggish. Prison would do that to him, make him appear meaner, maybe even more sinister than he had in the press, when he'd looked like someone anyone would be terrified to meet in the dark.

Considering his actions, they'd be right to feel terrified at any time of day.

In a tone she didn't care too much for she said, 'Are you interested to know what I'm doing too?'

Without hesitation he said, 'Always.'

So what should she tell him? She tried to think, but her mind had gone blank. In the end, she said, 'It's very beautiful here right now. I can send some pictures of that too, if you like.'

'Yes please.'

She didn't understand why he wasn't reacting to her snippiness, or why she was finding this so difficult. What was making her angry, or upset, or whatever it was she was feeling? She guessed it was a lot of things, the frustration of not being together, the surprise that he hadn't called before now, that he seemed to be coping better than she was, although she had no idea if that were true. Perhaps it was her failure to ask about Ben that was making her edgy, guilty, annoyed with Matt when really it was her own cravenness she was finding intolerable.

In the end, because she knew he was waiting, she braced herself and said, 'Do you want to tell me about him?'

Sounding relieved, though cautious, he said, 'I guess that depends if you want to know.'

She didn't, and yet maybe she did, provided it was what she wanted to hear, such as remorse, cooperation with the authorities, a connection with humanity. 'How was he when you last saw him?' she ventured.

'About the same as the time before that. Cocky, surly, bored . . .'

So he hadn't changed. 'Bored with you, or with where he is?'

With a laugh he said, 'Probably both. I keep asking him why he sends me a visiting order if it's such a chore to see me, and he says he doesn't want to deprive me of the highlight of my week.'

She didn't smile. Her son's teasing was possibly even more grating than his arrogance.

'He was surprised,' Matt continued, 'and I think put out, when I told him this week that I wouldn't be able to make the next visit.'

'Why can't you make it?'

'I can, I just didn't want him to think that my whole life revolves around him.'

'Why not, when it does?'

'Not entirely. I'm going to start writing again.'

Her heart gave an unexpected lurch. Though she felt glad for him, obviously, for some reason thinking of him immersing himself in another world that didn't include her, or Ben, or any part of their appallingly wrecked lives felt absurdly like a betrayal. Perhaps she was jealous. Wouldn't she seize the same escape if it were open to her?

'I thought it would be best to do it under a pseudonym,' he was saying, 'but Hayley isn't convinced.'

'Oh? Why?' she asked stiffly.

'She thinks a lot of people will want to read my next book in case it turns out to be based on what happened.'

Justine felt herself turn hot. 'Well, it's good to think our son's heinous crime is such a useful marketing opportunity,' she snapped.

'I'm not using my name,' he told her darkly.

'But you are going to write, presumably to keep Hayley happy?' How could she be making an issue of this when there were so many more important matters to discuss? Perhaps this one was just easier.

'I'm doing it to stop myself going crazy,' he replied. 'Whether it will be publishable in the end we'll have to wait and see.'

'Have you started?'

'Not yet.'

'And *will* it be about Ben?'

'Good God no. Why on earth do you think I'd do that?'

She didn't, she just felt so thrown by her own reactions, so detached from him and the life he was living, that she was scrambling around trying to find some sort of steady ground.

'How is he really?' she made herself ask. 'Does he . . . Does he ever talk about me?'

'Not really. Sometimes he'll ask if I've heard from you, but when I tell him I haven't he changes the subject.'

Did it give him a sense of satisfaction to know that his parents weren't in touch? Was it what he'd hoped for, to create a rift in their marriage that would punish them for crimes they'd never even committed? 'Has he spoken to a psychiatrist yet?'

'Not as far as I know, but he probably wouldn't tell me if he had. To be honest, I've been worried about him lately. He puts on a big show of having everything sussed in there, no one messes with him, he's got his mates' backs and they've got his, and all that sort of crap, but I'm pretty sure a lot of it is front. I don't mean that he can't take care of himself, if you saw him you really wouldn't want to mess with him, but underneath it all I think he's struggling.'

'You'd have to hope that anyone in his position would be,' she commented tartly.

Passing over the remark, he said, 'I've spoken to someone on the Safer Custody Team, and they promised to look into it, but I haven't heard back yet.'

'So is it possible that this *struggle* might mean he's finally discovering some sort of conscience?'

'I'd like to think so, but there are reports coming out all the time about the problem of depression in prisons and I think he's going that way.'

It was hard to feel sorry for him, yet she couldn't feel glad to hear it either.

'. . . and the suicide rates are high.'

Suicide. The word dripped through her like ice. Was

that what she wanted for him? How could any mother want that for her son?

Not every mother had a son like hers.

'Overcrowding is one of the biggest causes,' Matt was saying, 'but there's a fuss now about this new ruling to stop prisoners' access to books. Actually, I considered lending my voice to the protest, but then I realised having me involved probably wouldn't do the campaign any good.'

She understood what he meant. Who would give a damn about McQuillan's Monster not having access to books?

'Anyway, I hear it's about to be resolved,' he added.

'So does Ben read?'

'I'm not sure. I don't think so.'

Unable to stop herself, she said, 'Nor does Abby . . . Or Wes, or Chantal, or Connor, or Neil.'

He fell silent.

'Do you ever think about Abby, Matt?'

'What kind of question's that? Of course I think about her. All the time.'

Close to tears, she said, 'I miss her so much. I don't know why, but it seems to be getting worse as time passes. I keep thinking of what she'd be doing now, how she'd have completed her world tour and be starting uni . . . She might even have a recording contract.'

'Justine . . .'

'Do you know what really breaks my heart? It's that she was good enough to make it, but now she'll never get to experience Glastonbury, or the O2, or Radio City . . . She'll never be in love, or have children . . .'

'Justine, don't do this to yourself.'

'Don't you do it to yourself? Don't you wonder what it would be like if we could go back, if none of it had happened . . .'

'Of course, but it did happen, and nothing's going to change that, so we have to try to move forward. It's why you're there, remember, and I'm here . . .'

'Please tell me how you being there is moving forward? You're stuck with him. You don't have a life any more because you can't go out. You've lost all your friends, apart from Hayley . . .'

'I told you I'm starting to write, that's me moving on with my life, and do you really want me just to turn my back on him? I thought you couldn't bear the idea of that.'

'I can't, but I can't stand us living apart either. It doesn't make any sense. We should be together.'

'Do you want to come back here, is that what you're saying? Remember, you left because there was no place in this country we could go where we wouldn't be recognised or . . .'

'Of course I remember, I'm just saying that it's still all about him, and Lula needs her daddy just as much as she needs me.'

'Don't you think I don't know that? It half kills me to think of her growing up without me. But we've had this conversation, many times, and this was the only solution we could come up with that we thought we could make work.'

'Well maybe we can't.'

'We haven't given it enough time. It's only been four months.'

'Almost five, but who's counting?'

Sighing, he said, 'OK, five, and not a single day has been easy, for either of us, and I don't know if that's going to change, but I do know that if we're going to fight like this when we speak then maybe we should go back to our original decision and not have any contact at all.'

Stunned, she cried, 'You don't mean that.'

His silence told her that maybe he did.

'What about Lula? I thought you wanted to know all about her?'

'Of course I do, but maybe knowing and not seeing, not being a part of it, is going to be too hard.'

'This is crazy!' she shouted. 'We're married. We love each other and we're parents to a little girl who needs us both. Why isn't that coming first for you, because it is for me?'

'You know the answer to that, so why are you asking?'

'Well maybe he doesn't count any more. He certainly doesn't deserve to.'

'It was feeling neglected and abandoned that got him to where he is now.'

'No! He's there because he's not like normal people, or none that we know. He grew up in a decent family, he had everything any child could wish for, and yet he doesn't function the way we do. He doesn't care about what he's done or whose lives he's destroyed. Other kids suffer from neglect, I mean serious neglect, they're properly abandoned, even violently abused, and they don't do what he did.'

It was a while before Matt said, 'OK, he's not like

everyone else, but he's still my son. You can wash your hands of him if you like, but whatever anyone says, whatever *he* says, I am not giving up on him yet. Now, can we please change the subject so we don't end this call still angry with each other?'

Wishing she had his ability to step away from the heat of her feelings, to compartmentalise and bring forth something irrelevant or important for another reason, she said, 'I can't agree that we should go back to our original decision. I want to speak to you. We need to have contact.'

'OK, well let's think it through some more and see how we feel in a week or two.'

A week or two? 'And in the meantime do you want me to email photographs, or will they be too hard to look at?'

When he didn't answer she felt wretched for deliberately trying to hurt him.

'I'll send them,' she said.

'Thank you.'

'I should go to pick her up now.'

'OK. Give her a big kiss from me.'

'But don't say it's from you?'

He didn't respond.

'I'm sorry,' she sighed. 'It's the strain of everything . . . It'll be better the next time we talk.'

'It will,' he promised.

Trying to take comfort from that, she rang off and decided to distract herself in the few spare minutes she had left by checking her emails.

As usual there were a couple from Sallie Jo, both work-related, one from day care about a proposed field trip at the end of the month, another from Gymboree advising her that the clothes she'd ordered for Lula were about to be shipped, and, to her surprise, there was one from her mother.

Scooping Daisy up for a cuddle, and feeling bad that she'd forgotten to ask Matt about Rosie, she opened the message and seeing it wasn't very long, she decided to read it straight away.

Hello dear, I thought I might have heard from you by now, as Rob tells me you've received the package I sent. Shall I assume you haven't opened it yet? Perhaps you have and you don't want to talk. It would be nice to hear from you one way or another.

I think about you and Lula all the time. I wonder if you've forgiven me yet for not being more supportive before you left. I hope the letters in the package will go some way towards explaining that, but I will understand if you feel they don't.

With my love to you

Mum (Or should I be saying Mom these days?☺)

Her mother ending a message with a smiley face was almost as startling as the email was intriguing. (*Letters*, plural? She'd sent more than one?)

She sat quietly for a moment, smoothing Daisy, trying to work out how she felt, what she should do.

In the end, she hit return and typed,

Dear Mom (sort of getting used to it!)

I'm sorry, I haven't opened the package yet. Things took an unexpected turn here recently so I've been quite distracted. I'm presuming from everything – reactions here to Grandma's name, your secrecy and now how anxious

you seem – that I need to be in a good place when I find
out what you're hiding. To be honest there are times when
I'm afraid I might never feel able to cope with anything
bad again. So how bad is it?

I guess the answer has to be very, or we wouldn't be
exchanging emails like this. Just tell me, is it something
I really need to know? Will it change my life for the better,
or worse? Will I be able to get over it?

Love Justine xxx

She was about to hit send when she decided to add a smiley face of her own, even though it probably wasn't appropriate. She just wanted her mother to know she was being friendly rather than challenging or overly defensive.

Later that night she was playing with Lula in the bath when her cellphone rang.

Suspecting it was Sallie Jo, while hoping it was Matt, she quickly dried her hands and padded through to the kitchen. To her surprise she saw it was her mother and for a moment she almost didn't click on.

'You asked how bad it is,' Camilla began with no preamble, 'and I'm not going to lie to you, it isn't good. However, I spent a long time thinking it over before I sent the package and I think you should read what your grandmother has to say. If you decide not to, all you have to do is send it back along with the keys.'

Justine's insides were starting to knot. There was a letter from her *grandmother? There were keys?*

'To the lake house,' her mother explained. 'In fact, if you want to keep them and go into the house without knowing your grandmother's story that's fine. I don't know what kind of condition it'll be in after all these years, if it's even safe . . .'

'Why did you never tell me you still owned it?'

'Because I couldn't. If I were to keep my promise to your grandmother I still wouldn't be telling you now, but I think, perhaps, it's something you need to know. It might . . . Well, it might help you. Of course I can't be sure about that, but I have a feeling, or at least I hope, it'll be good for you to know how and why your grandmother's life wasn't, in some ways, so different from your own.'

Justine flinched. 'Please don't tell me she had a son like Ben.'

'No, he wasn't anything like Ben, but she did have a son . . . I know I've never told you about him, but it was a part of my promise that I wouldn't. It's the way she dealt with him, the mistakes she made, that we all made . . . Well, I believe she'd do anything in her power to make sure you don't do the same, and I think you're in danger of it. So that's why I'm breaking my word by sending the letter. If you decide to read it and you want to talk some more, you know where I am. I'd fly over to read it with you if I weren't in the middle of a filming schedule.'

Not sure whether she'd welcome that or not, Justine said, 'Will it leave me in pieces, because I'm really not up for that?'

'The first thing to remember is that it's an old story that happened more than thirty years ago. Times were different then, although sadly I'm not sure how very different . . . It'll shock you in its way and it'll also make you sad, but more than that, I hope it'll make you realise that a parent is not always responsible for the way their child turns out.'

With those words still ringing in her ears Justine promised to call after she'd read the letter, and putting the phone down she went to take the package from a drawer. Though she was naturally intrigued, and even slightly nervous, she was aware of Lula splashing about in the bath, so now wasn't the time to open it. Perhaps it should wait till morning when Lula was at nursery; after all, if it upset her she wouldn't want Lula to see her cry. However, reading it tonight and losing herself in her grandmother's story would surely be better than lying in bed tearing herself apart over Matt and whether or not he was using this separation to start a new life with Hayley.

It was almost ten by the time Justine curled up in the rose-shaded light of a single lamp, a mug of tea on the nightstand beside her, and the bedroom door ajar in case Lula stirred. Propped up as she was against the pillows, she could see across the hall to where Daisy lay snuggled amongst a halo of soft toys with Lula lying in her usual position, on her side with her small hands cupped around her sweet little face.

Because they looked so cute she'd taken a photo before coming to bed, ready to send to Matt in the morning with an assortment of others.

She wondered what he was doing now.

Was he alone; awake; lost in a dream?

Since it was three in the morning with him, she guessed she could reasonably assume it was the latter.

It would be easier if she did.

What would never be easy was thinking of Ben and wondering what he was doing now. Lying in his prison cell dreaming of his crimes? Did they haunt him the way they haunted everyone else? Did he think about any of the bereaved families at all? Did he think about her? Did he hate her, miss her, long for her, the way she hated, missed and longed for him? Did their separation tear jaggedly into his heart? Maybe he was too busy fighting to survive in a place he was never going to escape to spare a thought for anyone else.

Would she ever see him again?

Stricken by the thought that she might not, while knowing she didn't want it at all, she pulled apart the top of the package where she'd already cut it and shook out the contents. This was the only way she was going to get him out of her mind tonight, to focus it on something else.

There were three envelopes; the smallest though sealed clearly contained keys, since it said so on the outside. The second, unsealed, had her name on the front in her mother's hand. On the back her mother had written: *Read your grandmother's letter first; I hope this one will help to answer some of the questions you're likely to have when you've finished. Remember, I'm at the end of the phone.* The third, the prize, the jewel of the package, had a raggedly broken seal, her mother's name and the address of where they'd first lived in London on the front and part of a return address on the back, *..st Shore Drive, Culver, In 46511.* Though the date mark was no longer legible, it was evident from the colour and texture of the paper that the letter was old.

For a brief moment as Justine peered inside she picked up the scent of roses, or perhaps it was oranges. Something sweet, anyway, and it seemed to be stirring a memory, or a sense of something familiar, though it was too vague, too ephemeral to grasp.

Wondering if her grandmother used to perfume her letters, as many women of her generation once did, she took care pulling the pages from the envelope, half afraid they were going to fall apart in her hand. However they were sturdy, thick, almost like blotting paper, with elegantly ruffed edges that had become crumpled, slightly torn with the passage of time.

To her surprise, when she unfolded the letter, she found the pages were numbered, not in the same ink her grandmother had used, so presumably her mother had done it later to keep them in order.

Six pages altogether, and both sides of each were full.

Turning to the first and holding it close to the lamp, she felt her breathing quieten as she started to read.

My dearest Camilla,

Thank you for your last letter and the photographs you kindly sent of the children. I do so miss them, and they are growing up very fast it seems, I feel I hardly know them any more. Justine twelve already, and Robert almost ten. What joy they must bring to you and dear Tom. It pleases me a lot to hear of how well things are working out for you all in London, it is a city that Daddy and I always enjoyed, though perhaps not as much as Paris. What a thrill to live in Europe, although for me the United States will always be home. I wonder if you think the same, or if, over time, you will become so anglicised you might forget your roots. I'm sure that will happen for the children, which I confess makes me sad.

I'm afraid, my dear girl, that this is going to be a very difficult letter for you to read, and it is no less difficult for me to write. It probably won't surprise you to learn that it is about your brother Phillip's problem — Daddy used to call it an affliction, but I prefer to say problem. As you know, it is something poor Phillip has battled for many years and finds very hard to control, though he tries with all his heart. He assures me it is not the way he wants to be, and I believe him, for I have held him many times as he's wept tears of terrible despair. He tells me he wishes he'd never been born because of the distress and heartache his problem has brought to me and Daddy.

To you too of course, because I know your love and loyalty to Phillip were severely tested at the time Daddy took his own life.

Justine stopped abruptly. Her grandfather had taken his own life? No mention had ever been made of that.

You told Phillip he was responsible, and Phillip agreed. He has never forgiven himself, indeed it has been very difficult for him to live with the guilt, and I in turn have found it equally hard to forgive. But he is my son and I still love him in spite of everything, for I know that he cannot help himself. I only wish I knew what I had done to make him the way he is. I ask myself all the time where I went wrong, how I could have done things differently; should I have sought medical advice? There are those who claim that people are born the way Phillip is, but Daddy and I never believed that, and even Phillip has always felt sure he would grow out of it eventually, or perhaps someone would find a cure.

Even after all these years I remain deeply troubled by Daddy's decision to leave us the way he did when it is against everything we believe – and yet I now find myself facing the same end.

Justine flinched, and her eyes flicked back over the last sentence, needing to be sure she'd read it correctly. Her heart thudded with the shock. How terrible it must have been for her mother to run into her own mother's intentions like that, so unexpected and yet so obviously sincere. How panicked she must have felt, and afraid to read on. Unless she'd had some sort of forewarning, but there was nothing to suggest that she had.

With heightened and unsteady feelings she now understood what kind of letter she was reading, but made herself continue.

Phillip has confessed to me that being where we are, close to the Academy in Culver, is insufferable for him, but he is afraid to leave and try to make a life on his own. I admit I am fearful of this too, because if people find out the truth about him it will make him very vulnerable and the object of much scorn and abuse, even hatred. The revulsion his problem gener- ates is, alas, widespread and even understandable, as it goes against everything the Bible has taught us. He has talked of moving to a community where there are more people like him. I reminded him that if he does this he will be committing himself to a life of sin, and there will be no hope at all of a recovery or a life everlasting.

The only answer I could propose was that we should sell the cottage and move back to Pennsylvania, but he would not hear of me giving up my cherished home. I should have insisted, I realise that now; after all, he had warned me that this place was presenting a devilish temptation for him. It wasn't that I ignored it, but the only action I could see to take was to pray every day, many times a day, for his deliverance from this sinful obsession. He joined me in the prayers, as did Father Dominic, whom you might remember. He has always been very kind to Phillip in a way one might not expect of a priest, but I can't help feeling that his kindness was sometimes undermined by the frequency with which he directed us to Leviticus 18: 22–23 and 20: 13. Was it a threat? It was how it felt.

Though Justine had a fair idea what the Bible passages referred to, she put the letter aside for a moment and climbed the stairs to where she was sure she'd spotted a New American Bible just after they'd moved in. Sure enough there was one tucked between a copy of *The Freedom of Forgiveness* and Billy Graham's *Hope for Each Day*. Taking it back to the bedroom she paged through to Leviticus, and felt instantly appalled by the damning words: Leviticus 18: 22: 'You shall not lie with a male as one lies with a female; it is an abomination.' Leviticus 20: 13 : 'If there is a man who lies with a male as those who lie with a woman, both of them have committed a detestable act; they shall surely be put to death.'

Having no desire to read the words again, she closed the Bible and pushed it under the bed before returning to the letter.

It isn't easy for either of us to read these Bible passages, mainly because they leave Phillip with the greatest burden of shame. I believe that is Father Dominic's intention, as if shame in itself might provide a transformation, even a cure. For my part the guilt of knowing that I have not been able to help my son, that I have maybe in some way made his situation worse by trying so hard to protect him, grows with each day.

As you know, it was the police discovering Phillip with a young man many years ago that drove Daddy to do what he did. Had we been able to keep it a private matter things might have turned out differently, but the act was still illegal then, and no amount of Daddy's influence could prevent a prosecution. It was, and remains, a miracle that Phillip was not committed to an institution for psychopathic offenders, because that was the punishment back then for men with his problem. Today things have changed, men like him are no longer officially viewed as a criminal or deviant in the eyes of the law, but they are in the eyes of many, and of God. This of course does not in any way change how much I love my son, it simply makes me feel more helpless than ever to guide him.

And now I have no power at all.

I'm sorry to break it to you this way, dear Camilla, but we received confirmation last week that your brother has contracted the deadly HIV virus which has already developed into full-blown Aids. I ask myself, is this punishment for the sins he's committed? I fear that it is.

A few days ago I received a visit from the Principal of the Academy here in Culver. He was polite, as you would expect, but he didn't hold back on lecturing me about the dreadful disease that everyone is talking about and how it is threatening to run rampant around the world and so must at all costs be stamped out. I agreed, of course, how could I not? I daresay if Daddy hadn't been an alumnus of the school, and hadn't made such generous donations in the past, things might have gone differently. As it was, I was told that no charges would be brought provided the boy Phillip had apparently corrupted tested clear of the virus and Phillip moved away from the area.

I'm afraid I didn't have the courage at the time to admit to Phillip's diagnosis, but of course I have now, in a letter that I've already sent.

I have spent the time since then putting my papers in order and doing what I can to ensure as few diffi-culties as possible will remain when I have gone. I have already written to the authorities explaining my actions, and to Father Dominic asking him to pray for my and Phillip's souls. I realise I am committing yet another sin in the eyes of the Lord, and for this I am likely to suffer in hell, but I find that following Daddy at this time is meaning more to me than my eternal salvation. Wherever he is I shall go too, and in so doing I shall spare my son the suffering of a terrible, drawn-out death.

It is my intention to end our lives in the boathouse, and for the entire structure to be destroyed as soon as possible thereafter. I have left instructions for this in my letter to the authorities, with a further letter to my lawyers to make sure it happens. The cottage and everything else I own will pass to you, my dearest daughter. You must decide whether or not it should stay in the family. I admit it gives me some pleasure in these final troubled hours to think that one day, a long way in the future, Justine and Robert might enjoy it again, perhaps with children of their own. An old lady's fancy, but perhaps I am allowed one or two at the end.

To make it possible for them to enjoy it you must not tell them anything of what I am about to do. I want to feel your promise connecting us when I am on the other side, so please make it, Camilla, in your heart, deeply and truly so that it reaches me. There is no need for them to know of their uncle's shame, or my own for having failed him. I would like very much for you to close your own mind to this brief and unfortunate episode, so that all you allow yourself to remember are the many happy times we spent here in Culver, you as a teenager so leggy and wilful, like Daddy in many ways, but perhaps a little like me too.

As I sit here at my bureau, with the lake shimmering in the sunlight, I feel I can see you waving from Daddy's boat, dancing along the jetty, diving in for a swim. Do you remember how we loved to work on the garden together? You were always so knowledgeable about plants, I used to wonder where you got it from. I still have your first spade around here somewhere, the one with the red and blue handle that got broken one year when we replanted the Christmas tree. Daddy repaired it for you, but it was never strong enough to use again.

Funny the things that keep coming to mind, like the boy a few doors along, was his name Derek, who used to swim past our jetty and pretend he was drowning so we'd have to go and rescue him. He so loved to visit with us, didn't he? I remember my own mother coming here for the first time and telling us we were decadent to spend so much money on a summer house, but could she come every year? She did, until she died a few years later. You were too young to remember her, and I fear it's going to be the same for Justine and Robert. It is unlikely they will remember me.

Perhaps that is why I would so very much like the cottage to be kept for them. It will be a small part of their childhoods, returned to them with a great deal of love from their grandma.

It is, of course, your decision, Camilla. I will no longer be here to argue or approve of what you decide and I am sure Tom will want to have a say. Please know that if things work out the way I am planning there will be nothing in the cottage, or the grounds, to associate with my actions. No ghoulish reminders, or inappropriate shrines.

One of my greatest sadnesses today is that I am leaving you without having yet visited you in London. I know you understand why it has been difficult for me to come, as I didn't feel able to leave Phillip on his own once he'd moved up from Pennsylvania. Just as I understand why you stopped the children from coming here. I truly don't believe he'd ever have hurt them, you must surely remember how sensitive and caring he is, there is just this side to his nature that has ended up ruining all our lives.

I will wish you goodnight now, my dearest, and at the same time I ask you to try to remember how much you loved your brother as you were growing up. Try from now on to think of him in only that way. The lawyers will take care of our funeral arrangements so there will be no need for you to come to Culver if you would prefer not to. As I have no idea how much attention or scandal will attach itself to my actions, I have relieved Father Dominic of the problem of how to deal with our burials by requesting cremations. Another way of displeasing the Church, but I believe in my heart that God is all-seeing, all-powerful and all-forgiving.

I know you claim no longer to be a believer but I would ask you anyway to pray for me and for Phillip, as I, when I go to communion tomorrow, will make my final prayers inside a church for you, Tom and my wonderful grandchildren, Justine and Robert.

God bless you all

Your devoted mother
May

Justine's eyes closed as her heart filled with so much anguish and sorrow that tears ran down her cheeks.

Her grandmother had taken her own life and her son's because of bigotry and Aids.

Suddenly catching the sweet scent of flowers again she felt it softening the tension inside her, like a soothing hand, and opened her eyes. She was trying to imagine how her grandmother must have felt in those final days, and hours. It must have taken so much courage to do what she had, but at the same time she must have been very afraid. Everything was against her religion, the homosexuality, her husband's suicide and then her own. The killing of her own son to save him from a horrible death . . .

She had to presume that her grandmother had carried through her plans or she wouldn't be reading this letter now, or finding out about her uncle for the first time. She had no recollection of him; maybe her mother had insisted from the time she and Rob were born that Phillip was not to come anywhere near them. Her mother should have known better, and almost certainly did now, but there had been so much ignorance and prejudice back then, not to mention panic about the spread of this new and deadly disease.

Reaching for her mother's letter, she slipped it out of the envelope and held it to the light. It was true, she had many questions after reading her grandmother's last words, and she was more than ready to hear some answers.

Dearest Justine,

If you're reading this I'm going to presume you've come to the end of the last letter I ever received from my mother. It's been many years since I read it myself, and doing so recently has disturbed me in just as many ways, actually more, than it did back then.

We have all done things of which we are ashamed; where I differ from you and your grandmother is that I had a choice. I needn't have turned my back on my brother, but I did, and I will never forgive myself for that. I should have stood by him, and not added so cruelly to his pain after our father died. I should have stood by my mother too, and not encouraged your father to move us to London. Don't get me wrong, it was an excellent position and he wanted to take it, but for the right reasons, not for those I now admit to with such bitter regret.

Most importantly of all, what I want to say to you is that the shame you feel about Ben and that my mother felt about Phillip has no place in your hearts. She couldn't help the way Phillip was any more than you can help the way Ben is. You have no reason to feel any guilt either; it wasn't you who killed those children, and nothing you did drove Ben to it. Whatever he did is in his character, or the chemical make-up of his brain, not his upbringing.

Though I realise Ben's crime was very different to Phillip's, that the two can't even be compared, I think it's important for you to realise that you are in danger of going the same way as your grandmother. No, I don't think you're about to commit a murder, suicide, but I am sometimes afraid that only Lula, and a prison sentence, is saving you from that.

I understand that as Ben's mother you needed to get away; it wasn't possible for you to carry on living here in this country without everyone knowing who you were, and though not everyone blamed you, it's true that some did. It's all too easy for people to have opinions about those they don't know, have never met and are not even likely to meet; in my own small way I get it all the time. In your case I could see how difficult it was becoming, and I now deeply regret not helping you more. My only excuse is that I was so shocked, and then afraid when you decided to go to Culver, that I couldn't make myself think straight. I felt I had somehow to dissuade you from going; your grandmother had been very clear, she didn't want you or Rob to find out what she'd done, or know anything about Phillip. Yet, perversely, she dearly wanted you to have the house. It was in trying to reconcile these contradictory wishes that I went about everything in completely the wrong way with you when you decided to make Culver your home. I know I upset you, and of course I confused you very much indeed. This was most definitely not what you needed at such a difficult time in your life, and I can hardly begin to tell you how sorry I am.

I know you will have many questions going round in your head now, such as why did I keep the house and never visit? Why didn't I offer it to you when you decided to go to Culver? You might even want to know how your grandmother committed her final act.

Of course I wasn't there, but when we speak I can tell you what I was told and I've never had any reason to doubt it.

If you go to the cottage you will see that the boat-house has gone. I believe it was burned to the ground, but again I can only report what I was told. Your father and I didn't fly over for the funerals; this is another of my many regrets. I often think if I hadn't turned my back on her she might not have done what she did, although I remind myself too that there was no cure for Aids at the time Phillip was diagnosed, so perhaps there really wasn't anything I could do.

I know you've more or less turned your back on Ben, and of course no one can blame you for that. However, I implore you to let go of the guilt and shame you are feeling and start living again. As I've already said, it doesn't belong in your heart any more than it belonged in your grandmother's. You need to take your life back for your own sake and for Matt's. I say Matt and not Lula, because I think he needs you even more than she does right now. The decision you took to separate so you could give Lula a life was understandable, but wrong. I heard someone say recently that the experience of trauma has many far-reaching effects, and we certainly know that is true for us. You should not be allowing Ben to break up your family; he's caused enough damage already, you simply can't make it possible for him to cause more. If you do you'll forever be hanging on to your misplaced guilt and shame as a reason for why you can't have a full and worthwhile existence. You're punishing yourselves, both of you, for a crime not of

312

*your doing or making, and believe me no good will
ever come of that.*

*So, Justine, please listen to your grandma, because
I believe in her way she is talking to you now, through
me, through her letter, and through the feelings that
drew you to Culver. She doesn't want you to suffer
for something that you never had the power to control,
the way that she did.*

Call me when you're ready.

With my love

Mum

Keeping hold of the letter, Justine lay back against
the pillows and turned out the light. Her grandmother
and mother had left her with much to consider, and
already her mind was trying to sort through it all, to
make sense of why things happened the way they
did, or in some instances didn't happen at all. *I heard
someone say recently that the experience of trauma has
many far-reaching effects, and we certainly know that is
true for us.*

It would go on and on, Justine was in no doubt
about that. How could it not, when Ben's crime had
affected so many? She didn't have it in her heart to
forgive him, in spite of knowing that somewhere deep
inside she still loved him. Nor did she feel that her
forgiveness would carry any great significance; how
could it when it would be a mere drop in the ocean
of what was required?

She was tempted to call her mother now, if only to
thank her for showing an understanding and love
that Justine had never really credited her with before.

It just went to show how hard it was to really know someone, and how easy it was to get it wrong.

Aware of how tired she suddenly felt, she gathered up the letters and put them on the nightstand along with the keys. If she dreamt about anything tonight she'd like it to be something beautiful and simple, such as Lula and Daisy, the sun on the lake, the whispering fall of leaves from the trees. There would be time tomorrow to think about Ben and Matt, her grandma and uncle, and what else she might yet find inside the lake house.

Chapter Fourteen

Culver, Indiana

'Are you sure you're ready for this?' Sallie Jo asked warily.

Justine was gazing through the chain-link fence to where the gabled rooftops of her grandmother's mansion of a cottage were nestling amongst a canopy of bright coppery trees. There was no movement, no signs of life apart from the darting scurry of a squirrel crossing a power line, and the occasional drift of leaves as they meandered to the lawns below. From their neatness and the piles of fall debris stacked on the roadside, it was clear that the gardener had been since their last visit.

She was about to answer when she spotted the remains of a tree house in the outstretched limbs of a giant maple. She wondered if she was really remembering climbing the slats nailed into the trunk, or just wanting to remember it.

Finally responding to Sallie Jo's question, she said, 'Yes, definitely,' and holding on to Daisy she pushed open the car door. Though it was sunny and crystal-clear the temperature had plummeted overnight, and even now, in the middle of the day, it was struggling to make it past two degrees.

Reaching the padlocked gate she tried both the keys, but neither of them fitted.

Apparently amused, Sallie Jo said, 'Then I guess we're climbing this here fence,' and waiting for a passing car to disappear in the direction of the woodcraft and Academies, she slotted a foot into the chain-link, swung a leg over the sagging top and dropped nimbly down to the other side.

Handing Daisy over, Justine followed suit, wondering if anyone could see them from the neighbouring houses. Though both were a good twenty or thirty yards away, the change of season was offering brief glimpses through the trees of glinting windowpanes and red-brick chimneys. However, she felt confident that their unconventional entrance had most likely gone undetected.

Following Sallie Jo and Daisy along the cracked and uneven footpath, she caught herself thinking of Cheryl and how exciting she'd have found this peculiar adventure. Abby would have loved it too, and Chantal. Probably her mother would have liked to be here, but from their brief chat on the phone this morning she knew that much as Camilla might wish it otherwise, there was no real chance of her getting away until just before Christmas.

'I'd like to come then, if I may,' Camilla had added, managing to sound uncharacteristically humble, for her. She was worried, Justine realised, about how harshly she was being judged over the treatment of her brother. However, it hadn't been the time to discuss it, with Camilla on location and cameras likely to roll at any second. So deciding to put her mind at rest, at least for the time being, Justine said, 'Of course, we'd love that,' and she'd meant it. 'Will you fly out with Rob and Maggie?'

'I'll have to check when they're coming, but it would be nice if I could. When do you think you'll go to the cottage?'

'Today. Sallie Jo's coming with me.'

'That's good of Sallie Jo. I can't vouch for how safe it is after all these years, so you shouldn't go alone.'

'Would you rather I waited until you came?'

There was a moment before her mother said, 'You have the keys, it's as much your place to explore as mine, and I have a feeling Sallie Jo might expire with frustration if you told her you're not going in yet. Has she read the letters?'

She hadn't then, but Justine had given them to her when she'd arrived earlier, so she knew as much as Justine now, and was clearly every bit as intrigued about what they might find – though Justine was perhaps a tad more apprehensive.

Descending a set of crooked steps at the side of the house, where Daisy was sniffing around an abandoned bistro-style chair barely visible amongst a small forest of brambles, Justine almost collided with Sallie Jo as she stepped on to a ruined patio. It ran the entire length of the house and had apparently once been sheltered by some sort of wooden structure, the remains of which now lay rotting amongst the weeds and nettles pushing their way up through the old slabs of stone. The view of the lake spreading widely into the distance was exquisitely uninterrupted, due to how carefully the sloping gardens had been tended right up to the edge of the patio, where everything suddenly fell into disrepair. She saw no sign of a pier belonging to the property, nor of any other structure that could once have been a boathouse.

Turning back to the once stately old residence, whose formerly whitewashed walls and coal-black paintwork were almost lost behind a rampant ivy, she could only wonder why the gardener didn't clear the ragged clamour of briars and scrub that assailed the place with such vigour. It could only be because he'd received instructions not to go near the house.

Or maybe someone had told him it was haunted and he was afraid of disturbing the occupants.

With that cheering thought she used her phone to take shots of the exterior, careful to include the striking contrast between the forlorn-looking property and immaculate gardens. It was like coming across a once dignified old lady gazing nostalgically upon a shining array of young girl's clothes.

Following Sallie Jo past four lofty windows, all firmly shuttered from within, to a centrally placed set of double doors with rusted hinges and handles, she took out the keys again.

'Do you think these doors are going to fall apart when we open them?' she asked, struggling with the lock. 'We should have brought some WD-40.' Withdrawing the key to slot in the other, she started as Daisy gave a sudden yelp. The door was tipping towards them.

Managing to catch it, Sallie Jo said wryly, 'Well I guess you've got your answer to that.'

Slightly shaken, Justine stepped out from under it. 'Amazing that the wind's never taken it down, with it being so fragile,' she remarked.

After carefully leaning both doors sideways against the frame, Justine stepped cautiously into the dark, mouldering interior, just able to make out two weather-stained walls either side of her that opened out after a few steps to form a large, dome-ceilinged circle. There were doors all the way round the entrance hall and a very grand, exquisitely carved oak staircase was still struggling to look proud of its sweeping rise to the upper floors. Hearing something crunch underfoot as she moved forward, she looked down. Guessing much of the debris mixed with old leaves and ragged particles of carpet was made up of mouse droppings and perhaps even decayed animal bones, she glanced at Sallie Jo, pulled a face and inched on.

'Anything coming back to you?' Sallie Jo joked as Justine craned her neck to look up at the shadowy landing.

'Let's just say it's not happening yet,' Justine responded. 'Do you think it's safe to go up there?'

'Don't you want to look down here first?' As she asked, Sallie Jo pushed open a door to the right, went to go in and suddenly shrieked. 'I think it was a rat,' she gasped as Daisy shot past in hot pursuit.

Not doubting this was the long-term residence of all sorts of rodents, bugs, birds, maybe even snakes, Justine crossed to the door and peered warily into the room. Apart from Daisy sniffing at the scratched and rotting skirting boards there was no sign or sound of anything moving. 'We should have brought a torch,' she whispered.

'If we can get the shutters open, we'll be able to see,' Sallie Jo pointed out, and bravely striking forth she went to draw back the heavy drapes.

Minutes later, still fanning away clouds of silvery dust and picking off strings of clinging cobwebs, they were standing in a dazzling stream of sunlight, gazing around the spacious room. In spite of its shapeless mounds of covered furniture, mildewed wallpaper and crumbling cornices, its former grandeur was crying out to be recognised.

'Wow,' Sallie Jo murmured, taking it all in. 'This is one of the best examples of an early lake cottage I've ever come across.'

Justine was watching Daisy nosing around the hems of a dust sheet that clearly covered a sofa. 'You don't think anyone's still sitting there, do you?' she murmured drily.

Sallie Jo laughed. 'Actually, that might not be funny,' she decided. 'Oh my God, will you just look at that fireplace? I swear the only time I've seen anything like it was in a chateau in France. All that beautiful white marble and filigree work. The cherubs, the flowers and mouldings. I bet they had it shipped, or specially made?'

Deciding it was ostentatious enough to create a new level of style and elegance, Justine was about to go for a closer inspection when she caught the sweet scent of oranges. She turned, half wondering if she might find someone behind her. 'Can you smell it?' she asked Sallie Jo.

'Smell what?' Sallie Jo inhaled deeply and said, 'Yes, I can. It's like . . . Roses?'

'Oranges?'

'Maybe that. Where's it coming from?'

Undecided, Justine moved towards the window, as if following the scent, but it had disappeared.

'Daisy, what are you doing, honey?' Sallie Jo laughed.

Looking down to where Daisy was growling as she tugged at the corner of a dust sheet, Justine said, 'I hope she hasn't found the rat. Daisy, let go.'

But Daisy was on a mission and before Justine could stop her she'd dragged the linen cover to the ground, sending up a billowing cloud of dust – and in its midst, almost like an apparition, was an ornate lady's writing desk.

Justine almost gasped. 'Oh my God, this must be where my grandmother was sitting when she wrote to my mother,' she said, looking out at the lake. She felt sure she was picking up the sweet scent again, but could find no obvious source for it as she pulled open the drawers of the desk in search of stationery or perhaps some sort of pot pourri.

What she did find, however, was a handful of silver-framed photographs, the first of which showed a sharp-featured young man with slick fair hair and vaguely haunted dark eyes. She showed it to Sallie Jo as she came to look over her shoulder.

'Do you think that's Phillip?' Sallie Jo murmured.

'I'm guessing so,' Justine responded, noting his resemblance to her mother.

'He sure was handsome. How old would you say he is there?'

'Early twenties, maybe.'

Wondering what was going through his mind as he sat for the photo, how many fears and demons he was trying to hide, how much prejudice and misunderstanding he'd already suffered, she moved on to the next, and felt her heart give a sudden and painful lurch. 'This is definitely my mother,' she said hoarsely. 'I hadn't realised until now just how much Abby resembled her.'

'She's beautiful,' Sallie Jo remarked softly. 'Like a young Grace Kelly.'

Justine couldn't help but smile to think of how her mother would glow with pleasure at the flattering comparison.

Tearing her gaze from the face that was so like Abby's, she moved on to the next and gave a little laugh. 'This is me in a boat with Rob and . . . Oh my God, it's my father. Proof we were once here. I can't be much more than five, which would make Rob three. He's so cute, isn't he?'

'You both are.'

Thrilled that her grandma had kept a picture of her and Rob close by, Justine turned to the next photograph and felt herself melting with affection. 'Her wedding photo,' she said softly. 'Doesn't she look beautiful? Don't you just love her dress?'

'Your grandpa is very like Phillip,' Sallie Jo commented, and returning to the moody-looking young man in the first photo she held the two pictures side by side.

Justine wasn't going to say so, but she was sure she knew what Sallie Jo was thinking – of the two her grandfather looked the more effeminate, which made her wonder if it was his own suppressed sexuality that had caused him to find his son's proclivities so frightening and abhorrent.

She guessed they would never know – unless, of course, there was a diary waiting to be found.

Discovering in another drawer a small album filled with shots of her and Rob during their summers here, she wondered if she could take it away with her, but for some reason it seemed important for everything to stay as it was, at least until a decision had been reached on what they were going to do with the house.

'I wonder what happened to the paintings,' Sallie Jo pondered as she gazed around the walls. 'You can see where they were hanging . . . You don't guess someone has taken them?'

Justine had no idea.

'Maybe they're in storage,' Sallie Jo suggested.

Justine was about to return to the writing desk when the sound of something moving about upstairs made her stop.

She looked at Sallie Jo.

Sallie Jo looked back. 'Birds,' she decided.

Agreeing, Justine carried on riffling through the desk, finding more small albums, a bundle of letters tied with a blue ribbon that turned out to be from her mother, an assortment of pens and pencils, a dried-up bottle of ink and a small tin of breath-freshening mints.

By now Sallie Jo had moved across the hall and was

calling for her to come look at the amazing seventies kitchen.

Justine was on her way and already starting to smile at the vivid apple-green units and flowered wallpaper, when another sound from upstairs caused her to stop.

'Did you hear that?' she whispered to Sallie Jo.

Sallie Jo nodded.

Deciding once again that it had to be birds, she was about to move on when Daisy suddenly shot up the stairs.

'Daisy, come back,' Justine shouted after her.

Daisy wasn't listening; she was already charging up a second flight and quickly disappeared from view.

Sallie Jo came to join her and together they gazed up at the landing.

Telling herself that no one was up there, so there was no one to hear her, or to harm her precious little dog, Justine shouted, 'Treat,' while knowing it was next to useless, since Daisy had never been much interested in snacks.

Suddenly Daisy started to bark, but from a further distance than Justine might have expected, suggesting she'd gone into a top-floor room.

'I wonder what she's found,' Sallie Jo murmured.

Reining in her imagination, Justine waited for the barking to stop so she could call again, but it didn't seem it was going to happen any time soon.

Glancing at Sallie Jo in dismay, she said, 'I think we'll have to go and get her.'

Sallie Jo didn't disagree; however, neither of them moved.

'The stairs look quite sturdy,' Justine observed,

'provided we tread carefully . . .' Daisy suddenly stopped barking, but only long enough for Justine to call for her to come before starting again with renewed vigour.

Seriously glad she wasn't alone, Justine started towards the stairs.

'What are we going to do if someone's up there?' Sallie Jo whispered from behind her.

Justine's heart thudded. She had no idea. 'Let's just tell ourselves it's a trapped bird,' she suggested, and after carefully testing the first step with most of her weight, she started to climb.

Staying close, Sallie Jo called out to Daisy again, but the dog was clearly deafened by her own noise.

As they reached the first landing the barking suddenly stopped again. This time it didn't resume, nor did Daisy come when both women shouted out to her.

Not sure she had the nerve to go any further, Justine turned to Sallie Jo.

'We could wait it out,' Sallie Jo suggested. 'She'll have to come sooner or later.'

Thinking that might be the best course of action, Justine looked up to the next landing and to her surprise, and relief, she spotted Daisy watching them through the stair rails. 'Good girl,' she cooed. 'Come on down now.'

Daisy simply wagged her tail and trotted back to wherever she'd come from.

As the barking started again Justine braced herself, and attempted the next flight. The treads here were much more decayed, and the banister didn't feel stable either. Cautioning Sallie Jo not to lean on it, she kept tight to the wall as she rounded a curve, and not wanting to think about what might happen if they had to run she finally reached the top landing.

A moment later Sallie Jo was with her.

'She's in there,' Justine whispered, pointing to a partly open door only feet away.

Sallie Jo glanced down at the hall below.

Justine did the same and immediately wished she hadn't. It was a very long way to fall.

Accepting that it was her dog so she had to continue to go first, Justine bolstered herself with brisk strides towards the door, pushed it open and immediately screamed as something hit her face.

'Jesus Christ,' Sallie Jo muttered, quickly ducking out of the way. 'Bats! Ugh!'

Though Justine wasn't at all keen on them herself, she had no problem deciding they were better than many alternatives, and wrapping her coat around her head she ventured further into the room.

To her amazement she caught the sweet scent again, but so briefly she might have imagined it. 'Daisy, naughty girl,' she scolded, going to scoop her up.

'There must be a bat stuck behind these . . . *paintings*,' Sallie Jo declared with widening eyes. 'So they are still here,' and going to break open the shutters to let in some light and flapping her hands to shoo away the bats, she began helping Justine to haul off the heavy canvas. They knelt down to examine their find.

The first garishly ornate frames contained mainly portraits, they discovered, with small brass plaques saying who they were and when the likeness was done.

William Benson 1924; Matilda Benson 1926; Alexander Cantrell 1901; Edward Rossiter 1899; Emily Cantrell 1930.

'It's looking to me like you've got half your family tree here,' Sallie Jo commented delightedly. 'Do you recognise the names? Cantrell obviously . . .'

'I think Benson might have been my grandma's maiden name,' Justine said, slightly awed by the unexpected find.

'Oh wow, look at these,' Sallie Jo murmured, arriving at the landscapes. After a while she slowed to a halt, and sat back on her heels. 'I don't believe what I'm seeing here,' she stated incredulously. 'I mean, it can't be . . .'

Justine was barely listening. Her mind had suddenly flooded with images of the paintings Ben and Abby used to bring home from school. Abby's were invariably better. Had Ben sensed her preference?

'Look at them,' Sallie Jo urged. 'I don't recognise a single one, but the style, the feathery brushstrokes . . .'

Justine blinked as she focused on a hazy landscape in various shades of blues and yellows.

'This is full-blown Impressionism,' Sallie Jo informed her, 'and the quality, the workmanship . . .'

'I had no idea you knew about art,' Justine commented.

'I majored in it,' Sallie Jo told her, still rapt as she continued a careful study of each picture. 'Where did you say your grandparents were from?'

'New Hope, Pennsylvania.'

Sallie Jo's eyes widened in shock. 'You're kidding me,' she accused.

Justine laughed. 'Why would I?'

Sallie Jo didn't answer; she was gazing at the paintings again.

'Look, there's something written on the back of this one,' Justine pointed out.

Turning it so she could see, Sallie Jo read aloud, *'To William and May, great friends, Daniel . . .* Oh my God, *oh my God!'*

'Who's Daniel Garber?' Justine demanded, checking the name.

'Who is he?' Sallie Jo cried. 'Only one of the most famous of the Pennsylvania Impressionists. This is unbelievable. I just can't . . . Look at this one, it's signed to your grandparents again, this time from *JFF.* Holy . . . I think I'm going to faint.'

'JFF?'

'John Fulton Folinsbee.'

'Is he famous too?' Justine said incredulously. Was she imagining things, or was she really getting flashbacks of these paintings hanging on walls, bright and colourful, each one being described by someone she couldn't quite see?

It felt real, almost as though it was happening now, and then it was gone.

Sallie Jo was reading from the back of the next framed masterpiece, this one of a barn in the fall. *'Dear Will and May, splendid times, with love, Fern Coppedge.'* She looked at Justine. *'Spring on the Delaware* is one of her most famous works and one of my absolute favourites,' she told her.

'Is that it?' Justine asked.

Sallie Jo shook her head. 'I've never seen this one

before,' she admitted, and carried on through the collection, looking more now at the backs of the paintings than at the artworks themselves. Each name seemed to mean something to her. 'Roy Cleveland Nuse,' she murmured, 'Edward Willis Redfield – this is a *serious* find, because he burned a lot of his paintings . . . Daniel Garber again, George Sotter, Walter Baum . . . They're not all signed to William and May, so I'm guessing the other recipients are your great-grandparents, or even great-great-grandparents.' She sat back again, so flushed with awe and excitement that a layer of sweat had broken out on her forehead. 'I can't say this for certain,' she declared, 'but I reckon some of these paintings aren't even known about. It could be they were commissioned by members of your family and that's where they've stayed, in the family. Shit, Justine, this is blowing my mind.'

Seeing that quite clearly, and feeling slightly dazed herself, Justine forced herself to admit that she'd never heard of the Pennsylvania Impressionists before.

'I can give you plenty of stuff to read,' Sallie Jo told her, 'but they're mainly landscape artists from the turn of the last century through the fifties, even sixties. It seems likely your family knew a fair few of them, and if I'm right about this, and they do turn out to be genuine, I don't even want to guess at what this collection could be worth.'

Justine wasn't sure what to say.

'The Redfield alone could fetch something in the region of half a million dollars, maybe more,' Sallie Jo told her.

Stunned, Justine looked at the paintings stacked in

a closely packed row against a large French armoire that might have been put there to protect them from the damp brick wall. In the end she said, 'What are we going to do with them, if they're as valuable as you say?'

Sallie Jo was ready with the answer. 'First up, we have to get them looked at by an expert. I think I can . . .'

'But what about right now? Do we just leave them here?'

Though clearly not happy about it, Sallie Jo threw out her hands. 'What choice do we have? No way can we carry them down those stairs, and if they've been here for the past thirty years . . . Do you think your mother knows about them?'

'I've no idea. She's never mentioned them, but someone obviously arranged for them to be taken off the walls and stored up here.' Taking out her phone, she quickly tapped in a text. *Do you know anything about Pennsylvania Impressionists?*

Since it was almost time to pick up the children, they carefully re-covered the paintings with the canvas and were already downstairs, with Daisy, by the time a reply came back from Camilla.

Just that my grandparents, and various other members of the family were patrons for a while. Why?

Have found possible mega collection in the cottage. Did you know they were here?

No, I thought they were all sold when my mother moved from New Hope. I think they're quite valuable now.

That's what Sallie Jo says. She's an art major BTW.

We need to discuss. Will call as soon as I can.

330

Putting her phone away Justine checked the time, and went to join Sallie Jo at the front door. As she got there Sallie Jo put out an arm to stop her going any further.

Curious and startled, Justine looked in the direction she was indicating and to her amazement and alarm she saw a man standing at the shore of the lake, his back to them. They had no way of telling who he was, or how he'd got there, and they were none the wiser when he turned around and started ambling towards them.

'Do you think we should run?' Sallie Jo muttered.

'Why? He's the trespasser.' Then, worried he might have a gun, Justine felt her heart starting to thud. He could be some sort of maniac who'd been camping out here and considered the place his home.

Whoever he was, he wasn't dressed like a down-and-out, though his navy bib-front overalls, pale blue shirt and workman boots weren't especially smart either. His fair hair was thick and wavy, and he was so tall and bulkily built that he looked slightly daunting. Apparently he didn't feel the cold, since there was no sign of a coat – or, happily, a gun.

'Good afternoon, ladies,' he said amiably as he stepped on to the collapsed patio.

'Who are you and what are you doing here?' Sallie Jo demanded hotly. 'You're on private property.'

To Justine's surprise his arrestingly blue eyes sparked with humour. 'Now that was going to be my line,' he told her, stooping to give Daisy a ruffle. 'You're sure a purty little thing. Could it be you doing all the barking I heard?'

'Are you a neighbour?' Justine enquired, still trying to sound lofty.

'No, ma'am, me, I'm from midway between here and South Bend, but I happened to be not too far away when one of the neighbours alerted me to your presence on the premises.'

Justine could only look at him.

'Why would they do that?' Sallie Jo wanted to know. 'You don't own the place.'

'Now *that* is true,' he agreed, straightening up again. 'But I kinda keep an eye on it from time to time.'

Justine's eyes widened. 'The door fell off when we opened it,' she informed him, 'which suggests no one's been inside for a good long while.'

'Mm, I would agree with that,' and stepping forward he held out a hand to shake. 'Alastair Leith,' he told them, taking Justine's hand first. 'Most folks call me Al.'

Since he seemed friendly, or at least unthreatening, Justine felt compelled to introduce herself too.

'Cantrell,' he repeated in an interested drawl. 'So you're a relative of May's?'

Sallie Jo took over again. 'She's her granddaughter,' she informed him, 'which makes her the owner of this cottage, and I'm Sallie Jo Osborne.'

'Pleased to meet you, Sallie Jo,' he responded, shaking her hand too. To Justine he said, 'I'm guessing from your British accent that you're related to Camilla?'

Justine managed to stop her mouth falling open. 'How do you know my mother?' she asked.

'I don't,' he confessed. 'Or not any more. Haven't

seen her since she married your father. I was just a little biddy thing back then, so I guess she won't remember me. How is she these days? Still in London?'

Still thrown by his knowledge of her mother, Justine pressed, 'Who exactly are you?'

'Now that part's easy,' he replied. 'My father, Dick Leith, was May's half-brother, which kind of makes me a nephew once removed.'

Justine blinked. This man was a *distant relative*?

'So Camilla's taking an interest in the old place again,' he commented, looking up at the time- and weather-wearied facade. 'That's good. It's time someone brought the old girl back to life.'

'Do you . . .? How come *you're* taking an interest?' Sallie Jo asked. 'Are you . . .? I don't get . . .'

With a smile that almost made Justine's heart skip, he said, 'Don't worry, I'm making no claims on the place. It belongs to Camilla, always has, since May and Phillip passed. We just – my father and I – thought we'd keep a check on it until Camilla was ready to sell, or maybe come back. My pa knew how much it meant to May.'

Unsettled by how easily they were being taken in by this stranger, Justine said, 'Have you ever been inside?'

He shook his head. 'Not since May and Phillip went.'

She wondered if that was true, and what difference it made if it wasn't.

'So what do you do midway between here and South Bend?' Sallie Jo wanted to know. 'And where exactly is that? I'm guessing the place has a name.'

'The nearest town would be North Liberty,' he

replied. 'And me, I have myself a farm over that way. Hogs mostly, but some corn and soybean.'

Suddenly conscious of the time marching on, Justine said, 'I don't know what to do about the door. It's completely wrecked and we have to leave.'

'Oh, don't you worry about that,' he told her. 'There's a hardware store over in Argos, I'll bring some wood and seal it.'

'But then we won't be able to get in again.'

'Do you want to?'

'At some point, yes.'

'OK, let's board it up for today, then see about fixing up a door by the end of the week.'

'Do you think we can trust him?' Sallie Jo murmured as they left him estimating dimensions while they headed back to the car. There was an enormous Bronco truck parked next to it, which presumably belonged to him.

'I don't see that we have much choice,' Justine responded, knowing she wouldn't feel anywhere near as uneasy about him being there if they hadn't discovered the paintings. 'But listen, he's been able to get in any time he wanted for the past thirty years, so why would he wait for us to break the door down before seizing his chance?' After a pause, she added, as much to comfort herself as Sallie Jo, 'I think he's genuine.'

Sallie Jo nodded as they got into the car. 'And kind of cute,' she declared.

'Yeah, he's definitely that,' Justine agreed, settling Daisy on her lap, and feeling more than a little bewildered by how the day had turned out, she sat quietly beside Sallie Jo as they drove steadily back into town.

'Those paintings are still going to be there tomorrow, aren't they?' she asked as they pulled up outside the day care ministry.

Turning to look at her, Sallie Jo said, 'I can't believe that neither of us thought to get his card, or at least a number.'

'No,' Justine murmured faintly, 'nor can I.'

Chapter Fifteen

Present Day – Culver, Indiana

A lengthy phone conversation with her mother that night, plus a helpful Google search, revealed that Alastair – Al – Leith was indeed who he'd claimed to be, a cousin, albeit distant, and a North Indiana-based hog farmer. This was no small relief, considering how concerned Justine was becoming about the paintings and their possible worth.

Sallie Jo agreed, they had to get them to a safer place as soon as possible, and since she was the one with contacts she was already on the case.

Days passed, a security truck arrived at the cottage, and the artwork was carefully transported to a specialised storage facility in South Bend. By then Justine, along with most of her neighbours, indeed people all over the region, were cranking up their heating and splashing out on thick sweaters and down coats in an effort to keep warm. Heavy snow was forecast, though hadn't yet arrived. However, with such low temperatures and feisty gales there was no question of returning to explore the cottage any further just yet. Besides, she was more concerned for the moment with the arrival of a deeply unpleasant email.

So we know you're in Culver Indiana hiding away, pretending to the world that you're Justine Cantrell, when you're really Justine McQuillan. Lucky you finding an escape. There's not one for the rest of us. We continue to suffer thanks to your son. We just hope that you're suffering too.

'And it came to your current address?' Matt asked when she read it out to him.

'Yes, it did. I don't know how they found it, but I guess the publicity surrounding the rabbit rescue finally made its way to them.'

'Whoever they are. No clue from the ID?'

'It's just a series of numbers from a Hotmail account. I'm going to guess it's Melanie or Maddy.'

He didn't disagree. 'Forward it to me. I'll see if I can find someone to trace the sender.'

And then what would they do?

Probably nothing.

Since she was sitting in front of her computer she sent it right away, before closing the laptop down. 'I take it you've been receiving the photos of Lula?' she asked. *Why hadn't he acknowledged them? What was wrong with emailing back to say how beautiful his daughter was?*

'Of course. She's beautiful,' he said. 'I can hardly believe how fast she's growing up.'

'She's four now.'

'I know. I got the pictures of her party. Where was it again? The Lakeside Grill? Looks like you all had a great time.'

'We'd have enjoyed it more if you were there.'

Sighing, he said, 'It's not that I don't want to be, you know that.'

'Do I? You could have come.'

'Yes, but then I'd have to leave again and what would that be like for Lula? For us?'

Awful, but maybe better than not seeing him at all. They couldn't go on like this, surely he realised that.

'I'm not visiting Ben this weekend,' he told her. 'Apparently he's sent the order to somebody else.'

Justine drew back, startled, and immediately suspicious. 'Who else would go to see him but you?' she demanded.

'He won't tell me, but my best guess is he's agreed to receive drugs or some other sort of contraband for a fellow inmate. It might even be for himself, because he's seemed pretty spaced out the last couple of times I've been there.'

Hating that – her son, the drugged-up, bruised-faced, bloody-knuckled prison thug – she said, 'Is he getting into any fights?'

'Some, I should think. He doesn't tell me about them.'

'Then what does he tell you?'

'Other people's business, mostly. Who's picking on who, how long someone's been there, what they're in for, whether they'll ever get out.'

'Such edifying stuff. Have you told him we're in touch?'

'I have, but he had nothing to say about it.'

As all the harrowing, conflicting emotions surrounding her son assailed her, she put a hand to her head.

She had no idea what to read into his apparent dismissal of her, if there was anything to be read into it at all, so why was she trying?

'Are you still there?' Matt asked.

'Yes, I'm here. Do you still think he's depressed?'

'Probably. Most of them are in there.'

'Did you hear anything back from the prisoner safety people?'

'Only to say they're looking into it.'

Which didn't sound very reassuring at all. 'So what will you do at the weekend?' she asked.

He sighed. 'I'm not sure yet. Hayley's trying to persuade me to go to London for a change of scene; she thinks it'll get my creative juices flowing.'

A weekend with Hayley, but not with her and Lula.

Knowing she was in danger of being unreasonable, she forced herself to sound light as she said, 'Is she inviting you to stay with her?'

'I don't think so, but let's not go there, OK? We both know it won't end well, so tell me more about the lake house. Judging from the photos it's in a pretty sorry state.'

Forcing herself to go with the change of subject, she replied, 'Yes, it is, and it'll take a fortune to restore, if that's what we decide to do. Mum says she's happy to sign it over to us now, so it's up to me and Rob what we do with it.'

'What does Rob want to do?'

'He can't afford to put much into it, but he's willing to sell me his share at current market value if I want to buy him out.'

'How much would that be?'

'I'm not sure. Given its position and the amount of land it'll be a sizeable sum, and then I'd have to consider how much all the work would cost. It's a very big house, Lula and I would rattle around like peas in a barrel, and with it being on the East Shore, it's a bit far from town.'

She hadn't told him about the paintings yet, mainly because she was afraid – if they did turn out to be genuine – of how wrong it would seem for them to receive so much good fortune. A lake house *and* a cache of valuable artwork, when the result of Ben's actions was still causing so much suffering. It might seem like their grief, their punishment was over and the gods were smiling on them again. What a slap in the face that would be for the others. If there were a way of sharing the good fortune she'd do it in a heartbeat, except what would that entail, handing out a couple of paintings to each bereaved parent as though its monetary or investment value might make up for a house they couldn't sell, dreams that had been shattered, a child they'd never see again?

'Isn't Thanksgiving coming up?' Matt asked chattily.

'Next week. Sallie Jo's parents are coming back to Culver tomorrow, so they've invited us to join them at their place on the lake.'

'Is it anywhere near yours?'

Startled by the 'yours', she said, 'No, it's much closer to where I am here, on the South Shore. It's beautiful, old, another one of the originals, but obviously in a much better state of repair than May's.' That felt better, May's.

'So will it be roast turkey?'

'Of course, and at the weekend we've all of us, Sallie Jo's family included, been invited over to Al Leith's farm for a hog roast.'

'Al Leith your cousin?'

'Twice removed.'

'So you're getting quite friendly with him?'

'Not really. We've spoken on the phone a couple of times since we met at the cottage, and he came into Café Max the other morning while I was having breakfast.'

'So he joined you?'

'And Sallie Jo. She was there too.'

'Is there a Mrs Leith?'

'Not that we've heard any talk of. I guess we'll find out when we go to the farm.'

'Has he met Lula yet?'

'No, but Daisy seemed to quite like him. There's nothing much not to like. He's very easy-going, considerate, good sense of humour.'

'Is this going to end in pistols at dawn?'

Unable not to laugh, she said, 'I hope not, because I expect he's a much better shot than you.' The words and their grotesque reminder of Ben's skill smothered the humour like choking black clouds.

'I've been thinking,' she lied, because she wasn't sure she'd been considering this at all, at least not consciously, 'maybe I should write to Ben.'

Sounding surprised, and cautious, he said, 'There's no reason why you shouldn't.'

'He told me he wouldn't read it if I did.'

And why should she be allowed contact with her son when Gina, Melanie and Maddy would never have contact with theirs again?

As though reading her mind, he said, 'You can't make a difference for anyone else, but you probably could for him.'

'In a positive way?'

'That'll depend on what you write.'

She had no idea, couldn't even think how she'd begin. *I won't read it anyway.*

Maybe it would be easier to go and see him again, except that wasn't going to happen, at least not any time soon.

'Did I tell you that he gets quite a bit of mail?' Matt said.

She frowned. 'Who from?'

'Fans, he calls them. Women, girls, who consider what he did to be macho, attractive, even heroic.'

'Oh God,' she groaned in disgust, though she knew very well that many serial killers received this kind of attention. 'That is so sick.'

'Exactly what he says, but I think he writes back.'

'Maybe it's one of them who's visiting at the weekend.'

'It could be. I have no idea.'

Feeling queasy at the mere thought of Ben being allowed anywhere near a female who clearly wasn't of right mind herself, she said, 'I wonder if he'll write back to me.'

'I guess you won't know unless you write to him.'

'I'm not sure what I'd say. Tell me what else you

talk about when you're with him? Something to give me some guidance.'

'To be honest there are long stretches when we don't talk at all, just sit there like a couple of no-hopers waiting for the time to pass, but other times he'll tell me about something he's watched on TV, or a new kind of exercise he's trying out in the gym. When he's in the mood to wind me up he'll tell me about fights, or attacks he's planning. I don't know how much of what he says is true, but I'm guessing from the black eyes and bruises that some is.'

Repulsed, her eyes closed in hopeless despair. This was how his life was going to be, year in, year out, until he wouldn't be able to live any other sort of life, even if they allowed him to come out.

And all the time Matt would be growing old in his self-imposed prison a mile away.

Unless he went to London at the weekend with Hayley.

'Prison's a tough place,' Matt was saying. 'I guess we have to feel glad he can take care of himself.'

Has he been raped? She'd never ask, and couldn't imagine Matt ever did either. For all they knew Ben's savagery had turned him into a violator himself.

'Tell me,' Matt asked, 'have the letters from your grandmother and mother helped you let go of some of the guilt?'

Sighing, she said, 'I'm not sure. Sometimes I think so, but how can I ever feel anything but ashamed of what he did? How can you? It's going to completely dominate my life, I know it is. You know, there are times when I envy the parents in our position whose sons took their own lives after going on a killing spree. At least they don't have to tear themselves apart deciding whether or not to be in touch with them, what might be happening to them on the inside, if they're ever going to get a chance at normal life again, which of course they aren't. How do we carry on when we know he's there, hanging around like some awful nemesis, OK, paying for what he did, but never, *ever* making up for it? And let's not forget how he's constantly standing in the way of us properly mourning Abby, the way she deserves.'

Very softly he said, 'Let's talk about something else.'

Wanting to, more than anything, she closed her eyes, needing time to shut out the angst, fear, loathing, hopelessness and despair. Worst of all was knowing that in coming here she'd abandoned her son. Did Matt have any idea how much worse he was making her sense of guilt by staying, and having regular contact with him?

In the end she managed to focus on Daisy, who was tossing around a squeaky hedgehog. 'How's Rosie?' she mumbled hoarsely.

Instantly sounding upbeat, he said, 'She's great.'

'Will you take her to London if you go?'

'Sure. We go everywhere together, don't we, old girl?'

Easily able to picture Rosie's adorable face as she enjoyed the attention, Justine said, 'Except the prison.'

'No, she can't go there, but we make up for it after

by going for a long walk, or to an out-of-the-way pub where they allow dogs.'

Suddenly realising she wanted the conversation to end, she said, 'Will you let me know if you find someone to trace that email?'

'Of course.'

'And don't worry about calling again. Maybe you're right, it's easier if we don't talk.' She didn't mean that, wasn't even sure why she'd said it, except everything was feeling so mixed up and beyond her right now.

He didn't argue, simply said, 'We can always hope things will get better, maybe become clearer over time.'

Almost without thinking she heard herself murmur, '*Hope is the thing with feathers*,' and with a brief goodbye she put the phone down.

It was Thanksgiving Day morning. Justine and Lula were getting ready to go to Sallie Jo's parents at midday, packing enough to stay the night in case the cold winds rushing in from the Arctic decided to bring in a blizzard. The temperature outside was well below freezing, around twenty degrees Justine had heard on the TV, minus six in her previous life. Figure in the wind chill and she was sure it was colder than she'd ever experienced before.

Thank goodness for a good furnace, a generous-sized wood-burner and reasonably small rooms, which weren't difficult to heat. She just hoped Sallie Jo's parents' place wasn't as draughty upstairs as she feared. To be on the safe side she'd packed extra sleeping bags for her and Lula, and even a little hot-water bottle for Daisy.

She was allowing herself to look forward to the day, for in spite of everything she'd lost and had been through she had plenty to be thankful for, and that was what the celebration was all about. There would be plenty of time tomorrow to feel sad and troubled again; to worry about Matt and Ben, Cheryl and where she might be, Simon and Gina, and all the others who were still trying to pick up the pieces.

Today she was going to be a lively, entertaining guest for Sallie Jo's parents, who were as warm and friendly as their younger daughter, and who'd already gone out of their way to make her and Lula feel a part of their family. Angela, Sallie Jo's sharp-eyed, energetic mother, who looked far closer to fifty than over seventy with her glamorous blonde hairdo and peachy skin, had even made a point of setting time aside later in the day to tell Justine all she could remember about her 'dear grandmother, May'.

'We were none of us ever too sure about what happened back then,' she'd already confided, 'which was why I didn't want to get into conjecture when Sallie Jo rang. You can imagine, nothing like it had ever happened in Culver before, so in spite of what the police reports said everyone took to making up their own version of events . . . Some reckoned your uncle was a victim of the Ku Klux Klan and your grandma got in the way, and let me tell you, there were plenty ready to believe it, because the Klan were around this way back then, and not going after blacks, but Catholics. Others decided someone from

Pennsylvania with a grudge had tracked them down and got his revenge . . . I actually heard someone say once that there was some sort of Satanic ritual involved. Well, of course, those of us who knew May knew *that* wasn't true. She was the sweetest, sassiest, most level-headed woman with a saucy laugh you could wish to meet. Not that she socialised much, she usually preferred keeping herself to herself, and we hardly ever saw your uncle. Some people thought he had an illness of some sort, but of course no one really knew anything for certain, and they seemed to think it was more fun to make things up.'

Keen to hear more, even if the detail was scant and accuracy dubious, Justine finished wrapping the ham she'd insisted on baking and went through to check on Lula.

'Mommy,' Lula said thoughtfully as Justine waded through a sea of clothes into the bedroom, 'I'm not in a very good mood.'

Justine's eyebrows went up. 'Oh? Why is that?'

'I don't know yet, but I think it might be that time of the month.'

'What?' Justine cried with a laugh. 'You're not old enough to have times of the month.'

Lula frowned. 'How old do you have to be?'

'Well, in some cultures it can happen when a girl is as young as nine or ten, but with you, my darling, it probably won't happen until you're around twelve or thirteen.'

'So I won't get any bad moods until then?'

Justine was still laughing. 'What's making you ask about this? Did you hear someone talking?'

Lula nodded, but before she could answer the sound of a car pulling up outside sent her dashing off to find out who it was.

'It's Sallie Jo,' she shouted as Justine followed her into the kitchen. 'Oh Mommy, the deers are back. There are three of them this time. Please, please can we feed them?'

'I've already explained that we could do them more harm than good if we do,' Justine replied, while understanding the urge, since they looked so young and thin and adorably Bambyish poking about the edge of the woods. Their heads came up to watch Sallie Jo hurrying to the house to escape the biting cold, and went down again as she disappeared.

'We were just leaving to come to you,' Justine declared, shivering at the frosty air Sallie Jo brought in with her.

'I guessed you would be,' Sallie Jo responded, pulling off her gloves and scooping Lula up into a lavish embrace. 'I could have rung, but I wanted . . . to come . . .'

Alarmed by the catch in her voice, Justine said, 'Why? What's happened? Are you OK?'

'Yeah, yeah, I'm fine,' Sallie Jo assured her, sniffing and blinking back tears.

'Are you sad?' Lula asked, peering worriedly into her face.

'No,' Sallie Jo tried to laugh. 'My eyes are watering from the cold. You're looking very smart today in your lovely blue corduroy dress.'

'I chose it myself from Diva,' Lula informed her, 'and I got a coat too. Shall I show you?'

'Oh, yes please. I'd love to see it.'

As Lula hastened off to her bedroom with Daisy hot on her heels, Justine said, 'What is it?'

Sallie Jo's mouth trembled as she threw out her arms. 'First up,' she cried, 'my sister's car hit some ice and went off the road . . . It's OK, no one's hurt, but the car's wrecked so the breakdown service is taking them back to Indianapolis.'

'Oh no! So they're not coming today? Your parents must be really disappointed.'

'Tell me about it, but Cora Jane's not ruling it out. If the weather doesn't turn any worse they'll make the journey in her car, and aim to get here around five, which is about when my ex-parents-in-law are due to arrive, because they've been held up too, apparently.'

'So it means we'll eat later than planned. That's OK, isn't it?'

'Sure, I guess so. Yeah, sure it is.'

'There's more,' Justine prompted knowingly.

Sallie Jo didn't deny it, but Lula was back in her new coat – and fur-lined boots on the wrong feet. 'You are adorable,' Sallie Jo laughed. 'It is the most stylish coat ever, and I just love those boots.'

'We got them at Diva too, and Daisy's got a new coat that we sent for online. It's pink with pictures of snowflakes on it.'

'Why don't you go and put it on her?' Justine suggested. 'It should be in the drawer at the bottom of your closet.'

Off Lula zoomed again, apparently unfazed by her east-west-facing boots, and Justine turned back to Sallie Jo.

'It's David,' Sallie Jo informed her. 'He just told me this morning that he's been offered a job in Washington and he's already decided to take it.'

Justine's jaw dropped. 'Of all the . . .' Drawing Sallie Jo into an embrace, she said, 'I'm so sorry.'

'It's OK, I'll be fine. It's not like I wasn't expecting it.'

'But to tell you today . . . Why couldn't he have waited?'

'Apparently he didn't want to spend the day having to pretend. He thought it was fairer to let me – my parents – decide whether or not we still want to invite him. If we don't he says he'll understand.'

'So what are you going to do?'

Sallie Jo shook her head. 'I don't know. Mom says it has to be up to me, and I know what I want to say, but it seems kind of mean to make him spend the day on his own.'

'It would be no less than he deserves. How long has he known about the job?'

'A couple of weeks, apparently. He says it's too good an offer to turn down and he's not exactly making the best of his skills in Culver, which I can understand. He's played with the big boys in the past, so why wouldn't he want to go there again?'

'But what about you? Didn't he . . .'

'It's got nothing to do with me. We're not an item; he doesn't have any obligations towards me . . .'

'But he knows how you feel about him.'

'Even if he does it's not his main concern, and I'm a fool for actually believing it might have worked out for us.'

Hearing a yelp in Lula's room, Justine turned round as Daisy came scurrying in to be rescued.

'She won't let me put it on her,' Lula complained, appearing in the doorway with a cute pink anorak with four tiny sleeves and a fur-trimmed hood.

'That is just too ridiculous,' Sallie Jo spluttered.

Lula's eyes rounded. 'She'll catch a cold if she doesn't wear it,' she protested.

'Maybe you should carry her tucked inside your coat?' Sallie Jo suggested.

'But I want her to wear this one. Mommy put it on earlier and she looked really sweet.'

'Isn't it too small for Mommy?' Sallie Jo teased.

Lula appeared confused, until getting the joke she gave a shout of laughter.

Laughing too, Justine went to check her mobile as it rang, and seeing it was Matt her heart turned over. If she answered it would be the first time they'd spoken since she'd told him not to call any more, and maybe she didn't want to speak to him now, when Sallie Jo clearly needed to talk.

'I'll let it go to messages,' she announced, turning back to her friend.

'But if it's important . . .'

'It's not. So what are we going to do about David? Do you think you can bear to have him around after this?'

Sallie Jo shrugged. 'It would be easier if he'd just pull out instead of leaving the decision to me.'

'Is there anywhere else he can go for the day?'

'He mentioned something about one of his neighbours, but I don't know if it's really an option.'

351

Justine glanced at her phone as it rang again, this time to let her know there was a message.

'. . . or I guess he could go to Toby Henshaw's,' Sallie Jo was saying, 'unless Toby and Melissa are with her family over in Plymouth, and they usually are for Thanksgiving.'

'We could always ask Iris Longstow to invite him,' Justine suggested, only half joking, 'she's big on taking in strays at this time of year.'

Sallie Jo had to laugh, but her eyes darted to Justine's phone as it rang again. 'It's not him, is it?' she asked, anxiously.

Justine was experiencing a stirring of unease as she held up the cell for Sallie Jo to see that it was Matt.

'You should take it,' Sallie Jo told her.

Deciding she probably should, Justine clicked on. 'Hi, is everything OK?' she asked, turning away from Lula.

'Yes, I'm fine,' he answered, not sounding it. 'Is Lula with you?'

Frowning, she said, 'Yes, of course, why do you ask?' Her heart suddenly jolted. Had the email led to something? Was he about to tell her she and Lula were in some sort of danger?

'You need to sit down,' he said softly. 'What I have to say . . . It's not . . . It's going to come as a shock. Is Sallie Jo around?'

'Actually, she's right here. What is it?' She knew instinctively this was about Ben, but she didn't want to say his name in front of Lula.

'He's . . . I've . . . I had a call from the prison this morning. I've been there ever since . . .' He took a breath. 'I'd have called sooner, but the time difference . . . I didn't want to wake you . . .'

When he didn't continue she felt herself turning cold to her core. She didn't know exactly what she was thinking, but only because she didn't want to put it into words.

'They found him this morning, in his cell,' Matt was saying brokenly. 'He used a razor, apparently. No one knows how he got it . . .'

Justine was starting to sway. 'Are you saying . . .? Is he . . .?'

'Yes, I'm afraid he is.'

She sat down hard in a chair, tried to speak but couldn't. A week ago she'd told Matt how she envied the parents of the boys who'd killed themselves . . . For one bewildering moment she wondered if Ben had heard her, if she'd somehow willed him to do this . . .

Realising something was wrong, Sallie Jo took Lula and Daisy into the bedroom.

'I'm sorry,' Matt was apologising. 'I didn't want to break it to you like this. I'd have come to do it in person, but by the time I got there you'd have heard it on the news.'

Justine's head was spinning so fast she could barely catch the tail of a thought before it collided with another.

Ben was . . .

He'd used a razor . . .

Found him this morning . . .

She opened her mouth and a terrible cry erupted from the very depths of her. 'No, no, no,' she wailed. 'Oh God, no.'

Matt was saying something; Lula was rushing to her, crying, 'Mommy! Mommy!'

Justine could barely pick her up.

'What's the matter, Mommy?' Lula sobbed, trying to grab Justine's face.

'It's all right,' Justine tried to say, the words ragged, unintelligible.

'Mommy! Mommy!' Lula choked, wrapping her arms round Justine's neck as Daisy whined at her feet.

Gently taking the phone, Sallie Jo said to Matt, 'It's Sallie Jo here. Can you tell me . . .?'

'Is she OK?' Matt interrupted. 'She's taken it even harder . . .' His voice broke on a sob.

Turning from where Justine and Lula were clinging to one another, Sallie Jo said, 'Is it about your son?'

'Yes. He's . . . He's taken his own life.'

As Sallie Jo's face paled, she whispered, 'I'm sorry. I know things . . . I'm so sorry.'

'Thank you. Can you stay with Justine?'

'Of course. Will there be . . .? I guess there are arrangements . . .'

'I don't know anything yet. I'm going back to the prison as soon as I've finished this call. I should know more after.'

'Let me speak to him,' Justine insisted before Sallie Jo could ring off, and taking the phone she told Matt, 'I'm coming over. If I can get a flight today I should be there by morning. Can you meet me?'

There was only a brief hesitation before he said, 'Just let me know what time you're due in. Will you bring Lula?'

'Of course. I'll call Rob . . .'

'Don't worry, I'll do that. Are you sure you want to come?'

'How can I not? He's my son.'

Chapter Sixteen

Present Day – London, UK

So this was what it was like to be back on the other side of the corn-silk veil.

It felt strange, familiar but distant, danker, greyer, smaller, louder, kind of impervious to everything she was feeling, and everything that had happened. The world had moved on and were it not for the headlines and hounding of the press, Justine might have felt that she'd never been here before. That was in the good moments; in the bad she felt swamped by the nightmare all over again.

Six days had passed since Sallie Jo and Al Leith had driven her and Lula to Chicago to catch a flight to London. Al Leith? Who'd called him? Why would he have given up his Thanksgiving to take someone he barely knew to an airport?

She must remember to thank him. Maybe she should send a note, or email.

She kept worrying about having messed up the day for Sallie Jo's parents, but she'd already received emails insisting she hadn't, and expressing sadness for her loss. Before leaving she'd given Sallie Jo permission to let her parents know the truth about Ben; she couldn't tell by their messages how they'd received the news, but at least they were in touch. And apparently the day of celebration hadn't ended up with no guests at all, since Cora Jane and her family had eventually managed to get through, as had Hazel's other grandparents, and Al had managed to get Sallie Jo back by six. He'd stayed for dinner, but had driven home after in spite of a snowstorm.

Justine was still struggling to acclimate – acclimatise.

Although everything was in English it was feeling foreign, different, and she wasn't sure why. It was as though she'd stepped out of time and was trying to catch up, or slow down, or simply gain some sort of balance. The streets around Rob's felt cluttered and dreary. The sky was too low, the trees too bare with sad, spindly arms stretching to nowhere and small clusters of leaves clinging on to the last.

The media interest didn't let up for a minute. It was as though they couldn't get enough of reliving the crime, showing old footage over and over, bringing in the same so-called experts they'd found before, speculating on what had gone wrong, how the affected families might be reacting to the news of Ben's suicide.

None of those families had come forward to comment.

Not much had emerged about the suicide itself; all the police would say was that a thorough investigation was under way. However, Matt had been told that a young woman who'd visited Ben only days before the event was being questioned. It was possible that she'd managed to slip him the blade, though how he'd requested it, or even if he had, was not known. Fellow

357

inmates were also being questioned, but no one was hopeful of getting any useful information out of them.

Justine was still finding it hard to accept that her son was actually dead. Having not seen him for months she could easily persuade herself that he was still at the prison, and this was all a bad dream.

Or a good dream, depending on who you were.

Every time she remembered how she'd virtually wished him dead she felt swamped by guilt, grief, regret . . .

She hadn't meant what she'd said. It had slipped out in a moment of angry despair when she wasn't able to control what she was saying, or thinking. And yet, were she able to bring him back, she had to admit in her heart of hearts that she wouldn't. What would be the point, when his life had been all but over anyway? There could be no quality to it while he was locked away from society, and society would never want him back, or accept him if at some distant time in the future he was forced upon them.

She wondered if he could see them now from wherever he was, her and Matt, travelling in a Mercedes saloon with both their mothers, and Rob and Maggie, following a solemn black hearse containing a coffin where his body lay inert, bloodless, clean-shaven and dressed in the smart grey suit she and Matt had bought specially. Though the windows of their vehicle were blacked out, they kept their heads down as they passed the waiting press on their way into the crematorium, aware of flashes going off, voices calling out to them, cold and inquisitive eyes watching, waiting and hoping for only they knew what.

She shouldn't have come, but how could she have stayed away?

How could she never have written him a letter?

Had he wanted to hear from her?

He hadn't said so in the note he'd left for her.

It had arrived at Rob's address two days after his suicide, postmarked the day it had happened.

Why hadn't anyone at the prison read it? If they had they could have stopped him.

She hadn't given the note to the police yet, or to Matt, although he knew she'd received one. He hadn't asked to see it, and because of the things Ben had said she'd decided that she wouldn't be ready to confront them until the funeral was over.

There had been no note for Matt, and Justine knew how hurt he was by that. The father who'd stayed with him, had visited every week, sometimes twice a week, had not been considered worth a goodbye at the end: another demonstration of how Ben's conscience wasn't the same as most other people's.

She didn't glance at Matt now, but was picturing him in her mind's eye, pale, tense and with more grey hair and lines around his eyes than she remembered. His natural charisma, though dulled, was still there, she'd felt it the instant they'd found each other in the crowded arrivals hall, and when he'd stooped to Lula's height to reintroduce himself to his daughter, Justine could tell that Lula had felt it too.

'Hello sweetheart,' he'd whispered, 'do you remember me? I'm your daddy.'

Lula's eyes had rounded with awe. She looked at Justine as though seeking reassurance.

359

Justine nodded, and Lula turned back to Matt.

'You're very naughty because you didn't ring us back,' she told him earnestly.

Laughing and sobbing, he'd swept her up in his arms and buried his face in the sweet, little-girl scent of her. 'You're right,' he murmured, 'it's very naughty not to return someone's calls. We must make sure you've got my new number.'

They'd been inseparable since then, which had been harder to cope with than it should have been, mainly thanks to Ben's note, but at least it had given Justine time with her mother. Their reunion had been as emotional as she'd expected; she wondered now why she hadn't always felt close to her mother when it seemed to be happening so naturally, so powerfully. They'd talked a great deal, mostly about Grandma May and Phillip, with Justine doing all she could to help soothe her mother's guilt and grief, while Camilla did the same for Justine over Ben. A new and vital bond had developed between them that Justine was drawing strength from right now.

On reaching the chapel they got out of the car and Rob and Matt joined the funeral director's pall-bearers to help carry the coffin inside. Justine followed, holding on to her mother's arm, and feeling Camilla's long, slim fingers curled around hers. Justine was aware of the cameras searching her mother out; being the celebrity amongst them she'd make as many front pages tomorrow as her infamous grandson. It wasn't going to be easy for her having to live through the shame all over again, but she'd come to the funeral despite this, and Justine was reminded once more that her mother had been there for her more often in her life than she'd ever given her credit for.

Behind them Catherine and Maggie walked together, soberly dressed and heads bowed. To the rest of the world they probably appeared as no more than bit players in this unholy drama; to Justine and Matt they were as vital in their love and support as Camilla and Rob.

Matt had chosen the music for the service, along with the readings. He'd kept it traditional, unremarkable, not wanting to give the press any more reason to criticise, or to accuse them of celebrating the life of a killer.

When the time came the minister didn't speak for long, but he was generous in the way he commended Ben's soul to God.

There was no one else in the chapel, just the six of them, sitting quietly in the front pew watching a heavy curtain moving around the coffin to take it from view. There were no tears, no other movements at all, only a terrible, silent grief for all the children who'd gone.

Feeling Matt's hand reaching for hers, Justine let him hold it for a moment, not knowing whether he was offering strength or seeking it. Probably both. Their two eldest children were both dead. It didn't seem credible, it couldn't be true and yet it was.

There was a chasm inside her, so deep and black and unending it could never be filled.

Abby and Ben. How had this happened? What kind of malice had been at play when fate had mapped out their ways?

Justine's mind went to Lula, at home with Francine,

her round blue eyes watching, trying to understand, wondering why everyone was so sad. Perhaps they should have explained about Ben, but what could they say when for the past fifteen months she'd been encouraged to forget she even had a brother?

They were handling it all wrong. They needed some advice; Lula had to be counselled, and so did they.

Outside in the cold damp air Justine stood with her mother, Catherine and Maggie while Matt and Rob thanked the funeral officials. There were bouquets and wreaths spread out over the courtyard from a previous funeral; the only flowers for Ben were still on his coffin. Would they be burned with him, or set aside for . . . what? Justine didn't know and wouldn't ask. Later, the crematorium would organise the disposal of the ashes – there was nowhere to scatter them that felt right, and they didn't want any sort of plaque or memorial that might cause offence to others. It was more than enough, they'd felt, for reminders of their son to live on in the scars he'd left in their hearts.

Abby's ashes were still in a white marble urn, at the bottom of Justine's closet in Culver. Maybe when she got back she'd see about scattering them on the lake: that way she'd always feel close. This was provided Justine decided to go back, but she couldn't imagine not doing so. Culver felt much more like home now than anywhere in England.

Beside her Catherine murmured, 'I wasn't sure they'd come.'

Justine glanced at her, then followed her eyes. Her heart contracted to see Simon clasping Matt's shoulder.

Matt turned round, and after a moment the brothers moved into a powerful embrace.

Then Gina was there, pulling Justine into her arms and holding her tight.

'I've missed you,' Gina whispered.

Too emotional to speak, Justine simply hugged her back.

When she opened her eyes she saw that Maddy and Ronnie were there too, and Melanie and Kelvin, but they didn't come close, barely even looked at her, apart from Melanie who glared at her so coldly it almost felt like a weapon.

The only reason they'd come, Justine realised, was to make sure Ben really had gone, and perhaps to seek some sort of closure.

As they walked away Justine looked around for Cheryl, wanting desperately to see her, but there was no sign of her.

'Do you ever hear from Cheryl now?' she asked Gina as they started back to the cars.

'No,' Gina replied. 'I tried her mobile a few months ago, but she never got back to me, so I don't even know if she got my message.'

'What did you say?'

'I simply asked how she was. I wondered afterwards if she's found that cutting herself off from us all is the only way she can cope.'

Suspecting that was the case, Justine's heart ached with grief and pity for her dearest friend. She wanted to see her so badly, to be sure that she was all right, but the only person she could call was Cheryl's father, and why would he want to hear from her, much less assure her that his beloved daughter was recovering from the loss of her only child?

She'd never recover from it, Justine knew that, and being in touch with her would only reopen the very worst of the wounds, which was the last thing Justine wanted.

Though Matt invited Simon and Gina to come back to Rob's when the formalities were over, they gently but firmly excused themselves. There would be time, soon, Simon had said, for them to get together, but today they needed to go their separate ways.

'I guess,' Matt said in the car on the way home, 'that now Ben's gone they feel they can speak to us again.'

Justine didn't reply, though she'd reached the same conclusion. She could only wish Cheryl had felt the same way.

'I'm not sure how I feel about that,' Matt commented.

Justine wasn't either, but what she said was, 'You understand it, surely.'

Matt nodded and sighed. The day had clearly taken it out of him, out of them all, but Matt's strain was showing.

Justine's eyes went to Catherine. It would mean the world to her mother if her sons were reconciled; it would no doubt mean the world to them too, if they could manage it.

Taking out her phone she sent a text to Francine, asking her to let Lula know that Mummy was on the way home. Maggie had probably already alerted her daughter, but Justine had felt a sudden overpowering need for Lula, and for now this was the closest she could get to her.

It wasn't until after they'd eaten – and praised – the cake and sandwiches Lula had helped Francine to prepare that Justine felt able to say she needed a lie-down.

'I'll come with you,' Matt said, starting to get up.

'No don't!' she replied, so sharply that the others glanced up in surprise. Seeing the hurt and confusion in Matt's eyes she said, more gently, 'Stay with Lula,' and signalling to her mother to follow in a few minutes, she left the sitting room and went upstairs to the small guest suite Rob and Maggie had added to the house some years ago. It was warm and cosy, with toast-coloured walls and matching curtains and carpet. The bed was an English king-size, American queen, covered by caramel-striped bedding and cream faux-silk pillows. This was where she and Matt had slept for two nights out of the five she'd been back; the other three they'd spent at her mother's. She couldn't be sure now why they hadn't made love at the beginning; perhaps it was jet lag or grief. Since receiving Ben's letter she'd simply been unable to, in spite of wanting him more than she ever had in her life.

'Are you OK?' her mother asked, letting herself in the door.

Taking Ben's note from her bag, Justine handed it over. 'I want you to read this,' she said. With a sad half-smile she added, 'We seem to be reading a lot of letters lately. At least I do.' Oddly, the brief allusion to her grandmother brought a lump to her throat.

Taking the note and seeing the prison paper, her

mother's eyes returned to hers. She was looking older, Justine noticed, and tired, though whether that was overwork, or all the heartache she'd been through, it wasn't possible to know.

'When did it arrive?' Camilla asked. 'Before or after?'

Understanding she was omitting 'the suicide', Justine said, 'After. Matt hasn't seen it yet, but he knows I have it.'

Clearly baffled by that, Camilla said, 'Why haven't you shown him?'

'You'll see when you read it.'

Saying no more, Camilla unfolded the note and started to read.

Dear Mummy –

The way her mother's eyes quickly flicked to hers told Justine that she was wondering the same as Justine had on reading that childlike word – was it sarcasm, or had he reverted to being a little boy in his mind? The answer was almost instant.

It's all a load of bollocks really, isn't it? Life, death – good, evil – freedom, captivity – guilt, innocence. I don't get what all the fuss is about. We're all going to die one day, so why the big deal when someone makes it happen? What's wrong with having control, paying someone back for the shit they dished out? An eye for an eye and all that crap. I could always buy into that much more than turning the other cheek. What kind of fuckwit would do that?

I know everyone wants me to feel bad about what I

did, but sorry, I can't. I hated every one of those wasters and I have to be honest, it made me feel good to watch them squeal and panic when they realised what was happening. They knew it was me; and they knew they were paying for fucking me off. Dumb thing they did calling me a psycho, dumber still to laugh. Had to do something about that, didn't I, and what better than to prove them right?

BTW, if you're interested, Abby was the last to get it. She might have saved herself if she'd run, but only might, because I was on fire that day. She was screaming at me to stop. She didn't think I'd have the balls to take her out too, but she knows better now.

The funny thing is, Mummy, the only person I feel kind of bad about is you, and I'm still trying to figure out why. You looked so pathetic the day you came here, I wanted to laugh at you, but you ended up making me cry when you'd gone. Deffo hadn't expected that. Got over it pretty soon though, which was why I never wrote, didn't want you getting to me again, did I?

Dad told me you moved to America with Tallulah. Good long way from the psycho son, yeah? What's it like there? Don't worry about answering, I won't be around to hear it, just being polite, which I bet you'll say isn't like me at all. Anyway, I've been giving this some thought since I was offered a quick way out, and I reckon your life might be a lot easier if I wasn't around any more. Don't worry I'm not doing it for you, I'm doing it for me, cos majorly sick of it in here. When I'm gone you won't have to feel guilty about not visiting me – I know you do, because I know you – and you won't always be fretting over what's happening to me in here.

I'm not sure it'll make Dad's life much easier. I've been providing a good excuse for him to stay in England, wonder what he'll do when I'm not here any more. I told you, ages ago, there was something going on with him and Hayley, but you never wanted to believe me. You'll have to now, because there's more to it than just an affair, or maybe you already know they've got a kid together. A boy, not sure of his name, but he must be about four by now, same age as Tallulah.

He must have been going through a fertile patch back then, getting you both knocked up around the same time.

When Camilla's eyes came up again, Justine knew she'd reached the part about Hayley. She looked as shaken as Justine had felt when she'd read the words herself.

She felt no better about them now, even though she kept telling herself they couldn't be true. A part of her must believe it, or she'd have given the letter to Matt by now.

'Keep going,' she said softly. 'It doesn't get any better, but you might as well.'

Pressing a hand to her mouth, Camilla returned to the letter.

It feels weird to think I won't ever see you again, although I don't suppose I ever really expected to. Just never really thought about it before. I wish I could tell you something to make you believe you were a great mum, but why should I when you weren't, or at least not all of the time. Favouritism's not a good thing, it fucks with a kid's mind, gives him a sense of not belonging, or being wanted. That's what you and Dad did to me, but lucky I could handle it better than most, and I suppose you were better than I gave you credit for before I came in here. That's because I've had a lot of time to think since, and it's funny the way my thoughts keep going back to you. It's like that with mothers, I suppose, they always matter in the end even if they couldn't stand you.

This was where his pen had apparently run out of ink and he'd continued in pencil.

You know, I'm intrigued to find out what's on the other side, if there's anything at all, or if all that crap about afterlife, judgement, eternal hellfire, is just another load of bollocks. Maybe Abby and the others will get to take some revenge on me, or maybe they're in a place I'll never be allowed to go to. Anyway, whatever's over that side, anything or nothing, has got to be better than where I am now. OK, if I was going to get out one day, but it's not going to happen even if I start saying I'm sorry and acting all weird so they can label me a mentalhead and put me in Broadmoor.

So this is goodbye, Mummy. Guess what, I'm crying as I write this, like I don't want to go, but I do. I guess it's that I wish you were here to hold my hand, or tell me it's going to be all right, the way you used to sometimes if Abby wasn't around to distract you. I know it'll make you feel better if I say I'm sorry for everything I did, so I'm sorry for everything I did.

One last thing: I'm still capable of a good feeling towards someone and I hope you're glad it's you.

Ben

Justine watched her mother inhale deeply, push a shaking hand through her hair and eventually put the note down.

'I hardly know what to say,' Camilla murmured.

Seeing there were tears in her eyes, Justine passed her a tissue and reached for her hand. 'What do you think of the bit about Matt and Hayley?' she asked. 'And the child?'

'That it's nonsense,' Camilla replied. 'I don't know why he said it, but frankly we've never known why he does anything.'

Justine stared at the note. With all it contained it felt like a bomb that kept on exploding.

'You have to show Matt,' her mother told her gently.

After a while Justine said, 'What if it's true?'

'Justine, you know it isn't. This is Matt we're talking about – and Ben.'

Her eyes full of anguish, Justine said, 'I never believed my son could be a mass-murderer before it happened.'

Camilla almost flinched. 'It's hardly the same.'

'Why not? People can be capable of so much more than we ever suspect, and when I think of how Matt didn't seem to want to come to Culver, how he thought it was best for us to sacrifice our marriage for the sake of our children . . .'

'I thought that was your idea.'

'I guess it was both of us, but let's not forget how

Hayley's been there for him since I left . . . She hasn't let him down the way so many other friends have. She wouldn't, if they have a child together . . .'

Camilla picked up the note again, and after rereading parts she said, 'I hear what you're saying, and I understand why you're afraid to trust, anyone would be in your position, but the part that's not working for me is that Matt confided in Ben.'

It hadn't seemed likely to Justine either when she'd first read it, but after giving it some thought . . . 'They had to talk about something during all those visits,' she said, 'and why would Ben bother to lie?'

'To make mischief, of course.'

'But what would he gain from it when he had no intention of being around for the fallout?'

Though there were many ways of answering that, all Camilla said was, 'You have to show Matt the letter, and frankly I think you should do it now.'

Justine's insides dissolved into turmoil. 'And if it turns out he does want to stay with Hayley?'

Camilla's face was pinched, but her tone was firm as she said, 'It's not going to happen, but if it does we'll work it out. I'm not sure how yet, but I promise you, we will.'

It wasn't until much later in the day, after Lula was tucked up in bed and the others were watching a film downstairs, that Justine finally presented Matt with the note.

As she passed it over she hated noticing how pale and edgy he seemed, as though he'd rather be giving it back than taking it.

'Can I ask,' he said, 'why you've waited until now to let me see it?' He sounded like a stranger, someone whose voice was hollow, not really belonging to him.

Wondering what he was imagining, or dreading, and trying not to think of it herself, she told him, 'It's best if you just read it.'

She noticed his hand shake as he unfolded it, and the way he suddenly frowned told her his eyes had gone straight to *Dear Mummy*.

After that his expression wasn't possible to gauge, since he got up from the bed and kept his back turned as he read. She could sense his tension, almost feel the emotions tearing through him, or perhaps they were her own. She was aware of her heart thudding, yet she was hardly breathing.

The child was four years old. If he was real then he was somewhere right now with his mother, maybe waiting for his daddy to call, or come.

She could live with it if it would bring Abby and the others back, but it didn't work like that. There was no bargaining with fate, or destiny, or God if there was one. This cruel, never-ending suffering was how things were . . .

Matt was shaking his head and she suddenly felt herself being sucked into a terrible void where there was only darkness and devastation and no escape. She was going in deeper and deeper, gulping for air, shuddering, panicking, retching . . .

Matt's arms were around her, he was holding her tight, trying to soothe her, to make her look at him, to stop fighting him.

'You need to listen to me,' he told her. He took her face in his hands, forcing her to look at him.

'Tell me it's not true,' she gasped.

'Hayley has a child,' he replied, 'but he's not mine. I swear it. Hayley's son is *not* mine.'

The words were reaching her but she was afraid to believe them. How could she trust anything or anyone any more? 'So why does Ben think he is?'

'I've no idea what Ben thought. I never told him that . . .'

'How did he know the child even existed?'

'Because I talked about him sometimes . . . There was so little else to talk about, but never once did I say that Marcus was mine. Why would I when it isn't true? Marcus has a father. OK, he hardly ever sees him, and over these past few months he's probably seen a lot more of me, but he knows I'm not his daddy. He calls me Matt . . .'

'I don't know what that proves. You and Hayley were always . . .'

'*Good friends*, and we still are. It might not be what you want to hear, but since you went, I swear I don't know how I'd have coped without her. She's been there for me in a way you just couldn't be, because you had to put Lula first. We both did, and I still think we were right to do that, but I think we agree now that we went about it the wrong way.'

She couldn't deny that.

'I swear to God Marcus isn't mine,' he said softly. 'It's not possible for him to be when I've never slept with Hayley in my life. If you don't believe me, call her. She'll tell you it's true, and she'll tell you about

Marcus's father if you want her to. He's her ex-boss, and he's married, which is why he's hardly ever on the scene, and that's a shame, because Marcus is a wonderful little boy. You'd love him too if you met him, and I hope you will, because I don't want to cut him out of my life as if he doesn't matter. But if it's what you want I will, because you and Lula come first now. Ben's suicide is allowing me to make that happen . . . He's given me . . . He's done . . . He . . .' As he started to break down Justine folded him in her arms, crying too as their terrible, relentless grief engulfed them.

'I can't believe he's gone,' Matt sobbed. 'I keep thinking he's still there, at the prison, and this is all a sick joke . . . Or I tell myself it's for the best, but how can any of this be for the best?'

'It can't,' she replied brokenly. 'There is no rhyme or reason. We'll never understand why he did what he did, or what made him the way he was . . .'

'I'm the one who dropped him.'

'But you didn't. You caught him, just not quickly enough, and we still don't know if it's the reason he turned out the way he did. We'll probably never know. Matt, please, you have to stop blaming yourself. You're a wonderful dad, you did everything you could for him and for Abby . . .'

Matt's eyes closed as he murmured, 'Abby, Abby, Abby. Our precious girl. Oh God, Justine . . . I miss her so much.'

'I know. I do too.'

'I keep hearing her . . . It's like she's always there. I turn on the radio, the TV, and everything reminds me of her. I see young girls walking down the street, I hear someone laugh . . .'

Justine pulled him back into her arms, needing to hold him as much as he needed to be held.

They stayed that way for a long time, crying together, trying to comfort one another, and somehow make sense of why things had happened the way they had, even though they knew they'd never be able to give it any meaning.

'I don't know if we deserve to be where we are now,' he said in the end, 'but I do know that I can't carry on without you. I don't know why I ever thought I could.'

'You tried for Ben's sake,' she reminded him, 'and you'll always have that, knowing you were there for him when no one else was.'

His eyes drifted as he shook his head. 'And how did he repay me? By telling you something he knew wasn't true, and was going to hurt you, hurt us both, in a way that . . . what? Gave him pleasure?'

'Maybe he thought it was true,' Justine responded. 'Maybe the way you talked about Marcus . . .' Realising what she was about to say, she cut herself off.

'Maybe I sounded like a proud dad?' Matt continued for her. 'Maybe I made him think that I'd found a son worth caring for . . .'

'Don't,' Justine interrupted, putting a hand to his face. 'We're never going to understand what went on his head, so we have to stop trying.'

After a while his eyes came searchingly to hers.

'It's going to stop now, isn't it?' she implored. 'Please tell me that we don't have to go through any more, because I'm not sure I could survive it.'

'I wish I could make you that promise,' he replied softly, 'with all my heart I wish I could, but this I can tell you, if there is any more we'll get through it somehow, because we have to, for our own sakes, as well as Lula's.'

Of course he was right, she knew that, she just hoped all their challenges and heartache were over.

'We'll be fine,' he whispered, as though reading her mind.

She smiled, and her eyes closed as he kissed her. She wouldn't ask him yet about moving to Culver, there would be plenty of time for that later.

Chapter Seventeen

Culver, Indiana

Snow was falling so thick and fast it wasn't possible to see the lake, frozen as it was into a massive rink of daily thickening ice; or indeed to make out anything at all that was much further than the porch. Trees loomed white and shapeless in the flurrying cascades, while hedges stretched like frozen creatures trapped in the storm. This latest one had begun just over an hour ago, piling thick, icy stars on to the already snow-covered streets, creating deeper and more impenetrable drifts, turning the whole of Marshall County, perhaps the entire Midwest, into a winter wonderland.

Justine hadn't listened to the news yet this morning, she was almost afraid to, since the forecasts she'd heard over the past few days were predicting one of the worst winters in the region for several decades. All kinds of warnings were being issued – *make sure you have an emergency kit of salt, sand and shovel; if you have elderly folk nearby keep an eye out for them; don't call local law enforcement or 911 for travel information; be extra vigilant with small children when playing in the snow.*

'They're saying we could see a repeat of the Great Blizzard of '78,' Sallie Jo had told her on the phone this morning. 'Seventy or more people lost their lives in that storm, but everyone reckons we'll be better prepared this time around.'

Better prepared or not, flights in and out of both Chicago and Indianapolis were already affected, either by delays, or in some cases outright cancellations, and many of the Interstate highways were struggling to stay open. Thanks to the severity of the forecast Camilla and Rob, who both had heavy work commitments in the new year, had decided that they couldn't risk finding themselves snowed in after Christmas, if they even managed to get there, so neither of them was going to make it.

'Daddy's still coming, isn't he?' Lula asked for the sixth or seventh time that morning.

'I'm sure he is,' Justine replied, turning from the window and wrapping her cardigan more tightly around her, even though it wasn't at all cold in the house. They'd already decorated for Christmas with the tree twinkling colourfully in one corner, frosty garlands looped over the mantel above the wood-burner, and all sorts of stars, bells, Santas and reindeer that Lula had made herself at day care. They even had a little nativity scene on top of the fridge with everything from the baby Jesus to shepherds and three wise men.

Justine stood a moment watching Lula's efforts as she tried wrapping yet more presents at the kitchen table. She didn't want any help, she'd declared, she could do it herself. So far today she'd managed to create lumpy little parcels with glittery gold bows for a glistening amber bracelet for Hazel, a pair of pink woolly socks for Sallie Jo, some chocolate reindeer for Sallie Jo's parents, and a chocolate pig for Uncle Al, as she'd taken to calling Al Leith. 'Because he's got pigs at his farm,' she'd explained when she'd chosen it.

The biggest pile, already wrapped and under the tree, was for Matt.

'Let's get this for Daddy, and this, and this,' she'd cry every time they went into Diva, or Gail's Emporium, or Fisher & Co – she'd even found something at the café. So now they had everything from packs of coffee, to snowman cookies, to Jingle Bell socks, to a deep red and white Indiana Hoosiers bobble hat, to an assortment of other sporting and seasonal treats that Justine could barely remember. Lula was so excited about her daddy coming that it was almost impossible getting her to sleep at night, and on the days the weather allowed her to go to nursery she was coming home with yet another picture, or Play-Doh sculpture, or funny potato head for Matt.

They'd been back in Culver for almost three weeks by now, and as surreal as it had felt for the first couple of days, there was little doubt in Justine's mind that she'd been right to bring Lula home when she had. There simply hadn't been any point to hanging around in London, in spite of being urged by her mother and brother to stay awhile. Matt had tried to persuade her too, and in the end she might have given in had she not felt herself going downhill fast after Ben's funeral. She'd needed to get away, so she'd used Lula's desire to see Daisy as a reason to leave, and seeing Lula's little face light up when they'd come through to arrivals to find Sallie Jo and Hazel holding Daisy on a leash had been enough to convince her that she'd done the right thing.

No sooner was the reunion over than Lula launched into how Daddy and Rosie would be coming in time for Christmas, and that they were going to be living with them from now on. Afraid that Hazel might be feeling sad that her daddy wasn't coming, and that she didn't have a dog when Lula was now going to have two, Justine tried to distract Lula, but it was Sallie Jo who distracted her in the end. Apparently, as a parting gift to Hazel, David had bought her a three-month-old Coton de Tulear that Hazel had named Dizzy, because he kept running around in circles.

So at least Hazel had a dog for Christmas, even if she didn't have a daddy.

'They're going to be Dizzy and Daisy,' Hazel was telling Lula as they made their way to the car, 'and when they're old enough they can get married and have puppies together.'

Lula was so delighted by this that it was the first thing she'd told Matt when they'd rung that night. The second thing she'd wanted to know was did he have Rosie back yet and was he definitely going to bring her with him to Culver?

'Yes, and yes,' he'd laughed. 'I couldn't possibly leave her behind, I know you'd never forgive me.'

'No, I wouldn't, because Rosie was my first dog

and first dogs are very special. So is Daisy special, and Dizzy, who we haven't met yet, because he gets sick in the car so Hazel couldn't bring him to the airport. But we're seeing him tomorrow and I expect all the other days, because they don't live very far and he's probably missing Daisy already. Daddy, did you know . . .?'

It was amazing how long she could talk to her father on the phone, there was always so much to ask or to tell him, and half the time, after she'd handed over to Justine, she'd manage to think of something else and so would plead to speak to him again.

It was usually when she was at day care or sleeping over at Sallie Jo's that Justine really got to talk to Matt, although throughout their conversations she was careful to hide how wretched she was feeling. She knew grief was getting the better of her, and that she needed help, but she didn't want to saddle him with the worry, or make him feel that he'd rather stay in England than move to Culver and find himself having to cope with her deteriorating state of mind.

In the end, apparently sensing how bad things were getting, Sallie Jo insisted on taking her to the doctor, who prescribed a course of antidepressants. Since he'd warned that they'd probably take a while to kick in, she made an effort to distract herself by spending time with Angela, Sallie Jo's mother. Though they often talked about Justine's grandma, Justine never seemed to absorb much, since she could barely remember what had been said when she came to relate the stories to her mother.

As soon as the snow arrived the regular lunches and visits with Angela were forced to a temporary halt, and since then Justine had barely seen anyone, apart from the more elderly and infirm of her neighbours whose mail she collected from their boxes to save them skidding or falling on their drives. According to Sallie Jo, Al was due to come later to help clear the worst of the downfall so everyone in Justine's little enclave could at least get into town, perhaps even as far as the Park'n'Shop to pick up supplies.

'Daddy doesn't have to worry about being snowed in,' Lula was telling Daisy, 'because he's going to be living here from now on. So is Rosie. She's a golden retriever so she's bigger than you, and older, but I think you'll like her anyway. Mommy, Daisy will like Rosie, won't she?'

'Of course,' Justine assured her, though she had no idea if the dogs would get along. Right now it was hard to make herself care, but she had to force herself to try for Lula's sake, because everything was about Lula now.

Hearing a sudden banging from the side of the house she glanced at Lula, told her stay where she was and went through to the back door to investigate. She found Billy Jakes outside, hammering and chopping at her store of logs.

'They're going to freeze solid if you don't move 'em inside,' he told her. 'Won't be no good to you then. Got some place you can put 'em?'

Bemused, Justine looked around, trying to make a decision. 'Just here, in the hall,' she told him. Then she remembered to say thank you.

'No need for that,' he retorted gruffly. 'Get back in the warm. I'll sort this out.'

Doing as she was told, Justine returned to the kitchen and took the lasagne she was making for her neighbours, Maurice and Evie Gibson, from the oven. As she set it down on the countertop she wondered why her vision was blurred. It was as though the snow had somehow become trapped in her eyes, turning everything white and watery. She reached for some kitchen towel and was already dabbing her eyes before she realised she was crying, as silently and persistently as the snow was falling. She tried to make herself stop, but suddenly huge racking sobs were tearing through her, and Lula, shocked and frightened, was jumping off her chair and running to her.

'Mommy, what is it?' Lula wailed. 'Did you burn yourself? Does it hurt? Shall I kiss it better?'

Justine couldn't answer; she could only cling to her daughter and wish she was Abby.

'I love you too, Mommy,' Lula whispered.

Realising she must have spoken, Justine tried to speak again, but no more words would come, only terrible, heart-wrenching gulps of grief. She was scaring Lula, she could see that, but was unable to stop, or make out what Lula was saying. Nothing was making sense any more, everything was closing in on her and all she wanted was to sink to the floor and scream and howl for the return of her dead children. She couldn't go on without them. She'd tried telling herself she could, but it just wasn't possible. It was as though all the vital parts of herself had been ripped away, and nothing, not time, nor pills, nor counselling was ever going to heal them.

Entangled with it all she felt a desperate need for Matt. There was barely a week to go until Christmas and he still hadn't booked a flight. Even if he managed to get one now there was every chance it would be cancelled, or diverted to an airport that wasn't closed due to the freeze. And how would he get from there to Culver if the big blizzard hit?

Perhaps he didn't want to come.

'Justine, hey, hey,' someone was saying. 'You're going to be OK. Ssh, now. Come on, deep breaths, there's a good girl.'

'I think she burned herself,' Lula was sobbing. 'She won't let me see her hands . . . Mommy, please stop crying, please. Uncle Al will make the hurt go away.'

'Did you burn yourself?' Al asked, easing Justine on to a chair.

Realising her hands were jammed under her arms, Justine plucked them out to show that she wasn't injured. They looked strange to her, as if they belonged to somebody else. Everything was strange, the room, the people in it, the dazzling blaze of coloured lights, even the thoughts in her head.

'OK, I'm going to call Sallie Jo,' Al told her. 'I might have to go pick her up, but . . .'

'It's all right, I'm fine,' Justine whispered raggedly. 'I just . . . I'm sorry . . . It was suddenly . . . Suddenly . . .' Her voice broke on a sob, as her mind reeled into a terrible darkness.

'Too much?' he said, still holding on to her.

She tried to focus on him, but his face kept swimming away.

'Daddy's coming soon,' Lula told him, her earnest eyes still awash with tears.

'Sure he is, honey,' Al smiled.

'Are you OK now, Mommy?' Lula asked.

Justine put a hand to her dear little cheek and tried to smile. 'Abby,' she whispered. 'I'm sorry, I shouldn't have scared you.'

Lula looked worriedly at Al.

Justine noticed Daisy sitting upright on the floor, big black eyes fixed on her, ears down and an uncertain wag in her fountain of a tail. Was this a new game? What was she supposed to do?

Allowing Lula to climb on to her lap Justine suddenly started to shake, so hard she could barely hold her.

'Mommy!' Lula cried.

Justine's laugh was shrill. 'Abby, what are you doing?' she demanded. 'You're grown up now, you shouldn't pretend to be a child.'

'Mommy, I'm not Abby,' Lula wailed. 'I'm Lula.'

Going through to the back Al quickly asked Billy to go fetch Sallie Jo, then returning to the kitchen he eased Lula gently from Justine's arms, keeping her safely in his. 'Can you help me get Mommy into bed?' he asked with a reassuring smile. 'I think she needs to lie down.'

'Yes,' Justine agreed, aware of how ferociously she was wringing her hands, and hurting, and longing, and despairing. 'I need to lie down. I'll be fine once I've had a lie-down.'

*

She slept for the rest of that day and most of the next. By the time she woke up again she was feeling much better.

It was good to be back at the farmhouse, she decided. She'd missed it. She and Matt had been away too long this last time. She couldn't think for the moment where they'd been, but it would come to her. She wondered how the children were, if they'd behaved for Catherine, and how Cheryl had coped with the business.

She'd get out of bed in a minute to go and find out, but for the moment, she'd just carry on lying here, cosy in the feel of Lula and Daisy snuggled up next to her, both fast asleep.

'Hey Mum,' Abby said.

Justine looked towards the door where Abby was standing; how beautiful her darling girl looked with her cascades of wavy blonde hair and baby-blue eyes. 'Where's Dad?' Justine asked her.

Abby didn't answer. She was searching for something, turning her bedroom upside down. 'I can't find it,' she cried angrily. 'I have to find it.'

'What are you looking for?'

'Ben's hidden it, I know he has. Where is he? I'm going to kill him.'

'Too late, I got you first,' Ben guffawed from the tree.

'Come down!' Justine cried. 'Please. You've done a terrible thing.'

'You wish I was dead,' Ben snarled.

'That's not true,' Justine cried, frantically looking around.

'Sssh,' Sallie Jo soothed, tightening her hold on Justine's hand. 'You're going to be OK, just take it easy now.'

Justine tried to speak, but the words couldn't make it past the dryness in her throat.

She closed her eyes and sank slowly back into oblivion, down and down, deeper and deeper, all the way through the years to their flat in London where Abby was sitting on the bed with Matt and three-month-old Ben, reading them a story.

Justine went to embrace them and they laughed as they tumbled on to the floor in front of the fire in the farmhouse. It was Christmas, the tree was glowing with musical lights, snowflakes were sprayed on the windows, torn wrapping paper was all over the floor.

Ben snatched up his bow and arrow. 'This is a bad-luck house,' he shouted, fixing his aim on Abby.

'The place is cursed,' Maddy insisted. 'That's why you got it cheap.'

'I gave the girl the razor blade,' Melanie told her. 'She took it to him, because I wanted him gone.'

'Abby might have saved herself if she'd run,' Ben shouted. 'I was on fire that day.'

Lula was singing her a song, something about boogieing and dying.

'No, you mustn't die,' Justine broke in hoarsely.

'Why don't you try "Rudolph the Red-nosed Reindeer"?' Sallie Jo suggested to Lula.

Obediently Lula started to sing, and as she listened Justine watched her face changing to Abby's, who was in the school hall, playing her guitar, her beautiful hair swept over one shoulder as she sang 'Those Were the Days'.

'Stop!' Justine cried in distress.

Lula's face crumpled.

'It's OK,' Sallie Jo assured her. 'Mommy didn't mean you. She's having a bad dream, that's all.'

'I want her to wake up,' Lula said brokenly.

'I know, and she will soon.'

'Can she see me?'

'Sometimes, yes. She just needs to get lots of rest, and then she'll be able to see you all the time.'

A baby was crying and crying. It was Ben, begging her to come. 'Mummy, Mummy, Mummy.' The wind suddenly snatched it away, threw it into the clouds, turning it as loud and deep as thunder. 'MUMMY! MUMMY! MUMMY!'

Her delirium and exhaustion continued all through the weekend, and into the next week, with only short bouts of semi-consciousness when she was able to stumble to the bathroom or to down some soup.

She was dimly aware of people coming and going, Lula, Sallie Jo, Angela, the doctor, and a man who said his name was Al. She felt sure she knew him, but her mind wouldn't focus long enough to remember from where.

'Have you booked your flight yet?' she asked Matt.

'I'm sorry, but I won't be coming,' he told her. 'I have to stay with Marcus and Hayley.'

'Because he's your son?'

'Yes, he is.'

Abby was singing again, very softly, one of Justine and Matt's favourite songs, *When I fall in love, it will be for ever* . . .

Lula was there, her baby, cradling her little dog in her arms and trying to stop Rosie from licking Justine's face.

'Rosie?' Justine murmured hoarsely.

'Yes, it's Rosie,' Lula told her.

Justine held out a hand and Rosie buried her adorable furry face in her palm. 'Is she really here?' Justine croaked.

'Yes, and Daddy is too,' Lula answered.

Justine's eyes closed again. 'Daddy's not coming,' she said softly.

'He's here,' Matt told her, coming to sit on the bed.

Justine's heart twisted and she hardly dared to open her eyes.

Matt lifted her hand and pressed it to his lips.

She looked up at him and felt two large tears roll slowly, wetly into her hair.

'Hey you,' he said with an ironic smile.

'You've been asleep for a long, long time,' Lula told her.

'How long?' Justine whispered.

'Almost a week,' Matt replied.

She looked at him, half afraid he was going to disappear. 'When did you get here?'

'About an hour ago. Your cousin Al came to get us from the airport in his truck, thank God, or we might never have got through.'

Justine turned to the window. The night was illuminated by the brightness of snow. 'What day is it?' she thought to ask.

'It's Christmas Eve,' he replied, and as Lula leaned in to him he pressed a kiss to the top of her head. Justine had a quick vision of him kissing Abby that way, and felt more tears welling up from her broken heart.

'Are you really here?' she asked, tightening her fingers around his.

'I'm really here,' he promised.

Lula said, 'Billy Jakes brought us some rabbits. Not wild ones to eat, but little white fluffy ones that we can keep in a cage.'

'That was kind of him,' Justine murmured.

'He said they're for Christmas.'

Finally connecting with how special tonight was for Lula, Justine tried to sit up. She had little strength, and felt horribly sweaty and stiff, but with Matt's help she managed to swing her legs over the side of the bed.

'Go and tell everyone we'll be ready for dinner in about half an hour,' Matt said to Lula.

'Everyone?' Justine echoed, feeling vaguely light-headed.

Counting on her fingers, Lula announced, 'Sallie Jo and Hazel are here with Dizzy, and Hazel's grandma and grandpa. Uncle Al's just popped home for some things, but he's coming back, so that makes five. Oh yes, and there's you, me and Daddy. That makes eight.'

As she ran off with Rosie and Daisy at her heels,

390

Matt said, 'Sallie Jo and her family were worried you might not be yourself tomorrow, so they decided that instead of us going to them for Christmas, they'd come here. That way Lula wouldn't have to leave you, or miss out.'

Touched by so much kindness, Justine hardly knew what to say. 'They've been such good friends,' she finally murmured as Matt held her close. 'I don't know how I'd have managed without them.'

'They seem a very special family,' he agreed. 'I'm looking forward to getting to know them, and to seeing the house on the lake I've heard so much about, but I guess that won't happen any time soon with the weather the way it is.'

Remembering that she hadn't yet told him about the paintings, or even really considered what to do about the house, she gazed into his eyes, and decided it could all wait for now. He was as exhausted by everything they'd been through as she was, and she knew in her heart that there was still a very long way to go . . .

The holidays passed in a flurry of presents, log fires, baked hams, Christmas movies, snowman-building and hilarious skating sessions on Lake Maxinkuckee. Most of the town was out, flying about the solidly packed ice like angels, or heffalumps, depending on their skill. There were many ice-fishing and -sculpting competitions, ice-dance tournaments, snowball fights and much sledding down through the frozen summer camp at the Academies.

Though Justine was still weak, and nervous of

feeling happy in case it was brutally snatched away again, she knew she was improving now that Matt was there. What was concerning her mainly was how desperately hard he was trying to hide the ravaging depths of his own grief. Since leaving England and stepping into this new life she could tell that having no more duties, excuses, easy denials to hold him back from the edge it was drawing him closer all the time.

At the start of January severe blizzard warnings began hitting every news bulletin and weather forecast; by the fifth the storm was fiercely under way, with a biting polar vortex sending temperatures plummeting to minus twenty by day, and minus thirty by night. Most of the time it was too cold to go outside, since it took only minutes for frostbite or even hypothermia to set in.

To everyone's dismay, especially Sallie Jo's, Al was unable to make it from North Liberty for several days with most roads being impassable, and those crazy enough to try driving while conditions were so harsh usually found themselves stranded, and then fined.

Stay off the roads was the unequivocal message from NIPSCO – the Northern Indiana Public Service Company. *Don't let it be your abandoned vehicle that prevents the emergency services getting through.*

'Apparently they've closed the Academies,' Sallie Jo told them on the phone. 'A lot of students are on their way back after the holidays, but they can't get through, and Ed Forth, who owns one of the boat-storage companies, says the roofs of at least two of his buildings are in danger of collapse.'

'With everyone's boats inside?' Justine cried aghast.

'Exactly. We've just got to hope the owners have insurance in place, or they're standing to lose a lot of money.'

A day later the first building went down, destroying everything inside, followed by the second building the day after that. Boathouses and pontoons around the lake were also collapsing under their own burden of snow, and in some places power lines gave out too, leaving many homes without heat or light.

At the end of the month, following a longed-for break in the weather, the town was just beginning to function again when another severe storm hit. As soon as they knew it was coming, Justine and Matt arranged for Lula and the dogs to sit it out with Sallie Jo, Hazel and Dizzy at Angela and Frank's cottage on the lake. This way the girls would have each other to help alleviate the boredom of their enforced confinement, while Justine and Matt could have some private time to continue to deal with their grief.

Over the following days, as the polar vortex whipped its icy might through the whole of the Midwest, and more drifts built up around Waseya as though the weather itself seemed to recognise Justine and Matt's need to be alone, they began taking the threads of each other's memories and weaving them into such vivid episodes from the past that at times they were almost too painful to bear. They cried many tears together, laughed more than they'd have expected, and even found the courage to play some of Abby's songs.

All through those frozen months, while it wasn't possible to do much else, they did their best to start putting the past behind them in order to plan the future. They understood that in spite of the progress they were making, trying to advise and support themselves without proper help was like trying to carry a heavy bag from the inside. The outside would inevitably collapse and allow all sorts of demons back in. So they sought a recommendation from the doctor and made a pact that as soon as they were able to get to South Bend, they'd consult an experienced bereavement counsellor.

By the time they were able to get that far, April had come around, and several other decisions had been reached, not the least of which was that they were going to restore May's cottage. It might take a small fortune, but one thing they weren't short of was money, especially now the farmhouse had sold. Apparently a developer had bought all the properties in the vale at a knockdown price, with the intention of razing them and building a supermarket in their place. Matt and Justine had agreed that even a supermarket was preferable to the sick pilgrimages some people were still making to the scene of the crime.

The Pennsylvania Impressionist paintings, still in their storage in South Bend, were authenticated by two separate experts. However, after seeking a valuation and catching Matt as he pretended to faint, Justine decided against selling, and applied for permission to convert two empty shops on Culver's Main Street into one. Her plan was to turn them into a gallery for the Cantrell Collection. Sallie Jo wasted no time getting in touch with her old tutor, who immediately offered to fly up from Memphis to advise on restoration and display. Meantime, Matt began interviewing potential security companies and website designers, while Angela volunteered her services as chief marketer and publicist – a role she'd held for many years before her retirement.

It was an early April afternoon, with a glorious wash of bright sunlight helping along the big thaw, when Matt found Justine in the smaller of the two shops on Main Street, patching the damaged walls with filler. Since no one, including the town president, foresaw any problem with planning consents when the project was going to bring many tourists to the area, there seemed no reason not to carry on as though everything was already settled.

'Hi,' she said, glancing over her shoulder as he came in the door, 'you're back sooner than I expected.' His plan for the day had been to spend time over in Wakarusa with the Mennonite builders who'd come highly recommended for the work on May's cottage.

Before he could answer she went on, 'I had an email from Rob earlier confirming that he, Maggie and Francine, plus Mum, will definitely be here for Easter. Flights are already booked, apparently, so we're going to be quite a houseful with your mum, Simon and Gina as well. Luckily Angela's offered to let anyone stay at the cottage who wants to, so I'm thinking we should probably have our mothers with us so they can make a fuss of Lula, and the others can enjoy being right on the lake.'

'Good call,' he agreed, taking in the broken floor-boards and collapsing ceiling. 'Anyway, I hope you're in the mood for surprises, because I happen to have one.'

Her instant reaction was to tense; a beat later common sense prevailed. He'd never dress bad news up that way.

'Actually, it's quite a big surprise,' he cautioned, 'but I think you're going to like it.'

Intrigued, she watched him turn back to the door, open it and gesture for someone to come in.

The instant she saw who it was, tears rushed to her eyes. 'Cheryl,' she gasped, dropping her filler and tool.

Biting her lip to try and stop herself crying too, Cheryl came forward with her arms open. 'I've missed you so much,' she whispered hoarsely, as Justine wrapped her up so hard she almost crushed her.

'I've missed you too,' Justine wept. 'Oh God, I can't believe you're here. Let me look at you.' Holding her back she gazed wonderingly into Cheryl's lovely grey eyes, taking in her delicate cheekbones and jawline, the familiar wispy dark curls and quirky smile. She was the same Cheryl, although different in a way that Justine couldn't yet fathom. 'I can't tell you how happy I am to see you,' she murmured. 'I've been so worried. No one knew where you were.'

With a mischievous twinkle, Cheryl said, 'Wait for this: I've been at a spiritual retreat getting my head sorted out.'

Justine peered at her curiously.

'I needed help desperately after losing Chantal,' Cheryl expanded, using her daughter's name far more readily than Justine might have expected. 'Brad and I were no good for one another, so it wasn't long before we decided to go our separate ways. Then one day I found myself in a church begging Jesus, Mary, Joseph, anyone who'd listen to help me cope with my grief. And to my amazement it turned out that someone was listening, because in that very church on that very day I found a leaflet for a Christian retreat in northern France, and taking it as a sign I decided to go.'

An almost visible glow seemed to emanate from her as she spoke.

'And who should be waiting for me there,' Cheryl continued, 'but God himself?'

Justine was aware of Matt watching them, and since he almost certainly already knew the story, presumably having heard it on the way from the airport, he was no doubt waiting for her reaction

Still smiling in an impish way, Cheryl said, 'I truly never imagined myself becoming a religious person, but that's what's happened and I really couldn't be happier. It's helped me in ways I can hardly begin to describe, from my soul, to my confidence, to my view of the world and the people in it. Honestly, I have so much love in my heart these days that I hardly know what to do with it all, and since there's really no one I love more than you, I thought, why not come and tell you that? So here I am, hoping we can be friends again, and that you'll forgive me for not being around to support you during the terrible time you've had.'

'Oh God,' Justine sobbed, hugging her again. 'I'm the one who should have been supporting you. Oh, Cheryl, I'm so happy to see you, and I'm even happier that you've found God, because you look absolutely wonderful and if this is what it's done for you then perhaps we should all take a lesson from it.'

Cheryl gurgled on a laugh. 'I promise I'm not out for conversions,' she said, 'but if you are interested, obviously I'll be happy to discuss. Now, down to more important matters . . . First of all, how's Lula? I don't expect she'll remember me, but I certainly remember her. Such a sweetheart. Matt tells me she's at day care?'

Justine nodded. How brave Cheryl was to be able to talk about Lula so freely after the terrible loss of her own daughter. 'A Christian one,' she stated, hoping it would please her.

Apparently it did, if the shine in Cheryl's eyes was anything to go by. 'Matt also tells me,' she ran on, 'that you've found your grandmother's old house and you're going to restore it?'

'Speaking of which,' Matt said, checking his watch, 'I'm due to meet our builder there at four, so I'd better be on my way. Really good to see you, Cheryl. I'll let you tell Justine how you emailed me to ask if I thought she'd see you, and how we planned this surprise.'

As he rushed out the door, Justine took Cheryl's hands in hers and gazed into her eyes again. 'I don't want to stop looking at you,' she murmured. 'I was afraid I might never see you again.'

'I had the same fear until I realised that if I could find it in my heart to forgive Ben, it would clear the way for us.'

Justine's expression sobered as her son's guilt crushed her heart. 'I don't know how you could do that . . .'

'It wasn't so difficult when I had Jesus to help me, he took me through every step of the way, but I'm guessing that sort of talk is making you cringe . . .'

'No, no, it isn't. How could it when your faith has brought you all this way back to me?'

Bunching their hands to her chest, Cheryl said, 'You know, I'd love to see your grandmother's house. Matt told me during the drive how excited you are about it, so if it's all right with you, can we go there now?'

'Of course it's all right with me. I love nothing more than pottering about out there, in spite of it being a wreck as it stands.'

Minutes later they were in Justine's car heading down South Main Street, with Cheryl taking everything in as they passed.

'You must tell me what you're doing now,' Justine insisted, 'where you're living. Perhaps you're still at the retreat?'

Cheryl laughed. 'No, I left a couple of months ago. I've been staying with my dad and stepmum since then. Luckily I'm not too badly off for money now the house has sold, so I can take my time deciding how I'm going to use my new skill.'

'New skill?'

With dancing eyes, Cheryl said, 'I design and make

jewellery. Mostly silver and semi-precious stones, and believe it or not, I already have some customers.'

'That's fantastic.' Justine was genuinely thrilled for her. 'Do you have a shop?'

'I rent a stall at a market near my dad's every first and third Sunday in the month, the rest of the time I sell online. I have gifts for you and Lula – and for Sallie Jo and Hazel, who I'm longing to meet.'

'Matt obviously told you about them?'

'He did, so it seems you found some angels of your own.'

Justine threw her a quick glance. Yes, that was an accurate way of describing Sallie Jo and her family.

Cheryl smiled and winked, and a moment later Justine found herself wondering if she might be thinking the same crazy thoughts that were crowding into her own mind right now. They'd often come up with ideas, even outlandish ones, at the exact same time, so maybe that uncanny connection was still there.

'It's definitely worth considering,' Cheryl told her.

Justine blinked. 'You're kidding me,' she cried, realising they actually were reading each other's minds.

Cheryl laughed.

'I think it's the most wonderful idea,' Justine declared rashly. 'You can stay with us until you find a place of your own, and there's definitely room for a jeweller a few doors down from my gallery. I think there's even space for a workshop at the back. We can check it out. Oh God, Cheryl, I can hardly believe this is happening.'

Smiling, and gazing at the Culver Bible Church

they were passing, Cheryl said, 'It would be wonderful if it could, but there will be an immigration issue to overcome . . .'

'We'll put you in touch with the lawyer Matt's using. It's a bit different for him, as a writer, because he qualifies as being what they call "outstanding in his field", and of course he's married to an American, but I'm sure this guy can work something out for you. It might mean you having to leave the country every three months for a while . . .'

'Which would be fine. I can visit my dad and maybe do some travelling in search of inspiration.'

Reaching for her hand, Justine said, 'Please tell me I'm not dreaming.'

Laughing, Cheryl said, 'You're not dreaming. I'm really here, and from the little I've seen of it so far I think I could feel very comfortable in these parts.'

'Oh you don't need to worry about that,' Justine told her drily, 'this is a community of around twelve hundred people with no less than ten churches to choose from – all Christian I believe – so you should feel very at home.'

'Such heaven,' Cheryl sighed humorously. 'Do you ever go to any of them?'

'No, I'm afraid we don't, but that's not to say we won't. Everything is up for discussion . . . Now, if you look to the right, do you see the house at the end of the track, kind of hiding behind the tall hedges? That's ours, but I'll take you there later. I just wanted you to see where we are in relation to town, and to May's Cottage, which is what we're going to call it, officially.'

'Perfect. I'm sure she'd thoroughly approve.'

'I hope so. Honest to God, I sometimes feel that she's here, guiding me, or watching over me. I even think she had something to do with bringing me here in the first place, like she willed it or something.'

'I don't see any reason why that shouldn't be true,' Cheryl responded.

Justine wondered if she was going to expand on that, but she didn't seem inclined to, so they simply drove on along the South Shore chatting about what they were seeing as they passed the Venetian Village, turned by the Wetlands Conservation Area, took a left at Mystic Hills and eventually arrived on East Shore Drive.

Apart from a car and a truck there was no sign of Matt and the builder when they arrived at the cottage, which was still masked from the road – this time by lavishly blossoming trees.

'Wow, this is truly special,' Cheryl murmured, gazing up at the welcoming facade as they stepped on to the crumbling patio with its patchwork of left-over snow and assortment of budding wild flowers. 'And the view . . . It's so close to the lake . . . Are you going to live here when it's done?'

'We're not sure yet,' Justine replied, going first into the hall where Al had helped Matt to lay temporary timbers to make the floor more secure. 'It's quite cut off in winter, with most of the properties around only being used in summer, which would be OK for me and Matt, but not for Lula. So we're thinking we might try to buy the house we're renting at the moment, as we've become so fond of it, and do the same as our East Shore neighbours, come over here from around May to September, except we won't have as far to travel. It's an extravagance, but if we can persuade our families to spend time here during the summer there'll be plenty of room for everyone to stay. Including you.'

'You can count me in,' Cheryl twinkled. 'I'm loving it already. Look at this kitchen, it's so hilariously seventies . . . Are you going to keep it?'

'Alas no, the floors will have to come up for heating and plumbing to go in, and given its condition it's likely to fall apart as soon as we start moving it. We're taking plenty of photos though, because I don't want to forget how it was for May.'

After showing Cheryl the sitting room with the magnificent fireplace that was still, apart from mould, bird droppings and dust, more or less intact, and the furniture a group of Amish craftsmen had already inspected for restoration, Justine said, 'Sounds like Matt's in the cellar with the builder, so let's go upstairs. I haven't properly been through Phillip's or May's bedrooms yet. Do you know about my uncle, Phillip, and what happened?'

Cheryl nodded. 'Matt told me. It's so tragic but, as we know, your grandma wasn't the only one running scared of Aids and the stigma back then. Thank God times have changed.'

Agreeing, Justine said, 'My mother wants to go through his room when she comes at Easter, so I'm left to sort out May's. I'm not sure why, but up till now I've been a bit hesitant about starting, but with you here . . . Weirdly, it feels like this is the right time.'

Apparently amused, Cheryl followed her up to the first landing and all the way to the end where the master room was still largely under wraps, apart from the bed with its corroded iron frame and rotting linens. A couple of ladders were propped against one wall, left by Al and Matt who'd had to use them when removing the shutters.

'It's like a little mystery tour,' Cheryl murmured as she helped Justine remove the covers from a formerly pink, now putrid chaise longue. 'This was obviously exquisite once. Will the craftsmen be able to do anything with it?'

'I won't know until they've seen it, but let's hope so. I think that must be a tallboy over there, do you want to check it out while I do the nightstands?'

Apparently entranced, Cheryl went to drag off the heavy dust sheet and found a bookcase full of classic novels and biographies. 'She was obviously a big fan of Henry James,' she commented, counting as many as ten of his titles on the top shelf.

'There's one here,' Justine said, finding a damp and curled copy of *The Wings of the Dove* beneath some rosary beads in a bedside drawer. Seeing there was a bookmark she opened it to the page it was saving, and was saying, 'She must have been reading it before she died,' when her eye was caught by the back of a wooden frame propped against the wall beside the bed. Lifting it carefully she checked the handwritten inscription in the bottom right-hand corner, wondering if she was about to discover yet another Impressionist masterpiece.

What she read was, *Done by May Cantrell, August 1976.*

She turned it over and saw that behind the mouldy glass was a beautifully embroidered quotation.

Frowning as she looked round, Cheryl said, 'Can you smell oranges? Or is it roses?'

Justine nodded, because she could; in fact she felt surrounded by the scent, and when she realised what she was reading she understood why.

> *'Hope' is the thing with feathers*
> *That perches in the soul,*
> *And sings the tune without the words,*
> *And never stops – at all . . .*

Acknowledgements

So many enormous thank yous to the people of Culver:

First of all to Susie Mahler, owner of Café Max on Main Street. Thank you Susie for being there every step of the way, answering my emails so quickly and so informatively and for allowing me to use the café as a location.

To Sallie Jo Tardy Mitzell for an amazing tour of Lake Maxinkuckee and of her family's beautiful lakeside cottage. Thank you too, Sallie Jo, for letting me use your name for one of the main characters.

To Craig Mitzell for adding so much colour and character to the story.

To Jeff Kenney of the *Culver Citizen* for yet more colour and so many insights.

To Chief Wayne Bean of the Culver Police Department.

To Sheryl at the Child Care Ministry.

To Marcia Adams for generously sharing her historic knowledge of Culver.

Also to my dear and treasured friend Chip (Mitzell) Mitchell for introducing me to Culver.

And to my US editor Kate Miciak for the story about the rabbits and introducing me to the Pennsylvania Impressionists. ☺

Susan Lewis

No Place To Hide

Bonus Material

Susan Lewis

on
No Place to Hide

Dear Reader,

The question I've been asked most frequently since I began the research for this book, and throughout the writing of it is, how on earth did you, a Brit, come to choose Culver, Indiana for a setting?

It's a good question, given that my experience of living in the States has, to date, all been in Los Angeles, and the US cities I've visited are all major centres in their own ways.

However, I never seem to tire of reading about smaller towns and communities in the States, particularly those in the Mid-West, when I get a real sense of whom and what America is really all about. Being British it would be hard for me to do full justice to that without going to live in a small town for a considerable period of time, so in this instance I enlisted the help of a dear friend in LA, Chip Mitchell to set me on the right road.

It took no time at all, for when I asked Chip if he could recommend a small town in the Mid-West to set my story, he immediately put me in touch with his aunt and uncle, Dorry and Channing Mitzell, who have a long history with the Culver Academies and continue to live in Culver. I had no idea at that time what an absolute jewel of a place he was connecting me with, how unusual and inspirational it would turn out to be, or how enthusiastically his family and their many friends in Culver were going to embrace the story. Actually, I shouldn't really have been so surprised, as I've met many Americans during my travels around the world, and so have much experience of just how engaged and even gallant they can be. (I've been rescued from many a tight corner by an American, from Morocco to Manila, but that's for another time!)

So I travelled to Culver, hoping and praying that I was doing the right thing, after all I'm not American, and the way of life in the Mid-West was surely going to be very different to anything I'd experienced in the States to date. I needed to have no fear. Within minutes of arriving I found myself standing on a secluded beach at the top end of town, gazing out at the mesmerising waters of Lake Maxincuckee towards the glittering, multi-million dollar homes on the far shore. It was impossible not to be moved by such a peaceful and yet intriguingly different setting to the one I'd envisaged in my mind's eye. There was already something about this place that was getting to me.

Amongst the many experiences and enlightening conversations I enjoyed during my stay there are two that stand out as firsts for me: giving a talk to a creative writing group from the Culver Girls Academy, wonderful students, an absolute privilege to spend time with. And the invitation to be part of an exercise that would never happen in Britain, and one can only feel sad that it does in the US - shooter training at the local Elementary and High Schools. That really was a surreal experience.

Though many of my earlier books have whole chapters set in various parts of the States, this is the first time I've located so much of a book in a place I didn't know before. I'd love to write more set in America, so I'm very interested to know how well, or not, you feel I have portrayed this small town and the mainly fictional people I've used to bring it to life.

A very warm thank you for reading this one, as ever I hope you enjoy it.

With my warmest wishes to you all,

Susan

$\mathcal{S}$usan's travel diary

A trip to Culver for the book launch of *No Place to Hide*

Dear diary,

Wow! What a visit! This past week in Culver is going to live with me for a very long time, that's for sure. It's also going to be up there with some of the most enjoyable trips I've made.

I couldn't be happier that I decided to share the launch of *No Place to Hide* with the many friends and townsfolk who gave so generously of their time during my research trip a year ago. It felt right to do so; after all, the book isn't just about me and the characters within, but about all those who helped to create the story and give it a reality I couldn't have begun to achieve on my own. It felt like the perfect decision to host the launch in the very town the book is set.

Having set parts of other books in New York, Los Angeles and New Orleans, I immediately decided that this time I should choose somewhere in the very heart of America. So, I consulted my dear friend, Chip Mitzell, who lives in Los Angeles, to ask for some advice. He didn't hesitate. 'It has to be Culver,' he declared.

'Do you mean Culver City? LA?' I asked in amazement. Hardly small town America – he apparently wasn't getting this.

'No, Culver, Indiana,' he explained. 'It's about as Midwest as you can get – and boy, will you be in for a treat.'

I have to confess to feeling somewhat dubious when he first began describing the place – it might be in the Midwest, but this clearly wasn't your regular small town. In fact the idea of the Academies seemed a little terrifying from a distance; how on earth was I going to weave such a grand establishment of learning into a novel that was essentially about domestic trauma? And as for all those multi-million dollar cottages (cottages!)...

However, the more Chip told me about this very special place in his heart, and his family, the Mitzells, who many Culverites know well and hold dear, the more convinced I became that I must explore this extraordinary township. So my husband and I hopped on a plane to go and check it out. My reaction when I arrived, my thoughts, my surprise, are mostly captured in the opening chapter of the book – it really is a town of many contrasts, a secret, glittering jewel all tucked away beyond the vast and dreamy corn silk veil.

Right from the start I was reminded that one of the best parts of being a writer is exploring new places and meeting new people. You use the things you see, hear, smell, like invisible, magical pieces of a jigsaw puzzle to start putting a story together. And with the many introductions I was given by the Mitzell family, the book soon started to take on a life of its own.

It's not possible to go into detail of how the story was shaped by that first visit without giving too much away, but I will say that meeting Susie Mahler was like meeting one of my own characters. I had wanted the main Culver protagonist to be a real estate agent who also owned the local café, and there she was. Along with the Mitzells she jumped right on board with the plot and as their knowledge and insights began to merge, even shape my ideas for the story, so everything began to acquire the mystery and suspense I was aiming for.

Me and Susie at Café Max!

There are so many others who also gave generously of their time and knowledge: Sheryl Tompos and her colleagues at the Child Care Ministry; Marcia Adams for her wonderful guided tour; Dorry Mitzell and her delicious coffee and apple cake (as featured in the book); Jeff Kenny of *The Culver Citizen* – there is an editor in the book, but I have to stress he isn't actually Jeff! Police Chief Wayne Bean who opened my eyes in so many ways, not least of all for allowing me to attend a shooter training session at the local school. Then there's Sallie Jo Mitzell, who not only drove all the way from Indianapolis to take my husband and me around the lake and show us her family's beautiful home on the south shore, but who also allowed me to use her name for one of the principal characters.

It's true to say that I've never received the same sort of enthusiasm and help with a book as I did when I came to Culver to begin *No Place to Hide*. It carried on right through the following year as I sat at home in England writing it. Susie Mahler and Craig Mitzell kept in touch with me throughout the entire time, answering my questions almost as soon as they were asked, and giving me information about Culver that I wouldn't have even known to ask for. I've even stolen bits of their chatty emails and put them into dialogue.

So now the book is out there for all to read. The positive response so far has been quite overwhelming. To my great relief – and joy – most seem to love it in spite of how dark it is in places, and most importantly of all everyone seems to be enjoying the depiction of the town they know well, as well as engaging with the characters.

It was an odd experience for me, going back, as I kept expecting to run into Justine, the principal character. It felt as though she was there, going about her life, but I just kept missing her. Sometimes I even wanted to ask people about her to find out if they liked her and whether she was settling in OK. Nothing if not a little barmy!

Even as I started the long journey back to the UK, taking so many wonderful memories with me, I knew I was leaving a piece of my heart in Culver – I'm sure I shall go back one day soon.

At the beautiful Lake Maxinkuckee!

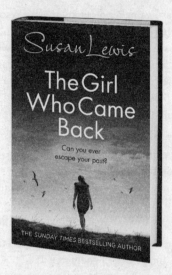

About *Susan*

I was born in 1956 to a happy, normal family living in a brand new council house on the outskirts of Bristol. My mother, at the age of twenty, and one of thirteen children, persuaded my father to spend his bonus on a ring rather than a motorbike and they never looked back. She was an ambitious woman determined to see her children on the right path: I was signed up for ballet, elocution and piano lessons and my little brother was to succeed in all he set his mind to.

Tragically, at the age of thirty-three, my mother lost the battle against cancer and died. I was nine, my brother was five.

My father was left with two children to bring up on his own. Sending me to boarding school was thought to be 'for the best' but I disagreed. No one listened to my pleas for freedom, so after a while I took it upon myself to get expelled. By the time I was thirteen, I was back in our little council house with my father and brother. The teenage years passed and before I knew it I was eighteen … an adult.

I got a job at HTV in Bristol for a few years before moving to London at the age of twenty-two to work for Thames. I moved up the ranks, from secretary in news and current affairs, to a production assistant in light entertainment and drama. My mother's ambition and a love of drama gave me the courage to knock on the Controller's door to ask what it takes to be a success. I received the reply of 'Oh, go away and write something'. So I did!

Three years into my writing career I left TV and moved to France. At first it was bliss. I was living the dream and even found myself involved in a love affair with one of the FBI's most wanted! Reality soon dawned, however, and I realised that a full-time life in France was very different to a two-week holiday frolicking around on the sunny Riviera.

So I made the move to California with my beloved dogs Casanova and Floozie. With the rich and famous as my neighbours I was enthralled and inspired by Tinsel Town. The reality, however, was an obstacle course of cowboy agents, big-talking producers and wannabe directors. Hollywood was not waiting for me, but it was a great place to have fun! Romances flourished and faded, dreams were crushed but others came true.

After seven happy years of taking the best of Hollywood and avoiding the rest, I decided it was time for a change. My dogs and I spent a short while in Wiltshire before then settling once again in France, perched high above the Riviera with glorious views of the sea. It was wonderful to be back amongst old friends, and to make so many new ones. Casanova and Floozie both passed away during our first few years there, but Coco and Lulabelle are doing a valiant job of taking over their places – and my life!

Everything changed again three months after my fiftieth birthday when I met James, my partner, who lived and works in Bristol. For a couple of years we had a very romantic and enjoyable time of flying back and forth to see one another at the weekends, but at the end of 2010 I finally sold my house on the Riviera and am now living in Gloucestershire in a delightful old barn with Coco and

Lulabelle. My writing is flourishing and over thirty books down the line I couldn't be happier. James continued to live in Bristol, with his boys, Michael and Luke – a great musician and a champion footballer! – for a while until we decided to get married in 2013!

It's been exhilarating and educational having two teenage boys in my life! Needless to say they know everything, which is very useful (saves me looking things up) and they're incredibly inspiring in ways they probably have no idea about.

Should you be interested to know a little more about my early life, why not try *Just One More Day*, a memoir about me and my mother and then the story continues in *One Day at a Time*, a memoir about me and my father and how we coped with my mother's loss.

Memoirs by
Susan Lewis

Read the true story of Susan Lewis and her family and how they coped when tragedy struck. *Just One More Day* and its follow-up *One Day At A Time* are two memoirs that will hopefully make you laugh as well as cry as you follow Susan on her journey to love again.

Available in paperback

5 minutes with

Susan

Where does the inspiration for your books come from?

I often write about difficult issues, as you well know.
I don't necessarily write from experience in these cases but
I rely on listening and seeking the experience of others
who might have witnessed or been through challenging
situations. It's important as a writer to imagine how you'd
feel if it happened to you. I enjoy doing it but sometimes it
can be quite distressing – sometimes I cry, which tells me it's
working. This is how I really bring my characters to life.

Do you have any peculiar writing rituals or habits?

Nothing too peculiar! I'm very strict about the hours I write,
starting at 10 in the morning and going through until 5pm
or 6pm, usually six days a week. Then, I love to have a glass
of wine at the end of the day as I read back over what has
happened in 'my fictional world' over the last seven or eight
hours, socialising with the characters and often wanting
to gossip about them with someone else.

What advice would you offer to aspiring writers?

Remember to listen: listen to the way people speak,
to the rhythm of the words you are writing (you're most
likely to do this in your head), and always give your characters
room to be themselves. They'll have plenty to say if you
just let them chatter on to one another, often giving
you ideas you hadn't even thought of!

What is the last book you bought someone as a gift?

A variety of children's books for the recipients of the Special Recognition Award that I'm sponsoring for the local secondary school. They've chosen the titles themselves and what a fascinating selection they've made – from *The Diary of a Wimpy Kid* to *The Curious Incident of the Dog in the Night Time* (one of my own favourites).

What's the best piece of advice you've ever been given?

If you want to be a producer you'd better write. I was working in TV drama and this was what I was told to get me out of the Controller's office! I took him at his word and the rest, as they say, is history.

If you had a superpower, what would it be?

If I had a superpower I'd rescue all the children and animals being subjected to cruelty.

What literary character is most like you?

Definitely Emma from Jane Austen's wonderful novel.

If you were stranded on a desert island what song would you choose to listen to, which book would you take and what luxury item would you pack?

That's a hard one. Song choice would have to be Just My Imagination by the Temptations. Book choice . . . *How to Survive on a Desert Island* by anyone who's been thoughtful enough to write such a useful guide. Luxury item: A double-ended stick with a toothbrush at one end and a knife at the other . . . I could give Bear Grylls a sure run for his money!

Have you read them all?

For a full list of books please visit
www.susanlewis.com

Connect with

Susan Lewis

online

Sign up to Susan's newsletter for
exclusive content, competitions and
all the latest news from Susan.

Want to know more? Visit

www.susanlewis.com

Connect with other fans and join in the
conversation at

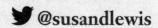 **/SusanLewisBooks**

Follow Susan on

🐦 **@susandlewis**